# HEARTLESS HEARTLAND

For Max
From Farrell

Enjoy!

# Heartless HEARTLAND

BY

## FARRAL BRADTKE

Sense of Wonder Press
JAMES A. ROCK & COMPANY, PUBLISHERS
ROCKVILLE • MARYLAND

*Heartless Heartland* by Farral Bradtke

SENSE OF WONDER PRESS
is an imprint of JAMES A. ROCK & CO., PUBLISHERS

*Heartless Heartland* copyright ©2006 by Farral Bradtke

Special contents of this edition copyright ©2006
by James A. Rock & Co., Publishers

All applicable copyrights and other rights reserved worldwide. No part of this publication may be reproduced, in any form or by any means, for any purpose, except as provided by the U.S. Copyright Law, without the express, written permission of the publisher.

This is a work of fiction. Both European American and Native American histories trace the forced emigration of the Sauk people from their native lands along the St. Lawrence Seaway to their definitive battle with the United States soldiers in northwestern Illinois. The histories also describe their use of the lands in Iowa and Minnesota, the frequent altercations with the Sioux in the northern Iowa-southern Minnesota region, and the establishment of a "no-man's land" by the U.S. government to separate the two peoples.

I used this bit of history to inspire this novel. Names, characters, places and incidents are products of my imagination or are used fictitiously. Any resemblance to actual events or locales or persons, living or dead, is entirely coincidental.

*Address comments and inquiries to:*
SENSE OF WONDER PRESS
James A. Rock & Company, Publishers
9710 Traville Gateway Drive, #305
Rockville, MD 20850
**E-mail:**
jrock@rockpublishing.com    lrock@rockpublishing.com
Internet URL: www.rockpublishing.com

ISBN: 1-59663-514-2

Library of Congress Control Number: 2006925101

Printed in the United States of America

First Edition: August 2006

*In memory of
Mae Patz
and
Mary Golat*

# Acknowledgments

Special thanks are in order to Detective Sergeant James Hoppes of the Forest City Police Department, for assistance in descriptions dealing with police procedure, and to Mr. Steve Sagataw of the Hannahville band of the Potowotamee, for assistance in description of the general culture of the Woodland tribes.

I also wish to thank Mr. Kenneth Golat, Director of Public Safety for the City of Manistique, and his wife Karen, who answered further questions regarding police procedure (many times on the phone as I worked into the middle of the night) with extreme patience.

I appreciate the effort and suggestions of my manuscript readers, including Tom Money, Theresa Schaedig, Gail and Garth Green, Janet Decker, Tondra Jaynes, Allison Lyles, and Nicole Brown. And I especially wish to thank my personal editor *extraordinaire*, Julie Hayes, who is able to fine-tooth a manuscript in a New York minute.

Each of these individuals offered both help and encouragement, without which this work would have been diminished.

F.B.

PART ONE

# The Curse of Heartless

# CHAPTER
## One

On an exquisitely golden summer's afternoon in 1972, a tiny, slim feminine figure sat in the sun-dappled shade of maple and oak trees on the bank of a river in northeastern Iowa. She might have been a teenager who had led a very rough life too terribly soon. Or, she might have been a much older woman who had seen too much and who had every innocence ripped from her, one by one. Either way, the lackluster blonde hair, the heavy droop of her shoulders, and the half-lidded, cloudy green eyes that stared into the water yielded the impression of someone who had finally had enough of what the world had offered her.

In a way, she was both. But 39-year-old Anna Baumann's thoughts were far away from self-pity. She didn't hear the cheerful chirpings and chitterings in the forest, or the soporific rush and gurgle of the river. She didn't feel the gentle breeze that caressed her pale cheeks, or the soft carpet of pine needles and grass beneath her. She didn't see the brilliant blue sky or the clear, undulating waters flowing before her, and she had yet to notice the form of a young, beautiful Indian woman who was watching her from the far side of the river. Anna's mind was indeed far, far away and long ago. At this point her body was merely a shell from which her psyche had taken flight. She was watching a movie in her mind's eye, one that was full of oppression, terrible violence, and blood.

Part of this drama was supplied by her own memories, both those that were easily called forth and those that were deeply buried in the need to simply get by in everyday life. The rest was supplied by the woman White Feather, the woman across the river, the one whose vicious murder over a century before would haunt this place and the fates of dozens of men, women, and children for all time.

In life, White Feather's heart had been light and loving, but she was a fierce protector of the innocent. Her spirit had graced this place ever since her death, and she interceded whenever she could. This living woman, this Anna, was a good woman; but she was losing her grip on her own essence, one very much like White Feather's own. And so she guided Anna's mind with her own, showing her the memories of White Feather, Anna Baumann, and this terrible place called Heartless, in the hope that Anna could survive the inevitable.

# CHAPTER TWO

White Feather's people, the Sauk, had had many trials, both with other Indian nations and with the white man. They first appeared in oral history as an Algonquin tribe, living in Canada in the area of the St. Lawrence Seaway. The arrival of white men from Europe and wars with other tribes forced them to move first to Michigan near the Saginaw Bay, and then to the territory of Wisconsin, near Green Bay. Finally, they settled at Saukenuk where the Rock River met the great Mississippi River in what we now know as the state of Illinois. In the mid-1700's they were joined by the few people of the Fox tribe who survived near-annihilation by the French. At Saukenuk, the Sauk and Fox were comfortable and happy; as Woodland people they could live in the town and farm in the summer, yet move to the forests to survive the winter. The fertile soil there yielded excellent crops of corn, beans, squash, pumpkin, and tobacco; the rivers were full of fish; and game was plentiful in the form of deer, buffalo, bear, and other, smaller animals. These were important for their stores of food, clothing, tools, and trade. The Sauk and Fox flourished.

In disputes with other tribes, the Sauk and Fox joined for a time with the Ottawa against the Illinois tribes, and their territory grew to encompass parts of what the United States now recognizes as the states of Illinois and Iowa. In other territorial disputes, the Sauk and Fox fought the Iowa, Winnebago, and Sioux tribes. These battles against the Sioux were the most bitter and devastating of all, costing both sides many lives. In particular, they arose over hunting grounds in the area where the border between the states of Minnesota and Iowa now stands. The United States Government stepped in to create a treaty between the two peoples, and marked out a strip of land twenty miles wide along the northern border of Iowa that was to be a No Man's Land for the warring tribes. Both sides agreed to the treaty, but both sides regularly violated the treaty and more battles erupted. To amend what turned out to be a bad idea, the U. S. Government then bought a twenty-mile strip of land from each the Sioux in the north and the Sauk and Fox in the south, giving control of that land to the United States Government. In this new treaty both sides were able to use this so-called "Neutral Ground," as long as they did it peaceably. This worked well for a time, but the implacable U. S. Government was not satisfied. In its need (and greed) for more and more land, the Government moved tribes of people through the creation of treaties, land purchases, and battle to areas that were unfamiliar to them. In 1832, the Government attempted to forcibly move the Sauk and Fox to western Iowa and Kansas.

The Sauk Chief Black Hawk spoke to the Sauk and Fox people, and convinced many of them to fight to keep their lands where they were, particularly the town of Saukenuk. Black Hawk led a war against the American soldiers in Illinois that turned out to be disastrous for them. The Americans killed most of the warriors and then went on to massacre escaping men, women and children as they attempted to swim to safety across the Mississippi River. In this war Black Hawk himself was captured, and the Americans bartered him for more Sauk and Fox lands.

The survivors were moved again and again, and their numbers were further decimated by white men's diseases, starvation, and their introduction to "firewater," which caused them to break into deadly fights against each other.

Driven further and further into the plains and away from their original beloved woodlands, many had to accept the white man's way of life or perish.

White Feather had died in 1832, just months before Black Hawk's war against the Americans, in the northeast portion of Iowa, not far from the southern border of the "Neutral Ground." No burial or effigy mounds are found there, nor *any* remains of Indian burials. No evidence has been found of a village or the things that made up daily life for the culture. But farmers have found thousands of relics of war, including bullets, arrowheads, and tomahawks.

There is every evidence that this spot has been, over at least the last two centuries, a very troubled ground that echoes of anger and spilled blood.

# CHAPTER
## Three

In the early summer of 1832, three young Sauk women were gathering the sweet grass that grew on the boggy side of the Mississippi River near Saukenuk. It was a beautiful day, and the women were excited. A great Council was to be held soon, and the great Sauk Chief Black Hawk had called for all Sauk and Fox warriors to come to the town. They chatted comfortably as they cut the stalks of grass. The sun was warm on their backs, and wildflowers were in bloom.

It made a pretty picture for the four white men who watched them from a thicket of trees. These were United States Government soldiers, and their company's duty was to patrol the "Neutral Ground" in Iowa and assure that peace was kept between the Sioux and the Sauk and Fox tribes. This was boring, time-wasting work that these men did not care for. They found it easy to desert their company and slip away to the Mississippi River, where European Americans had built cities at crossing points. These were four men in search of liquor and women.

Hezekiah Cook was the self-proclaimed leader of this group of men, and he hated all Indians with a passion that was hard to match. He watched the scene for a few minutes through narrowed eyes as he sipped from his whiskey bottle. The other three white men joked and jostled each other behind him, and he quieted them with one look.

"What are we going to do about them women, Zeke?" asked Art Bennett. Nobody ever called Hezekiah by his given name, or they would be sorry. Zeke muttered, "Get on your horse and ride around 'em. Make sure there's no other Injuns around, especially braves." He fingered the coil of rope in his hands. "Looks like we can have some fun, maybe. Keep quiet, though, and give us a signal when it's clear."

He turned to George Hoggins and Fred Green. "Fred, you go with 'im. When we hear your call, we'll creep up and surround 'em on foot. One yell out of *any* of 'em, cut her throat. After all," he smiled wickedly, "one of 'em's enough. Three would be good, though." He took his dirty, sweaty kerchief from his neck and signaled for the others to do the same. "Bind and gag 'em and we'll high-tail it out of here."

Fred and Art mounted up and circled carefully through the trees until they could see both the Indian town and the river. Something unusual was going on here, all right. Saukenuk had swollen to twice its normal size. On their way in from the north of their present position, they had seen signs of many people moving back and forth between camps on the river and the town, and there was a lot of activity in the town itself. Out here, however, there wasn't a soul. Except for the three young squaws, that was. Fred's mouth watered in anticipation, as if he were about to sit down to a great feast. He wiped his sleeve across his lips. Yeah, this would be good.

When he was satisfied that there was little danger of discovery, Fred nodded at Art, who cupped his hands around his mouth and called a single, loud, "*Kaw!*", the sound of a crow.

Zeke watched the girls. When they heard the call, they all looked up in the direction it came from; when it wasn't repeated, they went back to what they were doing. By that time, the two groups of white men were creeping through grass and high shrubs to surround them.

The attack was over in minutes. Taken completely by surprise, the three women were jumped upon and thrown face down into the boggy earth. Not a sound escaped their lips, but the white men hadn't counted on them fighting back. Each held a short knife for cutting sweet grass; two of the girls had dropped theirs out of reach. The third woman still held hers. She twisted and slashed viciously at Zeke, leaving a shallow gash across his cheek. He reacted quickly, and punched her in the jaw; that stunned her. Zeke bared his yellow, stained teeth close to her unseeing eyes and whispered, "For that, Squaw, you'll be the last to die." Drops of blood from his wound dripped on her face.

The women were all three bound and gagged in short order.

Knowing better than to mention Zeke's wound, Art reported what he and Fred had seen of the other Indians. "Where will we take 'em?" he asked.

Zeke considered, swiping absently at the stinging cut on his face with his sleeve. He knew there were temporary camps to the north, and that Saukenuk was to the east. They had intended to go south along the Mississippi, but that was too risky now with their human baggage. He looked to the west, across the river. At that point, the Mississippi was fairly wide but shallow; dunes could be seen peeking out here and there midstream. "We'll throw 'em across the horses and take 'em back over the river," he ordered.

"But Zeke, that's back the way we came," Art pointed out. "It's Sauk land all the way to the Neutral Ground, and then we've gotta worry about being shot for desertion."

"Not if we're smart." Zeke glared at him, and Art fell silent. In Zeke's estimation, Art was, without doubt, the dumbest individual to set foot on earth.

Gagged and bound hand and foot with their wrists behind them, the three terrified women were tossed roughly over the men's leather saddles. Zeke rode his horse across the river alone while the other three men led their horses. They crossed a dune on the way, and Art was given the duty of covering their tracks.

On the other side, the men pulled the women off the horses and cut the ropes binding their feet. Lengths of rope were tied to their hands and the other ends were looped around the men's waists. To put some distance between the Sauk and their party,

Zeke ordered that the women ride in front of the men through the narrow strip of woods and hills on the west side of the river.

They came to a smaller, swifter river and rode upstream in the shallows for about fifty miles to the northwest before coming to a fork in the river. Zeke led the party to cross the east fork of the river, and they rode the shallows of the west fork before he allowed them to camp for the night. The women were led to separate trees, forced to sit, and then were tied to the trees. Zeke removed their gags. He lingered in front of the woman who had cut him; he had come to think of her as Wildcat, and his. He intended to very much enjoy this woman, in his own special way. Now "Wildcat" glared back at him defiantly, and he grinned an evil grin. "Tomorrow," he promised.

There would be no fire tonight to alert the soldiers to the north or the Indians in the other directions. George would take first watch and see to the horses; then it would be Fred's turn to watch, then Art's. George offered water to the women, which they took, gagging at first. They would take no food. George thought it was just as well. No sense wasting food on squaws who were going to die shortly, anyway. He replaced their gags.

As the leader of this small pack, Zeke sat in the shadows made by the full moon, watching the women and listening. No bird calls floated through the night, but occasionally small animals scurried. He fueled the flame of his hatred for the people who were nothing but a damned pain in the ass to him. Over and over again, the Government made treaties with these people, and he was sent with his company out into the hot, burning sun or the freezing rain or snow to watch over them and make sure they didn't violate the treaty. If the soft Government would allow him, he'd massacre every damn Injun he saw—*that* would take care of the problem. He thought of his own brother, dying in a battle with the Indians; when he'd been found, he was naked, and he had been scalped. Now some warrior had Ben Cook's hair tied to his saddle. Savages!

Zeke felt the slash on his face. The pain was numbing as he drank more liquor, but he'd bet that Wildcat had marked him forever. He planned her demise the next day in detail, and his sexual arousal intensified at the thought.

He was still awake when Fred took second watch and George lay on the ground to sleep, but Zeke missed Art's watch. He finally slept. He shouldn't have.

When dawn came and Zeke opened his eyes, the first thing he saw was Art dying at the foot of a tree. His throat had been cut, and the three women were *gone!* He roughly roused the others and quickly assessed what had happened. Art had cut the bonds of one of the women to have sex with her. She had gotten his knife and stabbed him in the gut and slashed his throat before freeing the others. It had obviously happened only a short time ago, because fresh blood pooled at the foot of the tree, and Art was still gurgling, raising his arms weakly as if to ask for help. Zeke kicked him in the head and left him where he lay. Of all the girls, Arty had picked Wildcat to fondle. As far as Zeke was concerned, he deserved what he had gotten.

George and Fred had saddled three of the horses, and they mounted up. Those women had to be found, and Zeke had a pretty clear idea of which way they went: east, back to their tribe, as fast as their little squaw feet could carry them. They'd overtake them on their horses easily, he thought.

But at the edge of the trees, all that could be seen was a sea of tall grass. No movement could be detected out there. Those girls could be *anywhere*, and Wildcat had a knife. He gestured for George and Fred to spread out; they'd cross the grass in a grid pattern and flush them out. The men walked the horses silently.

Suddenly, Fred's horse whickered and backed up, and there was a rustling in the grass near him. Zeke and George galloped over and found the women huddled together. Wildcat squatted in front of the others protectively, Art's knife in her hand and her deerskin clothes stained with Art's blood. The horse had smelled the blood and backed away in fright.

The three men hurled themselves off their horses and fell on the women. Zeke disarmed Wildcat by twisting the arm that held the knife. On top of her in the long grass, he first broke all her fingers by crushing them in his fists. And then he got started in earnest.

Horses and pursuers forgotten, the men perpetrated every kind of sexual horror that they could imagine upon the hapless women. *Now* the women screamed and cried. When the men were finished with their sexual depravity, two of the women lay dead, the earth around them soaked and stained with their blood. Wildcat still lived.

And that was the way that Zeke had wanted it. He had planned it that way. Too used and weak to walk, the woman was dragged by her ankles to where the other women lay so that Zeke was sure she knew that they were dead. By then, however, her eyes were glazed over, and Zeke slapped and cursed her to wake her up. He wanted her *aware*. When he saw a flash of shock and hate spark her eyes, he grunted in satisfaction. He waved Art's knife in front of her face before first scalping her and then slashing her throat. And *then* it was over.

The men looked around, heaving from their exertions. They were midway between the two forks of the river, their horses scattered, and suddenly they felt exposed and alarmed. They were covered in blood and gore, and overhead, a turkey vulture soared. They all had to rope their horses to mount them, and with difficulty in handling their horses while stinking of blood, they made it west to the river again. They avoided their campsite and galloped north. Suddenly their freedom from the United States Government didn't appeal to them as much as it had a week ago. A stay in the stockade was far preferable to what awaited them if the Sauk found them.

# CHAPTER
## Four

The Sauk had indeed been searching for them, but there had been a delay before it was discovered that the three women were taken. With so many people in the town, it was difficult to find someone who had seen them earlier in the day. When it was discovered that they had set out to cut sweet grass, the patches along the river were searched. It wasn't long after that that the women's knives and bundles of grass were found. And when these were found, the searchers found dried blood as well. Now the whole community was on alert.

Art's attempts to cover their backtrail had been worthless. It was clear to the Sauk party that white men had taken the women because the tracks they left were those of boot heels and of shod horses. When the white men turned north on the river Wapsipinicon, however, and stayed in the water to travel, it slowed their tracking just a little, until, beyond the trees, a scout saw a flock of crows circling, landing, and taking off again. There lay death. And from the large numbers of birds, the searchers knew that there was much death there.

The Sauk searchers came upon the women. Horrified and angry at what they saw and the story they must tell to the Council, they split into two groups. Most of the search party went on to find the white men; some carried the bodies (or what was left of them) back to Saukenuk to be prepared for burial and to face the tribe with the news. Those Sauk who went on to look for the white men who had done this found their campsite in short order, including the men's gear, Art's body, and his horse. His horse would go back to the camp, as their property. They let Art's body lie where it was, to be picked apart by animals. Useful items were tucked away. But Art's uniform and items belonging to the U. S. Government would be taken back to be put in the hands of the Council.

Zeke's group had forgotten all attempts to hide their trail as they made all haste back to the Neutral Ground, and in the prairie that was ahead of them, there was little cover. Zeke was planning on pure speed to make it to safety. Unfortunately, their speed was their undoing. Their desertion had already been discovered, and Government scouts were on the lookout for the men. Shots rang out shortly after they crossed into the Neutral Ground, and Zeke, George, and Fred shot back, killing a soldier. The chase ended when the men realized that they were about to cross over into Sioux lands. They had run out of options; there was no point of the compass that was safe for them any more. Zeke stopped to make a last stand, and George stayed with him. They were far outnumbered, however, and after a brief gun fight, both men lay dead. Fred kept running north, but was pursued and killed.

To the south, in the Neutral Ground, the Sauk warriors observed this from a distance, and knew that the men who had been killed were those whose tracks they had been following. They watched in silent witness as the company's soldiers collected the bodies and placed them over the backs of horses to be taken back to their camp, and then they turned back toward Saukenuk.

There would be terrible grief and mourning in the town, for the woman who had been scalped was White Feather, the favored daughter of one of the Sauk ceremonial chiefs, Bear Who Sees. This incident would only anger the Sauk and Fox further, making them more determined than ever to battle the Americans who talked of peace but poisoned, stole, raped, and killed.

---

In the sweat lodge two nights later, the chiefs of the Council sat with Bear Who Sees. They had been fasting to help purify their bodies and minds, and the sweat lodge was hot and smoky and scented with the herbs and sweet grass that were burning in the fire. Bear Who Sees appeared to doze. When he at last opened his eyes, he grasped his medicine bag and set the sacred items it held in front of the fire. Haggard and weak from fasting and grief, Bear Who Sees grasped the thin strip of leather that held a necklace of black bear claws around his neck. He held them in his fist above his head and spoke to the others gathered there:

"The white men have killed and stolen and spread their poison firewater and disease to our people for too long. I will go with my brother Black Hawk to fight the white men to keep our lands, but my heart has been torn from my breast. I have seen the Spirit of the Great Black Bear, and he has shown me that the Great Spirit has seen what happened in the long grass between the forks of the river Wapsipinicon. As I am without heart, that place will be known as Heartless. It will be poison to the white men forever.

"The Great Spirit has sent the Spirit of the Great Black Bear to watch that place. He will listen to the voices of the Earth and Water. They will tell him when evil walks that land and it is time to come and purify the land with the blood of the white men."

The story was told over and over again, and the Sauk, together with the Fox, left to follow Black Hawk in August of 1832 in a war against the Americans with renewed anger and determination to live or die in the ways of their people. Most died in that battle, including Bear Who Sees, and the Americans took the land of the Sauk and Fox. But the place called Heartless remained, in the care of the Spirit of the Great Black Bear, for then and all time.

The Spirit of the Great Black Bear slept undisturbed for twenty-two years.

PART TWO

# The Curse Comes Alive

# CHAPTER
## Five

Heinrich Baumann was an enormously strong, tall, blonde-haired and blue-eyed man, the product of a long line of hard-working, hard-fighting farmers. He had married his wife Katrina in their native Germany and immediately the couple moved to America. He was a man who generally disliked being around too many people, and when it came time for him to take a wife, he chose to come to a new land rather than to share the family farm with his brothers. He found the eastern sea coast of America to be too crowded as well, so the young couple moved west to Pennsylvania to farm, settling near a community of German immigrants.

It was rough, back-breaking work clearing the land of trees and the ever-present rocks, but both Heinrich and his young wife Katrina were used to long, hard labor. Before too long the first fields were planted, and Heinrich had built a rough shack for them to share. Katrina proved to be as fertile as the land. In quick succession she gave birth to four sons; another two were born later.

Whereas Heinrich was stoic and did not like to part with a penny needlessly, Katrina was warm, generous, and outgoing. She truly loved her strong ox of a husband with all her heart, and was proud of what he was able to accomplish. She gathered her family to her with song and strength, and lived happily while she was close to other women, a church, and the social closeness of a German community in this new land. She secretly longed for a daughter, however, to share the comforts of close feminine companionship. Katrina would keep on trying, even though she suspected that it was too late for her.

The Baumann farm prospered, and Heinrich became a man known to their community as a good, honest, hardworking farmer. He accompanied his wife to church and social gatherings, and allowed his children to attend school during the winter months, despite his own awkwardness in crowds. He loved Katrina deeply, and had loved her ever since he had seen her smiling, open face looking at him over a barrel of potatoes in Germany. He thought she loved him as well, although the couple had never discussed it. At the time he had decided to make her his wife, he had simply gone to her father and made a bargain over several steins of beer. She had cost him two oxen, a desperately dear price; but when Katrina's father had called her to join them and told her she would marry Heinrich, the look of shy pleasure on her face was worth it.

And his instincts had proven right. Katrina would willingly obey him in everything. When she looked at him she made him feel strong and capable, and he would willingly move mountains for her.

Now, seventeen years into their marriage with six sons, well-established in the community and on their farm, Heinrich felt stifled. He dreamed of a farm so large that he could not see his neighbors except when he wanted to do so. Katrina was happily attached to several women of the town, and would take the buckboard and visit them for hours. Still, she never missed a chore or a meal for her large family. The older boys (Peter, Karl, Ruebin, and Stephan) worked admirably on the farm and he was proud of their abilities, even their ability to read in both German and English, a skill that Heinrich had never had time to master. However, when chores were done and time allowed, they were off to town on their horses, and Heinrich suspected that friends (particularly girls) were a great attraction.

Since he had no close friendships of his own, Heinrich felt as if he was losing his family.

One night he stood with a group of men at a wedding celebration, brooding about his perceived loneliness, when he overheard two men talking about a place called Iowa. This territory was far to the west across the great Mississippi River, but had been a state for eight years. Word had come from relatives who had pioneered the region that the land was very fertile and cheap, but they begged for more German settlers to come. They encouraged their families to join them in this great new land.

Heinrich was intrigued enough to ask questions, and learned that a small wagon train would be leaving after fall harvest. They planned to reach friends in Indiana, wintering there and starting out again as soon as they could to reach Iowa by spring. If Baumann was interested, they would invite the family to join them. The larger the wagon train, the less likely they were to be attacked by rogue bands of Indians who refused to accept the treaties, and more help was available in case of accidents.

Heinrich looked around the meeting hall and spied Peter, flushed and dancing with little Emma Krentz. Her father had been one of the men interested in the move west. Baumann grunted. Emma was tiny but would make a good wife for Peter when the time came. It would be a chore to keep the two separated during the trip so that no baby arrived before its time. And Emma could be a distraction from the hard labor that would lay ahead for settlers starting a new farm. He would have to work to control Peter, but he didn't think it would be too hard. Peter knew where his loyalties lay.

That night Heinrich lay awake long after Katrina slept and the house was still and dark. He knew he could sell his farm for a good price and that Katrina would move if he only asked. The boys were obedient in all ways, but Karl, his second son, had a look in his eye at times that told his father that he *thought* before he obeyed. Of all his boys, Karl would be the most likely to simply disappear one day if he did not agree to the move. It would be Karl, then, that he would have to convince. If he could do that,

Heinrich had a plan to gather his family back to him.

The next morning at breakfast Heinrich made the announcement: he had made the decision that the Baumanns would join the wagon train west to Iowa after fall harvest. Behind him, Katrina softly set the iron griddle she was holding back on to the stove and settled her hands on her husband's shoulders. Her eyes did not meet those of the boys'. Instead, she looked down at the huge, rough, calloused hand that settled on hers in gratitude. Heinrich looked around the table. Each of his sons looked only at his plate, except for Karl. For several seconds his troubled blue eyes looked straight into those of his father's; then he, too, looked at his plate. It was his family's sign of acceptance.

Later that morning Heinrich found Karl repairing tack for the horses in the barn. Incapable of a straightforward conversation about his personal feelings, Heinrich sat on a bench near his son and asked to see the leather that Karl was using, and Karl handed it over without a word. Heinrich tested the leather for its strength and examined it for cracks. Finding it to be acceptable, he handed it back, and Karl silently went back to his work. The silence stretched. Heinrich grasped his massive thighs and wondered how to begin. Finally, it was Karl who spoke.

"Iowa is far away."

With immense relief, Heinrich agreed, "Yes."

"We don't know what it will be like there."

"We only know what I heard last night at the wedding feast. It is a great, wide-open place with good farm land, and the people there are asking for more settlers," Heinrich told his son. "We could have a farm seven or eight times this size, enough for each of you boys to have your own farm one day."

Karl looked at his father with those piercing eyes. "What if I don't want to farm?"

Heinrich's jaw dropped. He had never thought of such a possibility. Farmers' sons became farmers. It had always been that way. "What would you do instead?"

"I would carve wood," Karl declared. "Come, I'll show you." He led his father to the back stall, where a small window let in the light of day. There, resting on burlap sacks of oats and barley, were sets of bowls, spoons in different sizes, and a small, ornately carved chest, all made of wood. The chest had small scraps of leather cut for hinges. Karl picked it up and handed it to his father. "This is for Mama's birthday."

Heinrich was shocked. "How did you learn this?"

"I started when I was six. I taught myself with the hunting knife I stole from you," Karl admitted. "I'm sorry, Papa." He hung his head.

Heinrich put out his hand and lightly touched his son's head. After a second he tousled the blonde hair. "So *that's* where that knife went to."

Karl looked up, hopeful. "You forgive me?"

"Will you give me a chest as well, for *my* birthday?"

"Of course!" Karl replied.

"Then all is forgiven. You are a woodcarver, I see. Would you teach an old man?" Heinrich smiled.

"You want to learn this?" Karl asked incredulously.

"If we never do anything new, then life is over. It's time for my son to teach his father," Heinrich said. He handed the chest back to Karl and grasped his son's shoulder. "Just one thing."

"Yes?"

"Farming first, carving when it's done. Agreed?"

Karl's face glowed. "Agreed!"

Heinrich left the barn, confident that he could gather his family to him once more.

---

As he had predicted, Heinrich sold his farm very easily, and for a good price. He bought another two oxen to join the two he already had; these cows would mate with the bull in due course, and he would be assured of reaching the end of his journey with supplies to see his family through. The Baumanns would be traveling in two covered wagons pulled by oxen, and their horses would be herded unfettered.

Although Katrina's heart contracted at the thought of leaving their friends and neighbors, she never thought once of doing other than what her husband asked. Peter was thrilled at the thought of traveling in the party with Emma. Karl seemed particularly close to his father and very agreeable these days. As for Ruebin, Stephan, and the younger boys Hans and Walter, they were excited about moving to the wild west. They begged their father for guns to use on the trip, but Heinrich only laughed at his smallest sons and furnished them with wooden ones that he and Karl had carved for them. He did not laugh, however, when he taught Karl, Peter, Ruebin, Stephan, and even Katrina to shoot. This was a necessary precaution; even if they were not attacked by Indians or roving bandits, hunting along the way would stretch their supplies.

The Koerner train, joined by the Baumanns, moved out in October, right after the first frosts. In all, it carried seven families and eleven wagons. By the time the first snows arrived in November, they had reached the safety of Koerner's friends in Indiana. Upon their arrival, the travelers staged a celebration; the wagons circled, neighboring settlers joined in, and Peter and Emma danced around the fire with other young couples. Hesitantly, Heinrich approached Katrina and invited her to dance as well. He picked her up, whirled her around and made her giggle like a schoolgirl. When the reel ended and the fiddler took a break to slake his thirst, they were both out of breath and holding on to one another. Tiny Katrina hugged her husband to her and allowed herself to be led back to their wagon. Heinrich sat on the bed and waited for his wife to change into her nightdress behind a curtain made from a blanket. Hans and Walter were already fast asleep in the other wagon; the older boys could see to themselves.

"Katrina."

"Yes, Heinrich?"

"There is something I must tell you."

"Tell me, husband."

"I must see your face."

Katrina pulled down the top of the blanket and peered over it at her husband. His features were in shadow and therefore unreadable. "What is it, Heinrich?"

"Come here, Katrina, and sit beside me," Heinrich said.

Katrina let go of the blanket and finished dressing in silence. What could it be? Heinrich had sounded serious. This was a time for merrymaking, not sorrow. Was he ill? Slowly she pushed back the curtain and came to sit beside her husband, waiting.

Heinrich took a deep breath. "Katrina."

She waited.

"Katrina, tomorrow morning we will awaken early. Before the others are up. We will pack up again and go on, to Iowa," Heinrich told her.

Katrina gasped in shock.

Before she could object, Heinrich went on. "We will reach Iowa by the worst of the winter, and find the best place for our farm."

"Heinrich, that is so dangerous! We will be alone! What if we are attacked by Indians? What if we are stuck in the snow? Who will help us?" Panicked, Katrina voiced the first objections she had ever made known to her husband in all their married life. The thought of such isolation was dreadful to her. "No one can help us if one of us is ill! And where will we live?"

Heinrich put his arm around Katrina and pulled her to his chest. "Katrina, my bride. You have grown soft from too much comfort, *hein?* Do you not remember leaving for America when it was only the two of us? We did not know a single soul in this land, yet you made friends. And when we started our farm in Pennsylvania, you were quick with child, yet you nursed me from my fever and worked the fields. You are stronger than you think."

"But Heinrich . . ."

"And now we have six boys. Six boys! They will help. Peter and Karl are *men*, Katrina, young men, yes, but *men!* Together we are eight. We will reach Iowa and find land near where the Koerners are going. They will be there in the spring. We will have already planted and be ready to help them start when they arrive," Heinrich whispered to her urgently.

Katrina picked her head up from his chest and looked into her husband's eyes, frightened tears glistening in hers. "Why? Why do this when it is so much easier and safer to wait?"

Heinrich met her questions with silence. How could he tell her that he was afraid of losing her and his sons? Finally Katrina rose and pulled the covers back from her side of their bed. "I will be ready, husband," she stated. She slipped beneath the covers and lay with her back to him.

Never before in their marriage had Heinrich felt this doubt, this coolness from Katrina, and he did not know how to deal with it. He pulled off his boots, washed his face and neck in the bowl by the door, and got into bed with her, staring at the back of her head. Finally he sighed and turned down the wick on the lamp. Outside, the party went on noisily, and light from the huge campfire danced strange shapes across the side of the canvas covering the wagon. On the other side of the bed, Heinrich heard a soft sob.

"Katrina."

"Y-yes, husband?"

"There is something I have never told you, but I think I must."

He could feel Katrina turning in bed to face him, but stayed where he was on his back.

"I should have told you this long ago, but I'm not used to speaking in such ways," he said. "I think I must tell you now. I love you, Katrina. I have loved you since first we met," he admitted, squirming uncomfortably inside. What if she did not love him?

Katrina had indeed been crying, but now she smiled through her tears. "I know."

"You know?"

"Do you think me a fool to leave my father's house, travel to a strange land alone with you, and have six of your sons without thinking that you loved me?" she asked, a laugh in her voice.

Heinrich considered this, but did not ask the question that was on his mind.

"Then I must tell you that I love you as well," Katrina said. "I always have, and I always will. And I will go with you tomorrow to Iowa or France or, or *Africa*—wherever you go. I *love* you, Heinrich."

The covered wagon rocked as Heinrich hefted his bulk to face his wife in bed. "I have been a fool," he whispered into her hair. "I should have guessed."

# CHAPTER
## Six

Heinrich Baumann stood outside his sod house in the hour of dawn, washing himself from one of a dozen buckets of water his sons had brought from the river the night before. He turned and grunted a greeting to his eldest son, Peter, now dressed and ready to join him in the fields. Peter only nodded in return, and bent to wash his own face and head from the same bucket his father had used. Heinrich Baumann allowed for no waste. At sixteen years old Peter was as tall as his father and already heavily muscled from years of manual labor, first at their farm in Pennsylvania, and now in this new state of Iowa. As far as farming was concerned, he was glad of the change in geography. The soil of Pennsylvania could be cultivated, but it grew as many rocks as ears of corn. He missed the trees, however, and badly. Wood for building comfortable houses and furniture, and for burning as fuel was plentiful back east. Here trees were plentiful only around the river. Oak, maple, elm, ash, walnut, and locust trees were most common, but had to be cut and then dragged by the horses or oxen to their homestead. He also missed Emma Krentz badly. Not a day went by that he didn't think of her and wonder if she and her family had made it through the winter and the journey without trouble. Soon now, soon, he would ride south to the settlement of Apple Springs and ask again if any word had arrived from the traveling party.

They had arrived on this land that his father had filed for with the Government about two months ago, in February. It had been a brutal trip. At first Peter and Karl had been sullen and angry at their father, working and eating with the family in stone silence. It had been Karl who had warmed first, for he was teaching Heinrich to carve wood. They had made a great celebration of their mother's birthday in January, and Karl had been able to give her the carved chest he had made. Heinrich had declared it a holiday for her, and while Peter and Karl killed a deer to roast for supper, he found apple trees along the wagon trail and was determined to peel the tiny, frozen apples to make a pie. Heinrich had never cooked before in his life, and finally his wife took pity on him and shooed him away from the cooking fire. He helped the older boys butcher the deer and teased Karl about the old hunting knife that his son had purloined. When the deer was quartered and the loin set aside for supper, he followed Peter to the wash buckets. He put his arm around his son's shoulders and said, "See here, you are truly a man. We depend on you. Look what you have done!"

After a moment Peter looked up at his father and smiled, and a silent truce was drawn. It was, however, the first time that Peter had harbored the adult thought that perhaps his father could make a mistake, and that was a thought that could not be forgotten. So far the trail had been rough but firm. It was cold, but no colder than it had been in Pennsylvania. Snow only dusted the ground; perhaps they would be lucky. Peter had wondered if they would make it in time to be ferried over the Mississippi River, which they would soon reach. If not, at least they would be around other people this winter.

That had not been the case, however. With the relatively mild weather, the ferrying business was still in full swing. Heinrich had allowed the family one day to rest in the comforts of civilization on the east side of the river, socializing and trading, and then the Baumanns were ferried across the great Mississippi without incident. They reached Iowa in February.

Their small individual train consisting of two covered wagons, a buckboard with dwindling supplies, and animals had made it two days past the Mississippi before the snows of February truly set in. Heavy, wet snow bogged their wagons down and the oxen were put to hard use to pull them out. Then the temperature dropped, sending icy flakes of snow. The winds of the prairie reached them, whipping the new snow into a frenzy. Sight was made impossible at times, and the younger boys were often sent ahead for just twenty paces to make sure they stayed in the track. No one bothered them, not Indians nor bandits nor traders. They were utterly alone in this wide, white world.

Heinrich consulted the map that Koerner had made for him, but without reading skills, it was necessary to have Peter help him interpret landmarks. Peter showed his father where Apple Springs was located with excitement. They were less than a day away, by his reckoning! To his astonishment, his father looked around at the snowy landscape made silver by the dark February skies, and pointed north. "We will follow this river north until we can cross it. See? There is this land between the two forks of this Wapsinicon River. That will be our home. You are right! We are only a day away from home."

"Papa, no," Peter uttered, shocked at his own words.

"*What?*" Heinrich looked at his son as if he were insane.

"Papa, we need to rest. We need to be warm. We do not need to head out further into the wilderness, not now. We should wait until spring," Peter asserted, straightening out his shoulders and tensing for a blow.

Heinrich instead put his hand on Peter's shoulder. "My son, I am your father. Please trust me. When we get to our new land we must settle on it so that I may file it with the Land Office. Then, we can have the oxen drag us a trail to Apple Springs."

Peter looked at his father and then away from him. He was tired of traveling, tired of hardship, tired of the decisions that his father was making without any assurance that they were the right ones. He came close to closing his hand into a fist and punching his father.

"Just trust me for a little longer, Peter. Please," Heinrich urged, sensing the tension and knowing full well the feeling that Peter was having.

Peter suddenly relaxed and nodded, turning back to lead the oxen north to the wilderness instead of southwest to safety. He would not abandon his father now.

But his doubt remained, and on this April morning his heart was still troubled.

---

It would have been wonderful to have had wood fires to combat the icy, rushing winds and frozen ground, but Heinrich Baumann would not allow it. They would build a wooden house and cut fire wood only after the fields had been planted. Their first shelter had been a crude lean-to formed between the wagons. The first wooden structure to be built had been completed last month: a barn for the animals. In the meantime, the family had moved into a hastily-made house of frozen sod, insulated only with bunches of the long grass that grew so luxuriantly here, and Baumann used their only chest of drawers as a door. Fuel for cooking and warmth was provided by the children roaming the fields and forests and foraging for dried buffalo dung, and by the smaller branches and bark stripped from the trees that had been used to build the barn. It was close and terribly stuffy in the sod building, and there was only a hole in the roof to let out the smoke and fumes from the small but long-lasting fires stinking of animal droppings. The family slept on long grass that had been gathered to cover the bare ground. Each family member spent time outside doing chores, walking, and taking advantage of as much daylight as possible; evenings were spent with Katrina trying to teach Hans and Walter to read in the dim half-light.

As could be expected with crowded, dirty conditions, arguments and scuffles broke out among the boys. Heinrich's size and authority had stopped any bloodshed, but there had been some close calls. Lately, it seemed as if they each had retreated into his or her own world, and few words were passed among them. It had been a miserable time, and Peter was glad to be out in the fresh air and in a hurry to start the planting. He swore to himself that as soon as the farm was up and running, he would move from this hateful place. He thought they were all getting stranger by the day, as if they slept inside poisoned earth.

Karl, Hans, and Walter appeared next. There was no greeting from any of them, only silence as they washed. Karl shook his head and hands to dry them in the chill spring air and went straight to the barn. Hans went to his father and said, "Mama's sick."

Heinrich looked at Hans, then back at the opening in the earth that served as their front door. "Nobody feels good right now, Hans. We'll feel better as it gets warmer and we get fresh air."

Peter turned with a flush to his father. "Mama is *sick*, Papa. We all know it. She needs a doctor. The least you could do is go and see her."

Heinrich, always slow to anger but as implacable as a bull when it happened, turned with reddening neck to his son.

"Are you telling me what I should do with my wife, boy?"

"Someone has to!" choked Peter, his fists doubling.

"I should have given you a lesson long ago, you *Kacker* of a baby!" Heinrich roared.

Out of the doorway appeared Stephan. "Papa!"

Peter and Heinrich were circling each other like fighting dogs, fists raised. Anger sparked like lightning between them. Hans shrank against the sod house, terrified.

"Papa! PAPA!" Stephan cried, and rushed forward to get between the two men. He pushed his father back. "Papa, come look at Mama!"

Heinrich ripped his gaze from Peter and looked at Stephan. For the first time he could hear his wife calling for him weakly. The blood left his face, and he turned his back on Peter and strode to the sod house.

There, in the moldy earth warmed this morning only by the glow of an oil lamp, Katrina lay on their bed. Sheets were twisted around her, and she had vomited on herself. Sweat soaked her nightgown and hair. Heinrich realized that she was horribly thin and pale. "Katrina!" he cried.

"Husband, help me. I must get outside, into the sun and fresh air," she begged, then gagged again. "I . . . I need water," she finished helplessly.

Heinrich picked her up and carefully aimed her prone body through the doorway. "Stephan, get the blankets and pillows from your bed," he ordered, and Stephan hurried to obey.

Peter saw his mother and immediately forgot his earlier anger. He ran to pull up fresh strands of long grass, and barked at the other boys to do so as well. They made a rough pallet while his father held his mother, covering it with the blankets. Heinrich himself tenderly washed the vomitus from his wife's face and hair, and ordered the boys to cut wood for a wood fire. It would be green and smoky, but it would be outside, and he could bathe his wife. While the boys were gone he stripped the nightgown from her to wrap her in a blanket. He gasped in surprise when he realized his wife was pregnant.

"How long gone are you?" he asked Katrina.

"Five months," she breathed.

"You didn't tell me. I wouldn't have made us come here if I'd known."

"I know," she smiled weakly, then clutched at his arm. "I think it's a girl. Don't let me lose her."

Heinrich kissed his wife's brow, smoothing back her hair and seeing for the first time how grime had inundated her skin. "I won't. We'll go to Apple Springs today, to the doctor."

"No, no doctor," Katrina tossed her head. "I'm only going to have a child. He would laugh."

"But you never got sick like this before, and you've had six children!" protested Heinrich.

"No doctor. Promise," Katrina begged weakly, and Heinrich agreed.

That day Heinrich decided to move his family from the sod house to the wagons until he and Peter and Karl could finish a house for them. As Peter returned with a load of firewood, he approached his son and admitted that he had been wrong. He asked Peter to help him build a house, and Peter whooped with glee. Quickly he called to Karl for help, hitched up the oxen and drove them toward the trees with a wood axe and a hand saw.

Even working every possible hour of the day while the younger boys planted, it took them three weeks to finish a log cabin. Peter made the trip to Apple Springs to bring back precious windows while Katrina was safely installed in the new house. While he was in town, Peter found that the Koerner party had made it to the settlement. Even though he had not taken the time to find Emma, he was heartened. He also secretly paid a visit to the doctor to ask about his mother, who was still nauseated and losing weight. Doctor Leipmann, who treated both humans and animals in this small frontier town, said that he would visit when he could. Until then, Katrina Baumann needed fruit and vegetables and milk. Peter had no money of his own, so the doctor gave him a dollar to buy canned goods and milk. The boy promised to repay him if it took the rest of his life, and thanked the doctor profusely. Doctor Leipmann waved it off, and said that this was a community truly like no other; they saw to themselves, and help would be given when it was needed. Peter rushed back with his cargo, arriving in the middle of the night. He explained the canned fruit, vegetables, and milk to his father by telling him that the windows had cost less than expected, and that Mama had asked for them when she was terribly ill one night. He didn't mention his visit to the doctor, but as the spring wore on he kept the younger boys busy picking berries and he planted their own vegetable garden.

Seven-year-old Hans and five-year-old Walter were happy to explore the woods, river, and fields. One day they crossed the river to the far side, creeping atop a tree that had fallen over the river to make a bridge of sorts. They could see red berries growing close to the grown with fragrant, glossy green leaves: wintergreen. If the wintergreen was there, sweet wild strawberries had to be close by! They searched a clearing until Hans noted that Walter was standing stock-still, staring into the trees.

Coming closer, he was amazed to see an Indian woman in full native dress standing there. Shyly, Walter waved to her. She smiled and waved back; then the wind suddenly gusted, tossing the leaves where she stood, and she was gone.

The young boys were thrilled. A real Indian! Excited and talking in gasps, they ran back to the log over the river to tell the rest of their family. As they crawled over the bridge, however, Hans suddenly thought better of the idea. He knew that white men killed Indians; maybe Papa would want to kill her. But this woman had seemed nice. She was a young woman. Perhaps she had children of her own. Maybe they should keep it a secret.

Walter was difficult to convince. He didn't really believe that white men killed Indians, anyway. At least, not nice white men. In a sudden brainstorm, Hans told Walter that he could be sure that Mama and Papa would never let them go into the woods alone again if they told them about the woman. If they told their older brothers, it would be the same as telling their parents. Walter did not want to give up exploring the woods, and so he agreed.

Over the next several weeks, they saw the woman only once more, this time in the wheat field. Again she smiled and held up her hand in greeting; again she disappeared as mysteriously as she had before.

The children could not know this, but the Indian woman was identical in appearance and character to White Feather of the Sauk, who was now long since dead.

To the family's intense relief, Katrina began to grow healthy and stronger. Doctor Leipmann visited ("No charge, just passing by and was curious about who lived here," he told them, and winked at Peter), asked Katrina when she was expecting, and if there was anything he could do for any of them. Both Katrina and Heinrich smiled their thanks, but denied that they needed help. Particularly since he was their first social visitor, they invited him to stay and have a piece of cake.

"You know, there's an old Indian tale about this area. Have you heard it?" he asked, as he finished his cake and pulled his chair back from the table.

"No, not a thing," replied Heinrich.

"Story goes, this is supposed to be protected ground. It's not an old burial ground or anything like that. I hate to tell you this, but the land is supposed to be cursed," the doctor told the family.

Heinrich and Katrina glanced at each other and the boys drew closer, eyes wide.

Liepmann continued, "The old Sauk Indians claim that the soil itself drives white men mad. If human blood is spilled in anger and hate on this ground, some great bear is supposed to be called by the Great Spirit to take care of the whole business."

"Really?" asked Hans, eager for details. "Were there Indian wars here or something?" He looked at Walter meaningfully.

"Yes, years ago, son," answered Leipmann, smiling at the boy. "People from Apple Springs have always avoided the area because of the story. The Indians call this place, 'Heartless.'"

Heinrich and Katrina looked at each other again, and Katrina shivered.

"Did you never wonder why no one else had settled here?" Leipmann asked Heinrich.

Heinrich took his time answering, then shrugged. "We started out with the Koerner party. Koerner had relatives in Apple Springs who told them about the river and how it divided, and how very few people had even come up here between the forks of the river to hunt." He looked sheepishly at the doctor. "I thought they were fools."

Doctor Leipmann laughed out loud. "Apple Springs has its share of fools, that is so. But does the isolation not bother you? Have you considered moving your farm?"

Heinrich glanced at his wife. Katrina read her husband's mind accurately: stubborn as a bull, Heinrich would not give up on a thing until he was *ready* to give up. And he was only beginning here. She smiled, and he returned her smile, confident that she knew his thoughts.

"We will stay," said Heinrich simply. "We do not believe silly Indian superstitions."

Doctor Leipmann nodded thoughtfully, then turned to Peter.

"Seen any bears around here?" he asked casually.

"No. In fact, no bear sign at all," said Peter.

"Well, if I can't convince you, be careful, and be good to each other," Leipmann said seriously, taking his hat. "I'll say goodbye now, Mrs. Baumann. All you have to do is send one of your boys to town to find me when the time comes, and I'll send a midwife out. I'm glad to see the canning jars. You be sure to have fruit and vegetables, and maybe Mr. Baumann will get you a milk cow or so, so that you and your baby and your growing boys can have some milk."

At the door the doctor turned back to the family. "You know, it's none of my business, Mr. Baumann, but it might be a good idea to get yourselves to town more often. Meet the people, take a rest from your farm. Do you good."

At Heinrich's silence, Dr. Leipmann opened the door and turned once more to the family before he left. "Just doctorly advice. Can't help it, I suppose. Thank you for the cake, Mrs. Baumann, and take care of yourself and that baby."

With that he left.

As the good doctor drove back toward town, Peter and Heinrich looked at each other. They both knew how close they both had come not so very long ago to spilling human blood.

It wasn't far off, though.

# CHAPTER
## Seven

The Baumann farm was doing exceptionally well. Spring rains had softened the ground and hastened their ability to plough and plant, and roughly eighty acres of corn, wheat, oats, and barley were fully grown and ready for first harvesting.

Heinrich had agreed with Katrina that once a month she and the boys would attend church in Apple Springs. On one such Sunday he carefully waited until the house was empty. When he was sure that no one could watch him, he drew a flat, heavy wooden chest, about the length and width of a suitcase, out from under the bed. This was made from heavy Pennsylvania oak, with a minimum of decoration; he fashioned it with his own hands from the teachings of his son Karl. He was certain that none of the family knew about the chest, since he had been very cautious with it. After all, what was a man without money? It was money he had earned with his own hands and back over the years, building his first farm.

He had no thought of Katrina's labors as a farmhand and his wife. In those days, a woman accepted the money that was gifted to her by her husband and was grateful for it. Heinrich had hidden it first in the bottom of the covered wagon where he slept during their journey to Iowa. Then, as he was making the sod house where they had wintered, he buried it beneath where he would sleep. He instinctively repeated his actions in his house when it was built. Groping even further under the bed, his fingers found the key in the corner of the head of the bed, under the mattress. Heinrich inserted the key and held his breath as he opened the lid. Yes! It was still there. Gold, pure $20.00 gold pieces that had substance as a man felt their weight in his pocket. He sat before the chest on the floor and sighed. His gratitude for his wife's regained health (and some guilt for her sickness) was such that he had decided to part with a large portion of it now, instead of later. He counted out a sizeable amount, and over the next days he would make several trips to the village alone or with Peter and Karl, bringing back chickens, sheep, a cow and a bull, pigs, and even cloth for clothes and window curtains. Heinrich replaced the chest and key, and that evening he made plans with his sons on their return from Apple Springs.

Katrina was delighted. She had never seen her husband spend so much money, and had no idea of how much Heinrich had hidden away. It would never occur to her to ask. As her belly grew and the heat wore on, she kept up with her daily chores of cooking, laundering, mending, and the like, but she found herself seeking the coolness of the east fork of the river several times a day. There she would sit in the shade of the trees with her bare feet in the water, or, when she was sure the boys were busy elsewhere, she would strip down and soak in the river naked. She would dream of the future and the happiness that was promised by their good fortune. They had a wonderful farm already, a baby (she *knew* it was a girl) on the way, and old acquaintances not *too* far away. Peter had confided to her about his feelings for Emma Krentz. She liked the young beauty very much and hoped they would settle near the family farm. And Heinrich was always surprising them with something new from town. She still couldn't get used to it.

She supposed it must have something to do with the corn liquor.

As she and the boys helped unload the wagon after each of Heinrich's trips to town, she noted her husband disappearing into the barn with two crock jugs. After supper each night he would melt away for a bit, and when he returned, he smelled of whiskey. He was more openly affectionate, both toward her and the boys, and had even made friends in Apple Springs. Katrina's thoughts darted to two friends of Heinrich's she did *not* like, two brothers named Herman and Johann Wolff. Whenever these men met the family in Apple Springs, they would seduce Heinrich away from his family. Katrina and the boys would leave the church or the stores, and more and more often Heinrich would be waiting for them in the back of the buckboard, drunk. It was embarrassing to find her husband snoring away in the middle of the day, smelling like a tavern. Katrina would hurry her children to leave for the farm at once, and it ruined their chances for an invitation to lunch or leisurely conversation with the townsfolk.

Of course Katrina investigated the barn and found the crocks of liquor. Well, her husband worked hard and deserved to relax. She was used to her own Papa snoring away in front of the fire in the evenings, an empty beer stein at his side. With some difficulty she uncorked one of the jugs and dipped her finger in, tasting what Heinrich had been drinking. *Ach,* it was awful! She was glad he did not bring it into the house.

Well, anyway, it was time to harvest the first plantings of field crops, and start the haying. *That* should keep her husband busy for a while. And they badly needed a root cellar, a large one, to store ice and vegetables and the jars of tomatoes, pickles, beets, preserves, and much more that would be produced in her kitchen. Also, they had heard of the terrible storms that could sweep across the prairies, called cyclones. A root cellar should be big enough to shelter the whole family, as well.

She knew just the spot. Their old sod house sat where they had left it, close by the barn. With a close-fitting door and some improvements, she thought they could easily make it into a strong cellar. Katrina would ask Heinrich about it tonight . . . *during* supper.

---

Supper was a lively meal. Katrina had made her husband's favorite meal, consisting of sausages, cabbage, potatoes, and blueberry pie with fresh cream. While Heinrich and the older boys worked on the covered wagons to transform them into cargo wagons for the crops that were about to be harvested, Hans and Walter had gone "fishing". That is, although they *carried* poles with strings and hooks that Heinrich had fashioned for them when they left that morning, they returned empty-handed just before supper. Their father teased them, encouraging them to tell tales of huge fish that got off their hooks. With each telling, the fish got bigger and bigger. Katrina dabbed tears of laughter from her eyes with her apron and begged her husband to stop. They both suspected that the young boys had spent yet another day looking for the cave of the fabled Indian bear.

As Heinrich finished his second piece of pie and sat back with a contented sigh, Katrina brought up the subject of the root cellar. Heinrich agreed at once. He would dig the floor deeper, and Karl offered to make a door. Peter would make shelves of leftover boards from the cargo wagons, and Stephan and Ruebin would cover the hole in the roof and add more dirt on top of the roof for insulation. The younger boys would drag wooden crates in to await potatoes, turnips, onions, and the like.

Heinrich figured the project would take a day. That evening, while Katrina happily washed the dishes with Hans drying them and Walter putting them carefully away, he stole away to the barn and his jug of corn liquor. He poured a little into a tin cup and savored its savage, acrid taste. The first sip always burned his mouth and throat, and as it hit his stomach it felt like it torched a fire. The second sip was always much better. Heinrich sat on a stump behind the barn, facing west and the sun as it sunk toward the horizon. Life was good, and he had accomplished exactly what he had hoped to do: he had gathered his family to him once more. He finished what was in the cup and started to return it to its place behind the jug, when he thought, *Is not now the time to celebrate? One more cup and I will sleep well, knowing that I have all I want.* He filled the cup again from the jug in the barn, and as an afterthought, decided to take the jug with him. Just in case.

*I should have Herman and Johann visit me here, to see my beautiful farm,* he mused, sitting on the stump again. He laughed to himself. *Johann makes me laugh so hard at his stories from the old country! Katrina would laugh, too, if she got to know him. She could make them sausages and cabbage, just like we had for supper tonight. They are such good friends to have.* He tried to think if the brothers were married, or what work they did, but the harder he thought, the further the information slipped from him. He knew they didn't have farms. When he visited them, they were always to be found in the tavern. A man couldn't farm and spend his days in the tavern all the time.

He drained his second cup of liquor, and wiped his mouth with his sleeve. It was still light out; perhaps he should go look inside the sod house now and see what kind of shape it was in. From where he was he could only see a small part of it. He hadn't been inside it since they had moved Katrina into the new house.

Heinrich hefted himself up off the stump and stretched his muscles, hearing a satisfying *crack!* as he leaned back. *That is the sound of a man who works hard,* he recalled his father saying. Well, it was true. He took his jug and returned to the inside of the barn, meaning to put the jug and cup away . . . but then thought better of it. Perhaps he should take them with him to the root cellar. On the way out of the barn he spotted the shovel, hanging from nails on the wall. Perhaps he should take that, as well, and just put it inside the sod house tonight. He picked up the shovel, but found it awkward to juggle the cup, jug, and shovel at the same time, especially since he was now swaying rhythmically on his feet. In the end he left the cup and headed for the sod house with the shovel and jug. He was proud of the perfectly straight line he thought he was walking.

Despite the strong sun's rays that still lit the western sky, it was dark in there. Perhaps some animal had made its home there. He felt to the right of the door and yes, a lantern and a tin of matches were still there. He lit the lantern and turned up the wick. All that remained of the first Baumann homestead was here: the lantern and matches. Heinrich looked around the tiny cave, amazed that eight souls had spent the dead of winter here in this tiny, cramped space. He thought of Katrina and her illness, and all his happiness left him. He sank to the floor, opened the jug, and slung it over his shoulder for a sip as he had seen Herman and Johann do.

Here on the dirt floor of the hovel there was a sickly, dead smell. *Katie, what did I do to you?* he thought, tears gathering in his eyes. *Peter was right all along. I was a fool to make you live in this hole in the ground.* He thought of what life without his wife would be like, and the tears coursed down his cheeks. He roughly scrubbed them away with his shirt sleeve, but he couldn't scrub away the sight of Katrina as he had carried her out into the open air that early spring morning, covered in vomit. He took another swig.

*You were a stupid, arrogant fool. You listened to no one but yourself, and took a fool's advice. You thought that because you were strong enough to do it, Katie would be strong enough, too. Katie and our little baby girl.* And he sobbed aloud.

---

In the house, Katrina had long ago finished the dishes and was sitting by the fireplace knitting. She *knew* she would have a baby girl this time, so she staunchly knitted with wool that had been stained pink. She dreamed of her daughter: she would be golden-haired with great blue eyes, so gentle and pretty. *I'll name her Illse, after my mother,* Katrina smiled to herself. *I will teach her to cook, and to sew, and to sing. While the boys work the fields, she will be with me.* She dropped her knitting beside her as the baby kicked at her belly, and cradled her girth lovingly.

*Heinrich has been gone for a long time tonight. What is he doing?* She rose and looked out the window that faced the barn, but couldn't see him. Just then, Peter came from the direction of the boys' bedroom and saw his mother at the window. "What is it, Mama?" he asked.

"Oh, I was wondering where your father was," Katrina said lightly, turning to face her son. "It seems like he's been gone a long time."

"I can go look for him. He may have found something that needed to be fixed on one of the wagons," Peter offered.

"You are right. He probably did find something to do. Thank you, Son," Katrina said gratefully. Each footstep at the end of these hot days was exhausting, especially after spending so much time over the stove cooking.

In less than ten minutes Peter was back, an odd look on his face. "Mama, I found Papa."

Katrina was knitting again. "Well? What is he doing?" she asked without looking up from her work.

"I think you had better come and look at him," replied Peter.

Katrina looked up at once, and put her knitting aside quickly. "Why? Is he ill?"

"Not really," Peter said slowly, "but you should tell me what to do with him." His face was transformed with fright and uncertainty.

Anxious and concerned, Katrina tottered as quickly as she could to follow Peter to the old sod house. As they grew nearer, she could hear Heinrich talking; but *who* was he talking *to*? At the doorway, Peter put a finger to his lips to warn her to be quiet, lit an oil lamp he had taken from the house, and held it as high as he could in the cramped space. There was Heinrich, kneeling on the dirt floor in the corner of the hut, digging with his hands in the dirt as if he were a dog. He didn't notice the change in light, nor did he see his wife and son, staring at him in shock.

Heinrich had reverted to German in his agitation, but Katrina and Peter understood him well despite the slurring in his speech.

*You are a dog, so dig like a dog! Find your chest of gold that you hid so well. Oh, you are useless! Dig deeper! The light is going!* This voice was deeper than Heinrich's usual voice, rough and angry.

*I can't find it! I know it was hidden right here, somewhere. Someone must have stolen it!* Heinrich whined back in the frightened voice of a child.

*Dig until you find it. Dig all night long if you must,* insisted the deep voice. *You buried it. Now FIND it!*

Katrina gasped and drew back, clinging to Peter's arm as she did so. "He has gone mad!"

Peter whispered, "He has his corn liquor with him. Do you think he's only drunk?"

Katrina glanced back inside the hovel. Black dirt enshrouded her husband's hair, face, arms, and hands. His jug was lying on its side and the oil lamp he used was burning low. "I don't know. I've never seen anyone act like this, not even your Uncle Kurt."

"I've never met Uncle Kurt," replied Peter.

"You were born here in America, and Kurt is your father's brother. He lives in Germany." She shook her head, bewildered. "Kurt often drank until he turned mean and angry, and wanted to fight. Heinrich would stay away from him when he got so drunk." Katrina considered the situation, and looked once more at her husband digging in the dirt, talking to himself. "Let's leave him here, alone. He will probably fall asleep soon, and in the morning he will have a big headache. When he feels better, I'll talk to him."

Nodding, Peter followed his mother back to the house. Inside, Katrina turned to her son. "Do not tell your brothers about this, Peter," she begged. "Your father would not want them to know about it."

Peter agreed, and when they returned to the house Katrina put her knitting away and dressed for bed. Heinrich did not appear in the house that night, but the first rays of dawn found Peter sitting in a rocking chair before the fireplace, wide awake and watchful. His father's shotgun, fully loaded, lay against the wall within easy reach.

## CHAPTER
### Eight

Hans and Walter were the first to rise the next morning. They wanted to finish their chores early so that they could continue their hunt for the bear, but first, they were hungry for breakfast.

Walter was the first to notice that Peter wasn't in his bed. "Where's Peter?" he asked his brother.

Hans looked at Peter's side of the bed that he shared with Ruebin and Stephan. It was empty. He shrugged. "I don't know. Perhaps he's already started working on the root cellar with Papa."

Satisfied, the boys dressed hurriedly and bounded out of the boys' bedroom, stopping short at the sight of Peter in the rocking chair. "Where's Mama?" asked Hans.

Peter stopped rocking the chair. "Mama's still sleeping," he said in a soft voice. "I'll make your breakfast." The thought of frying sausages and eggs and the greasy smell they would create turned his stomach over. "Since it's just us, let's have bread with honey and milk."

"Yes!" cried Walter. "That's a wonderful breakfast."

"Hush," warned Peter. "Wash your faces and hands, and you can eat." He hefted the crock of smooth, creamy milk Stephan had brought from the barn the night before and poured a cup for each of them.

While Hans and Walter were dripping honey on the thick slices of bread that Peter had carved for them, Katrina appeared. Quickly she looked at Peter. "Where's your father?" she asked.

Peter looked at her meaningfully over the heads of his young brothers. "He's already outside."

She quickly kissed each of her sons in greeting. "You two have a special job today."

Hans and Walter looked at each other in concern. An *extra* chore? When they had so much planned? Walter asked, "What is it, Mama?"

Katrina pulled a wide basket from the shelf above the stove. "I want you to take this basket and fill it with blueberries. But be careful. Bears like to eat blueberries, too, you know. You had better start early; I want to make jam today. Your brothers and I will feed the animals this morning."

Hans and Walter looked up at her, each of their mouths formed in a silent "o", and then looked at each other with delight. "Oh Mama, we will get you the biggest, juiciest blueberries in the world!" exclaimed Hans. "But what about the root cellar? We were going to help with that today."

Katrina shook her head. "We'll do it tomorrow. Today we'll make things to put *in* the root cellar. All right?"

At the lightning speed that only young children seem to achieve, the boys gulped the rest of their milk and dipped their hands in the wash water on the stove. In too much of a hurry to dry their hands on a towel, they wiped them on their shirts as they rushed out the door with the big basket.

Katrina sat at the table in relief after she had watched them disappear in the direction of the trees. "Well, that is one problem out of the way," she told Peter. "Did you look at Papa yet this morning?"

"No," Peter replied. "I thought I would let him wake up on his own."

"That's probably a good idea," Katrina sighed, "but what are we going to do about Karl, and Stephan, and Ruebin?"

"I don't know," Peter admitted. "But there is much to do on this farm, and not too many days to do it. Papa had better wake up soon."

At just that moment Katrina's remaining sons filed out of

their bedroom. Katrina moved to start breakfast for them, but Peter made her sit while he dished out milk, bread and honey. He started a fire in the cooking stove, and put a kettle of water on the stove to heat. "I decided to make breakfast for Mama today," he explained to his brothers. "For Mama, I will make tea."

Katrina smiled up at her son in tired gratitude. Peter was a wonderful, thoughtful son. He would make Emma such a good husband.

Suddenly, the air of the peaceful, warm summer morning was shattered with a tremendous, angry roar that seemed to go on forever. It was joined by the animals giving voice to their startled fear.

For an instant, all five of them sat as if mesmerized, eyes wide and breath held. Then Peter broke the spell by striding to the fireplace. He gripped the shotgun tightly and headed for the door.

"Peter, *NO!*" Katrina screamed as she struggled to her feet. Karl ran to the window nearest the barn, where it seemed the sound originated.

Peter set his face in a mask. "Not unless I have to, Mama. Not unless I must." He stopped at the door with his back still to his family. "Stay here." And he quietly opened the door and slipped out.

"Can you see anything, Karl?" asked Ruebin. "What is it?"

"Where's Papa?" asked Stephan at the same time.

"I can see nothing, nothing at all except Peter going around the corner of the barn. I don't know what it was; it didn't sound like any animal I've ever heard," answered Karl. He turned to Katrina. "Peter shouldn't be alone out there. I'm going to go with him." He took his father's old hunting knife from its place on the mantel of the fireplace.

Katrina put herself between Karl and the door. "No, Karl! I forbid it!"

As gently but as firmly as he could, Karl picked up his mother and set her aside. "He's my *brother*. And Papa is in danger, too."

Katrina cried, "Karl!" as he left. She sobbed great rending sobs; it felt as if her heart was being squeezed by a giant fist. Tears washed her face.

Behind her, Stephan and Ruebin were as determined to follow as Karl had been. This time, however, Katrina blocked the door with her body and held onto the frame with all her might.

"No! Stephan, you must take a horse to town and get help. Take Kurstin, she's the fastest. And bring the doctor, too."

As Stephan stood weighing the need to join a fight alongside his brothers and father, she pushed him. "Promise me you'll go! And run her as fast as you can!"

As Stephan silently nodded, she let go of the door frame and moved. "Hurry!" Katrina urged him. And she turned to Ruebin, who was looking mutinous.

"Ruebin, I know how you feel, but . . ."

Suddenly that terrible morning was split by another sound, one even more terrifying to Katrina than the first. It was the deadly *BOOM!* of a single shotgun blast. She screamed, "NO! Oh God, oh God, NO!" and staggered out the door herself, Ruebin close behind her. As he pushed past his mother on the neat porch, another enormous roar sounded, and this time they could clearly identify Heinrich's voice in it. Horses screamed and reared in their stalls; oxen and cows bellowed; chickens squawked and pecked at each other in the dooryard, feathers flying. Above it all, she heard one of her sons scream, "Papa! Papa, NO!"

Stephan had just mounted Kurstin, who he was fighting to control. The normally well-mannered horse's eyes were rolling in her head; she was trying to run away from the barn while Stephan struggled to turn her back. Katrina hurried to the back of the horse, screamed at Stephan, "I love you, Stephan! *Hurry to get help!*" and slapped Kurstin's rump as hard as she could manage. The mare bolted and took off like a shot, by instinct following the track toward Apple Springs. All Stephan could do was lie down on her mane and hold on for his life.

Katrina turned to find Ruebin, but it was too late. He, too, was disappearing around the corner of the barn in the direction of the sod house, where she knew the trouble was. She gasped a great sob and followed. She ignored the first labor pain. It was too soon. Still, she wrapped her arms around her huge belly protectively.

---

Morning's first rays of sunlight found Heinrich still toiling at his obsession of the night before. In his mind's eye he could only see the chest of coins that he had brought all the way from Pennsylvania with him and buried in the earth beneath where he had slept. All reason had left him. He forgot that when they moved to the new log house he had dug it up and put it under the bed. At this time, he was only sure that when he found the chest, all his problems would be solved. He did not stop to consider which problems he had; he *knew* which problems had to be solved. He had figured it all out last night. There was Katrina, first of all, a demon in the guise of a pretty, smiling woman who said she loved him while she secretly laughed at him. Peter, his first son, should have been grateful to Heinrich for bringing him into this world; but he had seen the challenge on his first-born's face several times. Young pup! He thought he knew everything, even more than his Papa. He would teach *him*.

Karl did not want to be a farmer. He thought farming was beneath him, and that made him *better* than his father. Carving in wood—child's play! And Stephan and Ruebin. They looked up to their older brothers like gods. They had forgotten that *he* was their *father!* In Germany, in the old country, this would never have happened. *He* had never forgotten who was in charge when he was living in his father's house. His father had made it perfectly clear to him.

His wrath deepened as he thought of Hans and Walter. Hans was seven years old and Walter was five, but every other word out of their mouths was *Mama!* And now they could both read. What good was reading on the farm? They wasted their time! They *all* knew how to read, all except him. Why had Katrina never bothered to teach *him*? Yes, yes, she thought he was stupid.

And so it all came back to Katrina. And now she was big as a sow with yet another mouth to feed. *If he could only find that money!*

Heinrich stood up to survey the fruits of his labors thus far. The sod house had been literally torn apart by hand. Where it had stood yawned a great pit, and at the bottom was a blossom of water. Heinrich Baumann had found a wonderful place for a well, but he himself would never see that well. His heart hammered as he realized that the money he sought was being lost forever as the water rushed into the pit. He roared, a great inhuman scream of madness and fury and frustration, and fell on his knees in the muddy mess, trying to dig blindly beneath the rising water.

And this is how Peter found him, cursing and muttering, wallowing in black mud that now covered him almost completely. Peter Baumann stood at the edge of the pit that had once been his home and was incapable of moving or uttering a sound. He had lowered the shotgun as he approached the great hole in the ground, wondering where the sod house had gone. In disbelief he stared at his father. Heinrich did not know that Peter was there; he had more important things to do.

But Karl was approaching from behind Peter, and had not yet seen what his brother had seen.

"Peter! What is it? Where's the old house?" he cried.

At that, Heinrich raised his massive, muddy head. The pupils of his eyes were so large that they could not be recognized as once having been blue, and the whites of his eyes were entirely red. He looked like a demon from hell. He grinned, and the flash of his white teeth in all that black sent icy fingers tickling Peter's spine from the neck down. Every hair on his body stood on end. He gasped and stepped back from the hole, grasping the shotgun to his chest once more.

"Peter." It was Heinrich's voice, croaking from the hole.

Peter didn't move.

"Peter, get down here and help me!"

Karl had reached the hole at Peter's side, and leaned forward to peer into it. Peter grabbed his brother's shirt and tried to pull him back, but he was too late. An enormous, black tentacle of an arm shot out of the hole and fastened on Karl's ankle, pulling the surprised boy into the muck. He landed on his back, his face disappearing beneath the rising water, and the knife he had held flung wide. Heinrich growled a deep, visceral sound of satisfaction and he fell on the boy, holding his head beneath the water while Karl struggled for his life.

Desperate, Peter aimed the shotgun several feet to the side of his father's head and pulled the trigger. The plug buried itself in the wall of the hole, but the blast turned Heinrich's attention from Karl. Heinrich stood and faced Peter while Karl scrambled to his knees, choking and vomiting mud.

"Peter!" he demanded. "Give me that gun."

"No, Papa. Come out of there and leave Karl alone."

"You fool! You have wanted to kill me for a long time. There you are with a gun in your hands and you don't even have the guts to use it, do you?" Heinrich taunted him.

"Papa, I don't want to shoot you, but you are acting crazy."

"Crazy now, am I?" sneered Heinrich, and laughed as he had done at the finest of his friends' jokes. He doubled over, and as Peter watched him guardedly, he jerked upright with the shovel that he had carried into the sod house the night before. He swung the blade of the shovel in a great, wide arc with all the strength he had, and chopped Peter in the side of his left knee, screaming in ecstasy. The shotgun flew from Peter's hands and landed several feet to the side of him as he crumpled to the ground.

Heinrich used the shovel as a crutch to help himself up from the hole and towered above Peter as the boy used his good leg and hands to try to stand, tottering perilously. Karl, able now to breathe but searching hopelessly for the hunting knife in the water, pulled the only solid thing he could find from the mud: the corn liquor jug. He clawed his way out of the hole on the side opposite his father, still lugging the heavy crock jug, and still gasping for air and sobbing.

Still chuckling merrily, Heinrich took his time in approaching Peter. Peter's lower left leg was broken, and white bone and gore poked crazily out of his bloody pants. Peter was growing weaker; his eyes swam with shock, and he shook his head to clear his eyes and mind. Behind Heinrich, Karl realized that his father was about to kill Peter, and he screamed, "Papa! Papa, NO!" He ran around the hole as fast as he could, but not before his father had raised the shovel over his head and buried the blade in the top of Peter's head.

The morning had dawned cloudlessly, but overhead dark, green-grey thunderheads suddenly blocked the sun. It was as if someone had blown out a lamp.

As Heinrich bent and struggled to remove his weapon from his victim, Karl flew from behind his father and crashed the heavy jug into his father's skull. Heinrich grunted and lurched, and Karl hit him again. This time the crockery split, and a jagged tear spewed blood from the side of Heinrich's head to mix in the black mud covering him. He turned and faced his next oldest son, crouching low to the ground.

Karl fell back. He had dropped the pieces of the jug when he had hit his father the second time, and now he had no weapon. As from a long distance away he could hear the horses screaming and the voice of his mother. Heinrich grasped a large shard of crockery in his fist, and approached Karl steadily. Karl turned to run, but his left foot slipped on the muddy side of the pit and he disappeared over the side. Heinrich jumped in after him and cut off his screams by slicing his throat with the piece of his liquor jug.

Heinrich Baumann sat in the mud and water of the pit panting, his second son's head lying on his knees. This was tiring work, and so much yet to do. If he could just rest for a bit . . .

Kurstin flew along the wagon track toward Apple Springs with every ounce of speed she could muster. Stephan at last had gained enough control to feel that he was riding her instead of merely flying helplessly atop her. Something was desperately wrong at the farm, and his family was in danger. He thought of his mother and how terrified she had looked, and he urged Kurstin on even faster. When they came to the crude bridge that Heinrich had built over the river so that the family might take a wagon across it more easily, horse and rider were as of one mind and avoided it and plunged through the shallow water. They raced to the village at a speed that Stephan had never before experienced.

He had made up his mind that he would go first to the doctor. Dr. Leipmann knew the way to their farm and could lead the sheriff and other men there while he gathered more help. Suddenly, the sky grew dark. He managed to slow Kurstin's gait to a trot and looked above and around him. Enormous clouds were moving quickly from every point of the compass to the land behind him; in the center they piled as high as the eye could see and churned with a sickly green and grey color. Stephan's heart pounded in his throat, and he kicked Kurstin back into a gallop.

---

Ruebin had stood at the corner of the barn and watched in horror as his father jumped into the pit after Karl, Peter's battered body close by. Karl was screaming for his father to stop, and then there was a sudden horrible silence from the hole.

The animals had gone berserk with the sounds of shouts, screams, and gunshot, and now they were able to smell blood. The walls of the barn shook as the horses kicked the sides of their stalls, and the bulls were charging the sides of their pens, snorting angrily. Above the chaos one sound broke Ruebin's shock: the weak voice of his mother calling his name. He turned, and saw

Katrina staggering toward him, hugging the outside of the barn. Ruebin leapt in her direction. He saw the dark color of wetness staining the front of the bottom of her dress, and from his memories of his younger brothers' births, he knew what it meant. Mama was about to have her baby.

He whirled his mother around to face the opposite direction, and scooped her up in his arms. Katrina fought him, crying, asking about her husband and Peter and Karl, but he would answer none of these questions. He strode as quickly as he could with his burden to the rows of corn and then into them. When he thought he had gone far enough, he set her down and put his hand to his mother's lips.

"Mama, Peter and Karl are trying to calm Papa down. Let them work. Hide in the corn until I come and get you."

Katrina didn't believe Ruebin; she had heard the shouts and screams, and she knew her sons were in trouble. "Ruebin, what happened to Peter and Karl?"

Ruebin dropped his gaze from her eyes, and she sobbed. "*Peter! Karl!!*"

"Mama, you must be quiet. Please, hide here," he begged.

"But Hans and Walter! Where are they? They will have heard the sounds and come running! We must find them!" and then Katrina moaned as a contraction wracked her body.

Ruebin wiped the sweat from his mother's forehead and neck, and laid her among the stalks. "I'll get them, and hide them as well until it's safe to bring them to you."

"What has happened to Heinrich, Ruebin?" Katrina moaned. "Oh God, what has happened to us all?"

Ruebin left her there, hurrying bent over through the stalks of corn back to the barn as quickly as he could. He didn't know how much time he had left, but he had to find a greater weapon than any that Papa had.

# CHAPTER
## Nine

Stephan reined Kurstin in hard in front of the doctor's office, so that she whinnied and blew. She was lathered heavily. He jumped off the horse, threw the reins around the post next to the doctor's wagon, and bumped into Dr. Leipmann as he blindly ran to the front door. The doctor had just finished breakfast, and was returning along the boardwalk.

"Hold up there, son! Is it Katrina? Is she having trouble?"

"Dr. Leipmann, it's not Mama, it's *Papa!* He's gone *crazy!* Please come now, and bring some help!" Stephan gasped, attempting to pull the doctor with him.

Dr. Leipmann started toward his wagon willingly enough, but then caught sight of the sky. "*Gott im Himmel!*" he swore, reverting to a language that he hadn't heard since his grandfather's day.

Clouds were apparently rushing from all parts of the globe, converging on the horizon in one spot as he watched. The light there was an eerie green, the clouds black from this distance. Flashes of lightning could be seen at the very tops of the enormous thunderclouds. He *knew*, there was no question: the Baumann farm could be found under those clouds, and Heinrich Baumann would be at the center of it.

"Wait, son, wait," Dr. Leipmann cautioned as he tried to pry Stephan's hand from his arm. "Let's not go until we get the sheriff and some help."

Stephan dropped his hand. "Hurry!" he begged.

"I'll be quick as I can. You're Stephan, aren't you?" the doctor asked.

"Yes, sir."

"Stephan, your horse is lathered and in no condition to keep up right now; it might be she won't even make it. Take a look." Dr. Leipmann indicated Kurstin.

Kurstin's sides heaved and her eyes rolled. She danced forward and backward, in obvious distress.

Stephan understood as soon as he turned to look at her. "But what can I do? I must get back to my family."

"Here, Stephan," Dr. Leipmann offered, holding out a few dollars. "Take Kurstin to the stables and find a man named Running Bear. Do you understand?"

Stephan nodded impatiently, looking along the street toward the stables.

"Tell him the doctor says 'it is time' and to take care of Kurstin," Dr. Leipmann finished.

"What do you mean, 'it is time'?" asked Stephan quickly.

"I'll explain to you on the way back to the farm. You can come in my wagon with me. Go now, and quickly. I'll get some men together," the doctor instructed. Stephan turned and picked up Kurstin's reins. Doctor Leipmann looked at the ominous sky covering the Baumann farm, and sighed deeply. As Stephan led his horse toward the stables, Leipmann started toward the sheriff's office. He shook his head. *Too damned bad,* he thought. *Heinrich was too hard-headed to convince, and now he and his family will pay the price. This is a terrible, terrible day, but we knew it was coming ever since they moved out there.* He reached the sheriff's office and went in, closing the door softly.

Sheriff Will Cooper looked up at the doctor's entrance. "Leipmann! Good to see you. Sit down and I'll pour us some coffee."

Then he noticed the doctor's face.

"What is it, John? You look like a man with something weighing heavy on his heart," Cooper observed. "Something like poison."

"Well, it *is* poison, Will. It's the Baumann farm," Dr. Leipmann spat bitterly.

The sheriff whirled to the window facing the street, but could see nothing but the tavern and a dressmaker's shop opposite his office and the town jail. He took his hat and gun from the desk and hurried to the office door. From the boardwalk outside he could see through a gap in the buildings where a new Government office was being built, and it was enough to sicken him. He stood with his gun holstered and his hat in his hand watching the sky in awe, and John Leipmann joined him.

"I never thought I'd see it in my lifetime," Cooper breathed. "It's real, then."

"Real, and worse than anything you'll ever have seen," Dr. Leipmann agreed.

"I thought it was just campfire stories the old folks told us to make us stay in bed after dark," Will Cooper said. "Damn me, this sure looks like what they told us."

"One of the Baumann boys rode into town looking for help. I sent him to Running Bear," said John Leipmann, catching the sheriff's eye and holding his gaze meaningfully. "You and I have some dark work ahead of us."

"I'll get some men rounded up. There's a wagon train headed for Oklahoma just outside of town, and I'm sure they'll want to help," Cooper assured him.

"Okay, Will, but don't hurry," Leipmann warned him.

"What? Why not?"

"Remember the story. I think that once it has started, we won't be able to get anywhere near the farm until it's finished. We have to let it play itself out. Nothing we can do," said Leipmann. "We'll know it's time to go in when the sky clears, not before."

Will Cooper sighed in frustration, and took off his hat to wipe the sweat from his brow. "Yeah, I remember now. The Great Bear Spirit is upon them, right?"

The doctor nodded.

"Well, somebody had better explain that to the Baumann boy. He's going to be in a lather trying to get back there."

Dr. Leipmann smiled a small, twisted smile. "Don't worry. Running Bear knows what to do."

---

Ruebin reached the open doors at the front of the barn, peering inside for any sign of his father. Heinrich was nowhere to be seen, but the horses were still restless in their stalls. As quietly as possible he closed and barred the front barn doors and lit an oil lamp. He set the lamp on the dirt floor at the front of the barn, near the doors and a bale of hay. He then crept toward the back doors of the barn, unfastening the doors to the horse stalls as he went, but leaving them closed. At the back doors he peeked through the cracks in the logs, trying to see if his father was still out there. As a middle child with strong, hearty, and taller brothers, he had learned not to depend on brawn, but to think problems through. Hans and Walter must wait. They would have heard the shot and shouts and screams, and would be coming back through the corn. Ruebin guessed that Hans would be cautious, with all the attention he had paid to Indian stories. He would watch before he brought Walter into any danger.

He had a plan, and a backup plan. First, he would open the back doors enough to let in the light of day; then he would stampede the horses out through the open barn doors. If he guessed correctly, they would fly out in panic and run over Heinrich Baumann before they realized they were running into the very danger they feared. With luck, Papa would be injured or delayed enough so that he could see to his younger brothers and Mama.

If something went wrong—if he opened the doors and for some reason the horses didn't stampede—he would run back to the front of the barn and set the hay on fire. The barn would catch fire, and the animals would undoubtedly panic. Ruebin would then slip out the front doors of the barn, blocking this exit by dragging the plow against the doors.

Either way, he would deal with Papa first.

His examination of the area behind the barn and the sides of the barn showed only Peter still lying there in the morning heat. He could see vultures circling overhead—circling but not landing. That meant that someone was still moving around out there. He checked again and again until he could see Papa rising from the hole in the ground, looking off in the distance with his lips moving, and sprang into action. Ruebin quietly removed the bar from the back doors, opened them, and ran back to the front of the barn. He picked up an empty washtub and a hammer and started beating the metal washtub and screaming. Immediately the horses reacted, rearing in their stalls. The first to find that his stall door was open was Storm, a young chestnut stallion with black mane and tail. His front hooves caught the door and he was free; he predictably ran from the source of the sound, toward the light and outside.

It took only a second for the rest of the horses to follow suit. They were stampeding, all right, straight out the back of the barn. Ruebin could see them run right over the top of his father.

He sat at the front of the barn on the floor, panting and watching for any sign of movement from Heinrich Baumann. What seemed like an eternity passed, and he slowly rose, turning off the oil lamp as he did so. Ruebin stopped at the back doors, watching. When his father still didn't move, he sighed and went in search of Hans and Walter, feeling as if a great weight had been lifted from his shoulders.

―――――

The black, rich soil steamed up around Katrina's head as she lay crouched in the corn in the moist heat of Iowa's July. The pains were, of course, coming faster and deeper, and she knew her baby must be born soon. She was almost numb with misery, however, from knowing that Peter and Karl must be desperately hurt by their own father. Just last night she had been so happy, thinking about her baby and thankful to God for their fortune; today all was lost. She was torn with another labor contraction. *Dear God,* she prayed, *I don't want to have my baby in the dirt, but if I must, let him or her be healthy. Help me to be quiet, and help Ruebin and Walter and Hans to be safe.*

This labor contraction was lasting too long. She was growing faint with the pain and with too little rest between contractions. Katrina must lay down or fall down. She fumbled with her skirt to take it off and lay it aside. She would need a clean cloth for the baby. Weakly she tore off her underskirt and spread it out in the dirt. Exhausted, she fell, clad only in her drawers from the waist down, onto the underskirt. The pain eased and she turned onto her back, feeling her belly and loosening her drawers. She found the baby's head high up under her ribs. Desperately she groped her girth; she could feel the baby's feet at her sides. *Breech birth!* The baby was in the wrong position, and without help she and the baby would both die out here in the field.

Another contraction started, and this time there was no gradual easing into it. She was at the peak of the pain instantly. It was enormous in its intensity, and she gave her body over to it. She could not feel her legs or feet, and her hands lay limply at her sides.

Above, the sun was blocked from her view by thick, ugly, sickly-looking clouds. The day cooled quickly. A quickening breeze bent the tops of the corn stalks and helped dry some of the sweat from her face. Katrina's mind wandered as she lay helplessly. She wished she could stand so that she might feel more of the breeze. It would feel so good against her skin. Suddenly she knew she wouldn't want to, even if she could. That smell under the wind . . . it reminded her of something, something she couldn't bear to think about. She tried to turn her thoughts away from it, but a sudden cold puff of wind hit her in the face *(But how can I feel wind down here on the ground among the corn stalks, when the tops of the stalks are not moving any more?*) and she remembered. Instantly she was back in Germany, the Germany of her childhood, in the house of her mother's parents.

She had been only four years old at the time, and was excited to be visiting her grandparents. Grandmama would show her how to make interesting things, and Grandpapa would let her ride a pony when she visited. She hadn't understood why all her relatives were grouped around in Grandmama's best room, the one reserved for holidays and company; nor had she understood why so many were crying. She only knew she wanted to see her grandfather. Little Katrina had gone from room to room looking for him, until finally she approached the closed door to his bedroom and turned the knob. Suddenly her mother's hands were on her shoulders.

"Katie, no. Do not go into Grandpapa's bedroom," Mama had told her.

"Why not? I want to ride the pony."

"Grandpapa is very, very sick. We must all be quiet and let him rest," Mama had explained. "Come now and look at some books, all right?"

"But I don't want to look at books. I want to see Grandpapa!" little Katie had exclaimed, tears starting in her eyes.

The bedroom door had opened in front of them, and a puff of air had assaulted her nose. Her grandmother had come out of the bedroom when she had heard Katrina's voice. "Let her come in, Illse. He has been asking for her, and it may be the last time she will see him."

The young girl frowned at the smell coming from her grandfather's bedroom. "It smells bad in there, Grandmama."

"Yes, *liebchen,* I know, but Grandpapa cannot help it. Go and tell him you love him," her grandmother had urged, kissing Katrina's forehead.

Katrina looked into the dimly lit room, and saw the form of

her grandfather on the bed. She approached him on tiptoes, not wanting to be there any more but compelled by fright. *Where is Grandpapa going?* she wondered. The smell grew stronger as she approached the bed, and she understood that the smell was coming from her grandfather.

Here in the corn Katrina smelled again the odor of mushrooms in the densest part of the forest, where no light reached; the foul odor of rotting chicken; the dusty-dry odor of her grandmother's parlor drapes when she hid behind them, teasing her grandfather.

It was the smell of Death, just before it arrives; and it was oh, so very close. She looked to her side and saw that someone was standing there. A young Indian woman looked at her sadly, and extended her hand to Katrina. *Everything is all right now,* Katrina thought, and died.

---

Hans and Walter had spent the morning in the forest on the far side of the river. The berry basket lay discarded on the river bank; they were too busy with their game of Hide and Seek to think about blueberries. This morning the Indian lady (Walter was convinced she was an Indian *princess*, exiled from her tribe because she was so kind and gentle) had appeared almost at once. The boys ran as fast as they could to where they had seen her, but she had disappeared among the trees. They searched and searched for her, but just as Hans had declared that she wasn't coming back, she appeared again, smiling broadly. Again the boys ran to find her, and again she disappeared. Each time they were about to give up the game, they would see her again. She never spoke; she only smiled and played the game.

It was a beautiful summer's day, and Mama was feeding the animals for them. Birds sang in the trees, and chipmunks chattered at them from the forest floor. The rush of the river water was near. And they were playing with an Indian woman in the forest. Both boys wore huge, goofy grins on their faces as they scurried through the trees.

Thus engaged in such hilarious play, the youngest Baumann boys did not hear the sounds coming from the farm. They had no idea of the horror taking place there. At one point they looked up at the sky beyond the treetops, because it seemed as if the sun were blinking off and on again, like a flame guttering to a halt. Hans said, "Look at the clouds, Walter! They look like they're running away from us."

Walter considered the idea and watched the sky for a moment, but then looked at the forest around him. "Hans, what is that smell?"

Hans detected the same odor that, unknown to him, his mother smelled as she lay in the corn. He looked around, then whispered to his brother, "Walter, *listen*."

Walter listened, and whispered back, "But Hans, I don't hear *anything*."

Hans shook his head. "This is *wrong*, Walter. Where are the birds and squirrels and chipmunks? And why can't we hear the river any more?"

Walter looked around the forest. He couldn't *see* the river any more, either, and it had been some time since they had seen the Indian lady. The spaces between the huge trees, formerly dappled with sunlight from above, were now dark. Nothing seemed to move. "Hans, I'm scared. I want to go home now."

Hans agreed. It looked like it might storm. However, he could see no familiar landmarks around them. Their game of Hide and Seek had taken them deeper into the forest than they had ever ventured before.

Frightened even more by his brother's silence and inaction, Walter whined, "Hans. I want to go *home. Now!*"

Hans was afraid, as well, but he couldn't allow his little brother to see his fear. He knelt next to Walter. "We must look at the trees. They will tell us which way to go in order to find home."

He looked at Walter's face; his small jaw was trembling in anticipation of tears. "Don't you remember what Papa said, Walter? He told us that moss always grows on the north side of trees. We came east across the river, and we must go west to go home."

Walter's eyes spilled over and the tears made tracks in his sweaty, grimy face. "I don't know where west is."

"But *I* will, as soon as we find a tree with some moss. Help me, Walter," Hans replied as he took his brother's hand.

Very quickly they located a massive maple tree standing away from the rest of the forest. There, on one side of the trunk, was a large clump of green moss. Hans stood facing the moss and held his arms out to either side of his body. As Walter watched, he looked down the length of his right arm and pointed his finger. "We go that way," he announced, and once again took Walter's hand.

The boys marched in that direction straight through the forest, checking their course every so often by finding more trees with moss. The day seemed to grow darker. Hans thought, *Maybe we have been gone all day. Maybe we've missed lunch and supper, and it's almost night. Papa will be very angry.* His stomach growled, and he remembered the blueberries they were supposed to be picking. *Mama will be angry, too,* he thought, and picked up their pace. How could they have gone so far into the forest without realizing it?

"Hans, I hear something!" Walter said excitedly.

They stopped to listen, and then, as if from a great distance, they could hear Ruebin's voice calling them. "*Walter! Hans! Where are you?*"

Both boys yelled at once, "Here! We're here, Ruebin!" and charged in the direction of the voice.

Still at a distance, they heard Ruebin call, "I'm on the other side of the river. I will wait for you here."

"We hear you!" Hans called back, and they rushed forward headlong.

It seemed to take forever to reach the riverbank. But this was not a part of the river that the boys had seen before, and the basket they had carried that morning was nowhere to be seen. There was no log across the river here. How were they supposed to cross?

Hans called, "Ruebin!"

There was no response.

Hans stepped right up to the river bank, cupped his hands around his mouth, and called again. "Ruebin! *Ruebin!* Where are you? We can't see you!"

He looked up and down the river, but could see no sign of his brother. He decided that after all, here was the river, and it looked calm in this place. He stepped into the water.

Suddenly sound came back into the world, but instead of the delightful music of a summer's day, it was a cacophony of nature. Flocks of birds whirled into the sky, *screaming* their song; huge black crows squawked and flapped their wings angrily as they took the place of the songbirds in the trees. Squirrels chattered a blasphemy as they fought each other on their ways to shelter in trees; the losers fell to the ground and raced to find another hiding place. Overhead, the sky was a deadly bottle-green color that roiled. Thunder and lightning split the sky, although not a drop of rain fell. The trees were tossed by a wind so violent that it threatened to knock the boys to the ground. At Hans' feet, the water that had been flowing so gently just a moment before now boiled blackly. It roared and foamed and spat at them.

With the wind blowing so hard that Hans could hardly open his eyes to see, he struggled back to the river bank. Walter had become so frightened that he huddled there with his arms over his head. Hans knelt beside him and held him, shielding him as best he could from the leaves and twigs and dirt that flew in all directions. He peered back over his shoulder at the river.

And someone or something was *there*, standing on the opposite bank! Hans squinted to see better. It wasn't Ruebin, but a *man* standing there with a wood axe! As he stared, he could make out that the man was as huge as his father, but covered in mud, and then the man roared.

"HANS! WALTER! Come over here right NOW!" the man shouted. "If you don't come over here, I'll come over there and GET you! COME HERE!"

Paralyzed with fear, Hans drew his brother even closer to his chest and ignored the debris hitting his face and eyes. *Is that Papa?* he asked himself in utter disbelief. *Is that OUR Papa?*

Suddenly the trees just behind their father parted, and an enormous, black shape roared a tremendous animal roar. The man fell to his chest as his legs were swatted out from under him, still yelling, "HANS! WALTER! COME HERE RIGHT NOW!" The man was dragged backward into the trees. There was a terrible splintering of wood, crunching of branches, and wordless screams. The thunder and lightning crashed and sizzled. Hans put his head face down on top of Walter's head (he could almost hear Walter's thoughts, *No, no, no, no, make it go away, not Papa, not Papa, go away*) because he could not bear to look any more. However, nothing could prevent him from *hearing*, and these sounds would haunt his dreams for years to come.

The worst was hearing the screams and roars stop.

The wind died; the water calmed; the storm stopped abruptly and clouds started to part. Brilliant sunlight proved that it was day instead of night. Above Walter's soft sobbing the only sounds they could hear were those of a huge, heavy animal pounding away downriver, hurrying through the underbrush and cracking twigs and branches as it left. Hans lifted his head warily, looking for signs of the man or the monster. There, on the opposite bank, was a wood axe, *their* wood axe, its sharply honed blade and its handle stained crimson. Beyond that was a wide path of what looked like blood. Trees as big as four and five inches across had been snapped like toothpicks, and gore adorned their ragged stumps.

Hans stood and dragged Walter up from the ground. He said in a clear, matter-of-fact voice, "Let's go. It's all over now," and promptly squatted down and vomited between his knees. Walter sank back to the ground next to him, not wanting to give up the feel of his brother's body yet.

When he felt well enough to stand, Hans walked to the river and rinsed his face and mouth. Walter said, "What will we do now, Hans?" and took his hand. Bleakly Hans noted that his brother had started sucking his thumb again, something that he had stopped three years before. He looked down at his little brother, who he loved dearly, and squashed the panic in his chest.

"That animal went down the river *that* way. Let's go *up* the river for a bit and then we'll cross if we get a chance. All right?"

Walter looked up at Hans and said around his thumb, "All right."

They walked a little distance, and Walter asked, "Where is Ruebin?"

Hans' breath caught in his throat. He suspected he *knew* where Ruebin was, but he answered, "I don't know. Maybe he got tired of waiting for us. But we should be quiet in case that animal is still around."

Walter didn't need convincing, and they walked along in silence.

Up ahead, Hans thought he could make out a log over the river, and pointed it out to Walter. As exhausted as they both were emotionally and physically, they began to run. Yes, it *was* a log, and here was the clearing where they had crossed early this morning! Reaching the clearing, the boys looked around for the berry basket. Walter cried out as he spied it. Standing behind it was the Indian woman!

They rushed toward her, trying to warn her and tell her what had happened, but she only put out her hand, palm outward, at chest level, signaling them to stop. They did, panting. The woman then pointed down at the berry basket and said the only word they would ever hear her say: "*Ill-sah.*"

And she turned and disappeared from their sight for the last time.

Walter walked over to the basket and looked inside. "Hans, it's a baby!"

Hans' heart pounded. The woman had said "Ill-sah"; did she mean 'Illse'? Illse was what his mother was going to name her baby. Was that his mother's baby?

Swaddled in a clean, soft deerskin hide was a tiny baby with red, puckered skin and white-blonde hair, fast asleep. Lying in a heap on the bottom of the basket, forming a thin palette, was a familiar cloth; yes, it was his mother's skirt, the one she had dressed in when she had come to breakfast that morning.

"Look, Hans, bear tracks!" said Walter excitedly.

Hans looked up from the basket. Behind the basket and all around it were the tracks of an enormous bear. Around their Pennsylvania farm and during their journey they had seen many bear tracks, but never were there any half as large as these. Suddenly uneasy again, he told Walter, "I think this is our little sister. Let's take the baby and go, now. Come on."

"But how can this be our sister? Where's Mama? And what about the bear?" protested Walter.

Hans didn't even attempt to answer the first two questions. "I don't think I want to see *that* bear," Hans assured his brother.

With Walter pushing the basket ahead of him on the log and Hans steadying it from the side as he waded across the river, the boys headed toward their home.

# CHAPTER
## Ten

Running Bear set Stephan gently in the back of Dr. Leipmann's carriage, and the doctor turned to thank him. When the boy had told him that the doctor had said, "It is time," Running Bear knew that the nightmare that he and the doctor had suspected would happen was now unfolding. Running Bear had instructed Stephan to sit and wait while he put Kurstin into a stall with water. The boy had been impatient and anxious, insisting that they leave at once; but Running Bear had only looked at him implacably and turned to pour hot water from the stove over some leaves in a cup. He swirled the contents, added a little cool water and turned to Stephan. "Drink this," he commanded.

"What is it?" asked Stephan. He looked into the cup; it smelled musty and looked like swamp water. "I don't want this. We have to hurry!" He tried to give it back to Running Bear.

Running Bear merely folded his arms around his sizeable chest and frowned. "Drink."

Stephan sipped the brew and decided it would not kill him, then sipped a little more. He looked up at Running Bear; the man had turned his back again and was gathering gear for horses. As he watched, Stephan's vision swam, and he fell from the stable stool to the floor.

Now he slept dreamlessly in the back of the doctor's wagon, unaware of the party that had formed at the edge of town. In addition to the doctor's wagon, there were two covered wagons driven by women. Nine men sat astride horses, including Sheriff Cooper and Running Bear. Silently they watched and waited until they could see the dissolution of the evil-looking clouds that had formed a fortress over the Baumann farm. At Running Bear's signal, they started forward.

What the party from Apple Springs found that day was incredible in its magnitude to them all, and it was a scene that they would never forget. None, even Running Bear, had lived through a similar experience. They would tell about it and write about it later, but that was a day of terrible and tragic labor.

When they arrived at the farm it was eerily quiet. Cows and horses roamed among the corn and wheat, and the oxen had wandered to the hay fields; only the pigs remained in their pens. The chickens were wandering the house's front yard and the rooster was perched on the porch's railing. No smoke came from the chimney atop the house. They called to the Baumann family, but there was no answer.

Sheriff Cooper found Peter and Karl behind the barn, and had some men help him heave Karl out of the mud and water. In the soaked ground around the pit where the sod house had been were the tracks of many horses' hooves; they could follow the trail with their eyes through the wheat fields behind the barn. Miraculously, none of the horses had fallen into the pit, but their prints told part of the story: about ten feet from the open back doors of the barn the grass was trampled with blood. The horses had split into two groups, avoiding the pit.

The house and barn were empty. The women drew their wagons behind the house and turned over the reins to the men; their work would be in the house, preparing food, hot water, and bandages. Dr. Leipmann was especially anxious to find Katrina, if she was still alive, and the women were prepared to care for her. Stephan was placed in one of the two beds in the boys' bedroom. Soon he would awaken and they would attend to him, as best they could.

When it was obvious that none of the rest of the family was nearby, the men fanned out in the fields to look for what was left of the Baumann family. They found Katrina first, lying in the corn amidst a pool of blood. When Dr. Leipmann examined her, he frowned. She had died before the baby was born, and not from an attack. Someone had cleanly cut the baby out of her belly; a sharply honed hunting knife lay next to Katrina's still body. Where was the baby? Was it still alive somewhere?

Next, the men found Ruebin in the forest to the east of the farm; he had died of vicious axe wounds to his neck and back. They went on toward the river, and walked into a bloodbath. On the bank of the river lay a bloodstained wood axe. Running Bear had found the tracks of an enormous bear, and followed the trail of tracks and gore downriver, until it disappeared into the water. Men searched the far side of the river for hours on that long day, but found only more bear tracks that suddenly stopped as if the earth had swallowed them.

As the group of men gave up their search for the day and were walking back to the farm house, one of them stopped to listen. Faintly, very faintly, he thought he could hear a baby crying from the direction of the wheat field. Again, they fanned out, and just before dark they came upon Hans, Walter, and a baby, huddled together in the tall wheat. The boys' eyes were wide from shock, and the baby cried from hunger. Walter insisted on holding on to his brother, and they all walked back to the farm house together, a silent group when there was nothing to say.

The body of Heinrich Baumann was never found.

# CHAPTER
# Eleven

Of the nine members of the Baumann family, only four survived that day, and the oldest was Stephan at the age of fourteen. Dr. Leipmann and his wife took the children in. Katrina, Ruebin, Karl, and Peter were buried in the town's cemetery; no one could bear to put a shovel to the earth of the Baumann farm. Stephan's bitterness was enormous. He found his younger brothers' stories of the Indian woman, the bear tracks, and finding the baby in their berry basket unbelievable. A terrible crime had been committed, and someone had to pay. He further did not believe that his father had killed his three older brothers.

Almost a year later, Stephan told the doctor that he wanted to revisit the farm. By that time, the crops had been harvested and sold, the animals had been gathered and cared for, and the children's personal belongings had long ago been brought to the Leipmann house by the people of Apple Springs. Throughout that year there had been a pervasive sense of joylessness in the town, a sense of loss, and guilt.

Dr. Leipmann insisted that he and Running Bear accompany Stephan. As the three rode horseback (Stephan once more on Kurstin), they talked of what had taken place on the farm. No one had all of the answers. Running Bear said little until Stephan, angry and confused, stated that he had decided to move the children back to the farm when he was sixteen and run the farm himself. At that, Running Bear pulled his horse up and in front of Kurstin until he blocked the boy's path. "You will listen," he said. Stephan stopped and fell into sullen silence.

"You must know that man cannot control everything on this earth. That land out there where your father put his farm is not like the land here. It cannot be ruled by man. I have heard stories of other such places as well. In such a place, the soil, the air, the water—all of them search a man's soul for his weaknesses and poison him with them. They make him very angry. When blood is spilled in anger, a Spirit will cleanse the soil with that man's blood."

"Papa was a very strong man!" objected Stephan. "He could plow a field by himself, *without* a horse or ox."

"Yes, your father was a great, strong man," answered Running Bear. "But I speak of what was in his heart, and every man has weaknesses in his heart."

Stephen fell silent. He had felt for a long time that if he had any courage, he would have stayed to fight. He would at least have gone to the farm afterward by himself.

"Let the land fall silent. Do not give it a reason to rise up again. Do not wake the Spirit of the Great Bear again."

Stephan thought of the huge bear tracks that the men had shown him by the river, and what Hans and Walter had told them of the Indian woman. He didn't think there was any spirit out there, but he did believe there was a giant bear hiding in the woods.

"I don't believe that we looked hard enough for the bear, and that's what I want to do now. If we kill the bear, there will be no danger," said Stephan stubbornly. He drew out his father's pistol from the saddlebag.

Dr. Leipmann interjected. "Stephan, let's say that all these stories are nothing but claptrap. Let's say that the mysteries of what happened that day, *including*, I might add, how your baby sister Illse ended up wrapped in deerskin *after your mother had already died*, were just mysteries. Let's say there is a *real* bear of the size that could do what it did to your father, and let's say we find it. Do you think that we could kill it with just our side arms?"

Stephan turned his head from them and gazed resentfully into the distance.

The doctor continued, "Son, I have been a doctor for many years now, longer than I care to remember. I've taken as many as five bullets from a man who was still conscious, and who lived to tell about it. Do you still think we can kill a bear like *that* one with bullets?"

Stephan turned stony eyes to the doctor. "There are other ways. Old ways."

The doctor and Running Bear glanced at each other quickly. "You mean like digging a bear pit," Dr. Leipmann replied.

"Yes," Stephan answered simply.

"So you would dig into the very soil that the stories say poisoned your father's soul," nodded the doctor thoughtfully. "If Hans wanted to do that, would you let him?"

"No!" cried Stephan quickly, then caught himself. "He's too little."

Running Bear grunted. "You want to do battle, to fight."

"Yes!" Stephan returned hotly. "My father brought us all here and worked that land so that we could have a place to live. We *all* worked hard on that farm, and it's all we know how to do. Am I to remember my father by running like a scared rabbit? Or should I *fight* to keep what he wanted?"

Dr. Leipmann said, "Son, sometimes you just have to accept things and walk away. It isn't cowardice, it's *wisdom*. And you are the head of the Baumann family now. It's not fair, but I'm asking you to be wise and strong for your brothers and sister. Forget about your own anger and do what will be best for them."

Stephan met the doctor's eyes steadily for a moment. "I'll think about it," he said.

And Stephan led the two men to his family's farm one more time.

---

John Leipmann and Running Bear followed Stephan as he examined the pit of water that had once been their sod house, the barn, and the house. They watched as he fingered his father's tools and his mother's hair brush. He ran his hands over the fireplace mantel that Karl had lovingly carved and stained himself. He walked to the dooryard, picked up a handful of soil, and let it sift through his fingers. The two men looked at each other; neither could tell what Stephan was thinking.

He went nowhere near the river or the forest.

Finally, Stephan sat with the others on the porch of the farm house, turning his hat in his hands. At last he spoke.

"Running Bear, you say that the *soil* here is evil, not the bear. Is that right?"

Running Bear sighed. "No, boy, neither is evil. The evil is inside man himself, as well as good. He chooses his path. When man touches the soil here, it seeks out his weaknesses to help him choose the evil path. It is a matter of the Great Spirit, who set aside this place as protected. If it is left alone, all is in harmony. If a man touches the soil in anger and blood, it protects itself with the Spirit of the Great Bear."

Now Stephan sighed. "I don't really understand."

"Things in nature are what they are, that is all," Running Bear said.

Again Stephan sat silently while the men waited patiently. Finally, he addressed Dr. Leipmann. "Sir, thank you for taking us in. May I stay with you another year?"

"Of course," said John Leipmann guardedly. "What will you do then?"

"I will build my own farm, much closer to Apple Springs, I think," Stephan nodded as he talked. "I will not sell the farm, but I will let it lie fallow to return as it was before we came here. The children will stay with you until they are older, if it is agreeable to you."

John Leipmann blew a pent-up breath of relief. "I think it is a wonderful idea. But what about the house and the barn? Will you burn them?"

"No," Stephan answered, "we built the place and nature may take them back. I cannot bear to burn what my family has made. We'll take the furniture and tools, but leave the rest."

Running Bear grinned the first smile that Stephan had ever seen on his face, and clapped him on the back. "This is a good plan," he said.

"I think so too, Stephan," said Dr. Leipmann. "I don't think anyone would disturb your family's things if we left them here until you are ready for them."

Before they left the Baumann farm, Running Bear went to the barn to group the tools that would be taken. Leipmann and Stephan examined the furniture in the farm house. As they entered Heinrich's and Katrina's bedroom, the doctor said, "Let's look at the mattresses and see if any mice have been at them. We might want to get rid of them if they have."

Stephan agreed, and pulled back the blankets on his father's side of the bed. No holes could be seen. He pulled up the mattress to look at the bottom, and spied his father's wooden chest and the key that matched it. He pulled it out with great effort; it was so *heavy*! Wonderingly, he fit the key to the heavy chest and felt his heart leap when he saw what was inside. He gasped, and the doctor came to his side to look.

"Stephan! Will you look at that! There must be a couple of thousand dollars in gold in there!" Leipmann exclaimed.

Stephan felt his heart lift for the first time since that awful summer's day a year ago. Here was money for clothes and food for the children, and more than enough to buy land for a farm! He looked at the doctor in delight. Now he could begin to see a future for himself and Hans, Walter, and Illse.

They finished separating the furnishings in the house quickly, finding no mice in residence. When Running Bear was finished in the barn, they hitched Kurstin to the buckboard that still stood in front of the barn and brought the chest, a few hand tools, and mementos for the children. Stephan hugged Kurstin's neck enthusiastically. He felt that on this day he had put an end to the tragedy and violence that had haunted him and his family, for now and for all time.

# CHAPTER
Twelve

Of course, Stephan was wrong about that. As Running Bear had said, things in nature are what they are, and Heartless was truly without mercy. The exception was the rare appearance of White Feather, who seemed to harbor a softness toward women and children. While the Baumann tragedy was fresh in men's minds, no one thought of living on the land again. Even down through the generations, stories and journals were passed on, and it was enough to keep Baumanns (and others) off the land for many years. But over time, men came to the place the Indians called Heartless several times. Some were ignorant of the curse; others had heard about it, but thought that it would pass them by.

In 1873, a group of railroad surveyors working for the United States Government came across the farm. Attempting to shelter themselves from the pelting rain outside, they rode their horses toward the buildings they could see in the distance. Although the house and barn looked well-kept and occupied, they could find no one at home. One of the men found that the barn was unlocked, and they brought themselves and their horses into the dimness of that structure. They waited a good hour for the rain to stop, but it didn't. It kept up at the rate of a steady downpour. Since it was getting dark as well, they decided to stay there for the night. If the owners came back in the meantime, they would pay good money for their emergency shelter.

Their supervisor was a man named Kent Durwood, a well-seasoned surveyor who was stocky and quiet, but honest and fair.

He cleared a place in the dirt of the barn's floor and laid his bedroll out right beside the other men's, and doled out their food supplies for supper: buffalo jerky and hardtack. They had water from their canteens, but a bottle of whiskey appeared, and the men all shared swigs of the liquor to ward off the cool air and dampness. Soon it was too dark to see, and the men groped their ways into their beds. They slept heavily.

Dawn found Durwood rummaging through the saddle bags of the other men, muttering to himself. Ed Stewart was the first to wake, aware that something was bothering the horses, and was shocked to see his boss going through their personal things.

"Kent. *Kent!* Whatcha lookin' for?" he called, and the others stirred.

There was no answer from their boss; he merely muttered louder, and sounded angry.

The men looked at each other, and Stewart approached Durwood from behind, touching his arm. "What in blazes are you doing?"

The men were totally unprepared for Kent Durwood's reaction. He spun around, and cold-cocked Stewart in the jaw. Stewart went down hard, spread-eagled, unconscious before he hit the ground. Durwood turned to the other men; they were stunned into immobility by what they had seen him do. They stirred quickly, however, when they saw the two-foot length of iron that he swung in his right hand. They were all on their feet in an instant, and backed up slowly in a semi-circle, back toward the front of the barn.

He advanced on his men, slapping the heavy cudgel into his open left hand. "I smell APPLES!" he roared. "Someone has APPLES in his saddlebag, and I want them NOW!"

The men quickly glanced at each other, questioning with their eyes. Fresh fruit on the trail was like milk and honey. None of them had seen an apple since they had left Illinois. "Boss, there's no apples here," one of the men ventured.

Behind Durwood, Ed Stewart's body still lay on the barn's dirt floor. He was breathing shallowly, but a small stream of blood was coursing from his split lip down his cheek to drip on the ground.

Durwood seemed to become even more enraged. "Seven weeks on the trail and no apples! I want those apples! Whoever has 'em, give 'em over, right NOW!"

Suddenly, a terrific wind rocked the barn. Dust fell from the beams, and Durwood plodded threateningly toward his survey team. The horses, tethered in their stalls, rolled their eyes and whinnied. Durwood slapped his palm with the cudgel, and every time he did it, he grinned and whisper-chanted, *"Apples! Apples! Apples!"*

One of the men tried to slip to the side so he could rush him, but Durwood craftily spun and swung the iron, *crunching* the man's skull. He stood over the dead man, smiled, and whispered lovingly, *"Apples,"* to the corpse.

Whatever thoughts the men had about capturing their boss and stopping his insane ranting were entirely lost at that moment. They turned as one and raced for the doors.

The wind, the damned *wind* was blowing so hard that it took two of the four men to hold the doors open so that the others could slip outside. Durwood took his time coming for them with his terrible grin. It seemed he knew he had all the time in the world. When the last man tried to slip through the door, he got stuck. He screamed for help, and the three who had made it outside pulled on both doors and his right arm as hard as they could. It was no good. Durwood stopped at the door, his own nose just inches from the other man's, and whispered, *"Apples! Where are the apples, you spineless toad?"*

And he swung the iron.

The first strike broke the man's left arm, bringing a scream of terror and pain from him. Durwood mocked him. "'*Ooooh! Oof! Ooooh!*' Is this a new language?" he sneered, then leaned up against the barn wall, his face just inches away from his victim. "What do I have to do to get those apples?" he asked conversationally. And then he swung again, and crushed the man's left knee cap.

The man fainted.

The wind howled, and the horses screamed and kicked at their stalls.

All of Durwood's good humor left him. He wanted an answer, and he wanted it *now*. "Don't you leave me! Don't you DARE leave me yet, you toad, you toad, you *toad!*"

And he bashed the man's head, face, and shoulders into pulp.

The men pulling on their comrade's right arm were finally rewarded when his body was released from the door with a sickening *SSSSHHHHTUP!* They fell backward onto the ground, two of them screaming because their dead friend's mashed and bloody body landed on top of them. Beyond the lifeless form, the barn doors opened as easily as if there were no wind at all, although it still blew dirt and grass into their faces and grit into their mouths, and Durwood stood there, triumphantly holding up his weapon.

They crabbed backwards on their hands and feet, and helped each other up. Without further delay they ran for their very lives toward the woods. Durwood called after them, "I'm coming! I'm coming, and I'll find you all! AND I'M GOING TO GET THOSE APPLES, *do you hear me?* I WANT THOSE APPLES!" He stood there in the barnyard, making short, vicious stabs and swipes through the air with the iron rod.

Before the sprinting surveyors lay a solid wall of bushes, vines, and trees, but the men crashed through and over it all. When they reached a river, they splashed through and kept on running. About a quarter of a mile on the other side of the river and up a slope, they stopped in a group, panting. Directly overhead, the sky was a clear blue, and there was no wind, *no wind at all.*

As soon as they could speak, they whispered a plan. Durwood couldn't get through all that foliage on the other side of the river without making plenty of noise; they'd know when he was coming. They would split up, and when he was on *this* side of the river, they'd make for the barn and their horses as fast as they could. They were all younger and leaner than Durwood was. Chances were they could make it out of there and to nearby Apple Springs before he knew he was aware of what was happening. Let the local sheriff deal with Durwood; he was *crazy*.

They split up, and found hiding spots where they could watch their backtrail and still see each other. They didn't have long to wait.

After about ten minutes, they could hear a tremendous thrashing and roaring that they recognized as Durwood's coming from across the river. They peeked out at each other; this was it, and they were ready.

Suddenly, the roaring was replaced by another roar; this one was an *animal!* One of the men had been to Africa, and had heard lions roar, but this was louder and more terrible, more *visceral*, more *greedy*. Durwood's roars turned to screams, and the thrashing escalated. Trees cracked and fell. Thunder rolled from the sky, from dark, angry clouds that stopped at the river's edge. And, just as suddenly as the holocaust started, silence descended. The clouds on the far side of the river fled, and the sky over there shone a clear blue.

The men rose from their hiding positions, white-faced and terrified. What in God's name had *that* been? As they stared in the direction of the river, they could hear a large animal moving off downstream at a fast pace. They decided, as one, to get moving.

On their jog back, they spied an area of forest that was *devastated*, with uprooted bushes, trampled ferns and vines, and splintered trees. It was covered in what looked like blood and bone and gore, and oh God, was that a *hand?* They didn't stop to investigate. They knew whose hand it had been, and they wanted to be gone from this land as fast as they could manage it.

They packed up all their belongings, wrapped the bodies of their two dead friends and tied them to the backs of their horses, and saw to Ed Stewart, who was just coming around and who couldn't remember a thing about that morning. They made for Apple Springs, visited the doctor and the sheriff, and sent a rider to the nearest telegraph office to inform the Government that Durwood had killed two of them and injured one, and had been killed himself by an animal. They referenced the local sheriff's office, and stayed in town until Stewart was able to travel. They didn't talk much about the incident; and, looking back on it, there hadn't been much questioning from the sheriff. Heading back to Illinois, the men were too tired and emotionally raw to talk of the incident. None of them ever surveyed the wilderness again.

---

During the last part of the nineteenth century, Heartless consumed hunters, campers, would-be squatters, and the occasional lost traveling party. The early part of the twentieth century was pretty quiet on the Baumann farm, and the local folks concentrated on attempting to diversify their main income from farming to industry. Various plants and factories were built; during this time the population swelled from just over a thousand to almost five thousand, and local politicians had dreams of establishing Apple Springs as a model small American city. Schools, two banks, and a hospital were built, and local incomes enjoyed a substantial boost. Good times and celebrations rolled, and so did the crime rate; Apple Springs experienced their first bank robberies. As modern and progressive as some in the town saw themselves, Apple Springs was a long way from large, urban sprawls and even further away from the current concept of "civilized." Nearly every man carried a side arm; brawls broke out frequently between farmers and factory workers, and all too often ended with someone lying shot dead on the street or in a saloon.

Apple Springs was just far enough away from the river boats

and the railroads to make transportation expensive for those who had to have materials, and dangerous for those who had to haul goods over land. One, then another, and another manufacturing firm closed its doors. In the 1920's, only one manufacturing firm still had its doors open, and that was a fertilizer plant. Apple Springs had come full circle to farming again, and the population plummeted. By 1924 the population was just under fifteen hundred souls.

That was the year that two prison escapees from Minnesota fled with Stillwater Prison guards hot on their trail. Abandoning their stolen car when it ran out of gas, the two men hitched a free ride in the dead of night on a train that they thought was eastbound. Jake Strickland had been convicted of double homicide, and his partner, Poker Joe Vinton, had taken part in a string of homicide-robberies. Both were desperate. Neither was willing to go back to the Minnesota penal system, and they both had far more enchanting plans than being punished for their crimes. Poker Joe had an old sweetheart who now lived in Chicago, and he believed he could charm her into putting them up while they took their slice of that fair city's money. In a city that size, he figured they could lose themselves and hole up while the Stillwater guards went round and round in circles looking for them. When the heat was off, they'd split their accumulated stash and their partnership.

Now, the problem was that Poker Joe wasn't overly educated, nor was he overly bright. And, of the two, he was the shinier penny. Jake believed every word Joe said. When they saw bright city lights in the distance, they assumed they were nearing Chicago. They jumped off the train, still in prison garb, and made it to the nearest house. After killing the surprised elderly couple who owned the house, they sat in the kitchen and helped themselves to a gargantuan meal of the food they found there. With the bodies of the couple still lying on the floor in the parlor, Poker Joe and Jake went upstairs and slept in the single bed. Late the next morning, they ate some more, cleaned themselves up, and dug through the old man's clothes to exchange their prison clothes for civilian ones. Neither Joe nor Jake was the same size as the elderly gentleman; they were both substantially larger than he had been. They could squeeze into his clothes, but shoes were a problem. They were stuck with the heavy, prison-issue work boots they had been wearing.

Then there was a *thunk!* at the door, and both men froze. Joe scuttled toward the front door, a butcher knife in his hand. Looking out the lacy curtains of the side window, he saw the back of a mailman retreating down the sidewalk, whistling a tune. He waited until the mailman was out of sight, and then opened the front door just far enough so he could snag the mail from the mailbox nailed to the front of the house by the door. He read the address written on the single envelope and swore loudly. The letter was addressed to Mr. and Mrs. Albert Messersmith in Des Moines, Iowa! Jake came over to look at the envelope.

Jake said, "I wasn't too good in school, Joe, but ain't Chicago in Illinois?"

Joe kicked him in the knee.

"Yes, you dummy, it is. And *we're* in *Iowa!* We got on the wrong train," Joe growled.

"Well, what are we gonna do?" asked Jake, rubbing his knee.

"Wait—was there a car out there in the yard?" asked Joe.

"I didn't notice," said Jake, and ducked a slap from Joe.

"Could you *look?*" asked Joe, who was getting exasperated. Bringing Jake along had seemed like a good idea at the time. He wasn't afraid of getting his hands dirty, he never questioned Joe's authority, and Joe was pretty sure he could get Jake to do any bullwork that needed to be done. But *damn*, Jake was dumb. Just look at him—Joe could slap him, kick him, do anything or say anything to the big dumb oaf, and Jake just took it. Dummy.

Jake pulled the drapes open in the parlor. Bright sunlight splashed into the doily-laden, flowery front room and across the dead faces of the house's former occupants. "Yep," he said in satisfaction, "there's a Ford sittin' right there." Joe came around the corner and cursed again at his partner.

"You *idiot!* No *wonder* you landed in the joint!" he yelled at Jake, who was now cowering away from him. Joe pulled the drapes shut before pedestrian traffic could see them. "Do you want the whole neighborhood to see us?"

"No?" ventured Jake.

"'No' is right," Joe said. "Let's find the car keys."

He bent over Mr. Albert Messersmith and searched his pockets. "Phew! Albert here is stinking up the place!" Joe straightened up with Albert's wallet, pocket change, and keys in triumph. "Gotcha!"

With part of a great getaway plan in hand, the pair only had to wait until dark, so that they wouldn't be seen in the Messersmith's car. Jake shrugged and went back to the kitchen to see whether Albert had stocked any liquor. Joe thumbed through magazines and newspapers, and brought up a prize: a folded map of Iowa. Sweat broke out on his brow when he realized they had traveled deep into the middle of the state. Further examination, however, showed that Illinois was right next to Iowa. All they had to do was travel north and east, and they should hit a road leading to Chicago. Joe relaxed, and looked around the house some more. Jake sure was taking a helluva long time in the kitchen. Well, they had a long time to wait until dark, anyway. Joe moved over to the pictures on the fireplace mantel.

*There they are,* he chuckled to himself, *Mr. and Mrs. Albert at their wedding. Mr. and Mrs. Albert and their first baby. Baby Albert takes his first friggin' steps. Baby Albert starts walkin'. Holy shit, Baby Albert's havin' a birthday party! And there's Baby Albert graduating from high school.* Suddenly he stopped, thunderstruck. *And there he is, a Des Moines City Cop.*

Poker Joe knew, he just *knew,* that Baby Albert the Cop checked on Ma and Pa Albert every day. Panic reached in and grabbed his intestines and *squeezed.* They had to get out of here, *now!*

"Jake!" he yelled. "Jake, get over here!"

There was no answer.

"Jake, get your ass over here. We're gettin' out right now!"

Still no answer.

Joe loped to the kitchen in search of Jake. He found him easily enough. Jake had found the Messersmiths' home-made wine stock, and had emptied a bottle and a half. He was sitting at the kitchen table, where he had knocked over a toothpick holder, and where he was attempting with all his concentration to replace each toothpick one by one. "Jake, you asshole!"

"Huh?" Jake could barely take his eyes off the toothpicks.

Joe swept the toothpicks off the table. Jake almost lost his balance trying to follow their flight to the floor. "Whudja do *that* for, Joe?"

"Listen, Fathead. We gotta get outta here right now. These old geezers have a son who's a cop. Sure as shit he's gonna poke his nose in the door any minute," Joe informed him.

"Jeez, Joe, you shouldn't get upset like that. You're gonna get an ulcer," Jake warned him.

"*You wanna see upset? Upset is when we get shot for killing his mommy and daddy! Now come ON!*" Joe yelled.

"Okay, okay," Jake agreed, shaking his head at Joe's anxiety. "But Joe, it's still light out."

"I know, I know. I'll tell you what. I'll get the car started. You watch for me, and when I give the signal, you run for the car and get in." Joe plucked Messersmith's hat from a hook near the kitchen door. "I'll wear this."

"What am I gonna wear?" Jake asked.

Joe pulled the lace table cloth off the kitchen table. "Put that over your head," he suggested.

"Aw, Joe, I'll look like a *girl*. Let's look for another hat."

"We don't have the time! Come on, try it," Joe insisted.

With a great deal of grumbling, Jake pulled the lace tablecloth over his head. A few toothpicks stuck up willy-nilly. Joe sighed. Well, it was only to get them out of town. He took a look inside the wallet and came up with eight dollars. Together with the change, they had a princely sum of $8.62 to get them to Chicago. Well, if they could find the right train somewhere along the line, they could ride free the rest of the way. Right now, however, they had to make it out of the city, and fast.

He opened up the kitchen door and darted to the car with the keys. It was unlocked, of course; these people were so *trusting*. It started easily, and he beckoned to Jake to get in the car.

Joe watched with amazement as Jake first got the tablecloth caught on the doorway behind him and fell on his rear end. Trying to get up while inebriated was no small task. Jake got lost in the tablecloth and finally ripped a piece of it off on the door jamb, leaving the back door wide open. He arranged the remainder of the ragged cloth over his head and staggered over to the car, finally managing to get in.

"That was the most stupid thing I've ever seen," Joe commented as he roared off down the residential street. Jake didn't say anything at all. He was used to hearing this. In the meantime, he sure was sleepy. While Joe was jabbering something about north and east and watch for this and that, his head tipped forward until his chin touched his chest, and he snored.

Joe looked over at his partner and sighed again. Well, it was probably better this way. They had a full tank of gas, and Jake was useless anyway. He could probably do a better job of getting away on his own.

It wasn't too long before he found a wide road that was heading in what seemed to be the right direction, toward the sun. If only he had thought to bring the map! But the road was almost empty, and they were moving at last. He pushed the accelerator as hard as he dared, and soon they were out of the city and heading through miles and miles of farmland. They breezed along.

Everything seemed to be going smoothly until Joe spotted a sheriff's car pulled over on the side of the road. He pulled his hat down over his eyes, and watched his speedometer to make sure he wasn't speeding. He gave the cop car a wide berth, touching the brim of his hat as he passed; he thought it was a nice touch. He glanced in the rear view mirror afterwards, just to make sure that the trooper wasn't following him. *Shitfire!* There he was, right behind the Ford, with his lights on!

Joe didn't give it a second thought. He had to outrun this cop. He downshifted, pushed the accelerator to the floor, and when the Ford's engine was screaming he shifted back up into third gear. It worked; he drew well ahead of the cop. The cop turned on his siren. To Joe's right, Jake snorted a couple of times to mark the occasion, then returned to his deafening snore.

Up ahead there was traffic slowing, and ahead of the cars Joe could see a farmer with his horse and wagon just poking along on the side of the road. Desperately Joe looked around for an escape, and saw it: people were turning onto a gravel road off to the left and speeding up, leaving clouds of dust from the road behind them.

He took the turn at a perilous angle, almost overturning the car, but fought the wheel and brought the car back under control. A look in the rear view showed him that the cop was still coming. The gravel road curved through acres and acres of corn that stood six feet high, and Joe took the second dirt road that led through the corn. He cut the speed to stop the dust from tattling his position to the cop, and watched the rear-view mirror. Sure enough, the cop whizzed by with lights and siren, and there was no sign that the trooper had even glanced in the Ford's direction.

Joe didn't take any chances. He drove on into the corn slowly, over ruts and through shallow mudholes, and was relieved to find another gravel road after half a mile. He took a turn on that road. In fact, he took almost every turn he came to, sweat pouring down his face and his chest. Jake snored on. At last, Joe saw a road sign for a town: APPLE SPRINGS 9 MILES. Thank God. They didn't have a watch between them, but his stomach told him it was mid-afternoon. He had to eat and visit the men's room, and it was high time Jake did something besides sleep.

Apple Springs looked like a pretty nice, quiet little town. Joe poked Jake in the ribs with his index finger, hard, as they passed the city limits. Jake woke up at last, yawning hugely. "Where are we?" he asked.

"Apple Springs," Joe said, and then before Jake could ask the stupid question that was coming, he finished it. "And I don't know what state we're in."

"Let's find a gas station. They have maps there," Jake said.

"Good idea," Joe muttered. Every once in a while Jake came up with a gem, it was true.

They found a gas station and pulled in. While Jake waited in the car, Joe went in and picked out maps of Iowa and Illinois. Heading back to the car, he froze when the man from behind the gas station counter yelled, "Hey, Mister!"

Slowly he turned around and faced the man, who puffed up to him. "Your wife's dress is sticking out of the side of the car," the man told him, pointing. Joe took a look back at the car and stifled a curse. Jake's tablecloth was indeed sticking out of the car door, trailing in the dirt. He figured there was a good two yards of it flapping in the wind while a cop followed them in a high speed chase. Somewhere back there was a state trooper wondering why in the hell an old man and his wife were running away from him when all he wanted to do was tell them that her dress was sticking out of the car. "I hate to say it, but it's probably ruined," the man said apologetically.

Joe swallowed his hair-trigger temper and only said, "Thanks. I guess I'll have to get her another one."

The man winked and shook his head. "Women, huh?" He looked Joe up and down doubtfully, noting the clothes stretched across his frame and the length of leg between the hem of his trousers and the top of his black work boots. "You, uh, you just get married?"

Joe gave him a dirty look, which the man missed. He went away, but Joe heard him chuckling as he hurried back to the station to attend to his business.

Joe headed over to Jake's side of the car in a savage mood. He flapped the maps on the window, and Jake rolled it down. "Well? Where are we?"

Joe hit him across the face with the maps and then picked up the ragged yardage from the ground. "You've been waving this at all the Staties in Iowa, Dope. Open your door."

Back in the car, Joe ignored Jake's whines about having to piss while he looked at the maps. There it was, Apple Springs, Iowa. Northeast Iowa. Not too bad; they were heading in more or less the right direction. They still had half a tank of gas. He figured they should probably get some food and some clothes, but he didn't want to pay for either of those, not if he didn't have to.

Slowly they cruised down the main street of town, which only took ten minutes. Couple of banks; another gas station; three bars; a five-and-dime; Sheriff's office; Mom's Eats; a drug store; a general store; lots of closed businesses. All no good. In this tiny berg they would be remembered if they stole something, especially since Jake had left the tablecloth sticking out of his car door. By supper time the whole town would know about crimes they pulled. Joe's stomach rumbled, and he finally gave in to hunger. He made Jake stay in the car while he parked in front of the general store and went in to get food.

Joe selected cold cuts for sandwiches, bread, mustard, and several bottles of beer. He eyed the shirts and other clothing items in the store, but decided that they'd spend the Messersmith's money only in the case of an emergency, like food. Or maybe gas.

Jake made a grab for the food and beer, but Joe made him

wait. He backed out onto the main street of town and slowly left Apple Springs behind. They'd eat in the woods.

Not too far down the road they came upon a dirt road to the left. No street sign. There had to be a farm back there. Joe pulled to the side of the main road and regarded the turnoff with some interest. If it was a big farm, they could hide out for a day, rest up, eat, rob the people, maybe even find better fitting clothes and guns.

"You gonna go down there, Joe?" asked Jake.

"Yep, I'm gonna try it. If we meet any men along the way, I'll just say we took a wrong turn and come on back out here. If we meet women, you just let me do the talkin'. You ready?"

"Can I take this off my head yet?"

Joe looked at Jake with disgust. "It don't matter. Doesn't make you look any better or worse than you already look."

"Joe, I have to piss somethin' fierce. Can we stop?"

"Hold on, I've gotta go, too," Joe told Jake, and Jake held on. Joe steered the car left onto the road, and pulled off onto some grass.

Joe left the motor running, opened his car door and left it open, and stood in front of the car with his back to the car. The relief was tremendous. He could just imagine how Jake felt after drinking all that wine and having to hold it all this time, and started laughing to himself. He turned to find Jake, but Jake wasn't there!

"*JAKE!*" he whispered as loudly as he dared. "*Jake, where in the hell are you?*"

"*Right here, Joe,*" came the whispered reply, but still Joe couldn't see his partner anywhere.

"Where are you?" Joe asked, slightly louder.

"*I'm behind the car,*" Jake answered, still whispering.

Joe fastened the fly of his too-small trousers with great difficulty and walked around to the back of the car. There was Jake, bare-ass in the breeze, taking a dump behind the car. Steam was actually rising from the tremendous pile, and flies the size of small dogs were lighting on Jake's rear end and fighting for space on the foul-smelling mountain of excrement.

"Jesus Christ, Jake!" exclaimed Joe. "What are you doing?"

"I hadda take a dump, too, Joe."

"Well, why didn't you do it in *front* of the car, like I did?"

"I didn't want anybody to see me," came the reply.

Joe sighed and looked back at the main road to town, just a few yards behind the car. "Jake, did you ever stop to think what you're gonna wipe that big ass of yours with?"

Silence.

Then, in a very soft whisper, Jake asked, "*Will you see if there's a Sears and Roebuck's in the back seat of the car?*"

Joe wanted to kick Jake, but with his luck he'd slip on the pile and land with his head in it. He cursed, went back to the passenger side of the car, and grabbed the lace tablecloth. "Here, use this," he told Jake.

"Thanks, Joe."

Joe turned on his heal and went to sit behind the wheel again, totally disgusted. Jake was going to be the death of them both. He couldn't wait to get to Chicago and dump him.

A few minutes later Jake returned to the car and slammed the door. "Ready to go," he said.

Joe turned and looked at him. "Where's the tablecloth, Jake?"

"I left it back there."

"Why?"

"Well, I don't want it any more."

Joe closed his weary eyes and rested his forehead on the steering wheel. "Jake, don't tell me you used the *whole tablecloth* to wipe your ass."

Absolute silence filled the car.

Then Joe erupted. "Get out there and bury it, shithead! It's a dead giveaway as to where we are!"

Silently Jake opened his door, found a good-sized flat rock, and started digging while Joe fumed. Twenty minutes later Jake got in the car again. Joe didn't ask any more questions; he didn't feel like listening to any more of Jake's answers at this point. He put the car in low gear and bumped back to the farm road. Glancing in the rear-view, Joe saw what he *thought* he'd see: a big mound of freshly dug dirt with a flat rock sitting on top of it. *Yep, that's Jake all over the place*, he thought, and continued on down the road. *Christ, I can't stand it any more. I'll just get rid of him here. I can't take another day with him, I just can't.*

Presently they came to a bridge made of logs roped tightly together; on the other side of the bridge was a gate made of a single strand of rope across the road and hand-lettered signs painted on plain boards: PRIVATE LAND. NO TRESPASSING. NO HUNTING. NO CAMPING.

Suddenly Joe's day just got brighter. *Nobody is home*, he thought. *Perfect!*

Untying the rope and moving the boards to let the car pass through was as easy as pie. Joe personally re-tied the rope and made things look like they had before with the signs. This was too important to entrust to that dunce Jake. He got behind the wheel again, and they rolled on down the road.

Soon it became obvious that although this was prime farmland, it wasn't being farmed. An occasional stalk of corn grew here and there, but nobody had planted this land in a long time. Up ahead Joe could see a big red barn and a farm house—but no tractor or other vehicle. He rolled down the window: no smell of manure. In fact, you couldn't even hear birds or bugs out there. Creepy.

Nonetheless, they approached the farm house. To be on the safe side, Joe ran the car out behind the barn to park it. Then Joe and Jake together cased the house and barn. It was fast and easy, because nothing was locked.

Nothing. Not a stick of furniture. Not a bread crumb. Not a leftover pair of underwear. No guns. In the barn, however, there were several bars of iron that looked like leftover parts of some hay wagon. Not easy to conceal, but Joe thought one of them would do nicely to lay old Jake to rest. His fingers itched. *Why not do it now?* he thought. *Get it over with.* He turned to see where Jake was. For some reason he was standing about six feet away, just looking at Joe thoughtfully. "What you lookin' at?" Joe demanded, startled.

Jake just shrugged and continued on to the back of the barn.

There was something there in Jake's mind, all right, Joe decided, but it couldn't be anything serious. Jake was Stupid with a capital 'S.' Outside, he headed back toward the car.

*Well, at least we can eat our lunch and drink our beer in peace*, Joe decided. *And Stupid there can shit all over the place and I won't care.* He grabbed the paper sack of groceries and bottles of beer from the back seat of the car and headed off in the direction of the trees.

"Where we goin', Joe?" asked Jake, jogging to keep up.

Joe felt a moment of generosity and decided not to kick Jake's ass. "We'll eat by the river, where it's cooler."

"Good idea, Joe! Hey, I'm sorry about that tablecloth, Buddy. I just didn't think."

"Forget it," Joe said.

"You're a good guy, inviting me to come along with you, Joe. I just want to say thanks," Jake said.

"Forget it," Joe said.

"No, I mean it. Most of the guys I know don't want me around because . . . well, I do dumb things once in a while."

Joe rolled his eyes but said nothing.

"So I just wanted to say thanks. You're a good guy," Jake finished grandly.

Joe considered himself to be a saint for putting up with Jake so far; his temper had landed him in the pen once (and he had only been *moderately* irritated when he had shot and killed two of his fellow poker players). Jake had already used up more than his portion of Joe's patience. "You're welcome," he said. "Now can you shut up?"

"Yes," Jake answered. And they continued on toward the river in silence.

The woods on the edge of the field was a wild tangle of vegetation, and Joe used Jake like a plow to break through before he followed. He felt it was only fair, since he was carrying the food. Jake did it willingly enough, but his seldom-seen temper flared several times when the vines he pushed aside bit back with thorns. "Shit, that stings!" he yelled, as a vine slapped him across the face and gouged his skin viciously. For some reason this tickled Joe, and he giggled like a girl. In fact, the more irritated Jake got, the funnier it seemed, until finally Joe was guffawing and tears were streaming down the sides of his face. The top button on his britches flew off with a *snap!* as he bent over, laughing.

By then they were past the vines and in clear sight of the river, but Jake turned and glared at Joe. "What's so freakin' funny?" he asked in a low tone.

Joe didn't notice the difference in Jake's demeanor. "You! You are!"

"Joe, that's mean," Jake stated flatly.

"Oh, have a beer. You'll feel better," Joe said, trying to stifle his giggles.

Jake ignored the bottle that Joe held out toward him and turned toward the river. He sat on the bank, took off his boots and socks, rolled up his trouser legs as far as he could, and waded in. He splashed water on his head and face, washing off as much of the blood from the scratches as he could and keeping his back turned toward Joe.

Joe tore open the paper bag and used it as a makeshift dining table. By this time he *did* notice a definite change in Jake, and felt just a little sorry about laughing at him. He made him a salami and mustard sandwich (spreading the mustard straight from the jar with his dirty finger and wiping off the remainder on his pants), and opened a bottle of beer for him with old man Messersmith's key ring. "Lunch is served," he called to Jake.

Silence from Jake.

"Aw, come on, Jake. Things have been pretty tense all day, and you slept through most of it. Gimme a break. Come on and have a sandwich. You'll feel better," Joe told him.

Jake finally turned around and waded back to shore. "I *am* pretty hungry," he admitted, and picked up a sandwich. He took a giant bite and said, "Jeez, Joe, this is good. I guess I was starvin'. Thanks, hey?"

While they were eating and drinking on the ground in the shade of a maple tree, Joe told Jake about the high-speed pursuit of the sheriff's car just outside of Des Moines. Jake thought it was pretty funny, and said he was sorry he missed it.

A little of Joe's good humor left him. *We wouldn't have been chased if it hadn't been for you, Dipshit,* he thought. He opened another beer for himself.

"Can I have another beer, too, Joe?" asked Jake.

"Get it yourself," Joe shot back. "I'm busy." He tipped his head back, taking a long, leisurely slug of the brew.

He didn't see Jake's face fall.

Jake rose, walked around behind Joe, and picked up a beer bottle. "How am I supposed to open this?" he asked.

"Any way you want, Retard," Joe snapped. "Figure it out." And he took another pull from his bottle.

Jake's full bottle of beer flew in a roundhouse slam, whacking Joe's left temple squarely and sending him flying sideways into the dirt. Blood spurted from his head. Joe wasn't knocked unconscious, but he was stunned. His vision blurred and his head ached fit to split. What had happened?

He struggled to sit up and shake his head to clear his vision. It *did* clear, too, just about the time he heard the breaking glass and smelled the odor of spilt beer. It cleared just in time for him to see Jake coming for him with the jagged remains of the beer bottle. He felt Jake shove his face back, mashing his nose and exposing his throat. There was a searing pain across his throat and all his breath left him. And then Poker Joe felt no more.

And the land came alive and had its own tasty snack. The tale of Poker Joe Vinton and Jake Strickland and their wild escape from justice in Minnesota ended on a farm in Iowa. All that remained there for anyone to find, when they did, was a stolen car behind the barn, some broken brown glass by the river, and a very strange burial site for a lace table cloth.

# CHAPTER
## Thirteen

In 1929, Jeremy Baumann, who was Stephan's great-great grandson, lost all he had as a result of the stock market crash. A week later, the factory where he had worked almost all his adult life closed its doors and he was out of a job in Chicago. He found himself suddenly and inexplicably deeply in debt without the means to pay the bills, and joined the queues of similarly stricken men looking for any type of work at all. There was none. Desperate to keep his family alive and together, he wrote to the Mayor's office in Apple Springs to make sure that the farm was still Baumann property and that no one else was living there. The news, for Jeremy, was better than the best: not only was the land vacant, but Stephan had prospered on his new farm well enough to invest his money in an attempt to assure that no other family suffered the fate of his own. A trust fund paid the taxes on the Heartless land in perpetuity, as long as the land was not sold outside the family. As the oldest living direct descendent of Stephan Baumann, Jeremy was the heir and sole owner at this point; the title and deed to the land would be passed on to him at his convenience.

Accompanying this news was an urgent appeal to contact the law offices of Koeppel, Sloan, and Koeppel in Apple Springs, Iowa, before any decision to occupy the aforementioned land. By the time that he received this letter, Jeremy had no telephone. For that matter, he would soon have no address. His mortgage on his house had been recalled due to non-payment, and there were just days before his family would be forcibly evicted. He felt he had little choice: he could either attempt to sell the land in Iowa in an attempt to keep his house and starve in Chicago, or try farming in Iowa. He never would contact that law firm, although they could have told him a lot about the history of the land and the many reasons there were to leave it alone.

Jeremy moved his wife Amanda, his four sons, and two daughters to the farm. After seventy-six years the barn and house were still standing as if Heinrich Baumann and his family were just on a trip to town. Tornadoes, hail storms, snow, dry rot, infestations of animals and insects alike were simply nonexistent on the farm. Although this was very puzzling to Baumann and his wife, they took it as just another good omen. Another good luck charm was heaped upon the family when they found that Stephan had replaced Heinrich's chest under the bed, filled with gold pieces. Jeremy didn't know that Stephan had emptied the chest before sliding it under the bed as a part of the original homestead. He simply closed his eyes and thanked God for his good fortune.

Jeremy improved the property by personally digging a well for a hand pump, and paneling the inside of the house. His family noted with surprise that he gradually started acting differently from his normal, even-tempered self. Although the farm's soil was extremely fertile—very little effort was required to grow just about anything they wanted, and they always seemed to have enough rain while the rest of the region went dry—he found fault with everything and every one. He became obsessed with money: saving it, hiding it, ferreting it out when it wasn't in his pocket. He was convinced that there was a treasure chest buried somewhere on the property and dug again and again to find it. He had used the money in Heinrich's old chest, replaced the chest under the bed, and then promptly forgotten about it.

It wasn't a year before tragedy struck again, and the Spirit of the Great Bear cleansed the land.

In shock, the people of Apple Springs dug out old letters and journals, and revived the stories about Heartless, but the official causes of death reported in the town records were listed as, "Death by Misadventure." Again, only the youngest family members survived, and these were taken in by the townspeople. By that time the farming community had troubles of its own. Memories of the horrible deaths of members of the Jeremy Baumann family grew dim as the nation's great Midwest became a dust bowl. Banks had no money, and farmers had no way to survive off the land. Most lost their farms and moved away, and this included the family that took in the Baumann children, who cleaned out the portable parts of the house and barn before moving on. And so the original Baumann farm rested, once again untroubled by human hands.

PART THREE

Rudy's Battles

# CHAPTER
# Fourteen

In early 1972, Jeremy's only surviving son found himself at one of those crossroads in life where he had to make a choice, and the Baumann farm in Iowa seemed like a better destination than where he was headed. Long forgotten were the tales of a curse attached to the land.

Rudy had been only two years old when the savage deaths of his parents and three older brothers had occurred, and he remembered nothing of the incident. He and his sisters had been taken in by a deeply devout and outrageously strict Christian family with eight children of their own. The Richters had been farmers, as well, and the extra mouths to feed had been paid for by the sweat, tears, and blood of the Baumann children, particularly when the entire family moved to join relatives on farms in Minnesota. Stanley Richter fully believed in the old adage, "Spare the rod and spoil the child," and applied his beliefs to Rudy particularly. All the Richter children and Rudy's sisters feared Stanley. Rudy feared and *hated* the man, yet, in later life, he became more like Stanley Richter than any of them. Upon graduation from high school, he became a carpenter's apprentice with the local union. Eventually he became a full carpenter with a union card, able to take up employment wherever he wished.

The building trades in Minnesota in the 1950's and 1960's were booming. Work was plentiful, and so was the pay. Rudy moved to Duluth on the far western edge of Lake Superior, and bought a home there not too far from his favorite bar. Beer had become his almost constant companion when he was off the job, and to him, life was a riot. He had plenty of women friends, all of whom he had met at various bars and parties, and all of his friends were willing to buy him a beer or be there if he wanted to stand a round. He became a confirmed bachelor. He had never wanted to marry, and considered all of his married friends to be fools.

He partied on well into his late twenties; that is, until he met Anna Christianson.

Anna was in her early twenties, a tiny blonde with sparkling green eyes who made his head swim when she laughed up at him. She was from a small town, Kenton, in northern Minnesota where Rudy's work team was assigned for several weeks, and worked as a teller at the local bank. They met when Rudy cashed his pay check one week. One look was all it took for him; he was head over heels in love with her at first sight. Anna's first impression of Rudy was that he was a "diamond in the rough". Word spreads quickly in small towns, and he had a reputation for being a bear for work and for having an endless thirst for beer. Alcohol was not allowed in her father's house, where she still lived, but she understood that after working long hours in the hot sun a man (a *real* man, she modified to herself) would want something to wash the dust from his throat. He had a temper, she heard—but so did her father.

He was a consummate hood and she was an angel bored with her corner of heaven.

He immediately asked for her name and if she would go out for supper with him. She put him off, telling him she hardly knew him. He argued that she had to eat anyway. Anna glanced quickly at the bank manager, who was otherwise engaged, and then at the other bank tellers. Two of them had noticed the tall, handsome blonde man staying at her window just a little too long, and Anna blushed bright red. Her friends giggled and motioned to her encouragingly. They knew that Anna didn't date. She didn't find any of the local bachelors attractive or interesting, or even mildly ambitious. They also thought it was high time that she got out from under her father's oppressive thumb.

When she still hesitated, Karen Swanson excused herself from the customer at her window and approached Anna. "Excuse me, Anna," she said sweetly, "but will you look at this for me?" Suspiciously, Anna excused herself to Rudy and stepped back to talk to Karen. Karen held a blank deposit slip in her hand.

"What are you doing, dummy? This is blank!" Anna exclaimed as she examined the slip. "What do you want me to look at?"

"Shush, Anna, and keep looking at it and nodding, okay?" Karen said, pointing to a blank on the slip. Anna nodded dutifully.

"He wants to go out with you, doesn't he?" Karen asked boldly.

"Yes, but I don't know him," Anna said, handing the slip back to Karen.

"That's no excuse. Just who do you *know* that you *will* go out with?" Karen remonstrated.

Anna blushed again, and turned back to Rudy with determination.

She turned him down flat.

At 3:15 that afternoon, as she walked out the back door of the bank, Rudy was leaning against the building, smoking a cigarette. He crushed it out as soon as she appeared.

"What are *you* doing here?" Anna demanded.

"I'm waiting for *you*," Rudy said.

"I told you I won't go out with you."

"Why not? Are you engaged?"

"No," Anna said, hurrying along the alleyway with Rudy close behind her.

"Married?"

"No!" she exclaimed.

"Does that mean you don't *want* to get married?" Rudy asked, finally catching up.

"No! I mean, yes! I mean . . . I mean . . . Mr. Baumann, I will *not* go out with you!" Anna exclaimed, turning onto the sidewalk. He followed her.

Anna stopped, wheeled around, and planted her feet apart on the sidewalk. She placed her hands on her hips; green eyes flashed a warning. "Now, STAY!" she commanded. Rudy stopped, his mouth open.

Anna fled the four blocks to her home. If anyone had passed her they would have probably thought she was crazy. She alternately blushed bright red, and then would burst out laughing. Apparently Mr. Rudolph Baumann responded best to dog commands. "*Fetch! Sit!*" she whispered aloud to herself, and had to stop and hold on to a tree as she doubled over in laughter.

For two weeks after that, Rudy Baumann still came into the bank to cash his checks, but he went to other tellers' windows. Each time Anna marked him from the corner of her eye, but pretended not to notice him. Instead, she would heap her considerable charm upon whoever happened to be her (very grateful) customer at the time. Rudy would stare longingly at her, and leave dejectedly when his business was finished. He never waylaid her in the alley again.

During those two weeks, Anna's friends at the bank had plenty to say about Mr. Baumann. He asked about her each time he came in, and they all felt sorry for him and rather irritated with her. "If he was looking at *me* the way he looks at *you*, I'd be on Cloud Nine!" Karen told her.

On Rudy's next visit, he came in just before closing time and waited in a long line at Karen's window, right next to Anna's. He didn't spare Anna a glance that day, but he did seem to be taking an awfully long time cashing his check. His and Karen's heads were bent over in whispered conversation. Anna found she couldn't concentrate, and had to count her deposit money twice. What were they *up* to?

When Anna's customer left, she pretended to busy herself with organizing receipts at her window while she strained to overhear

Karen and Rudy. She kept her head down, and was startled when Karen touched her shoulder. Anna looked up, and saw that Rudy was now at *her* window. She looked at Karen questioningly.

Karen cleared her throat. "Ahem. Miss Anna Christianson, please allow me to introduce Mr. Rudolph Baumann. Mr. Baumann, this is Miss Christianson." Karen stepped back a pace. "*Now* you know each other. Get on with it." And she turned back to her window as if nothing extraordinary had happened.

Anna took a deep breath and turned to explain *one more time* that she would not go out with Rudy, when she took a good look at him. He had attached a very large dog's collar and leash to his neck, and was offering her the leash's handle. He put up his paws, doggie-style, and asked, "*Now* will you take me for a walk?"

The entire line of tellers erupted in laughter. Anna finally said, "Yes", and a cheer went up. Mr. Brown came out of his office and put on his glasses, looking around and wondering what was going on in his bank. Fortunately for Anna and Rudy, the collar and leash had disappeared behind the counter by that time. Mr. Brown never did get a clear answer as to why his tellers were so noisily happy that day.

That was their first time out together, consisting of an ice cream cone apiece and a walk through the park. Despite his extensive experience with women, Rudy had never found one he wanted to impress as much as he did Anna. She was *beautiful*. She was *beyond* beautiful to him. When she looked at him with a smile, he never wanted her to take those eyes off him. She was smart, and kind, and funny. She made him feel ten feet tall.

Anna was also the first woman who was able to get Rudy to talk about the way he felt about things. It was easy for him to kid around with the girls who hung around the bars. Hell, they never required much more than a first name before they let him take them to bed. But there was something about Anna that made him want her to really *know* him, and he instinctively felt that she would treat him kindly. He told her what he knew of his family, the tragedy in Iowa, and his terrible years with the Richters.

She listened with sympathy but without pity, for which he was grateful. Anna then told him about her own life. She said that she still lived with her father, not so much because she couldn't afford to move out, but because he would be alone if she did. Her mother had died several years before of cancer, and since that time Harold Christianson had changed into a bitter, hard man who saw no joy in life and condemned those who did. She was his only child, and he held on to her with a fierce grip. She had hoped, in time, that he would soften and that life would become easier for him, but Harold Christianson was as hard and cold as a tombstone. A tear appeared in her eye as she ended, and Rudy offered her his handkerchief in silence. She took it, dabbed at her eyes, and then gently touched his hand. Pure, unadulterated joy coursed through his soul.

They met each day for a week, walking, talking, drinking coffee, picking up hamburgers, holding hands, and truly enjoying each other. They always met during the day, and always in the park. Never once did Rudy make a move to kiss or touch her other than to hold her hand. He desperately wanted to do those things; the nights in his motel room were getting longer and longer, and he ached for her. But he knew he wanted something more from her than a roll in the hay, something much more precious. He wanted *her*.

At the end of that week, Rudy had to tell Anna that he would be returning to Duluth the next day. When she responded with extreme disappointment, he gently explained to her that he had been taking vacation time from work this whole past week. The rest of the crew had gone on to another job. He didn't want to leave her, not at all, but he had to work.

They walked along in silence for a while, and then Rudy asked, "Do you ever go to Duluth?"

Anna looked up at him quickly; her thoughts had been going

in the same direction. "I've been there shopping a few times," she answered. "I don't have a car, so I take the bus and . . . and I stay overnight."

His grip on her hand strengthened, and she squeezed back.

"You might as well know that I love you, Anna," he said quietly, his head down. She stopped walking, and so did he, finally looking into those beautiful green eyes. "And I love you, Rudy," she said. And, glory of glories, she stood up on her tiptoes and kissed him warmly, full on the mouth, in broad daylight.

Rudy took her in his arms and stepped into the warmth of her, and kissed her back. He only meant to embrace her, to hold back, but what he felt in that kiss was so passionate and full of wanting that he helplessly responded. When she finally pushed weakly at his shoulders, they were both breathing in short gasps. Anna looked down, and saw the full length and breadth of his manhood. It couldn't be hidden. Rudy tried to turn away, but she caught him and lightly stroked the length of him. It brought a gasp from them both. Anna felt a warm wetness between her thighs; it was a new experience for her, but she instinctively knew why it was there.

"*Rudy,*" she whispered. "*Oh Rudy, I want you.*"

"Good Christ, Anna," Rudy croaked. "We have to stop or I'm going to pull you into those bushes."

She swallowed and stepped back, her eyes huge upon his face.

"I want you more than you could possibly know," Rudy admitted, his breathing still ragged. "I have wanted you since the first day I ever laid eyes on you. But not like this, not here, not now. And not in that seedy little motel room, either. It's just not good enough for you."

"What are we going to do, Rudy?" Anna asked helplessly.

"I don't know. I didn't expect to fall in love here," he complained, and then they both laughed. "Can you come to Duluth?" Rudy asked hopefully.

"Oh, yes!" she answered with feeling.

"Anna, let's write down our telephone numbers and addresses. We'll plan on it. But I think we should wait a couple of weeks," Rudy said.

"Why wait?" she frowned. "Rudy, we love and want each other so much! Why should we wait?"

He seriously regarded her flushed face and bright eyes. "Honey, you're a virgin, aren't you?"

She hesitated, but only for a moment. "So?"

"So this will be your first time. I want you to want *me*, not just sex, and I want to feel the same about you. If we wait a little bit and feel differently, okay. We'll forget it, no harm done. I don't want to take your virginity if we're not truly in love," Rudy explained, kissing her brow.

"I'm not a baby, Rudy," Anna said staunchly, and her green eyes flashed.

"You sure aren't," he smiled, and they laughed again.

They had walked across the park to the spot where they usually parted, Anna to return to her father's house and Rudy to find his way back to the motel. They stopped and turned to each other.

Rudy searched his pockets, but could only find old deposit slips in his wallet for paper. Anna came up with a pen from her pocketbook. They traded phone numbers and addresses, as planned, and Anna put her hands on Rudy's shoulders. They kissed warmly but with much more reservation with a warning from Rudy ("Don't do it to me, Babe, or I won't be able to walk"). Then they said goodbye. As Rudy watched her trim back walk away from him, she said over her shoulder, "I might be a virgin, Sweetheart, but I'm sure you'll teach me the right things. And you're the only man in the world I want to learn them from." And she was gone.

Rudy walked on air all the way back to the motel.

———

He came back down to earth the next day. Back on the job, he was greeted with a considerable amount of mostly good-natured teasing by his workmates. Rudy hadn't taken a vacation day since his first day of work, so that in itself was unusual. He *never* had let a woman come between himself and his beer. Well-aware that he had stayed back at the motel while the rest went on to the next job, and *why*, the building construction workers hurled sexual innuendo and downright bold remarks throughout the day. Rudy took it well but without letting a single detail out to his buddies, and this mysterious reaction spurred them on to even greater heights of what he called, "verbal diarrhea".

There were a couple of guys who made obviously vicious remarks; Rudy ignored these as well. Calvin and Bert had always been his best drinking buddies. They'd come around. He figured that they were jealous of his relationship with a beautiful woman. Well, if he had to trade them off, Calvin and Bert for Anna, there was no contest. Anna was precious to him. Without his drinking friends, there would still be beer in this world. Without Anna, however, he would be lost, and he was smart enough to know it.

That afternoon, after leaving work for the day, Rudy went home and sat in silence, alone, on his living room sofa. He didn't know what to do with himself. Yesterday at this time he had been with Anna, and his life had been so full. Now it was just . . . empty. Normally, he'd already be at Calhoun's, eating peanuts from the bar for supper and ogling women as they walked by. He had no taste for that tonight. In fact, the thought of it made him a little sick. Working, drinking, fighting, and nailing women. How had he lived like that for so many years?

He got up and wandered to the refrigerator in the kitchen, in search of something to eat. Rudy was horrified to see that the refrigerator's only occupants were beer, a gallon jar of pickled eggs (what year had he bought *that*, for God's sake?), and six pizza boxes, each boasting one mummified piece of pepperoni pizza. He searched the cupboards, and found only a half jar of rancid peanuts.

His appetite for food left him temporarily, and he roamed the house, looking at it as Anna would see it when she came to visit—*if* she came to visit, that was. This house had been his home for six years, but he never spent more than just the necessary time to shower, sleep, dress, and occasionally have Calvin and Bert over to watch a football or baseball game on TV. It was a mess, and that was putting it mildly. Empty pizza boxes and beer bottles littered every possible surface. Newspapers were flung on the floor after he finished reading them, and stayed there until he noticed them and put them in the trash. The tub and shower upstairs were almost black with accumulated grime and mildew. Now that he thought about it, he had *never* changed the sheets on his bed since he had moved in. He did laundry when he absolutely, positively had no wearable underwear. Otherwise, wearing apparel was relegated to his bedroom floor.

Rudy sat on the bed, overwhelmed. It was not humanly possible to change this house into something that he wanted Anna to see. How had he become such a pig? Suddenly, he wanted a beer, and badly. Yep, a beer would help calm him down and let him think about how to start. He headed back downstairs to the kitchen. The phone rang as he passed it, and he put out his hand and answered absent-mindedly, his thoughts still on a cold beer.

"Hello."

"Rudy? Rudy, is that you?" It was Anna's voice! His heart jumped in his chest, and he found he had difficulty breathing.

"Anna?"

"Yes. Rudy, I . . . I just called to see how you are. I miss you so much." Anna's voice murmured sweetly in his ear, and his knees weakened. He put out a hand to steady himself against the living room wall.

"I'm fine, just fine! But I miss you, too, Honey," he replied.

"Look, I can't talk long. I'm calling from a pay phone, and I don't have much money on me. I just wanted to hear your voice," Anna said.

"You sound beautiful, Anna. You don't know what you've done to me! I don't know what to do with myself," Rudy replied.

"It's the same for me, Rudy, believe me," Anna admitted. "I kept thinking about you all day and losing track of what I was doing. I'm going to get fired if I keep it up! But tonight's going to be the worst. It's going to be a long, long night."

Rudy laughed ruefully. "I know what you mean about that." His voice softened and grew husky. "I had a *very* long night last night. I kept thinking about your lips and the way it felt when you kissed me, and how I almost . . ."

Anna interrupted him. "Me too! Things are happening to me. I'm having feelings I've never had before."

There was a moment of silence on the line as they each digested the situation. Rudy broke it. "Honey, when I get you in my arms again, I'm not going to want to let you go."

"I don't *want* you to let me go, Rudy."

"Just remember that I love you, Anna."

"And I love you, Rudy." There was a click on the line. "Rats! My three minutes are up. I'll . . ." and Anna was cut off in mid-sentence.

Rudy held the handset to his chest for a moment after the line went dead. *Anna . . .*

He replaced the handset into the receiver and walked out to the kitchen. He opened the refrigerator and lugged out the gallon jar of sickly-looking pickled eggs and the pizza boxes, and fished out a trash bag. Once he started, he just kept on cleaning. He hauled out eight extra-large trash bags to the curb that night, washed a load of laundry and ate at an all-night diner. He decided he'd better learn to cook. After all, he couldn't survive the way he had been living, and eating out was expensive.

Back at home again, Rudy couldn't bear to shower in the shower-and-tub combination until it was cleaned, and he had never thought to buy cleaning solutions. He gave himself a birdbath in the kitchen sink instead. Exhausted, he sought his bed.

What was that *smell*? He finally realized it was the sheets: years of sweat and grease and God alone knew what else. Had he really brought women home to sleep in *that*? He spent his restless night on the living room sofa instead.

After work the next day, Rudy drove first to a department store to purchase an entire change of bed linen and towels. While he was at it, he bought two new pillows, as well. Next, he drove to a large supermarket and bought an enormous load of cleaning supplies and equipment, and real food. Lost and confused in the supermarket's aisle of cleaning aids, he approached a middle-aged woman who looked like she knew what she was doing. She was extremely helpful, choosing products that would help him as he described the situation at his house. He thanked her profusely when she finished.

"You're welcome, Sir. Now, you don't have to answer this, but I'm wondering if your girlfriend is coming to visit you for the first time?" the lady twinkled at him.

Rudy flushed, and the lady laughed. "Well, good luck. I can tell she's really special."

Later that night Rudy threw his old sheets into the trash, remade the bed, and tackled the shower. Armed with a scrub brush, scouring powder, and cleaning rags, he plunged in. An hour later he was cursing the shower and wondering how much it would cost to replace it. No matter how hard he scrubbed, the black mildew would not leave the grout between the tiles surrounding the tub and shower. He had a brainstorm, and fetched the jug of bleach. He would let chemicals do the work for him! He doused the tiles and drain with full-strength bleach, and backed out of the bathroom, his nose running and tears gushing from his eyes. How did housewives do it, day afer day?

He was monstrously hungry, and he went to the kitchen to make his own supper. Rudy knew how to make coffee, and put on a pot to brew while he made peanut butter and jelly sandwiches. As soon as the coffee was ready, he wolfed down three entire sandwiches with relish. Thank God he knew how to make those things. They were easy, he didn't have to turn on the oven, and he only had to wash a butter knife and a cup.

Upstairs again, he turned on the bedroom light and took pleasure in its neat appearance and freshly-aired cleanliness. Rudy planned to shower and relax in front of the television set for a while, before turning in for the night. He opened the closet to grab his robe and felt his heart sink. That, too, was a horrific mess. Why, there were clothes in there that he had worn in high school! Somewhat daunted and disgusted with himself, he closed the closet door and headed for the bathroom. Although it smelled quite strongly of bleach still, the tub and shower were gleaming. That brought a smile to his face. Then he looked down at the floor. Wherever he had accidentally sloshed bleach, the linoleum floor dazzled with its original color. He could tell exactly where the bleach had spilt, and where it hadn't. Funny; he had assumed that the bathroom floor was grey all along. Turned out, it was *white*. Who knew?

And so Rudy learned throughout the next several days three of the woes of housewives all over the world: keeping a clean house is hard, back-breaking work; clean one thing, and it makes the rest of the house look terrible; and the work never stops. He much preferred his regular job, where the work was hard and back-breaking, but there was a definite starting and stopping point. And he got paid for it.

In the meantime, he thought constantly of his new love interest. One day the mailbox contained a letter from Anna, and he tore it open and read what she had written before he reached his front door. He read it again as he dialed her telephone number, and waited for it to ring ten times before he gave up. He was elated. Although Anna hadn't written much in the way of news, she had repeated her feelings for him and the way he made her feel. Once again he was buoyed up with hope for the future and by the warmth of her regard.

Later that night, Rudy tried again at a time when he was sure that Anna would be at home. After three rings, the connection went through, and a deep male voice said, "Hello?"

Rudy swallowed. This must be Anna's father.

"May I speak to Anna, please?" he said, in his most ingratiating voice.

"Who is this?" the man asked rudely.

"Sir, my name is Rudy Baumann. Is Anna there?" Rudy asked again.

There was a hollow *Clunk!* as the phone was dropped, and Rudy could hear the man call in the background, "Anna! Phone's for you!"

After a short wait, Anna picked up the phone breathlessly. "Hello?"

"Anna, it's me," said Rudy. "I just got your letter today."

"Oh, thank you. That's very interesting," she said formally.

"Anna, what's wrong? Why are you talking like that?" Rudy asked, sensing the difference in her voice and demeanor.

"Well, that's hard to say," Anna responded.

"Is your father standing right there?"

"Yes, that's true."

"Honey, you're not a little kid anymore. Tell him that this is a private call and that you need some space," Rudy told her, frowning.

"This isn't a good time. I'm in the middle of making supper. I'll call you back tomorrow, okay?"

"Anna, I . . ." and the line went dead.

Rudy replaced the phone and sat there in silence, staring at it. What was going on? Was her father that controlling that he wouldn't let his twenty-two year old daughter take private calls? He had pictured (in his most private thoughts) that one day Anna would marry him. Was her father going to be a problem? He hoped not. It would be rough on Anna and uncomfortable for him. Or was there another reason that she had sounded so cool on the phone? Had she changed her mind about him?

Sleep was impossible for him that night, so he finally gave up on it and went down to the kitchen. Maybe a beer would calm his nerves. Now that he thought about it, he hadn't had a drink since he had first started seeing Anna. He shook his head. *Man, she's got me turned upside down, but good,* he thought. There on the kitchen table was Anna's letter. How could she sound so warm one minute and so cool the next? He thought he'd read it again. Maybe there was a clue there. Once again, she sidetracked him from his beer, and he sat at the kitchen table and opened the letter.

No. After re-reading the letter over and over again, there was no mistaking how she felt about him. The problem had to be her father.

He sighed. Family problems. He'd had enough of them to last a lifetime. It had been years since he'd seen his own two older sisters, even though they were married and living with their families right here in Duluth. He didn't even know his nieces and nephews. He rubbed the back of his neck to ease the tension there. Well, it was his own fault. When he'd left the Richter household, he hadn't wanted anything to remind him of those terrible days, so he closed his life to both of them, as well. His days and nights had narrowed to a slim track: work and drink. There was no room in there for family ties. And they'd made it pretty clear the last time they had seen him that they didn't approve of his life choices, nor of the company he kept. They both told him separately that he was not welcome unless and until he stopped drinking and carousing.

At the time, he thought he could do without them. Rudy was, after all, the lone male survivor of their family, and he had made it without them for years. If they didn't accept him and his ways, he certainly didn't need them telling him about it.

Except now, if he and Anna should have a future together, it sure would be nice to introduce her to his sisters and be welcomed into their homes again. Surely where there were family ties, there was forgiveness. After all, family was supposed to be family. Wasn't it?

He slept on the sofa that night, missing Anna's soft voice and her hand in his terribly. But his dreams were rent by terrible nightmares, one right after another, in which his sisters carried and dragged him through the corn.

*It was hot, the sun swallowed by evil black clouds, and he wanted a nap; he wanted Mama! Sarah told him to hush, that Mama would come, but Mama didn't come. Sarah and 'Lissa had pushed him facedown into the black dirt between the rows and covered him with their bodies. He couldn't breathe! It was too hot! Suddenly there was something or somebody crashing through the corn, and Sarah picked him up again, and she screamed, "NO! PLEASE, NO!" and she and 'Lissa ran fast with him and then she fell and then 'Lissa helped her up and carried him and now they were in the woods and the vines tried to trap them and scratch them and oh it was so hot and he was crying for Mama . . .*

Rudy fell on the living room floor with a crash and woke up. He was drenched in sweat, and his cheeks were wet, as if he had been crying. *What a terrible dream!* he thought, trying to slow his galloping heart. He went to the kitchen, turned on the light, and poured himself a glass of water. Catching sight of himself in the reflection of the kitchen window gave him a shock. His eyes were wide, his hair wild, and he looked *haunted*. Despite the heat he had felt in the dream, he shivered now as goose bumps trailed across his neck, shoulders, and arms. He drained the glass of water and then drew more in the sink to splash on his head and chest. As he dried himself with a dish towel, he tried to remember the dream, but all he could catch now was the smell of fresh corn and dirt, and a great, bright heat. *No more sleeping on the sofa for me,* he decided, and climbed the stairs to his bedroom.

# CHAPTER Fifteen

Anna had indeed been having a tough time with her father.

During Rudy's last week in Kenton, she had come home from work later than usual, by as much as two hours, without telling him exactly where she'd been or the company she had been keeping. Each of these days he had come home from his realty office to an empty house, and it was frightening to him. He nagged and complained about her "lack of consideration" and carelessness with his feelings. He told her that the least she could do for her free room and board in his house was to let him know where she was at all times.

She had never told Rudy.

At the end of that week, after she had said goodbye to Rudy in the park with a kiss that had left her hormones running amok, she grew impatient with her father. When he started to complain once again, she had turned squarely to face him.

"I've been seeing a man, Dad," she said flatly.

"A *man*? Who is he?" her father exploded.

"He's a friend, Dad. Someone I'm quite fond of. I hope to see him again," Anna stated.

"Do I know him?"

"No."

Harold Christianson slapped the newspaper on the table. "You picked up a complete stranger and have been sleeping with him! Tramp!"

Anna flushed, this time with anger to match her father's. "He's *not* a stranger to *me*, Dad. And we have *not* been sleeping together! How *dare* you call me a tramp?"

"I won't have this going on in my house! I don't care if you are my only child! If this is the way you want to live, you can get out now! *Out!*" Christianson carried on, his face purpling.

Anna was quite aware that her father had a heart condition; she was also aware that he was beyond reasoning at this point. She knew from long experience how to stop his tirade by withdrawing, but this was too important to her. "Stop it," she said, calmly.

"What?" cried Christianson.

"Just stop it, Dad," she repeated, just as coolly. "You know very well that nothing has been going on in this house that you wouldn't approve of. As for leaving, I guess I'm certainly old enough for that. I've had several invitations to share apartments with my friends. I have places I can go. Is that *really* what you want? For me to move out during a stupid *argument?*"

Harold Christianson stared at his only daughter, upon whom the heavens had seen fit to reflect all the features of his dead wife. Tears gathered in his eyes, and his color deepened even further. He bent his head and a low sob shook his frame.

Anna went to him at once.

Putting her arms around his shoulders and hugging him to her, she soothed him. When he was calm, Anna suggested that he take a short nap while she fixed supper. He did, and appeared to have forgotten the whole incident when he came to the table. Anna avoided the subject for the rest of that night.

For the next several days, her schedule returned to normal, and she and her father re-entered the daily cycle that had evolved in the Christianson home since her mother's death. But Rudy's phone call had caught Harold's attention again, and reawakened the fear that he would be left alone.

As she put the phone down she could feel his eyes on her back; he was standing just a few feet behind her. He spoke first.

"He said his name was Baumann. Rudy Baumann."

"Yes," agreed Anna.

"I don't know any Baumanns."

Anna turned and folded her arms across her chest. "Would you like to meet him?"

Christianson blanched. "No," he said. Then: "Is he the one you were seeing?"

"Yes, Daddy, he's the one."

"What did he do, dump you?"

Anna bit her lip to hold in the angry reply that wanted to burst out. "No, he didn't. He just finished his work here in town and went back home."

"Where does he live?" Christianson persisted.

"In Duluth," Anna answered truthfully. *In for a penny, in for a pound*, she said to herself. *Might as well get this over with.*

"Duluth! That's a good distance from here. Guess you won't be seeing him again, will you?"

"Honestly, Dad, we plan to see each other as often as possible. I think this is going to be a serious relationship."

"What do you mean, 'serious'?"

"We love each other, Dad," Anna said boldly.

Harold Christianson stormed past her into the living room. He picked up his newspaper from his chair, then tossed it aside. "*'Love'*! What do *you* know about it? How long have you known this Baumann?"

Anna dropped her eyes. "Just a couple of weeks." She looked back up at her father, her green eyes clear and bright. "But we know already. We know as much as anybody does, I guess."

Christianson sank into an armchair, his face pale. He remembered his wife, Eva, and the day that they had met. She had come into his realty agency as an applicant for a secretarial position. One look at her was all it took; his heart and body were on fire. They, too, had known after only a few days that they were in love. She had been twenty-one; he had been thirty years old. Now he was fifty four years old, and felt a hundred. How could life be so cruel as to snatch her from him when he wasn't nearly done with her yet?

Anna picked up the dishcloth she had been holding when she had come to the telephone. "It's time for me to try, Dad. I love you; I'll *always* love you. But I have to get on with my own life. I think you should, too. You're way too young to give up on living, but it's your choice. I can't stop you. But I can help myself."

She walked into the living room and sat on the armchair next to his. "Dad, I think it *is* time that I moved out on my own. Not because we're arguing. It's just *time*. I love Rudy, Dad, and I know there's no guarantee that things will work out with him. I hope so, but I'm not foolish enough to believe in such a miracle. If it doesn't, I have to keep trying. Can you understand that?"

Her words made perfect sense to Christianson, but he decided to play his trump card anyway. "Anna, I have a *heart condition!* Who's supposed to take care of me?"

Anna felt the full strength of the knife plunging and twisting in her heart, but she knew that if things stayed the way they were, she would never marry and she would end up as an old maid living with her father. "Dad, who takes you to see the doctor? Who buys your pills? Who sits down and counts them out for the next day, *every* day? Who tells me what groceries to buy and what to make for meals so that you have healthy food to eat? *You do,* Dad. You took care of yourself before Mom and I ever came into your life. You can do it again. You know how."

In desperation, Christianson tried the truth. "I'll be all alone, Anna, *all alone*. I don't want to be all alone." He raised sad, heart-rending eyes to his daughter.

"Then *do* something about it, Dad," she told him.

He lowered his eyes again and sank his face into his hands.

*Oh Dad, how did you get like this?* Anna asked herself. *How did you change from the strong, caring, fun-loving man you used to be, into this . . . this whipped puppy?* Aloud, she said, "I have to finish making supper now. It'll be ready in another fifteen minutes, Dad," and she rose and walked past him to the kitchen, her heart heavy.

The next morning, at breakfast, Christianson barely said a word to Anna before he left for work. By the time she arrived at the bank, her father's silent treatment had taken its toll, and Anna started her work day with a splitting headache.

At the next window, Karen noticed Anna's pale face and silence. As soon as they had a break in the lines of customers, she asked Anna what was wrong. Anna decided to tell her friend about her argument with her father.

"Are you really ready to move out?" asked Karen, excitedly.

"Yes, I think I am," answered Anna, although she couldn't generate any enthusiasm about it at the moment.

"*Perfect!* My old roommate just moved out to move in with her boyfriend, and I'm in the market for a new roomie. Why don't you come over after work, and I can show the place to you?"

Anna smiled weakly at her friend. "All right. It just bothers me that Dad is acting this way. I really wish he would be happy for me, but I don't think that's going to happen."

Karen sighed. "Parents. They can really bring you down. But Anna, what you told me about what you said to him last night was really true. I hope you're listening to yourself, because you're saying some very good stuff."

Anna's headache wore off by the time she finished work for the day, in large part due to her friend's bubbly personality and understanding. By the time she had freshened up and retrieved her purse, she was feeling much better and looking forward to seeing Karen's apartment.

Youth sees the world differently than the jaded eye of older adults. Karen's apartment was the entire third floor of an ancient, run-down house on the outskirts of town. The landlady, Sylvia Sherwood, lived in the rest of the house, and she regarded Anna suspiciously when Karen introduced her to the young woman.

"Do you have a job?" she asked, daring Anna with her eyes to lie to her.

"Yes, I do. I work at the same bank that Karen does," Anna told the woman.

"Any pets?"

"No."

"I don't like loud Rock 'n Roll. It gives me a headache," Mrs. Sherwood warned her.

"Well, if I *do* end up moving in, I'm sure Karen will help me not to make mistakes. I wouldn't want to do anything to bother or upset you," Anna answered.

"Hm. Well, you can take a look upstairs, and then you can find me outside in the garden," Mrs. Sherwood said in dismissal. "I don't go all the way up to the third floor *unless I have to*," she added meaningfully.

When the landlady had left, Karen and Anna looked at each other and giggled. Karen said, "She likes to pretend she's tough, but she's pretty nice. I haven't had any trouble with her at all, and I've lived here almost three years." They climbed the stairs together.

The third floor of the house had been hastily made into an apartment by the addition of Sheetrock walls surrounding the head of the stairwell, and a door at the very top of the stairs. The entire space was open, with the exception of a small bathroom in one corner, so that the two beds, the living room furniture, a dinette set, and the stove and refrigerator were all in one large space. The carpet was threadbare in places, the wallpaper was faded and old-fashioned, the appliances were ancient and noisy. Laundry would have to be carried to the basement and was scheduled for Wednesday nights. Frankly, it was old, inconvenient, and starkly lacking in privacy. But that's not what Anna saw.

She found it charming and spacious. And the price was right; it would fit well within her budget from her earnings at the bank. Excitement grew in her. She was looking at freedom at last! Karen did a remarkable sales pitch, and in the end, Anna agreed to move in, if Mrs. Sherwood agreed.

Outside, they found her kneeling in the dirt and pulling weeds in the garden, a floppy hat protecting her head from the bright sun. "Well? What did you think?" Mrs. Sherwood asked abruptly.

Anna smiled. "I think it's *gorgeous*," she replied. "Will you allow me to move in?"

Mrs. Sherwood sat back on her heels and peered up at Anna. "You're Harold Christianson's daughter, aren't you?" she asked, evading the question.

"Yes."

"Is this your first apartment?"

"Yes," Anna admitted uncertainly. *Do you have to have experience in order to move into an apartment?* she wondered.

"Harold Christianson is a very responsible man, a *business* man in this town. I would expect you to be just as responsible as he is," Mrs. Sherwood told Anna. "All right, you can move in. Rent's the same as the amount I charge Karen, and it's due on the first, *all of it*. I'll only charge you $35.00 for the rest of this month."

Anna and Karen hugged each other, squealing in joy.

"Thank you so much, Mrs. Sherwood. You won't be sorry, I promise," Anna said, as she dug the money out of her purse.

Mrs. Sherwood took the money, double-counted it, and nodded. "Okay, you can move in at any time now," she said, and waved the pair away. Anna and Karen were halfway across the wide lawn when Mrs. Sherwood spoke again.

"Anna."

Anna widened her eyes at her friend and turned around. "Yes, Mrs. Sherwood?"

"Did your father ever re-marry after your mother died?"

"No, Ma'am," answered Anna, glancing sideways at Karen and stifling a giggle. Mrs. Sherwood nodded thoughtfully.

When it was obvious that Mrs. Sherwood was finished with them, Anna and Karen walked to the street and made their plans.

Anna would move in that weekend; she would tell her father that night. Before Karen turned to re-enter the house, Anna wrote down what would be her new address and phone number; she could hardly *wait* to tell Rudy! Excitement and the feeling of starting her own life, her own *adult* life, carried her across the small town to her father's house.

---

Life in Harold Christianson's home was tense and stilted over the next few days as Anna packed and prepared to move. She had tried to phone Rudy, but there was no answer. Anna squashed any doubts that sprang to mind. Of course she couldn't expect Rudy to sit by the phone every minute, just in case she called! She busied herself with her packing, and the Friday night before she was to move she decided to try to break her father's silence. She wrote down her new address and phone number and tried to give it to him, but Christianson refused to take it. "I'm a realtor in this town! I know exactly where you're moving to!" he scoffed. "I'm just surprised that that old biddy Sylvia Sherwood is still alive!" he added with a dour look on his face.

"Dad, Mrs. Sherwood is probably younger than you are," Anna smiled, aware that she was treading on thin ice.

"Well, she's still a biddy! Never had much use for her. She's *grumpy*."

Anna bit her tongue.

"Dad, I'm moving out in the morning. How about if I fix us pancakes for breakfast?" she offered, aware that she was holding out an olive branch.

Christianson had been counting out his pills at the kitchen table, and looked up. "With strawberries?" he asked.

Smiling widely, Anna agreed. "Strawberries it is."

He looked down at his pills again. "You, uh, you need any help moving all those boxes? It'll go faster and easier if I help, and if we use my car."

Startled, Anna opened her mouth, then closed it. She moved to the table, where her father was sitting with his head bent, and kissed his cheek. "Thanks, Dad. I think I'll need all the help you can give."

So it happened that Anna moved out of her father's house at the age of twenty two, while her would-be lover (and the initial reason for the move) remained unaware of the fact. As soon as her father had left her new apartment, muttering something about how Sylvia Sherwood could be a lot more attractive if she wasn't such a sourpuss, Anna flew to the telephone and dialed Rudy's number. There was still no answer. She hung up the phone thoughtfully, her bubble about to burst.

"What's wrong with *you*?" Karen asked, passing on her way to the bathroom. "You look like you're about to cry."

"Well, I'm not. I just can't get hold of Rudy. He doesn't even know I've moved yet," Anna explained.

Karen shrugged. "Maybe he's out of town on one of those construction jobs, like the one he was on when he met you."

Anna's heart went cold. Was Rudy kissing another woman in another town? She couldn't bear to think of it.

She busied herself unpacking and rearranging the furniture in her 'bedroom,' and made herself wait until she had showered and dressed for bed before trying again. The phone rang four times, five, six, seven . . . and then Rudy answered, and a hot flush invaded her entire body.

"Rudy, it's me, Anna. I've been trying to call you, but you've been out," she blurted breathlessly.

There was a pause on the line.

"I've been in and out. Actually, I thought you had lost interest in me, from the way you sounded the last time we talked," Rudy said coolly.

"I thought you understood that my father was standing right next to me, and that I wasn't free to talk to you!" Anna exclaimed.

"I figured that out, but then when I didn't hear from you

again, I thought maybe you had some second thoughts," Rudy responded, still cool and distant.

"Oh no, Rudy, no! In fact, everything's changed now—I've moved out!" Anna assured him, and went on to describe the details of her move. "We can talk any time we want, now," she finished.

Rudy warmed up immediately. "That's great! I guess we just have to watch our phone bills." His tone softened. "I miss you so much, Honey, it's terrible."

"I know what you mean," Anna said in a husky voice. "I need you, Rudy."

"Anna, did you forget that this was the weekend that you were supposed to come to Duluth?" Rudy asked, a little hesitantly.

"Not for a minute," she answered promptly. "That's why I've been trying to call you day and night," she added. "Where were you?"

"I started out waiting around to hear from you, but when I didn't, I felt like you were finished with me. I've been going out to a bar, Anna," Rudy said truthfully.

"A bar! But I thought you didn't drink," Anna objected.

"You never *saw* me drink, but believe me, when I start, I can out-drink anybody. Anyway, this is Calhoun's, just down the street from my house. It used to be my main watering-hole. One night I was feeling pretty discouraged, so I went back there, to try to pick up again with my drinking buddies."

"What happened?" Anna asked. Her heart paused in its beat.

"Nothing. I ordered a beer, took a sip, and realized I didn't want it. I also realized that my best drinking buddies, Calvin and Bert, were just a couple of losers who only wanted me around so that they wouldn't feel like the only drunks in the bar. And the women who came in looked *ugly* to me. I kept looking for *you*." He paused.

"But you kept going back," Anna said, feeling her heart constrict. Was Rudy an alcoholic?

"Yes, I did. But just to get food. They serve some pretty good meals there for reasonable prices." Rudy laughed. "It turns out I'm a lousy cook."

They laughed together as they talked. In fact, when Rudy described his housecleaning efforts, Anna laughed so hard she cried. It felt wonderful to hear his voice again, as if he were standing right beside her. Except he *wasn't*.

"Rudy, can I come to Duluth next weekend?" she asked, a little timidly.

"Are you free next weekend?" he asked, a smile still in his voice.

"All my weekends are free, to *you*," she responded with a hint of shyness in her voice.

They made their plans. Anna would take a Greyhound on Friday after work, and Rudy would pick her up at the bus stop. They would have the whole weekend alone together.

When they had finished saying a very warm and prolonged goodbye, each felt jubilantly, totally in love. At last they would be together again.

# CHAPTER
Sixteen

Rudy paced the floor of the Greyhound bus stop in Duluth. *Why* hadn't he just picked Anna up in the car and brought her back with him? He *hated* waiting. A young woman with long blonde hair pulled back in a pony tail was bending over a suitcase, and he had started toward her when she looked up, smiled, squealed with delight, and jumped into the arms of a slick-looking black-haired man, obviously a city type. It wasn't Anna, after all. Rudy sighed and sat down again, his knees on his elbows and his chin propped in his hand.

He was deep into his own thoughts when a light touch on his shoulder startled him. He turned quickly, and there she was! Anna's smile was nervous and tentative, but his wasn't. He moved quickly to take her into his arms, but she faltered back a step. "Anna, Honey, I'm so glad to see you! Aren't you glad to see me?"

She let out her pent-up breath and smiled a more genuine smile. "Of course, Rudy. The bus ride just took so long that it gave me a chance to get really nervous."

"I've been nervous, too," Rudy admitted. "Look," he said, "let's just grab your things and get out of here. It's still early. We can go back to my house, I can show you around, and you can change if you want. Then we'll take a drive and relax. How does that sound?"

Anna's look of worry left her face completely. Somehow she had imagined that Rudy would push her to the floor of the Greyhound Bus waiting room and take her virginity on the spot. She was willing to give it, but needed more time. This sounded like he would give her some time to catch her breath.

And he did everything to put her at ease. Their stop at Rudy's house was brief, and the ride afterward was long. They toured Duluth and ate at a casual diner. Talking to him in person was just what Anna had needed. The same feelings of *connectedness*, of *rightness*, of *yes yes yes* came to her again, especially when he held hands with her and looked into her eyes. They sat talking in the diner over cups of coffee long after their meal was finished.

Finally Rudy looked around and noted that every other diner had left the place, and the waitresses were standing in a row, leaning against the counter and watching the two of them, smiling at each other. His face colored and he hurriedly suggested that they leave. As he approached the cash register with the bill for their meal in his hand, "Verna" (or so it said on her name tag) smiled widely and winked at him. "Have a wonderful evening," she said in a suggestive voice.

"What was that all about?" asked Anna when they gained the sidewalk outside.

"What?" Rudy asked, although he knew very well what she was talking about.

"That wink. That sly look the waitress gave you," Anna asked.

He looked at her. *She honestly didn't know,* he thought with a moment of panic. Rudy realized that he would be Anna's only teacher in the art of lovemaking between a man and a woman, and the idea both thrilled him and horrified him at the same time.

"I don't know," he lied. "Maybe she acts like that to everybody. It's the first time I've been in there." *Well, at least I told the truth about something,* he thought as he steered Anna into his car.

Rudy got in the driver's side and suddenly realized that he didn't know what came next. He turned the motor on, then turned to Anna. "What would you like to do now?" he asked, hoping she would suggest a movie or a walk along the lake.

Anna regarded him seriously. "I think it's time we went back to your place and made love," she stated unequivocally, and pinned him in place with those wide green eyes.

Rudy's pulse leapt to approximately that of a hummingbird's. Whatever he had thought Anna might say, it certainly wasn't that. He knew the answer that was expected of him, however, and he gave it immediately. "I think so, too." He maneuvered the car out into the street and turned toward home, thinking, *I know a bolt of lightning is going to come out of the sky and kill me for this.* They drove in silence for a minute, and then he thought, *Well, we all have to go sometime, somehow.* He smiled to himself. May all his problems be ones like this.

---

They entered his house via the kitchen door. Fortunately, there was just enough dusky light left for him to find the light switch. His thoughts were in such a whirl that if it had been dark, he would have been left to grope the walls in search of it. The overhead fluorescent brightness glared at him. Anna, however, seemed to be perfectly poised. She hung her jacket up on a peg and walked straight through to the living room, where she turned on one table lamp and perched on the sofa expectantly. Rudy took his time hanging up his own jacket, then hesitated at the threshold between the two rooms.

"Want something to drink? A soda? Or water?"

She shook her head 'no,' and patted the sofa next to her.

"I've got coffee, too, or at least I can make some," he offered.

"Come here, Rudy," Anna said.

"Want to watch some television? There might be a movie on," Rudy stalled.

Anna shook her head again. "No TV," she said.

Rudy paused, then hit upon an idea borne of desperation. "I've got to go to the bathroom," he told her. "All that coffee, you know. I'll be right back." And he bolted to the stairs.

He took his time, trying to bring his emotions under control. Washing his hands for the third time, he thought he might possibly be ready. Rudy dried his hands, straightened his shirt, and opened the bathroom door, ready to go back downstairs and do what he had set out to do three weeks ago: divest a virgin of her maidenhood.

A light glowed softly from his open bedroom door, and he turned toward it slowly. Anna was lying on the bed, fully clothed except for her shoes, which she had kicked off to one corner. The curtains were closed, and she had turned on one lamp. She was waiting for him.

"Rudy, come and kiss me," she invited.

And he accepted that invitation.

It only took a moment of her soft mouth touching his before all thought ceased. They lay together as man and woman and delighted in each others' touch. In a way, this was the first time for Rudy to make love as well; the rest of his couplings had been entirely sexual in nature, and they were hurried and rough in comparison. He found it was another matter entirely to make love with a woman who was in love with him, and he wanted to experience every sensation to its entirety.

Anna was equally swept by the moment, relishing every caress of Rudy's hands on her back, her hips, her thighs, her breasts—and she followed his movements with her own. It was everything she had dreamed of these past weeks, and more. She murmured his name again and again, and he loved to hear it. His fingers found the hooks of her bra, and she arched her back in eager anticipation of his touch on her nipples. When he finally touched one, she cried out in pleasure.

Rudy was rock-hard, harder than he had ever been in his life. His control was slipping as it was, and when Anna cried out, it was all he could do to keep himself from taking her at that moment. He removed his hand and rolled back on his own pillow, breathing heavily.

"Rudy, don't stop," Anna begged.

"Honey, I have to stop for just a minute," Rudy answered in a ragged voice. "You don't know what you're doing to me, and this is your first time. I don't want to ruin it."

"Baby, nothing you could do would ruin it for me. I want you so much," Anna responded, her breath tickling his ear.

He backed away from her on the bed. "Now, listen, Anna," he began in a lecture-style voice.

"Yes, Teacher?" she said, looking up at him from under her lashes.

He laughed with her, then said, "This is serious. This is your first time. There's going to be blood, and it might hurt. That's the way it is with all virgins."

"I know."

"What do you mean, you know?" Rudy asked. She had his full attention.

"I asked my friend Karen how it would feel. She's a lot more experienced than I am," Anna told him.

"And just what did Karen say?" asked Rudy, in amazement. He had never once thought that women would talk about such things to each other.

"She said there would be some blood, but, you know, we women have blood regularly," Anna said primly. It was amusing to Rudy to see this primness when her sweater was hiked up over her bare breasts and the fly of her jeans was undone. "It's really no big deal."

"And what else did she say?" he asked, fascinated.

"She said that lovemaking is as good as you make it, and that if you want it enough, it will be wonderful," Anna finished.

"Do you believe her?" Rudy asked, reaching over to trace the line of her cheek with one finger.

"I believe her, especially the part about wanting it enough," Anna said. "So come here, Rudy Baumann, and let me find out."

He kissed her for that, and helped her take her clothes off.

Quickly they were both nude and more than ready for each other.

Gently, carefully, he spread her legs and entered her. With that, the rest of the world disappeared for both of them.

And the deed was done. It was, as Anna's friend had predicted, as good as they both wanted to make it. Anna and Rudy cleaned themselves up in the bathroom when they were finished, and five minutes after that, they were back in bed making love again. That first night together was a blur of sleeping naked in each others' arms, interspersed with one or the other waking only to kiss and caress the other into another orgasm.

Rudy woke on Saturday morning alone in bed. He instantly missed Anna. He noted the sun's brightness behind the bedroom curtains and looked at the clock. Eleven o'clock! He quickly threw on a shirt and jeans and went in search of her. He found her in the kitchen, making coffee, wearing (apparently) only one of his T-shirts, which was miles too big for her. She didn't see him immediately, and he watched in amusement as she sang and danced to Rock 'n Roll on the radio. The morning sun danced across her hair, making it glow gold, and the only thought in his head was that *this* was what he *must* have.

They spent that first weekend together making love more times than he had ever thought possible, and when he finally allowed her to get on the bus back home, he was exhausted. Anna was exhausted, as well, and slept all the way back. Her friend Karen met her at the station and drove her to their apartment, prying for details the whole way insistently, but all Anna would say was, "Wonderful. It was wonderful."

---

And Rudy thought so, too. He was head over heels in love with Anna, no doubt about it at all. They shared such a close emotional and physical bond that he ached for her when she left at the end of the weekend. His thoughts turned more and more to marriage and commitment. Rudy banished all thoughts of beer, drinking, fighting, and girl-trolling from his mind. In his present mental state, he was horrified that he had ever lived that type of life. He applied himself to his work and his future, laboring for a promotion and status. He even called both of his sisters and tried to mend those bridges. He was rebuffed on both counts, but he thought that they would come around, in time.

That first weekend led to another, then another, then another, and suddenly the summer and fall were over and the first winter snows started. By the time that Rudy's crew experienced the usual annual slowdown in building construction, he and Anna were tied irrevocably to each other. So, on the weekend when Anna nervously broke the news that in late May he would be a father, his first (and genuine) reaction was one of total delight. He asked her to marry him immediately, and she accepted.

To Rudy, it seemed only natural that there be no delay. Since winter layoffs were nearing, he called his supervisor and asked for time off for a civil ceremony and a honeymoon, and received both permission and heartfelt congratulations. Hank Masters was impressed with the changes in Rudy Baumann that had evolved over the last several months, and would gladly authorize a promotion and raise for him when he came back to work.

Rudy was baffled by Anna's reaction to his conversation with Hank Masters.

"Rudy Baumann, I can't believe you did that," she said sternly. Rudy had just hung up the telephone and wasn't aware that Anna had been standing behind him. He jumped guiltily. The phone clattered into the cradle. Turning, he saw a very different Anna than the sweet, pliant beauty he was used to. Instead, her hands were on her hips, her green eyes glinted with anger, and her chin was thrust forward.

"Huh?" Rudy answered. "Anna, Honey, I *have* to ask for time off. If you don't show up for your job, they fire you."

"I know that!" she snapped. "I mean I can't believe that you just arranged our marriage and honeymoon on the phone with your *boss* instead of *me*! Maybe I don't want to get married right away. Maybe I need time to tell my father that he's going to be getting a son-in-law *and* a grandson pretty soon. Maybe I need to give *my* boss some notice so that he can replace me. I have friends that would want to know, as well, and maybe I'd like to have my father and friends there at the ceremony. And maybe I want it in a church instead of at the courthouse." She folded her arms across her chest, and a mulish expression changed her features.

Rudy staggered backward from the onslaught and sat on the sofa, his mouth open. In all the weeks they had been seeing each other, they had never had a cross word between them, and now here it was, staring him in the face.

"Well?" Anna asked, demanding that he explain himself.

"I, uh, I didn't think . . . I mean, I thought that you'd want . . ." Rudy stopped, his neck and face flushing lobster red. "I'm sorry," he finally finished lamely. "I guess I'm not used to having to think about anybody else except myself."

Anna regarded him with narrowed eyes. She had enough of being bullied by her father over the past several years to last a lifetime. But Rudy *did* look lost and sorry, and her heart melted a little.

"Okay," she said at last, and sat down on the far end of the sofa. "Let's talk and agree about what we want, before we start telling others about our plans. Fair enough?"

"Fair enough," Rudy agreed. However, he was more than a little shaken.

Hours later, they had agreed upon a civil ceremony with friends and relatives in attendance, a honeymoon in Chicago, and that it would take place in one month's time. Of course, Anna would be a little further along in her pregnancy by then, but with her slim figure and the circumstances, it shouldn't make much of a difference. They also agreed that Rudy would drive Anna back on Sunday, meet her father, and help her break the news. They slept together in Rudy's bed that night, but it was the first time that neither of them felt the spontaneous fire of passion that had so far marked their physical relationship.

The next morning, Anna was showering when Rudy sneaked downstairs and called Hank Masters back.

"Hank? This is Rudy Baumann again," he said.

"Hi, Rudy. What happened? You didn't change your mind about getting married, did you?" Hank joked, intending it as a good-natured nudge.

Rudy flushed red all over again. He had lain awake for a long time the night before, thinking about this moment, and imagining the shame he would feel when he had to admit he had jumped the gun on his wedding plans.

"Uh, no, no, we're still getting married," he answered, trying to force some return humor into his voice. "But Anna wants to wait for a month to get things together."

Masters laughed. "Yeah, I remember that myself. I thought while we were dating that Susie thought just like I did, but as soon as we decided to get married, I found out that she had a mind of her own. Well, no problem. Just let me know when you won't be available to work. Am I invited?"

The two men discussed the wedding plans briefly, and Rudy was in the kitchen making coffee when Anna came downstairs, freshly showered and dressed. She stood on her tiptoes, kissed the back of his neck and hugged him as if nothing of consequence had happened between them.

Rudy stood stiffly and continued to fill the coffee pot, but mumbled, "Good morning."

Anna didn't answer. Instead, she changed the direction of her kisses toward his ear and cheek. By the time she had twisted her body around his side and had reached the corner of his mouth, Rudy's mind had gone blank, and he let his body take over. He let go of the coffee pot, grabbed Anna's tiny waist, and set her on the kitchen counter. He kissed her passionately, and she returned kiss for kiss and caress for caress. He looked at her eyes, dark green now with only smoldering need in them, and said, "Damn, woman, you're going to drive me crazy."

She laughed huskily and answered, "Don't forget, I'm going to be on that same trip with you."

---

Rudy rolled to a stop in front of the Christianson house that Sunday afternoon at about 2:00. They had agreed that Anna would visit with her father first (*soften him up,* she had said) and then Rudy would arrive. He was very nervous for himself and for Anna. He knew that her father was important to her, and he wanted Harold Christianson to accept him.

Anna answered his knock. She allowed him to briefly kiss her on the cheek, and then led him into the living room where her father was sitting.

"Dad, this is Rudy Baumann. Rudy, this is my father, Harold Christianson," she said formally.

Christianson folded his newspaper and put it aside before standing. "Baumann, huh? I think I remember you calling here for Anna once this last summer."

"Yes, that was me," Rudy said.

Christianson ignored Rudy's proffered hand. "Have a seat," the older man said, indicating the sofa across from his chair, and both men sat. Anna appeared to be dancing from foot to foot with anxiety, and both her father and Rudy looked at her as if she were going to say something. "Want coffee?" she blurted.

"Sure," Rudy said.

"Okay," said Christianson.

She whirled and darted to the kitchen. Once there she hurried to make coffee, thinking, *Oh please don't say anything without me, Rudy! Why did I offer them coffee? What are they talking about?* She started the coffee and returned to the living room as fast as her feet would allow without actually running.

It seemed that she needn't have worried. In her absence, her father had turned on the television, and he and Rudy were watching a basketball game. For a full five minutes their only comments were about the teams, other teams, other seasons and games, player statistics, and other sports topics that had nothing to do with marriage or children. Those five minutes were long, and she finally left Rudy on the sofa alone to check the coffee in the kitchen. She was absolutely disgusted. How long did a basketball game last, anyway?

Anna returned to the living room with a tray laden with mugs of steaming coffee for all three of them, and handed them out. The men continued to talk nonstop as the action on television dragged on. She was about to wring both their necks when a commercial finally came on, and she plunged in.

"Dad, Rudy and I have something to talk to you about," she said, turning the sound on the television down low.

Both men looked at each other. Christianson said, "Well?"

Rudy cleared his throat. "Sir, I've asked Anna to marry me, and she's agreed."

Christianson's face froze. He turned to Anna. "Is that so?"

"Yes, Dad," she said confidently.

Christianson looked back and forth between Rudy and Anna. "Seems to me that you two barely know each other."

"I've been visiting him in Duluth, where he lives," Anna explained. "We know each other pretty well."

"What do you do for a living, Baumann? Are you going to be able to provide for my daughter?" Christianson shot the questions.

Rudy answered truthfully.

By that time Christianson had thought of some more interesting questions.

"And where does my daughter stay while she's in Duluth? Are you two sleeping together?"

Anna gasped. "Dad! That's none of your business!"

Rudy turned white.

"Well, Baumann, speak up! It's a fair question—she's my daughter!"

"I'm your *adult* daughter, Dad!" Anna protested.

Rudy quietly said, "Yes."

"Rudy!" Anna yelped.

"He's going to find out anyway, Anna. Sir, Anna's going to have my baby. The doctor told her to expect it in late May," Rudy said, watching the older man carefully.

Now Anna turned white. Perspiration dotted her forehead and upper lip; she felt faint.

"YOU SON OF A BITCH!" Christianson screamed, and vaulted out of his chair. His face was purpling. "I knew it! I *knew* it! You knocked her up as fast as you could!"

Rudy stood as well; he only wanted to calm Christianson down and get them both out of there. He stretched out his hands in a placating gesture, and said, "Sir, it wasn't like that . . ."

"I'm not a fool! There's only one way to get a woman pregnant, so don't tell me it wasn't like that!"

"That's not what I meant!" said Rudy, raising his voice a bit.

"You turned her into a whore! Whoremaster! How many other women have you gotten pregnant? I know men like you—you have a woman or two in every town! How dare you pick on my daughter for your recreation! I ought to knock your teeth out! And you come to me talking about getting married," Christianson sneered.

"Dad," Anna began weakly, "stop. Please stop. Both of you, sit down. Please. I'm not feeling well."

The two men glared at each other for a moment, then looked at Anna. Rudy sat beside her immediately, and pulled her to him, brushing her hair away from her face.

Christianson growled, "Take your hands off from her!"

Rudy snapped, "She looks like she's going to faint! Shut up and sit down."

Christianson shut up, but he refused to sit. He was simmering inside, itching to get his hands around Baumann's throat. He glanced at Anna as he paced the living room. She *did* look awfully white. But of course, she was pregnant. *Damn* the man!

Rudy was mopping Anna's face with his handkerchief, murmuring to her. She whispered back. Suddenly Harold Christianson went limp, and he sat, watching them. He might as well be on another planet, for all they cared. He was out of the picture. His heart twisted—it was like watching his wife with another man. First Anna had moved out of his house, and now she would move to Duluth. He would truly be alone if she did that.

Anna finally sat up and took a sip of the coffee that Rudy offered her. "I feel better now," she said, but kept Rudy's handkerchief to wipe the tears on her cheeks. She took another, longer sip of coffee gratefully, and smiled at Rudy. Christianson's heart lurched again.

Rudy turned to Anna's father. "Sir, we *are* getting married in one month, and we would like you to be there for it. Anna needs you. And we want to be able to visit you and have you visit us."

Christianson stared at him, his features twisting from rage to hurt and back again.

"And I know you're angry right now, but you're going to have a grandchild, and that grandchild will need a grandfather. My own parents are dead. Please, just think this over for a while. I'm asking you for Anna's sake," Rudy said soothingly.

Christianson rose once again from his chair. "I've already thought about it as much as I'm going to. Anna, if you marry this man, *you will no longer be my daughter.*"

Anna sobbed. "Dad, don't make it be this way!" she begged.

"That's my last word, except to ask you, Anna: are you going to marry him or not?"

Anna nodded her head mutely, crying hard.

"Then get out! Both of you! And don't come back!" Christianson ground out. He shut the TV off and went upstairs; there was a muffled but decisive *thump!* as he slammed his bedroom door.

Anna got up and went to the foot of the stairs, but Rudy stopped her from going after her father. "Anna, he's had his say, and if we keep after him, he'll only get angrier and more upset," he soothed. "Let's go. He may change his mind. We'll let him know about the wedding, and we'll keep trying, but right now we need to leave him alone."

Anna allowed herself to be pulled to Rudy's chest, but she couldn't be comforted. Rudy took her back to her apartment and stayed with her late into the night, even though Karen and Sylvia Sherwood, her landlady, were there to fuss and cluck around her. He made Karen promise to call in sick for Anna the next morning, and when Anna finally fell into a heavy sleep, he left to drive back to Duluth alone, mentally exhausted.

―――――

During that next month, Anna felt as if she were being emotionally pulled apart. Her friends rallied around her, supporting her upcoming marriage to Rudy. She knew her future was with Rudy. What few relatives she had were distant geographically, and although they wished her the best, they did not attempt to intervene on her behalf with Harold Christianson. Her father was as immovable as a mountain, and as cold and distant. It seemed as if nothing would heal the rift between them. Her landlady had known Christianson since they were in school together, and even she tried to approach the man.

One Sunday after church, she purposely dallied on the front steps, searching in her purse for something. As she saw Harold descending the steps from the corner of her eye, she turned and acted surprised to see him.

"Why, Harold Christianson! I didn't know you were here today!" she exclaimed loudly, gaining the attention of several passing church members.

"Hello, Sylvia," Christianson said. He attempted to push past her, but she grasped his arm.

"I can't find my car keys. Here, hold these," she said, and without waiting for his agreement, she handed him her sunglasses. He reflexively took what she handed to him.

"For goodness' sakes, I *know* I had them when I went in," Sylvia fussed, rummaging even deeper into the depths of her purse. "Here, hang on to these," she told him, handing him her checkbook and a comb.

Harold's hands were getting full, and he was uncomfortably aware that he was trapped with the church congregation milling in front of him on the steps, and the pastor talking to people at the church doors behind him. "For heaven's sake, Sylvia, what all have you got in there, anyway?" he grumbled in a low tone. "Why don't you just throw half of that stuff away?"

"Oh, Harold," Sylvia giggled girlishly. "You know that women have all sorts of necessary things they carry around with them."

Harold impatiently shifted his weight from one foot to the other. "Did you look in your pocket?"

Sylvia dipped her hand into her coat pocket, and drew out the car keys. "Well, look at that! Thank goodness I didn't lock them in the car!"

She started replacing items into her purse one by one, straightening things and taking an unnecessarily long time doing it. "Thanks for helping me, Harold," she said. "I haven't seen you visiting Anna lately."

At the mention of his daughter's name, Harold stiffened. "I won't be coming by any more."

"Why ever not? Don't you want to see your daughter?"

"No."

Sylvia shook her head in disappointment. "That's too bad, Harold. You only have one daughter, and it looks like you're throwing her away."

Harold's face and neck reddened. "She threw herself away." The crowd had moved off toward their cars, and the pastor had returned to the inside of the church. "Look, Sylvia, I know what you're trying to do here, and it won't work. As far as I'm concerned, I have no daughter." He piled what was left of the contents of Sylvia's purse into her arms. "Anyway, it's none of your business. Keep out of it." He brushed past her and continued down the church steps.

"Harold Christianson, you are breaking her heart! That's a lousy thing for a father to do to his daughter!" Sylvia called after him. "And don't pretend to *me* that it doesn't matter to you. It might work with Anna, but I'm a little too smart for that!"

He didn't answer.

"When you quit feeling sorry for yourself and start thinking of *her* instead, you'll come around!" Sylvia yelled after him. He kept walking, and Sylvia gave up with a stamp of her foot and a disgusted, "*Hmpf!*"

She didn't tell Anna about that encounter. As the day of the ceremony neared, Anna tried to busy herself with finishing her last few days of work, packing to move, and visiting with well-wishing friends. Her telephone conversations with Rudy reflected the strain and desolation that she felt, but he was unable to console her. All he could do was remind her that soon they would be together forever, and that her father would have plenty of time to re-think the matter.

And life *did* go on. The days passed, Anna's things were moved into Rudy's house, and the ceremony took place at the courthouse in Duluth, as planned. Anna's friend Karen, Sylvia Sherwood, and a few others from the bank where she had worked traveled down together for the day and were present. Rudy had invited his sister's families and Hank Masters. Sarah and Melissa both attended the brief ceremony and met Anna, but left quickly afterwards. His supervisor congratulated them warmly and presented them with a sizeable check as a wedding present. Before they had time to register that they were officially married and legally bound to one another, Mr. and Mrs. Rudolph Baumann were on their way to Chicago for their honeymoon.

Rudy did his very best to see that it was a good honeymoon for both their sakes. He kept Anna busy with sightseeing, shopping, nightclubs, dancing, and lovemaking. His aim was to bind Anna to him so firmly that he would lessen the impact of her father's coldness, and he succeeded. By the time they made their way back to Duluth and the house they would call home for several years to come, Anna was decidedly *Rudy's* wife.

# CHAPTER
## Seventeen

Anna lived in a dream world that Rudy created for her, full of nothing but him. He went back to work, taking on side jobs to finish the inside of buildings while she stayed at home, creating their nest and a place for their child. She still wrote to her old friends and occasionally talked to them on the phone, but when Rudy came home from work for the day, her attention was for him alone. Rudy came to depend on that attention and drew emotional nourishment from it. He couldn't remember ever having anyone place such importance on him in his life, and it felt wonderful.

As winter's frigid grip loosened into spring, Anna was more than ready for the baby to be born. She had no transportation during the day except for the bus system, and her girth made it difficult for her to get out to shop or do other errands. Even her daily chores around the house were made slower and more tedious; she was sick of the television and of the few books she had checked out from the public library. Mindful of her doctor's advice to exercise, she walked every day. Instead of being thankful that walking outside was made easier by the disappearing snow and ice, she grew resentful of her limitations. She would have loved to climb a ladder and remove last fall's leaves from the gutters, or give the house a good spring cleaning by washing the walls and windows.

Anna's profile, when viewed by her in the mirror, reminded her of a walrus. Despite Rudy's constant assurances that she was lovelier than ever, she wondered how he could stand to look at her. She was tired of her clothes, tired of the isolation and Rudy's long work hours, and, she feared, she was tired of Rudy himself. She hadn't made any real friends in Duluth, and desperately needed the stimulation of other people.

One day in mid-May, her friend Karen called. As they talked, Anna realized how desperately she missed her friend, and suggested that Karen come to Duluth for a day. It would be fun to shop with another woman, and show her what she and Rudy had done to the house to prepare for the baby. Karen was excited by the idea as well, and by the time the conversation ended, they had made plans for the following Saturday. Karen would drive up for the day, spend the night on the sofa, and drive back on Sunday.

That evening, Rudy arrived home as dirty, sweaty, tired, and hungry as he had been ever since he had taken on extra work to prepare for the baby's birth expenses. All he wanted was the comfort of his wife's company, a shower and meal, and to rest his head on his pillow. Anna, however, chattered on and on about Karen and her friend's impending visit. She followed him as he showered, waiting impatiently while the water was running, and began again as soon as he turned the water off.

Rudy leaned against the wall of the shower for a few seconds before opening the curtain, his eyes closed. A slow burn was starting in the back of his mind. There was something there that he resented, but he couldn't quite put his finger on it. In the meantime, Anna continued: Could he clean the leaves out of the gutters before Karen arrived? Could she buy a play pen while Karen was there? Karen knew how to sew. Maybe Karen would teach her, and she could make more clothes for the baby. And it went on and on; Anna was so excited that she never waited for answers to her many questions. Rudy gritted his teeth and said nothing, however, he did whip the shower curtain back a little more briskly than usual and toweled himself off vigorously, forcing Anna out of the small bathroom and back into the hallway.

It continued through supper, right up until bed time. Rudy finally told Anna that he was going to fall asleep on his feet if he didn't get to bed. He told Anna that he was glad to see her so happy (actually, he felt ambivalent about Karen coming to see her; Anna was just a little *too* happy about that). However, he was exhausted and he just *had* to get to bed, *right now*. He turned his back on her and went up the stairs without saying good night. Anna never noticed his relative silence or his curt manner. She was too involved in her own plans. She hummed merrily along with the radio as she did the dishes and made a list of possible things to do before Karen arrived in two days' time.

Upstairs in the darkness of the bedroom, Rudy set the alarm clock and fell into bed. He was sure that he would fall asleep as soon as his body was horizontal, but to his chagrin, he lay awake, mulling over that smoldering feeling. Something was wrong here.

He tossed and turned, willing himself to keep his mind blank unsuccessfully. His thoughts constantly went back to Anna.

*I work like a madman all week long, and now she wants me to clean gutters,* he fretted. *For Karen. The gutters were fine for me and Anna, but Karen has to have clean gutters.* He sat up and punched his pillow to fluff it. *Anna's got me and she's got a baby on the way; isn't that enough? She doesn't get that excited to see* me, now, does she? *Oh, and now she has to go shopping with Karen and spend some more of my hard-earned money!*

He tried his hardest to let it go, to relax and get some rest, but it wouldn't go away. And the less sleepy he became, the angrier he got. *God, I need a beer!* The thought surprised him. He hadn't had a similar one in months, even when Anna's father had disowned her. The harder he tried to push the thought away, the more it appeared in his mind's eye: a cold, frosty one right from the tap; his buddies, laughing and joking and teasing the women in Calhoun's; not a care in the world except getting to work the next day and getting to the bar the next night.

Rudy fell into an exhausted, unrestful doze just before Anna got to bed.

For the duration, Rudy decided to concentrate most of his mental powers on two things and two things alone: getting through Karen's visit without an angry outburst and without having a beer. He fought a mighty battle.

Saturday morning found him dutifully cleaning the leaves out of the gutters when Karen pulled up in her Volkswagen bug. Anna had been waiting since dawn for her friend, and as soon as the car engine stopped, Rudy saw his wife throw open the front door and trot ungracefully to embrace her friend. The two women screamed and squealed, and the sound hit him between the eyes like an icepick, reminding him of long-ago hangovers. He plastered on a smile and climbed down from the ladder, approaching Karen to say hello.

Anna and Karen were bouncing up and down in each others' arms, but Karen stopped long enough to brush Rudy's cheek with a quick kiss and to say hello. He carried her overnight bag into the house, turned to ask Anna where the aspirin was, and found he couldn't break into their excited jabbering. Hell, he couldn't even *follow* it. The headache gave a mighty throb, and he climbed the stairs to look in the medicine cabinet in the bathroom himself. He found them, shook three out of the bottle, and dry-swallowed them, just as he had when he had been drinking and woke up with a headache. He pushed *that* thought away in a hurry.

Downstairs, the two women had their heads close together, laughing and talking and drinking coffee. Rudy hadn't seen Anna so happy in months. He slipped out the front door and knew that neither of them had noticed.

About a half hour later, Anna and Karen barreled out the front door together to the VW. "Rudy!" Anna called to him. "We're leaving now!"

Again he forced a giant grin, and waved. Anna blew him a kiss, and they roared off down the street. As soon as the car disappeared, Rudy got down from the ladder and put it away. As far as he was concerned, *maple trees* could grow in the gutters forty feet high before he got up there again. He went through the back door to the kitchen and the refrigerator, opened it, and was looking for something when he realized in horror that he was searching for a beer.

Rudy turned to the coffee pot instead. It was empty. All right, he'd make himself some coffee. While it was brewing, he searched for something to eat for lunch, but didn't have the slightest idea what Anna had in mind for him to eat. He didn't even know if she'd be back for supper. He made a peanut butter and jelly sandwich and wolfed it at the sink, washing it down with strong, hot coffee.

Well, if Anna was going to play today, so would he. Rudy set himself up on the sofa in front of the television set, found a sports channel, and opened the newspaper.

The next thing he remembered was the sound of the front door opening and the cacophony of female voices. It was growing dark, and Anna and Karen were just returning from their outing. Groggily, he struggled to sit up and listen to their explanations of where they had been and to look at what they had bought, but it was no use. He simply couldn't understand the energy that flowed between them. He *did* comprehend that they had just finished eating at a diner, and Anna suggested that he make himself a sandwich for his own supper. Suddenly the headache was back, worse than ever.

Rudy went up to the bathroom, urinated, and swallowed more aspirin. When he came downstairs, Anna had cleared his newspapers and coffee cup from the area around the sofa and made up a bed there for her friend. The television was off. She and Karen were now in the kitchen, drinking sodas and talking. He felt displaced; now there was no place for him to go to escape them but the bedroom. The headache throbbed.

He went out to the kitchen and put his hands on Anna's shoulders from behind her chair, which got her attention. "Aren't you hungry, Honey?" she asked.

He bit back a foul reply.

"I have a bit of a headache, and I'm going to go out for a walk," he told her instead. "Maybe I'll get something while I'm out, if I feel like it."

"Are you okay, Rudy?" Anna asked, suddenly full of concern.

"Oh, I'll be fine when I get some fresh air, I think," he said with a fake smile. "You girls go on and visit."

Once outside, Rudy stalked down the sidewalk. *Damn* that Karen! He couldn't wait for her to leave and have Anna back the way she had been before Karen's visit. He stopped at the mailbox, reached in, and pulled out a single letter addressed to Anna. He didn't recognize the handwriting. Rudy squinted at the return address in the dim glow of a distant streetlight. It was from her father! Harold Christianson had finally written his daughter a letter.

Rudy turned back toward the house, instinctively meaning to give the letter to Anna immediately. Two steps later, he stopped and stuffed the letter into the pocket of his jacket. *Let her wait for it,* he thought nastily. He continued back toward the street.

He was coming up on Calhoun's, and looked in the front window as he passed. Yep, there were his old friends, slouched over the bar, talking to the bartender. His footsteps slowed. Calhoun's served sandwiches and other short-order meals, he remembered. It couldn't hurt just to go in and *eat*, could it? He pulled the pub's door open, and a strong draft of heat, smoke, beer, and frying onions billowed out. Rudy went in.

Bert looked back over his shoulder when Rudy walked in, and he called out with a sneer. "Well, look who it is, everybody! Good old Rudy Baumann is coming in to visit us common folks!"

Calvin turned and looked at Rudy, who only waved and passed on down the bar to an empty stool. Immediately the two put their heads together.

Rudy didn't recognize the bartender; he probably had been hired since the last time Rudy had haunted Calhoun's. Rudy guessed that he was probably in his mid-twenties. "Yes, sir, what'll it be?" the young man asked.

"You still serving sandwiches?" Rudy asked.

"Yes, the grill's still open for another half hour. Do you want a menu?"

"Yes, thanks," Rudy answered, and accepted the single laminated sheet from the bartender. He looked it over and ordered a cheeseburger, fries, and coffee.

"No problem," the young man said, and went to the back to turn in the order.

Rudy lit a cigarette and looked around. Except for Bert and Calvin, he didn't recognize any of his usual drinking crowd in here tonight. He reached for an ashtray and pulled it toward him. All of a sudden he was shoved half off his bar stool. Rough hands reached for him and pulled him back up. "Hey, there, good buddy, be careful!" Bert said.

"Yeah, *Rooooody*, you might get hurt," Calvin laughed behind him.

Rudy decided to let it go. They obviously had been drinking steadily for a while now, and he remembered playing roughly when he had gotten in that kind of condition.

"Hi, Bert," he said, and added, "Calvin."

"How come you're sitting down here by your lonesome? You too good for your old buddies?" Calvin asked.

"Thanks, but I'm just in here getting something to eat," Rudy told him.

"Wooohooohooo!" Bert crowed. "Did your pretty wife throw you out?"

"No, Bert," Rudy said patiently. "She has a girlfriend visiting, and I decided to give them some space, that's all."

"Oh, *right*. All these months you've had your nose buried up her skirts, and now you show up here. You know what, Cal?" Bert said, turning to his buddy. "I think his wifey's lonely right now. Whaddya say we go visit her?"

"Good idea! We could show her some sweet tricks," Calvin said.

"Come on, guys, cut it out, okay?" Rudy said, feeling a nervous stir in the pit of his stomach.

The bartender returned and placed a mug of steaming coffee on the bar in front of Rudy. "Here you go, Sir," he said, and looked at the two chronic troublemakers behind Rudy.

"We're just going to the toilet," Bert said, catching Calvin's eye. They had both just finished a furlough from Calhoun's for fighting in the bar. In fact, this same bartender had thrown them out and told them not to come back in for a month. "See ya later, Buddy," he said, clapping Rudy's shoulder a tad harder than he had to. The pair continued on to the back of the bar.

Rudy's food appeared before him, hot and delicious and greasy. He ate hungrily, and finished quickly. He looked up from his plate, and saw that Bert and Calvin had apparently gone from the bar; their stools had been taken over by two others. He considered having a soda and a cigarette to round out the meal, but decided against it. It was past 11:30 now, and he imagined that Anna and Karen were both in bed. He'd creep in, go to bed, and before he knew it, Karen's visit would be over. He'd have Anna to himself once again.

Rudy paid his tab and left the bar, lighting a cigarette and heading straight for home, when he heard quick footsteps behind him. He started to turn when his arms were grabbed from behind and his wrists shoved up toward his shoulder blades. He raised his head to see Bert grinning at him in the glare of the street light.

"We forgot to give you our wedding presents," Bert said cheerfully. He sucker-punched Rudy in the stomach, doubling him over. "*That* was from Cal." Rudy's rich, greasy meal burned a line back up to his throat. As he looked up, winded and grimacing in pain, Bert sliced an uppercut to his jaw. "And *that* one was from me. Congratulations, *Old Buddy*," he jeered, and Calvin let him drop to the sidewalk. Rudy felt his right eye smack onto the cement. The two ran back in the direction of Calhoun's and then past it. Rudy lay on the sidewalk, trying hard to breathe, remain conscious and keep his supper on his inside. He lost both of the latter battles.

He had no idea how long he had lain there unconscious—probably just a minute or so. When he came to, the street was just as deserted as it had been when Bert and Calvin had jumped him. His jaw and head were splitting with pain, and he tasted vomit and blood. Rudy sat up and gingerly felt his jaw and mouth. Both were swollen, and his lip was split. Where he had lain was a puddle of steaming vomit. He pulled himself away from the mess, sure that just looking at it was going to make him throw up again, and swallowed repeatedly.

Just then a man and woman passed him walking, giving him a wide berth. When they had hurried by, Rudy heard the woman mutter to the man, *"Oh, my God! Look at that drunk just sitting there in his own vomit!"*

*Not fair*, Rudy thought, and then stopped thinking because it hurt to think. This was definitely worse than any hangover he could remember. He gained his feet carefully, tried his balance, and found that he could walk, after all. Taking off his jacket, he mopped his head and face the best he could, then rolled it in a ball with the worst part of it on the inside. His walk home was as careful and concentrated as any that he had accomplished back in his drinking days.

His house was dark except for the light over the back door. Rudy left the outside light on and entered that way, leaving the kitchen light off to creep to the doorway to the living room. He could just make out a figure on the sofa and soft, feminine snores. That was good. He wasn't in the mood to explain anything tonight. He switched off the light for the back door, locked up, and climbed the stairs softly in the dark, feeling his way. The bathroom was down the hall and diagonally across from the bedroom he shared with Anna. Both were also dark, and that was good, as well.

With the bathroom door locked behind him, Rudy turned on the overhead light and closed his eyes until he could adjust them to the light. What he saw in the mirror horrified him. Dried vomit and blood was smeared from his chin up through his hair, which was standing stiffly up straight on the left side of his head. He did indeed have a swollen jaw and split lip on the left; in addition, his left eye was swollen almost shut. As awful as he felt, he needed to shower, clean out his mouth, and rinse out his jacket before he went to bed.

Rudy unrolled the filthy jacket he'd carried all the way home and poured water in the sink. He took his keys from one pocket, and reached into the other pocket to find the letter that Anna's father had written to her. While the jacket was soaking, he examined the envelope. It was stained with blood and vomit, as well, and Anna's name was smeared. He tried to rinse it off, but that only made it worse. He decided that he would cope with it tomorrow, and put the letter aside on the top of the toilet tank while he showered.

The soapy steam felt good. Rudy shampooed his hair and used a washcloth to carefully dab the left side of his face. He wiped himself dry, and then wiped the steam from the mirror to see if he looked any better. Well, the mess was gone, but the swelling was definitely worse, and his lip had started bleeding again. He could use some ice to take down the swelling, but he wouldn't go back downstairs tonight. That was just too chancy. He rinsed out his jacket, wrung it out, and hung it over the shower head to dry. He closed the shower curtain, hoping that both Anna and Karen would miss it in the morning.

Rudy was aware that this process was taking a long time, much longer than he had thought, and it was no surprise when a light knock sounded on the bathroom door. "Rudy?" Anna asked in a sleepy, quiet voice. "Are you in there?"

"Yes," he answered, checking to make sure that the door was locked. He dabbed at his bleeding lip with toilet paper.

"Are you all right? It's late."

"I know it's late, Honey. I just wanted a shower before I went to bed. Go back to sleep. I'll be right in," Rudy said.

"All right. I love you, Honey."

"I love you, too," Rudy answered quickly, and then listened for the bedroom door to close. It did, and he sighed.

He carefully brushed his teeth and rinsed with mouthwash, wincing at the eye-watering sting of it, took more aspirin, then wrapped the towel around his waist and sat on the lowered toilet lid. He'd better give Anna a minute to fall back asleep. He picked up Christianson's letter. What a mess! It occurred to him that if he let it dry this way, the pages would be welded together and Anna would never be able to read it. With a touch of guilt at opening his wife's mail, he easily peeled the flap of the envelope open and separated the two pages that he found inside. They were blurry, but still readable.

He couldn't help it. He read the letter, which was short but to the point. Christianson wrote:

*Dear Annie,*

*I hope you are feeling okay and that everything is going all right with you and your husband. I know that your baby will be born soon, and I hope that everything is going all right with that.*

*I've been a stupid, stubborn old man, Annie, and I hope you'll forgive me. I'm sorry for what I said to you. You're my daughter and I love you and I miss you. My only excuse for what I did is that I thought I'd be lonely—and here I am, lonely.*

*I was going to call you, but like the coward that I am, I was afraid you or your husband would hang up on me. Just remember, Annie, if that man hurts you or if you ever want to get out of that marriage, my door is always open to you and to your child.*

*Call me if you can forgive me. If you can't forgive me right now, give yourself some time, like I did. Just remember I love you.*

*Love always to my little Annie,*
*Dad*

Rudy read the letter through twice, then clenched his jaw so hard he thought he would split it himself. He forced himself to open his mouth and breathe. He got up, flipped open the toilet lid and put the seat up, then tore the damp paper into tiny pieces and flung them into the toilet. He urinated on the pieces—a long, steady stream—then watched as he flushed to make sure all the pieces went into the sewer. That was one letter that Anna would never see.

---

Sunday morning broke with a warm, grey drizzle and thunderclouds that threatened a real downpour in the near future. Rudy had managed to sneak naked into bed in the dark without disturbing his sleeping wife. He had expected a restless night, but fell fast asleep almost immediately. Now Anna was shaking his shoulder and calling his name. At the moment he was asleep on his left side, with his back toward the bedroom door. As soon as he opened his eyes, he felt the terrible ache in his face and abdomen, and full recollection of the past evening came to him. He feigned sleepiness, however, hoping that he could put off getting up and facing Anna until after Karen had left. If she knew what had really happened, she would have a full glimpse into his past life, and right in front of her friend. That shamed him. He didn't want to take a chance on losing her.

"Hey, Sleepyhead! We're waiting for you down in the kitchen," Anna said cheerfully. "Pancakes and bacon—your favorite!"

"Mmm," Rudy said, with closed eyes.

She kissed the back of his neck, usually a sure thing in the way of waking Rudy up.

"Oh, Honey, I'm tired," Rudy said in a sluggish drawl. He drew the comforter up over his head and turned his face into the pillow.

"Rudy, Sweetie-Honey-Babe," Anna whispered into his ear, tickling it.

He turned his mouth to the side and said in a muffled voice, "You go ahead and eat. Say goodbye to Karen for me."

"Oh no, you don't, Lazybones," Anna laughed, and pulled the comforter and sheet down to the foot of the bed. "MMM, look what I've found—a naked man in my bed!" She crawled over her husband's body and knelt in the middle of the bed, facing him. "I'll have to kiss him awake!"

"Anna, come on," Rudy complained, and reached for the comforter. As he moved, Anna gasped.

"Rudy! Oh my *God*, what happened to you?" she cried.

Rudy gave up and sat on the side of the bed, wincing as he did so. Anna got up and came to stand in front of him, and dropped to her knees at once. "Rudy, you've got to go to the hospital! You look like somebody beat you up!"

"Well, they did," Rudy said. "But I'm not going to any hospital, Honey. It's not as bad as it looks."

"Not as bad as it looks? Come and look in the mirror!" she exclaimed.

Painfully, Rudy got up and walked, still naked, to the full-length mirror hanging on the bedroom wall. What he saw was horrific. The entire left side of his face and jaw was swollen and bruised. His split lip had broken open in the middle of the night, and both dried and fresh blood decorated his lips and chin. Skin had been scraped from an area on his cheek bone below his left eye, and the eye was hopelessly swollen shut. To top it off, a large, purple bruise flowered over his lower abdomen. "Well, maybe I should see a doctor," he said, trying to talk without moving his lips. It didn't help; fresh blood splashed on his chest.

Anna ran to the bathroom and returned with a washcloth

that had been soaked in cold water. "Here," she told him, "hold that on your mouth to stop the bleeding. I'll get your clothes ready and help you get dressed. We've got to get to the Emergency Room."

He acquiesced weakly to her ministrations, numbly accepting her choice of a loosely-fitting jogging suit. The taste of fresh blood in his mouth was making him nauseous, and he could only imagine the pain of tossing his guts again. As he sat on the edge of the bed and let Anna put on his socks and shoes, he saw the blood-soaked pillowcase on the pillow where he had slept, and waves of dizziness flashed over him. Anna made him lie down again while she ran downstairs and explained the situation to Karen. While she was out of the room he spat blood into the wash cloth and turned it over.

Karen and Anna both came pounding back up the stairs and into the bedroom. "Oh Rudy, I'm so sorry!" Karen cried when she saw him. "Anna, how can I help?"

"Run back downstairs and turn off the coffee pot, Karen, and put the milk away. We need two more wash cloths soaked in cold water and folded; look in the linen closet in the bathroom," Anna instructed. "Rudy, Honey, where are the car keys?"

Rudy pointed to the top of the dresser wordlessly. Anna grabbed them and put on her own shoes, and by the time she had guided Rudy into the hallway, Karen had prepared the wash cloths. She took the soiled one from Rudy without a word, tossed it into the bathroom sink, plugged the drain, and ran cold water to soak it.

Downstairs, the sofa held a folded blanket with a pillow and the sheets Karen had used neatly stacked on top of it; her suitcase was sitting on the floor by the front door. The smells of coffee and bacon coming from the kitchen reminded Rudy of his supper the night before, and his stomach turned over. He moaned, and Anna's eyes grew wide. "What's wrong, Honey?" she asked.

"Bring the wastebasket," he managed, and gagged as he staggered toward the front door.

Karen looked around wildly and spied a small wastebasket near a stuffed chair. She grabbed it and her suitcase, and locked the front door after them.

"I'm going to follow you two to the E. R. and wait until I know you can manage things, Anna. If everything's okay, I can leave for home from there," Karen offered.

Anna nodded gratefully, and soon they were speeding down the relatively empty streets toward the nearest hospital. It was fortunate that Rudy had asked for the wastebasket, because before they arrived, he had used it twice. His nausea was still not relieved.

It was a long, long day for Rudy. He was examined, x-rayed, and had to provide blood and urine specimens. Anna stayed by his side, holding a compress to his mouth, soothing him, and urging him to be quiet; there would be time for explanations later, she said. Rudy closed his eyes and let his misery surround him while they waited for the doctor to come in with his diagnoses. It took a while; an emergency room in a city hospital is a busy place. Finally, the curtain swished aside, and the E. R. physician attending to Rudy's case entered with a clipboard.

"Well, Mr. Baumann," Dr. Snow began, "you're pretty well banged up. You've had a mild concussion. You have hairline fractures in the bone below your eye and in your jaw. You'll need stitches inside and outside of your mouth to stop the bleeding and let it heal. You have abrasions on your cheek, which we can attend to. Your urine and blood specimens don't reflect any internal bleeding, but I'd like to keep you in the hospital a day, just to make sure."

He turned to Anna. "This way we can keep him quiet and take care of any . . . problems that might arise, Mrs. Baumann. Do you know what happened?"

"I only know that he was beat up last night, Doctor," she answered.

"Son, I have to call the police about this. It's assault and battery," the doctor said.

Rudy closed his eyes and shook his head, "No."

"I have to; it's the law. Were you mugged?"

Again Rudy shook his head.

"Any witnesses?"

Rudy opened his eyes and shook his head for a third time.

"Well, we'll stitch you up and get you upstairs into bed, and maybe by the time the police arrive you'll be able to give them the information they need. Mrs. Baumann, I'm going to need you to fill out some papers," the doctor said. "Can you come with me?"

"Of course," she said, and after kissing Rudy gently on the cheek, she followed the doctor out of the cubicle.

Rudy closed his eyes again. He wasn't sure whether or not to tell the police about Calvin and Bert. He worked with them, and they knew where he lived. Under the best of circumstances, they each could be vicious and vengeful. When they were drunk, the only way to handle them was to make sure you were drunker and meaner than they were.

The problem was that the bartender from Calhoun's had marked them the night before. The police would eventually talk to him, and he could point them out as individuals who had been giving him a hard time in the bar.

The situation went around and around in his mind, and he dozed. When he woke, he opened his eyes (as far as he was able) to a brisk nurse wheeling in a tray of gleaming instruments and bandages; the doctor was right behind her. The nurse briefly explained that Mrs. Baumann was in the waiting room with her friend, and would walk up to his room with him when he was finished here. Rudy then gave himself over to a world of hurt as they cleansed, stitched, and bandaged him.

―――――――

Earlier, Dr. Snow had led Anna to the small desk area where the clerk had taken Rudy's identification and insurance information upon his arrival. Now he had hospital admission papers for

Anna to sign. Up to this point, she had been full of concern for Rudy; now she realized that her husband was to be hospitalized, and she burst into tears. Dr. Snow silently handed her a box of tissues.

When she had gained some control and finished signing the papers, Dr. Snow asked, "Mrs. Baumann, has anything like this ever happened to your husband before?"

"No, never!" Anna exclaimed. "Well, at least since I've known him. I met him about a year ago, and he's never told me about being beaten before."

"Well, the urine and blood tests show no traces of alcohol or drugs in his system. These are the kinds of injuries you usually see with a mugging. Your husband says it wasn't. It doesn't look like a bar fight, or his hands and knuckles would be bruised or cut. Where was he when this happened?"

Anna explained that she had been visiting with her friend while her husband went for a walk alone. She had no idea where he had gone, only that he had returned after she had gone to bed.

"Do you live in a rough neighborhood? The reason I'm asking is that you are obviously near to giving birth, and I hate to send you home alone to an area where there is violence."

"No, it's usually not rough at all. You never see the police around. We live on a street with older houses and a lot of older people. It's very quiet."

Dr. Snow sighed. "Okay. But just to be safe, could you stay with someone tonight?"

"I could ask my friend to stay with me one more night," Anna said thoughtfully. "But I'm sure I'd be all right alone."

"Do me a favor and ask her, would you?" Dr. Snow insisted, as he showed her the door to the waiting area. Karen immediately rose to her feet when she saw her friend.

"I will," Anna promised, and thanked the doctor. She walked over to Karen and sank into an uncomfortably molded waiting room chair.

"Well?" Karen asked. "What did you find out?"

Anna sighed and massaged her extended abdomen absently. The baby was kicking, as it had been regularly over the past month or so. It was good to know that *something* was normal. "I don't know anything more about what happened last night," she told Karen, "but Rudy's got to stay here in the hospital until tomorrow." She listed the diagnoses that Dr. Snow had told her. "Karen, he suggested that I stay overnight with a friend. Is there any way that you . . ."

"Say no more," interrupted Karen. "It's a done deal. I'll just call in to work tomorrow morning. Is Rudy going to be all right?"

"Yes, except for being in a lot of pain right now. He'll also have to eat and drink very carefully for the next week or so." Anna said. "I have to call his boss, too. His name was Masters, Hank Masters. I hope he's in the telephone book."

"I'll help you look," Karen offered, and pulled her friend to her feet. "Anna, are you sure *you're* all right? You look awfully pale and sweaty."

Anna laughed ruefully. "It's just hefting this baby everywhere I go that's got me tired. I'll be okay."

Together they found a "Henry" Masters in the telephone book for Duluth, and Anna dialed the number. To her relief, it turned out to be Rudy's boss, and she quickly explained the circumstances and that he wouldn't be coming to work the next day. He extended his concern, and told her that Rudy shouldn't worry; they could cover for him. Anna then asked him if he knew where Rudy had been working his side-jobs. She thought she should try to contact them, as well.

"Anna, I have no idea. I knew that Rudy was taking on extra work until the baby came, but he hasn't told me exactly who he's been working for. Don't worry; they'll call you if they miss him. If I hear anything from this end, I'll have them call you."

"Thanks so much, Hank," Anna said.

"No problem. And if you need anything, you have my number now. Do you have a place to stay tonight?" Masters asked, mindful of Anna's condition.

"I'm going to stay at home with a friend," Anna told him. "Thanks for asking."

She replaced the telephone and carefully copied Hank Masters' number onto a scrap of paper from her purse. She and Karen then sat down to wait.

About a half hour later, they were informed that an orderly was getting ready to transfer Rudy up to a hospital bed. Both Anna and Karen walked beside the gurney. Rudy was a mass of bandages and stitches and scrapes and bruises, and he couldn't talk very well. As soon as he was settled in his bed, nurses whisked in to examine him. They swished the curtain around his bed, and once again Anna was made to wait.

Karen told her, "Anna, take this chair." She had found a metal folding chair and was preparing it for her friend.

"I think I will, Karen. I'm so very tired," Anna said.

While they were waiting for the nurses to finish, a physician walked in and joined the medical team at Rudy's bedside. One nurse immediately left and returned with a syringe, a metal rack, an IV bag filled with a clear liquid, and clear tubing. Anna watched their feet as they bustled around Rudy's bed, and was amazed at how efficiently they worked together, never bumping into each other or tripping over equipment. Soon the curtain was swished aside.

The ward physician, Dr. Hebron, introduced himself to Anna and Karen and shook their hands. He told them that the IV was to make sure that Rudy didn't get dehydrated, and that he had given Anna's husband a shot for pain, which would put him to sleep for a few hours. "He's lucky that whoever did this to him didn't finish the job," he said, indicating Rudy with his head. "And you have no idea what happened?"

Anna repeated what she knew of the previous night's events.

"Well, the police have been informed. They'll be by later, after Mr. Baumann has had a chance to rest and get some fluids into him," the doctor told her. "In the meantime, Mrs. Baumann, I think you'd better go home. You look exhausted yourself. We'll call you if there's any change."

Anna looked past the doctor to her husband's prone body on the hospital bed. "I want to see Rudy first," she said, her jaw set. Dr. Hebron took one look at her stubborn expression and excused himself.

She went to his bedside and took in the IV needle inserted into the back of his hand, the bandages, and his waxen face. Her heart clenched mightily at the sight. She simultaneously felt love, and fear, and a lightning bolt of hate for whoever had done this to her husband. She gently laid her hand on the side of his face that wasn't bandaged. Rudy opened his eyes. "Anna," he croaked.

"Darling, don't talk. Just rest. You're going to sleep for a while now, and I'm going to go home for a few hours. I love you so much, Rudy. I need you so badly. Just get well for me, okay?"

Rudy's eyes filled with tears, and as she kissed them away, Anna stifled a sob. She waited a few minutes until she was sure he was asleep, and then turned to go. She was startled by Karen, who was standing right behind her.

"You love him so much, don't you, Anna?" Karen sympathized.

Anna only nodded jerkily, and walked as quickly as she could to the door of the hospital room. Once there, she turned the corner, leaned against the wall, and broke into tears. "If I were to lose him, Karen, I . . . I think I'd die." Karen held her friend and soothed her, and then took her home in her own car.

---

*She knelt in the endless field of corn, willing her heart to stop its pounding so she could hear. What was out there? Which direction would it come from? The trees . . . she would be safe if she got to the trees, and Ruebin would be waiting for her there. She tried to rise and run to safety, but her legs wouldn't move, and her heart pounded even more loudly. A rogue wind swirled the tall stalks of corn behind her. What was that? She commanded her legs to move, but they were dead weight. All around was the smell of ripened corn and the heat of a summer's sun on the earth, even though the sky was black with clouds. She twisted to pull herself through the corn with her hands, but suddenly there were arms around her shoulders, holding her back. She screamed . . .*

But in reality it only came out as a squeak. Someone was shaking her, calling her name.

"Anna! Anna, Honey, wake up! You're having a bad dream!"

Anna opened her eyes with a gasp. She had been sleeping so deeply that for a second she couldn't remember where she was, or who this woman was. It came back to her in a rush: she was at home, this was her friend Karen, and Rudy was in the hospital. She was lying on the living room sofa. She struggled to rise, but her legs were tangled in the single blanket that Karen had placed over her as she slept. Karen untangled her and helped her to sit up.

"Wow, that was a Lulu," Karen said, sitting on the sofa next to Anna with her arm around her friend. "Are you all right?"

Anna was straining to remember the dream. "There was corn, and oh, Karen, it was so hot and I was so scared . . . and who's Ruebin?"

"Honey, it was just a dream. You're under stress because of what happened to Rudy. Of course you're scared." Karen hugged Anna. "Let me get you some water and a cool cloth."

"Rudy!" Anna sat up, electrified. "What time is it? Did the hospital call?"

"Sshh, Anna. It's okay. They didn't call, but I did. Rudy's still fast asleep, and he's looking a lot better, they say. We've only been here about two hours; you fell asleep as soon as you laid down. Okay?"

"I think we'd better get back to the hospital," Anna said, starting to rise, but Karen made her sit where she was.

"All this running back and forth is no good for you, Anna," she said. "Please, just relax and let me take care of things for a little while, all right?"

Anna considered, rubbing her abdomen absently, then nodded. "But as soon as he wakes up, I want to go see him. Promise me," she begged.

"All right. No problem. Now relax. I'll be right back with the water," Karen said.

In the kitchen, Karen poured cold water into a glass and added a couple of ice cubes from the tray in the freezer. Anna worried her. What if all this stress brought on the baby's birth? She had heard of such things happening. It would be horrible if Rudy and Anna both ended up in the hospital at the same time. She shook the thought away. No use inviting trouble. Things were bad enough as it was.

She poured cold water on a clean dish towel, wrung it out, and folded it. When she entered the living room, Anna was sitting as she had left her, but was staring out the front window at a steady downpour of rain. Distant thunder could be heard. She had slept through a thunderstorm, in fact. Anna meekly accepted the water and allowed her friend to gently wipe her face and neck.

"Anna, you haven't eaten anything all day, and I've made some soup and sandwiches. Let's go into the kitchen and eat," Karen suggested. "It'll take just a minute to re-heat the soup, and I'll make some coffee. How does that sound?"

"I'm not hungry, Karen," Anna said, sounding far-away. Just then her stomach growled loudly.

"Ah, ha! *Somebody's* hungry, even if you're not," Karen smiled, and evinced a tiny smile from Anna. "You have to take care of that baby, whether he's inside or out."

Anna cheered at the thought of her baby. "So it's a "he," is it? When did you decide that?"

Karen helped her friend off the sofa. "Only a man would be that suggestible." They laughed together, and went to the kitchen.

While Anna had slept, Karen had stripped the bed and replaced the linens, cleaned the bathroom (finding Rudy's jacket in the shower and marveling at what it could be doing there), cleaned the kitchen, and done a load of laundry. As they ate, she wondered how Anna planned to manage after the baby was born, with her husband working such long hours and being new to motherhood. "Anna, do you have help for yourself and the baby after *he's* born?" she asked, adding a teasing note to a serious question.

"Rudy was going to quit his extra jobs and stay home with me for a couple of weeks," Anna explained. "I hope he'll be all right," she added, with a touch of worry.

"Of *course* he'll be all right," Karen said confidently. "One day in captivity and then he'll be yours to baby. And, speaking from my limited experience of boyfriends, when they're sick they *love* being babied. Trust me, he'll milk it for as much as he can get."

Anna laughed. "He hasn't even had as much as a cold since I've known him," she said. "I was beginning to think he was invincible." She sipped her coffee gratefully. She had been *ravenous*, it turned out, and had consumed double portions. Suddenly she asked, "Karen, do you ever see Dad? Do you ever hear from him?"

Karen paused and lowered her eyes. Harold Christianson had not contacted her once since Anna had left, and she thought it was terrible. She decided to tell her friend the truth.

"Not a word, Honey." She noted Anna's eyes clouding, and added, "Men can be so stubborn. I'll tell you what: the minute the baby's born, I'll call him myself and chew him out. He can hang up on me, but at least he'll know he has a grandchild. You'd think that at his age he'd figure out that life's too short to let pride break up his family. I'll just remind him of that."

Anna studied her coffee cup. "I miss him so much. I don't want this baby to grow up without a grandfather, not if he doesn't have to."

"Do you ever hear anything from Rudy's family?"

"Nothing," Anna sighed. "I think that deep down it hurts Rudy, but he won't admit it. I guess that after all, we just have each other."

"And *me. And* your baby. All things considered, you're pretty rich," Karen inserted, determined to keep things light.

Anna laughed. "All right, I'm lucky, lucky, lucky," she said. "Does that satisfy you?"

"Yes, it does," Karen smiled, and the phone rang.

It was the hospital. Rudy had just awakened and was asking for his wife. The nurse assured Anna that he was much better, and that the doctor thought that there were no signs of internal bleeding. "Take your time getting here, though," the nurse added in a lowered voice, sounding as if she had cupped her hand around the mouthpiece of the phone. "The police are in his room with him now."

---

Almost as soon as Rudy woke up, a Duluth city policeman had walked in with a nurse, who admonished the officer that he had fifteen minutes and then she would be back. She emphasized this warning with a meaningful look, as if to say, "This is *my* jurisdiction, not yours." The officer introduced himself as Herman Kroelowicz, "But I know your mouth hurts, so don't even try it." He shook Rudy's unencumbered hand, pulled up the folding chair, and pulled out a pad of paper and a pen. "I'm going to ask you questions. If you can say the answers without pain, go ahead, but I've got these (indicating the pen and paper) in case you have to write the answers. All right?"

Rudy nodded, and the slow process of writing out answers to the policeman's many questions began. When they were finished, Officer Kroelowicz summed it up. "So this is your statement: You went for a walk last night about 10:15 because you had a headache and your wife was visiting with her friend. You went into

Calhoun's, just a few blocks from where you live, and had supper and coffee, no alcohol. You left about 11:30 or so, and you started to walk back home. You heard footsteps behind you, started to turn, and someone grabbed your arms from behind. Whoever it was held you while some guy punched you in the stomach and hit you in the jaw. They didn't say anything, and you didn't recognize anybody. They dropped you, and you passed out for a minute. To your knowledge, nobody else was around. You walked home yourself and got there about 12:30 a.m. Is that right?"

Rudy nodded.

"Seems strange. Are you *sure* you didn't recognize either of them?"

Rudy nodded emphatically.

"And they didn't take your wallet?"

Rudy shook his head, "No."

The officer regarded Rudy silently for a moment. "Let's say we find out who did this. Are you going to press charges, Mr. Baumann?"

Rudy looked at the officer. He had made up his mind. Getting Bert and Calvin arrested would only do harm. Silently he shook his head.

Officer Kroelowicz closed the pad of paper and replaced the pen in his pocket. "Well, that's it, then. Will you sign a statement, at least? That way, if there are any other assaults in the area, we'll have a record. You might change your mind if that happens," he suggested.

Rudy nodded.

"I'll be back later with the statement, then," the officer said, and was shaking Rudy's hand when the nurse popped her head into the door with a severe look.

"You have had fifteen more minutes than you were given, Officer. My patient needs his rest, and you will leave now," she ordered.

Officer Kroelowicz drew himself to attention, mock-saluted

her, and said, "Yes, *Ma'am!*" That drew a tiny smile from Rudy, and the officer winked at him and said goodbye, giving the nurse a wide berth as he passed her.

The nurse took his vital signs, cranked up the head of the bed, helped Rudy to lean forward while she rearranged his pillows, offered him water through a straw, and was still working on her patient when Anna walked in. Rudy saw her and beckoned with his free hand. She came to him and tenderly embraced him. "Is he going to be all right?" Anna asked the nurse.

"Oh, yes. His vital signs are normal, and I think that the rest of your information is up to date," the nurse said. "Your friend Karen called us every half hour to find out, you know," she added with a frown. "You can tell her to stop calling us now." And the nurse left Anna and Rudy alone.

Anna struggled to keep her facial features calm. Rudy looked at her quizzically. "Karen's staying over another night while you're here to make sure I don't give birth alone while you're in the hospital," she explained. "I took a nap, and I guess Karen must have bugged them a little too often about how you were. Are you feeling better?"

Rudy nodded, and pointed to the right side of his mouth. Anna kissed it gently, and stood back. "I saw a policeman getting on the elevator. Did he question you?"

Rudy nodded.

"Do you remember anything more?"

Rudy shook his head, then pointed to Anna's swollen abdomen with his right eyebrow raised in a question.

"The baby's fine, and so am I. Karen's taking good care of me," Anna responded.

Rudy closed his eyes. *Karen. Always Karen,* he thought resentfully. *If she hadn't come, none of this would have ever happened.* He opened his eyes and mimicked writing with his hand and fingers.

"You want to write? Let me see what I've got in my purse," Anna said, and rummaged until she found a receipt and a pen.

She loaned Rudy her purse to back up the tiny scrap of paper, then looked at what he had written.

"Karen go home?" she read aloud in amazement. "Oh, you mean *when* will she be going home. Well, she'll stay tonight with me, and then we'll pick you up tomorrow morning when you're discharged. She'll go home when you're back at home with me and *I* can take care of you," Anna said cheerfully. She tucked the paper back into her purse. "Now, Sir, what can I do for you?"

The unaffected side of Rudy's lips lifted in a smile, and he lifted the covers to display his hospital johnny, which had rucked up to his waist. Anna's eyes traveled back from that sight to his face; his right eyebrow had cocked up in a leer. She laughed and whipped the covers back into place. "You *are* going to be all right! I guess it takes more than cuts, bruises and cracks to stop Rudy Baumann!"

She leaned over the bed, kissed the right side of his mouth more warmly, and placed his hand on her breast. "Well, Sweetie, all I can say is that you're going to have . . . to . . . *wait!* That nurse is ready to string me up as it is."

Rudy murmured something; to her it sounded like, "Tomorrow." And, if it *was* what she had heard, it was a promise he kept.

---

The next day, Karen helped pack Rudy into the passenger side of his own car and followed them back to the Baumann house. On the way, Anna had to stop at a pharmacy and get Rudy's prescriptions for pain medication and a preventive antibiotic filled, and Karen waited in the car with Rudy, sitting in the driver's seat.

Anna was in the drug store about a half hour, and the silence from Rudy was making Karen uncomfortable.

"Rudy, are you in pain right now?" she asked.

Rudy shook his head, "No."

Silence.

"I'll bet you're glad to get out of that place and go home."

Silence. Rudy stared straight ahead through the windshield.

"Anna had a good night. I think she and the baby are doing fine."

Nothing from Rudy.

Karen searched for something to say to fill the silence. "I'll have to go back as soon as we get you home and settled," she said. "I made sure that you two have groceries for a week, so that Anna doesn't have to go out for that." She laughed. "I included some straws and plenty of things for you to drink."

Rudy swung his head and glared at her. Karen's heart went cold. Was that *hate* in his eyes? What had she done to *him*? Chills crawled up her spine. "Y-you know, I think you'll be all right. I'll just wait in my own car," she stuttered.

Rudy turned his head forward in response.

Karen got out of Rudy's car and into her own as fast as she could.

Anna was a little puzzled when she came out of the pharmacy and noted that Karen was in her own car, but her friend only waved. She wedged herself behind the steering wheel next to Rudy. "Are you okay?" she asked.

Rudy nodded, and gave his half-smile to her. She started the car and drove to their house.

Karen helped carry things in when they got there; Anna had all but bought out the store of dressings, ointments, and the like. As soon as Rudy was seated in the living room, she told Anna she would be leaving. "I'm glad you're all right, Rudy," she called over her shoulder as she walked out the front door. Anna followed her.

"Karen, are you all right? You're acting like someone poured cold water on you," Anna said.

"I'll be fine. I'm just anxious to get back and get things ready for work tomorrow," her friend responded. "Take care of yourself, Anna, I really mean that. Call me *at once* if you need anything."

"I'll be *fine*, Karen," Anna assured her, kissing her cheek. "Rudy's home now."

"I know," Karen said. She took one last look at her friend and drove away.

Anna shook off the feeling that something was very wrong here. She had the *next* part of her life before her, after all: getting Rudy well and welcoming this new baby. She squared her shoulders and went back inside.

It turned out that Karen knew men pretty well. Rudy was pitiful in his pain and fairly demanding that day. Anna fetched and carried for him until she was almost exhausted. She was doing the supper dishes, thinking about how good it would feel to just sit down, when she heard what sounded like knocking coming from the living room. She dried her hands on a dish towel and peered into the room. Rudy had called her by rapping his knuckles on the coffee table; he gestured that he wanted something to drink. She stared at him in disbelief.

"Rudy Baumann, if I recall correctly, your injuries did *not* include anything to do with your legs or feet," she declared, placing her hands on her hips. "You know where the soda is. It's time you get it for yourself."

With that, she spun and went back to doing dishes. Rudy didn't come out to the kitchen, and by the time she had finished the dishes and swept the kitchen floor, guilt had inserted itself in the place of righteous irritation. Anna opened the refrigerator, took out a bottle of orange soda, removed the cap, and placed a straw in it, thinking all the while that it was probably a mistake, but that the guilt felt worse than her feet.

Rudy was absent from the living room, although the television was still turned on. She climbed the stairs in search of him, and found him lying on the bed, staring at the ceiling, his arm over his eyes.

"Rudy," she said softly, and he took his arm down and looked at her. He looked so pitiful. "I'm sorry for snapping at you, Honey. I'm just so tired lately. Here, I've brought you a soda."

He raised his hand as she walked over, and accepted the drink she offered. He sat up, took a long draw on the soda, and then patted the bed next to him. Anna sat down and sighed gratefully. It had been a long day. She kicked off her shoes, and Rudy put his arm around her shoulders. She leaned against him. "I love you, Rudy," she said, kissing his neck.

Rudy took his arm away and patted the pillow next to his.

"Oh, I'd *love* to lie down. My feet are killing me," Anna said, and crawled to her pillow. She lay on her side, facing Rudy, and closed her eyes.

But Rudy had other ideas.

His mouth was out of commission for the moment, and he had acted like he was totally helpless, but his hands weren't—at least when Anna was lying in bed next to him. He started gently, smoothing her hair back from her brow and caressing her neck. Then his fingers trailed down to her chest, where pregnancy had swollen her breasts to unbelievable proportions. He wanted to see those breasts now, feel them. Soon there would be a child suckling there; he had plans to do the same. He ran his thumb over Anna's nipple through her shirt and bra, and it hardened to his touch. She moaned, and her eyes opened, a smoky green.

They made love in the way that lovers do when one of them is very pregnant, and then Anna slept, exhausted. Her last thoughts before she fell asleep were, *My life is so complete. I love Rudy and my baby so much. No woman ever had so much as I do.*

She had forgotten about her father.

She had forgotten about Karen.

She had completely lost memory for the nightmare she had, the one about the corn and someone named Ruebin.

It didn't occur to her then that all of her life beyond the walls of this house was slipping away from her. Not then.

# CHAPTER
# Eighteen

A week later, Rudy was off the pain killers and able to drive. It was fortunate, because Anna's baby had dropped. They both saw their respective doctors on the same day—Rudy to get his stitches removed from his mouth and to be rechecked, and Anna to be rechecked by the obstetrician.

Rudy waited impatiently in the waiting room of the obstetrician's office, uncomfortably aware that he was the only male amidst a sea of pregnant women. Outside of curious glances when he first sat down and searched the pile of magazines next to him for male reading material, the women ignored him and continued their comments about how their pregnancies were progressing. He found a Reader's Digest and thumbed through it, but parts of the women's conversation intruded so that it was difficult to concentrate on any one story.

"Well, with my *first* pregnancy I was in labor for 36 hours," one woman confided.

"My water broke while we were having supper in a *restaurant*," another said. "What a mess! The man at the next table fainted dead away."

Rudy felt like fainting dead away, himself.

"Is your husband going into the delivery room with you?"

*Not on your life,* Rudy thought.

"Oh, yes, he's been through this with me twice before."

One young woman asked another, "Do you know what an episiotomy is?"

The other answered, "Oh yes, Dear. They have to clip the flesh between the openings to allow more room for the baby to come through sometimes. That's an episiotomy."

The young woman asked, "Which openings are you talking about?"

And Rudy left the room.

*Oh my God,* he thought. *I need a beer. I need a six-pack. Or a keg.* He paced the hallway outside the obstetrician's office until Anna poked her head out, looking for him.

"What are you doing out here?" she asked.

Rudy grimaced. "I couldn't take it any more. I was the only man in there," he told her, indicating the waiting room with his head. "Are you all finished?"

Anna smiled. "I'm all finished *here*. But the doctor wants me to pre-register at the hospital. He says it could be any day now. I'm dilated *two centimeters*."

On the way to the car, Anna explained that the baby had dropped, and the opening to her cervix (through which the baby would pass) was starting to open. Rudy looked doubtfully at her nether regions as they walked. Would her water break while they were on the way to the car? Anna explained that, particularly with the first child, this could take days. The pre-registration was to make sure that everything was ready for her arrival at the hospital.

Anna looked at Rudy out of the corner of one green eye. "The doctor asked me if you wanted to come into the delivery room with me," she said. "I told him I didn't think so. Was that the right thing to say?"

"Yes!" cried Rudy in heartfelt earnest, and Anna laughed.

"I didn't *think* you'd want to be in there," she smiled.

So they prepared for the baby's arrival. Anna packed her hospital bag, stocked the refrigerator with plenty of food for Rudy while she would be gone, and checked the baby's room to make sure that all was ready. Rudy went back to work, leaving word at the office that he was to be reached at once if Anna or the hospital were to call. The administrative staff, all female, smiled and assured him that they wouldn't let him miss this for the world.

Rudy's workmates had plenty of questions for him about his injuries—he was still healing, and his face was a veritable rainbow of colors—but he was vague in his replies. Bert and Calvin were working the same job, but they steered clear of him when possible. No mention was made of their encounter outside Calhoun's. At least, not until the end of the work day when they were getting ready to go home.

Bert approached him as he was changing his shoes. "The police have been by, asking questions," he said, looking around to make sure they weren't overheard.

"So?"

"So I told them I didn't know anything about it," Bert said, a little nervously. "I know you didn't finger us, because we didn't get arrested. What did you tell them?"

Rudy coolly finished tying his sneakers, then straightened and looked at Bert. "I decided to let this one pass, for old times' sake," he said, and Bert breathed again. "Just this one time, Bert. That's it. You and Cal were my friends once, but things changed. They *changed*. Those days are over. It has nothing to do with either of you. I just want a different life now."

Bert nodded in relief. "Okay! Pals, then?" and he offered his hand for Rudy to shake.

Rudy ignored it. "Let's call it a truce," he said, and walked away.

Bert looked at Rudy's retreating back uneasily. One thing he knew very well about that man, from his drinking days: Rudy had a long, *long* memory. He sure hoped Rudy didn't start drinking again.

---

It was 3:00 a.m. two days later. Rudy was fast asleep, but Anna was shaking him awake. He rolled over and said, "Let me sleep. It's not time to get up yet."

But she kept shaking him, and suddenly the word, "baby" came through.

He was awake, now.

"Rudy, my water broke, and I've started labor, I think. We'd better call the hospital."

He sat bolt upright in bed and looked at Anna. She was standing next to the bed; she had already gotten dressed and turned on the lights in the room. Spears of pain flashed through his eyes as he squinted, trying to see.

"Are you sure?"

"Look for yourself," Anna said, pointing to the sheets on her side of the bed. They looked like they had been bathed in pink water.

Rudy shot out of bed and down the stairs to the telephone. It was fortunate that Anna had been down before him and had turned on the lights, because he would have broken his neck in the dark. He called the hospital and reached the emergency room, rather incoherently announcing that he was bringing his wife in to have a baby. The desk clerk, used to late night calls of this type, was patient. When Rudy had finished his shouted announcement, she calmly said, "Congratulations, sir. Now, just tell me: what's your wife's name?"

"Anna!"

"Anna . . . sir, what's her last name?"

"Christianson!"

"Anna Christianson. All right, we'll be ready. Drive safely."

"No! BAUMANN! Her name is Baumann," Rudy corrected himself.

"Sir, you don't need to shout. I can hear you," the clerk "All right, I see that she's been to the hospital for pre-registration. Your name must be Rudy."

"Yes!"

"Okay, Rudy, bring her in. Drive safely. And, Mr. Baumann?"

"What?"

"Remember to bring your wife," the clerk snickered. She just couldn't resist. The line went dead.

Rudy stared at the phone in his hand, then remembered to hang it up. He raced up the stairs to dress, and met Anna coming down.

"Are you all right?" he asked anxiously.

"Yes, I am, Rudy. Are *you* all right? I heard you shouting," Anna said, a twinkle in her eye. She seemed so calm, so sedate.

"I'm fine! I'm fine! I'm going to get dressed now."

"That would be a good thing. Rudy, slow down, and don't shout. We don't want your stitches broken open, do we?"

He stopped talking, dropped his hands to his sides, and kissed her right there on the stairs. "You're going to have a baby," he said in wonder.

"No stopping it," she said.

"I'll get dressed," he repeated, and went up the stairs at a slower pace.

Upstairs, he was astonished to see that Anna had changed the bed linens, soaked the soiled ones, and hung them up over the shower curtain rail to dry. He grabbed clothes without looking at them and brushed his teeth. He thought about shaving, and decided that this wasn't the time; there was half a chance that he'd cut his own throat. He had turned off the lights upstairs and made it to the head of the stairs when Anna reminded him, "Remember my suitcase," and he had to turn back to snatch it from its place by the bedroom door. He descended the steps.

"Honey, we have plenty of time. We live pretty close to the hospital. The contractions are light, and about ten minutes apart. Just don't hurt yourself," Anna told him.

"Right," he answered.

All the same, Rudy was as nervous as any first-time father could be. He squealed his tires taking off from their driveway, and Anna rocked in the seat. "Rudy! Remember, I'm in the car, too! Be careful!"

Somehow he got her to the emergency room and checked in. He had expected to wait for hours in the emergency waiting room, but immediately an orderly put Anna into a wheelchair and led him upstairs to the maternity ward. Rudy didn't want to go, but put on a brave face. Anna was tightly holding his hand.

Upstairs, nurses assisted Anna in changing into a hospital gown and then into a bed. Anna's doctor had been summoned; he examined her and announced that she was dilated nine centimeters now. Everything was proceeding normally. Rudy was allowed to sit by her side and wait.

And wait.

And live through her contractions.

Rudy thought he was going to die. Previously, when he had thought of Anna giving birth, he had pictured one medium-sized pain followed by a squirt of baby and peace. He was unprepared for the ordeal that was taking place.

By the time Anna was fully dilated it was seven hours later. Both of them were drenched in sweat. Rudy's hand, where Anna had gripped it, was numb, and when they took her to the delivery room the blood rushed back with a vengeance. He shook his hand and massaged it, wondering what to do with himself.

It turned out there was *another* waiting room, this one for expectant fathers. The nurse showed him where it was and assured him that the doctor would be out as soon as his baby was born. There was only one other occupant, a big, beefy, red-faced man with an unshaven face. He hung his head and wept openly into his hands, bringing out a red railroad man's handkerchief to blow his nose noisily. Rudy bought himself a cup of coffee from the beverage machine located there, and approached the man, clearing his throat to warn him he was coming. The man looked up, and Rudy saw absolute terror in his eyes. Rudy introduced himself. The other man choked out that he was Jacob Smith.

Rudy sat down gingerly next to Jacob. "Is your wife all right?"

Jacob sobbed, "Yes."

"Is this your first baby?"

"Uh-huh," Jacob said. "But she's so little, and I'm so big! *Why* did I do this to her? That baby's going to rip her in two!"

Rudy paled, and silently returned to the other side of the waiting room to think while Jacob continued to sob.

Twenty minutes later the door to the waiting room opened, and a doctor appeared with a baby in his arms. Both Rudy and Jacob rose. "Jacob Smith?" the doctor asked, looking at both of them. Rudy returned to his chair, and Jacob stepped forward. "This is your son."

Jacob finally stopped crying and awkwardly held the bundle that was offered to him. "Is this all of him?" he asked.

"Uh, yes, he's all there. Very healthy. Seven pounds, five ounces. Your wife's been taken back to her room."

Jacob looked up in alarm. "Is she okay?"

"She did wonderfully. You can go see her now, Mr. Smith."

The waiting room door closed behind them; Rudy could hear Jacob saying, "But he's so *tiny*," as the door swished closed. And Rudy was alone.

It was 11:00 in the morning, and he finally realized that he had forgotten to call work to let them know that Anna was having her baby. He dug in his pockets for change and was about to insert a dime into the pay phone when the door to the waiting room opened again. His heart skipped a beat, but it was only another crumpled father being led in to wait out his wife's delivery. Rudy was connected to the administrative office where he worked at once.

"Rudy, is that you?" asked a female voice. He thought it was Susan.

"Yes," he said.

"Did your wife have her baby?"

"She's having it right now. I'm sorry I forgot to call in," Rudy apologized. "Let Hank and the others know. I'll be off for two weeks now."

"We figured it out when you didn't show up this morning and didn't answer your phone at home," Susan laughed. "Just do us a favor and give us a call when the baby's born, all right? We're all fairly excited about it."

Rudy agreed, and hung up.

He sat down again and regarded the other man occupying the waiting room. He was just about to get another cup of coffee and introduce himself, when the waiting room door opened once again. This time it was Anna's doctor, holding a blue bundle.

"Mr. Baumann."

He had Rudy's attention at once. "I'm Rudy Baumann."

"This is your son, Mr. Baumann." He gently laid the baby in Rudy's arms and instructed him on holding the boy's head. Rudy eagerly looked at him for signs of himself or Anna in the baby's features, but the baby only looked red, wrinkled, and chinless. He looked up at the doctor questioningly. "He's absolutely perfect; eight pounds, one ounce. Anna's doing fine. She's very tired, but you can see her now. Follow me," the doctor instructed, and held the door open for Rudy. The new father cradled his son to him as if he were the most precious thing on earth. He threw a backwards glance at the lone man seated there as he left the waiting room; he had a wistful expression on his face. Rudy knew how he felt.

Anna was sitting up and smiling tiredly as Rudy entered the room. *Is it this light or is she glowing?* marveled Rudy. He knew how agonizing her labor had been. How could she smile now? He carefully handed her the baby and watched as Anna looked down at the wrinkled gnome with absolute adoration, and he knew why she was smiling. He kissed her and the baby gently.

The baby started fussing, and Anna calmly exposed her breast and guided him to her nipple as Rudy watched. She looked up and smiled again, and reached for Rudy's hand. "We agreed that if it was a boy, we'd call him John Rudolph, right?" she asked, and Rudy nodded. "I love you, Rudy."

"I love you so very much, Anna. You're such a beautiful mother," Rudy said with deep sincerity.

In what seemed to be no time at all, a nurse came in to take John from Anna and put him in the nursery with the other babies. By that time, the baby had been fed and was fast asleep. She turned to Rudy. "You can visit as long as you'd like, but Anna here needs some rest. I bet you didn't get much sleep last night, yourself."

"No, I didn't," Rudy admitted, but he felt wide awake and ready to take on the world. The nurse smiled and left with the baby.

"She's right, you know," Anna said. "Why don't you get some rest? And oh, please call Karen and let her know. Her phone number is in the back of the phone book at home."

Rudy nodded, kissed her, and was almost to the door when she called him back. "Rudy, I know it's probably no use," she began, then bit her lip. "Do you think . . . do you think you could try calling Dad to let him know? Johnnie is his first grandchild. I would so like to see him."

Rudy stiffened, remembering the letter he had destroyed. He forced himself to relax and appear normal. "I'll try. I'll be back again after supper. That should give us both some time to rest, okay?"

"Okay, Sweetie," Anna smiled and slid down into the sheets.

Rudy sat in his car in the emergency room parking lot, wondering what to do. Anna's father and her friend Karen were both potential troublemakers. Now that he had his own wife and son, nobody else was needed. But Anna had asked him to call. Well, he would call, but he could make sure that neither of them felt the need to intrude in his home.

He called Karen first. She was at work, and when Rudy announced that John Rudolph Baumann had joined the human population, she squeaked and announced it to the other tellers. There were many questions and squeals of delight. Karen said,

"Tell Anna I'll be there to see her this weekend, and I'll bring as many of us as my car can hold."

"I really don't think that's a good idea, Karen," Rudy told her. "Anna's very, very tired, and the doctor's instructed that she have complete rest."

"Was there a problem with the delivery?" Karen asked in a worried tone.

"Not really. It just took a long time, and it wore her out."

"Well, how long do we have to wait to see her?" Karen persisted.

"Karen, I really can't say for sure. How am I supposed to know? I'm not a doctor," Rudy said sharply.

There was a pause on Karen's end of the line.

"Well, anyway, she wanted me to tell you, and I have," Rudy finished abruptly. "Goodbye."

And he hung up the phone.

The next call to tackle was to Harold Christianson. Rudy debated about whether to make the call at all. If he told Anna that Christianson had hung up on him and told him never to bother him again, how would she know the difference? Unless that loudmouth Karen called him and spoiled everything. Yeah, he'd better call him.

Rudy called him at the real estate agency, hoping that Christianson would be out showing a house, but he was out of luck. The secretary transferred him at once.

"This is Harold Christianson. May I help you?"

Rudy took a deep breath. "This is Rudy Baumann. You remember, your daughter's *husband?*" He added that last with the edge of a sneer in his voice.

There was a sharp intake of breath on the other end. "Is Anna all right?"

"Yes, she's fine. She just had her baby."

Christianson waited for more details. When it was obvious that no more were coming, he asked, "Well, was it a boy or girl?"

"We had a boy."

"What's his name?" Christ, it was like pulling teeth getting information out of this Baumann.

"John Rudolph."

"My father's name was John," Christianson said. Quick tears stung his eyes.

"Yes, we know that. Well, I just thought I'd let you know."

"Baumann, wait! What hospital is she in?" Christianson demanded. Now that his grandson was born, Anna *couldn't* refuse to see him.

"Anna asked me to call you, *Harold*," Rudy let his full disdain creep into his voice, "but just to let you know. I don't think you should try to see her."

"Why not? She's my daughter!"

"She wants *us* to have a family, and *you* want to split it up," Rudy snapped. "Just like in the letter you sent to her. You'd just upset her, and she doesn't need that."

"Anna showed you that?" Christianson gasped, disbelieving.

"Of course she did! You disowned her, remember? Threw her out when she was pregnant. Well, we don't need you. I don't want you in my house, and I don't want you bothering my wife. Got it?" Rudy barked.

Christianson did indeed get it, and Rudy got what he wanted: Christianson slammed the phone down in his ear.

Satisfied, Rudy replaced the phone. Now he could truthfully report to Anna that he had called and told her father about Johnnie, and that her father had slammed the phone down on him. He climbed the stairs, whistling, and in no time at all, he was sleeping peacefully in his own bed.

---

It was a very somber Anna who rode home from the hospital with her new baby and her husband a few days later.

"Why so quiet?" Rudy asked. "Are you feeling all right?"

"I'm feeling fine, Honey," Anna answered. "I just can't believe that Karen didn't come to see me in the hospital."

"Well, don't let that worry you. People get on with their own lives. Maybe you'll hear from her soon," Rudy said, patting Anna's knee. *I wouldn't count on it, though,* he smirked to himself.

"All the other mothers had tons of visitors, family and friends, and I only had *you*," Anna said, looking out the side window of the car sadly.

"Are you complaining?" Rudy smiled.

"Oh, Honey, you know I loved seeing you," Anna said quickly, touching his hand. "All the same, though, I felt a little jealous and lonely."

"Well, you have nothing to feel jealous about. You've got tons of flowers and plants and gifts," Rudy told his wife, a little irritation seeping into his voice. "Don't forget, I had to carry them all to the car."

It was true. The inside of the car smelled like a flower shop.

"I guess it's just those post-partum blues they told me about," Anna said thoughtfully. "Yes, I guess that's what it must be. After all, I have the best family in the world all to myself now."

"Exactly," Rudy said, cheering up a little.

"I must be a fool. I thought that when you called Dad, he'd forgive me and come running," Anna murmured thickly, tears threatening. "I can't understand why he'd slam the phone down on you like that."

"I'm sorry, Anna," Rudy lied. "I couldn't understand it myself, but you know your father better than I do. All we can do is hope he comes around in time."

A tear escaped Anna's eye and rolled down her cheek; she wiped it away impatiently with the back of her hand. "You're right, of course, Rudy. I guess I'll have to let him make his own decisions."

"Right," Rudy answered.

At home, he settled her and little Johnnie quickly inside, unloaded the car, and closed and locked the front door of the house. *Now,* he thought, *real life begins. I have my family and I will keep them. Things will be just the way I want them.*

Rudy hadn't thoroughly thought the situation out, however. He hadn't reckoned on the effects of having a new baby in the house. Johnnie demanded almost all of Anna's attention during her waking hours, which were few, since she was still breast-feeding him. The tidy little house soon became a foreign mess, with baby things all over the place. Johnnie woke and cried to be fed and changed every few hours, and it soon exhausted both of them. Although Anna loved her husband's attentions and affections, she made it clear that sex was out of the question, for the moment.

It wasn't long before spats eked out between the new parents. "Can't you shut that kid up?" Rudy would complain, waking in the middle of the night to Johnnie's howls.

"Why, yes, I can," Anna would say tartly. "I can get up and feed him and change him, if you'll let me go."

In the absence of friends her own age, Anna had befriended old Mrs. Kleigman next door, who had had plenty of experience in raising her own children. When she had questions about the baby, she would take Johnnie next door and spend time with the old lady, who was glad for the company. Rudy also resented this. He had his own ideas about how children should be raised, and that old bat certainly wasn't needed. When he told Anna that, she merely turned up her nose and marched straight out the door to Mrs. Kleigman's house, leaving Rudy to simmer and stew.

When his vacation days expired and he finally went back to work, Rudy was more than ready to go. He was sick of hearing nothing except what little Johnnie did today, and he yearned for adult male companionship. Back at work, he was treated as a hero, which he quite enjoyed. And it felt good doing familiar, physical labor. When he arrived home, he was greeted warmly by Anna. Although he had to listen to everything that the baby did all day while he was gone, her attitude toward him had warmed in his absence. She was genuinely happy to see him every day. And he had to admit that even though Johnnie was still a pain in the ass, the little kid *was* cute, at times. He had a special time with Johnnie after supper and before the baby was put down for the night, during which the house and baby were both clean. He'd play with the baby during this time and enjoyed Johnnie's gurgled language. On the more pleasant weekends weather-wise, he'd take Anna and Johnnie for drives or for walks in the park, and he also enjoyed the women who would invariably stop them to coo at Johnny and comment on how much he looked like his father.

The only downer now was his sex life, which had ground almost to a halt. According to Anna's doctor, it was perfectly all right to resume normal sexual relations, but at the end of a day with Johnnie, Anna was exhausted and fell asleep almost as soon as her head touched the pillow. And, if she *did* condescend to a little roll in the hay, little Johnnie would usually start crying before Rudy was completely finished with her. That baby's cry was like a bucket of ice water being thrown over both of them. Anna would immediately freeze up and get up out of bed to attend to him, and Rudy would lie there in the dark, stewing and waiting for her. By the time she got back to bed, she was no longer in the mood, and if Rudy insisted and she complied, it was like making love to a corpse. Rudy's manhood would shrivel, and he blamed Anna for what he perceived as a lack of prowess on his part.

As time went on, his anger and resentment grew more difficult to control, and it roiled black and green under the surface.

# CHAPTER
# Nineteen

Anna's friend Karen felt as if a part of her life had been ripped away. She had been the one to convince Anna to see Rudy in the first place; and she and Anna had been so close at one time. Now, if she believed Rudy when she called to try to talk to Anna, her friend had no time for her at all.

She consulted her landlady. Mrs. Sherwood was of the opinion that Anna's father had hurt her so deeply, that she had shut all thoughts of the town of Kenton out of her mind. She clucked and shook her head. "Harold and Anna. Who would think that there were two such stubborn people on this planet? Maybe I have to work on Harold some more."

In the meantime, Anna's father wasn't about to give up on his daughter. Like Karen, his every attempt at communication with his daughter was blocked by Baumann. However, he had resources that Karen didn't have. He hired a private detective.

After two weeks of watching the Baumann home, the detective could only report back that Anna and Rudy seemed reasonably happy together, and that Anna seemed to be totally devoted to her husband and son. Christianson was left out, and he felt it with every bone in his body. Sylvia Sherwood's campaign to soften him up had worked, but it appeared that it was too little, too late. He gave up on his daughter and grandson, and grieved. Sylvia was there to soften the blow, and somehow, life went on.

Rudy fought a brilliant battle against his resentment and the need to drink. It lasted until after John was two years old.

*Finally*, the little shit was walking, talking, and sleeping throughout the night. Rudy's sex life was back to the pre-Johnnie days, and Anna initiated encounters as often as Rudy did. He quite enjoyed that. And he discovered that Johnnie was like a miniature adult, with his own personality and preferences. Most importantly, as Johnnie grew, he began to look like Rudy's twin brother. Blonde hair, blue eyes, tall—he even had Rudy's chin. Daddy was so proud.

Then Anna got pregnant again, and Rudy was *livid.*

She told him one night while they were having coffee after supper. Rudy had seemed to really come around to enjoy being a father, and Anna half-expected joy from him. The other part of her remembered those first very uncomfortable months with Johnnie, and worried that they would come again.

To her shock, Rudy jumped up from the kitchen table and *screamed* at her.

"*How could you let this happen?*" he raged. "Aren't you on some kind of birth control?"

Anna closed her gaping mouth and set her jaw. "It happened *exactly* the way that it happened when Johnnie was conceived," she spat back. "I was there, but *so were you.* And it seems to me that you didn't mind a bit when it happened. As for birth control, I don't *want* to take pills, and I don't have the money for them, anyway. Why don't you just use a condom?"

Johnnie began to cry from his play pen in the living room. "Mama, Mama!" he called tearfully.

Anna threw Rudy a dirty look and started to move past him to attend to Johnnie. "*Now* look what you've done!" she scolded. "Johnnie's all upset."

Rudy's fingers hooked into claws; he wanted to strangle her. Instead, he grasped a kitchen chair and threw it against the back door. It landed with a crash, shattering the door's window panes, and sending shards of broken glass all over the kitchen. The vinyl and metal chair lay on its side in the middle of the mess.

Johnnie screamed in fear.

Anna gaped, then glared at him. "Are you *crazy?*" she yelled. "What's the matter with you?"

Rudy glared back. He wanted to crush her skull. Instead, he grabbed his jacket from the hook on the kitchen wall and stalked over the broken glass out into the evening, slamming the door behind him. It rocked the house satisfactorily.

There was no question here, no question at all, folks. He needed a drink, and he needed to be away from that hell hole he called home. Rudy headed to the bars.

It was if he had never left his party life. All of his single friends were still single, still drinking, and still ready to buy him as much beer as he could stand. He ended up at Calhoun's, where he willingly joined Bert and Calvin at the bar, and spent the hours until closing time complaining about the cunning little bitch at home who had trapped him into marriage. Once his sworn enemies, beer made them fast friends again. Cal suggested that he kick her and the rugrat out. After all, it was *Rudy's* house.

Rudy fully agreed with him.

Anna spent the night packing her and Johnnie's things.

When Rudy arrived home he was ready for battle. He had decided that Anna *must* have been whoring around. That was what she must have been doing with all her free time while he was at work, trying to make enough to pay the bills. One kid was bad enough, he had decided. There just wasn't room for another in his life, especially when the little brat wasn't even his. Anna could just pack her and Johnnie's things and move in with her pimp.

When he walked into the house, Anna was sitting at the kitchen table writing him a good-bye letter. Johnnie was asleep on the living room sofa, and her packed suitcases were by the front door. Anna flashed him a scathing look as he tumbled into the house, and informed him that she was leaving him. It was the last time she would ever do that.

Whereas just minutes ago he had wished his pregnant wife and child out of his life forever, *nobody* would just up and walk out on Rudy Baumann. By God, something like this would have serious consequences! He knocked Anna out of her chair and onto the floor with his first punch. When he was finished with her, Anna had suffered two black eyes, a broken nose and arm, various cuts and bruises, a loose tooth, and a kick to her right kidney.

When he was finished with her, Johnnie was screaming again, and Anna could barely move. Rudy sat down heavily on one of the kitchen chairs, swaying. He was drunk to the point of almost passing out, and he struggled to wind his thoughts around what had just happened. Anna had to call the ambulance herself, and crept outside to wait with Johnnie in the dark while Rudy sat bewildered in the wreckage of the kitchen. He didn't know why Anna wanted to leave him and he had no idea why he had become so violent with her.

In the hospital Emergency Room, the young doctor in charge of her case asked her what had happened. Crying hysterically, Anna refused to answer; she was only concerned about the baby she was carrying inside her. "Is my baby all right?" she asked, over and over.

Holding his questions for the moment, the doctor examined her, pronounced the baby safe, but told her she would need her arm set and that she would need several stitches. She would have to stay in the hospital, and find someone to take care of her son while she recuperated. Where was her husband?

When she wouldn't answer, the doctor excused himself and returned with a social worker. Marion Handley was seasoned in the specialty of family violence; she had seen plenty of it over the years and it looked just like this. She introduced herself, and held the sleeping Johnnie in her arms as she sat next to the gurney with the tiny, broken girl curled on her side.

"Mrs. Baumann, the people here are going to take care of you. I need to know some things, though, okay?"

Anna nodded.

"Did your husband do this?"

Anna said nothing. She only closed her eyes.

"If he did, you can press charges and have him arrested. He'll be put in jail," Marion informed Anna.

The green eyes flew open. "No!" she croaked.

"Then he did do it?" Marion pressed.

Anna cried some more and nodded in the affirmative. "But don't send him to jail," she begged. "He's never done anything like this before. We were arguing earlier, and then he went out and got drunk. He only hit me because I was going to leave him."

Marion busied herself with shifting Johnnie to put him over her other shoulder while she thought sardonically, *Nope, never heard* this *one before.* "Mrs. Baumann—Anna—you have to stay in the hospital for the next few days. Do you want me to send your son back to your husband so that *he* can take care of him?"

Anna vigorously shook her head 'no.' "Rudy has to work, and anyway, he doesn't have the patience."

"I have someone who can take care of Johnnie for a while, in a safe place," Marion informed her, "but you have to think of what you're going to do and where you're going to go when you leave here. Do you have a place to go?"

Anna's lips started to tremble. "I don't know."

"Do you have any money?"

"No," Anna answered, "but the doctor said not to worry about it."

"I'm not worried about the hospital bill, Anna, I'm just thinking ahead to what you'll do when you're able to take care of yourself and Johnnie again," Marion told her gently.

Anna began to cry again. Everything seemed upside down and inside out. "I just can't think now," she wailed. A nurse rolled in a tray with instruments and bandages.

"I understand. You're in a lot of pain and you've had a shock," Marion assured her. "Look, they need to get started with you, and I need to get this young man to bed. I'm going to leave my card with the doctor, and he's going to make sure you have it. I'll be back to see you tomorrow afternoon to give you a report on how your son's doing and see how you are."

She stood and Johnnie woke up. "Mommy!" he called, reaching for Anna. Marion patiently held him so that Anna could kiss him and tell him he was going to go to bed. Johnnie yawned hugely and dozed as Marion shifted him to her shoulder again. The cubicle's curtain swished, and they were gone. Anna gave herself over to the doctor and nurses.

---

Morning light poured through the windows, and still Anna slept on. She had looked terrible in the Emergency Room the night before, but she looked worse now. Both eyes were swollen shut. Her face and arms and legs were a mass of bruises, and tape and stitches dotted her face. Her left arm was in a cast from the wrist to the elbow, and an IV was attached to her right hand. Her blonde hair had been washed of blood and hung limply on her pillow. Rudy was horrified. He couldn't bring himself to approach the bed or to wake Anna. He stood there in the doorway of the hospital room with his arms full of flowers and candy, as if glued to the spot. Anna's roommate, a middle-aged woman awaiting surgery, said loudly, "You the husband?"

Rudy jumped. He hadn't been aware that anyone else was in the room. "Y-yeah," he stuttered.

The lady glared at him. "Did you do that to her?"

Rudy's heart pounded, but under that knowing gaze he couldn't lie. "Yes," he said quietly. "I didn't mean to. I don't know what got into me."

"I really couldn't care less *why* you did that. But you did. You deserve to go to jail, and I hope she divorces you and takes everything you've got. If I were a man I'd fix it so *you* were in a hospital bed looking like she does," the woman said heatedly.

"I'm so sorry," Rudy started.

"Sorry doesn't cut it, mister. Sorry doesn't help a broken body or a broken heart. *I know.* My first husband did the same to me," she continued relentlessly. "I hope you aren't going to give her any of that bullshit about not doing it again, because you will. And next time it'll be worse. And the time after that it'll be worse yet. Men like you don't stop."

Rudy was so stunned by the woman's onslaught that he didn't notice that Anna, who couldn't open her eyes, had awakened and was weakly trying to pull herself into a sitting position.

"I *promise* I'll stop. I'll quit drinking and get myself right," Rudy said with true sincerity in his voice. "I *love* my wife."

"True love, huh?" Anna's roommate snorted. "I bet she's really glad that you don't *hate* her or she'd be dead. Look, just get on out of here. She doesn't need flowers or candy. And she doesn't need *you*. She needs medical care and rest, not for *you* to come to her sniveling because *you* beat her up." With finality the woman picked up the morning paper and shook it out noisily, blocking her face from Rudy's view.

Without leaving the flowers or candy, and without saying another word, Rudy *did* leave. He walked the streets of Duluth for two hours as the flowers wilted and the chocolate melted in his hands, and ended up throwing them in a trash can. It looked like his brief marriage was over.

---

Marion Handley wished Anna and little Johnnie good luck as she stowed them into a taxi at the front doors of the hospital. It had been fifteen days since she had first met them in the Emergency Room. Anna's face still showed signs of swelling and bruising, and she would wear the cast for a while yet, but she looked a million times better. Anna had made arrangements to talk to a lawyer about a divorce. Until the divorce was final, she planned for herself and her son to stay in the family home while Rudy moved in with one of his buddies. Marion shook her head with worry. Although Anna had sounded strong emotionally and reasonably determined, there were too many things that could possibly go wrong with this plan. When the taxi was out of sight, she returned to her office. *Well, Anna,* she thought, *my prayers are with you. It's your choice, whatever you do. You're an adult, and I can't make you do what I want you to do. Please, God, let her be all right.* And she turned to the next file on her stack.

Rudy wasn't at home when Anna let herself in. The house felt cold, empty, like its heart had died. Anna walked around the house, just looking at things, while Johnnie plowed into his toys with enthusiasm. Their bags were still packed and where she had left them, but the house was uncharacteristically immaculate, considering her lengthy absence. Upstairs, on the bed, she found a letter from Rudy. She set down the bag of hospital supplies and medication with which she had been released, and sat on the bed staring at the letter. With some misgivings, she finally opened it. She remembered that Rudy didn't even know that she had overheard what had been said between him and her roommate, and he hadn't returned to the hospital. Who knew what he had written?

It began, *Dear Anna.* Anna got that far and blinked at the sting of quick tears. She pulled a tissue from the box by the bed, wiped her eyes and read on with determination. *I don't know when you will be home or even if you'll be home, but I've left this letter for you. I'm so sorry, Honey.*

At this Anna dabbed her eyes again, and when they were clear enough to see, she continued reading.

> *I love you so very much. I've always loved you. I haven't had a drop of beer since that night I hurt you. I never will again. My whole attitude is different. Please believe me. I wish you would give me a chance, just one more chance, to show you I've changed. I realize that you may have already made up your mind to divorce me* (here his writing wobbled

a little) *and I know I deserve it. I won't stand in your way, if that's really what you want. Just tell me, and I'll do whatever you want me to do. But Honey, if you can remember the good times, and if you love me at all after what I did, please give me another chance.*

*I love you, Honey.*
*Rudy*

Anna dropped the letter back onto the bed. Suddenly she wanted a bath, a hot bath to take away the ice that had formed inside her stomach. She checked on Johnnie downstairs and found that he had fallen asleep in the midst of his toys. Awkwardly she carried him up to his room and slipped him under the covers. She retrieved her suitcase from the living room, and hefted it onto the bed. When she opened it, the first thing she saw had been the last thing she had packed—almost as an afterthought. It was their wedding picture. It was a shock, but she carefully laid it aside on the bed and dug out her bathrobe, slippers, and clean clothes.

In the warmth of the bathtub, she held her left arm out of the water wrapped in a garbage bag and tried to keep her thoughts free-flowing, but always they came back to that damned picture. *Love, honor, and obey.* That was what she had agreed to when she married Rudy. And she had meant it. She still loved Rudy. She had never stopped loving him. But honor and obey? Not if he was going to beat her. Not if he didn't want the child she carried. *Until death do you part.* She shivered with sudden goose pimples. Was she willing to go on living with him for the rest of her life knowing he was capable of ending it? She thought of living out her life without him, just a single mom with two children in this house. Could she ever love anybody else?

The water was just not warm enough to soothe her. Anna got out and dried herself quickly. Despite the chill that she felt, the mirror was clouded over with steam, and she flapped her towel at it to get rid of the moisture faster. When she did, she saw her reflection and wished she hadn't thought to look at herself. Without thinking, she grabbed for her makeup and applied it, doing the best she could to hide what her husband had done. In the bedroom she applied perfume and searched for a blue top, Rudy's favorite. She had unpacked both her and Johnnie's things and was in the kitchen giving Johnnie his supper while she waited for the right time to pop the meatloaf in the oven before she realized she had made up her mind already.

She was stricken. *Is that all it takes? Just a note from him, and you're ready to come back?* Anna thought, furious with herself. *After all that reading and talking and counseling you went through at the hospital, you make it so easy for him. What's the matter with you?* And another part of her said, *Yeah, but they don't understand. We love each other. It'll never happen again. I can do my part to prevent it. I was pissed that night, royally pissed and out of control myself. Just see what happens.*

An hour later the aroma of baking meatloaf and potatoes filled the house, and Anna was watching cartoons on TV with Johnnie, when she heard the kitchen door open. In an instant Johnnie was up and running, yelling, "Daddy! Daddy'th home!" She sat where she was, and in a minute Rudy walked into the room holding Johnnie in one arm. He had lost weight, and his eyes looked haunted. He set Johnnie on the floor and stayed where he was.

"Hi, Anna," he said.

"Hi, Rudy," she answered, and then she was up and in his arms.

That night she slept soundly and dreamlessly in the cradle of her husband's arms. She had accepted his promises at face value; he had treated her like a princess. The future once again looked bright. *People can change,* she had decided.

It was a year before he yelled at her again, after Larry had been born. It was two years of verbal haranguing and threats before he touched her in anger again. After that first shove, it took very little time for things to nosedive into slaps, kicks, and punches for both her and the children. Each time he promised not to do it again. Each time she accepted his promises. And each time there was a shorter 'honeymoon' before it started again, even worse than before. Life became, for Anna and the children, the litany of Rudy Baumann: "Now pay attention, because, by God, if you *don't* pay attention, there will be consequences. *Serious* consequences!"

Looking back at it, Anna thought that the hospital social worker, Marion Handley, and her hospital roommate had both been right. It *was* an old pattern, and she had fallen into its trap. But *she* had also been right. People *could* change. She and their three boys (the last of whom was Frankie, conceived one night when Anna had refused sex and Rudy had performed a drunken rape, and who cost her two broken ribs and a concussion when Rudy found out she was pregnant again) had learned to predict Rudy's behavior and pretty much steer clear of him. It was a lonely life in many ways, but it was a *familiar* life, and Anna grew too weary to think of trying anything else.

The Anna she had known had gone to sleep. *This* Anna was a robotic shell who lived her life waiting to die.

# CHAPTER
## Twenty

Anna and the boys saw little of the fruits of Rudy's labors. It was his personal opinion that the family was only as happy as the head of the household, and it took several beers in several different bars each night to make Rudy think he was happy.

The winters were the worst for them. Minnesota winters were harsh, to begin with; there would be consecutive weeks at times when the temperature never reached zero degrees Fahrenheit. Fierce prairie winds that blew in from the west, or worse yet, from the north, dropped the wind chill factor to tremendous depths. Minnesota winters were also long, and if a building was not framed in by the middle of November so that carpenters could continue inside the building, there were layoffs. Rudy was always happy to take a layoff and draw his share of unemployment insurance from the Government. However, it also meant that the head of the household was available to pursue his personal hobby, that of drinking, full time.

Rudy was a cheerful, entertaining drunk (or so it appeared to him and his drinking buddies) when he started, but by the second six-pack he was able to see a myriad of faults in others, and happy to share his opinions. This was thirsty work. By the third six-pack he became sullen and argumentative, and true destruction started with the fourth six-pack. Chairs were likely to be thrown through windows or at Anna, and Rudy was handy with his fists and his belt alike with his wife and children.

During those times the older boys were glad to go to school

to get out of Rudy's way, which left Anna at home all day with him and little Frankie, and sometimes with his drinking friends as well. She looked for work outside the house to supplement their income and get out from under Rudy's feet, and was hired as a bookkeeper for a small department store. She paid Mrs. Kleigman next door to look after Frankie for several hours each working day, and truly enjoyed her brief respite from home life.

Her employment lasted less than two weeks. Anna was just about to take her lunch break one day when a commotion in the front of the store caused her to look out between the Venetian blinds that separated the office from the store. It was Rudy, roaring drunk and demanding to see his wife. The store owner and two salesmen tried to nip it in the bud by escorting him back onto the sidewalk outside, but he stood fast and bellowed for Anna.

Humiliated, Anna grabbed her coat and purse, and held her flaming face down as she hurried to the front of the store. It was the Christmas season, and the store was packed with holiday shoppers who were now staring at the spectacle her husband had caused. When Rudy saw her, he shook himself loose from the hold of the three men and towered above his petite wife, shouting that laundry was piling up at home while she sat on her ass at work all day. The best Anna could manage in the situation was to walk outside so that Rudy would follow her. Later that day she returned to work while Rudy slept on the sofa in front of the television, and tried to resume her book work. It wasn't very long, however, before the store owner came into the office and told her he couldn't afford to keep her at the store. Her husband had scared several customers away and erased the spirit of the season from many others, who fled the store after dropping prospective purchases where they had been standing. Anna was fired.

When she returned home, Rudy was awake, hungry for his supper. When she told him that she had lost her job, he punctuated his disgust with her by slapping her face, hard. Ashamed of her swollen lip and black eye, she sent John to collect Frankie from the neighbor's house. When her tears were shed and the house work finished, Anna went to bed alone that night. She mourned the death of her love for her husband, and briefly considered divorce for a second time. But where would she go with three boys to raise alone, and how would she do it? She was too tired; she had no money; the thought of starting a new life was overwhelming to her; she had no family or friends to whom she thought she could turn.

In the depths of her depression, she was as firmly caught in Rudy's web as he had ever hoped. She determined to be a better wife and mother, and would never try to work outside the home again.

---

Another four years of their seventeen years of marriage passed with Anna in an emotional coma, her sons fending for themselves, and Rudy trying to make himself happy.

It was without any real surprise that Rudy eventually started drinking at work as well as away from work. When he was caught, he was fired. He easily landed another job on his general reputation as an excellent carpenter, and repeated the process of getting fired. After his third job termination because of drinking and fighting on the job, Rudy was blackballed by building contractors, and couldn't even get a job digging holes and clearing away trash for them.

Hank Masters, the supervisor from his first job, spotted him at Calhoun's one night when Rudy first entered, ready to start his evening's entertainment. Hank pulled him into a back booth, and convinced Rudy to put off his first beer of the night by ordering food and coffee for them both. Rudy would never turn down free food, so he sat back easily on the bench. As they ate, Hank told Rudy outright that there was plenty of work for him in this city *as long as he stayed sober on the job*. Otherwise, there was nothing.

Always ready for a fight, Rudy leapt to his feet, but Hank was ready for him. He pulled him back down into his seat even as Rudy was on his way upward, and continued as if nothing had happened.

"Rudy, don't you have a wife and three kids?"

Rudy stared at him belligerently. "So?"

"So how are you supporting them? Where does your money go?" Hank asked.

"Well, for your information, I got bills—hell, everybody's got bills," Rudy replied. "And those boys eat like horses."

"And is your family happy?" persisted Hank.

"Who the hell cares?" snapped Rudy.

"Rudy, I just bought you a meal and coffee. *I* care," Hank said. "You know what I think? I think you drink your money away and you beat your wife and kids just the same way you beat on others. And it's all because of the alcohol. You've already lost your work, Rudy. Don't lose your family, too."

Rudy stared at his former boss. No one had *ever* questioned *anything* he did since he ran away from old man Richter. No one except Anna. And *that* was far in the past, no question about it.

Rudy leaned toward Hank over the table. "Just who do you think you are?" he said in a low, menacing voice. "All this has nothing to do with you, *nothing*. My life is none of your damned business. I'll handle it."

"Like you handled your last job? I heard you were with another man on some scaffolding, drinking your lunch, and when he told you to get rid of it you knocked him twenty feet onto the ground. Broke his nose and his leg. Now *he's* out of work and his family is suffering, just because you couldn't keep your lips off your beer bottle long enough to do your job." Hank shook his head with disgust. "Aw, you're right, Rudy, old buddy. Your life is totally in control. You're doing just fine in your career—your career as the town drunk, that is."

Hank rose and threw some money on the table to cover the

bill and tip. "I'm sorry I cared enough about you and your family to talk to you. Better get busy. You're about a six-pack behind." He turned and left, leaving Rudy sitting in the booth, open-mouthed.

Recovering his composure, Rudy hunched over the table, rearranging the salt and pepper shakers. Soon the waitress approached, checked the bill and money, and asked if he wanted anything else. Rudy opened his mouth to order a beer . . . and closed it. Instead, he said, "Can I have some more coffee?"

He wanted to stay in the bar alone a while by himself, just drinking coffee and ice water and thinking. Hank Masters had left Calhoun's without knowing that his words would have an astonishing effect on Rudy and the lives of his family members. In his own mind, Rudy Baumann was the king of a castle where *he* called all the shots. Hank had pointed out a possible—just a *possible*—weakness in the defenses.

Eventually, Rudy went to the men's room to relieve the pressure on his bladder. *Would* he lose Anna? Lord, was it even *possible*? If it was obvious to Hank Masters, it could be obvious to anybody, and therefore maybe a *real* possibility. He thought back over the years to when they first met. She was tiny, with that bouncy, shiny blonde hair and sparkling green eyes, always smiling or laughing, it seemed. He smiled as he washed his hands, and then caught a glimpse of himself in the mirror as he reached for a paper towel. *Oh God*, he thought, *is that me?* Staring back at him was a man supposedly in the prime of his life. What he saw instead was long, greasy, messy hair, a day-old beard, bags under his eyes, and bleary blue eyes. He squinted, not used to the bright lights. That didn't make it any better. He threw the waste paper in the trash, missed, and bent to pick it up. *Funny,* he thought. *I can remember pissing on the walls in here and dumping the trash, thinking it was funny as hell. God, that is disgusting.*

Back in the booth, he ordered another cup of coffee and his attention was drawn to two men in the front of the bar. They were obviously drunk, staggering all over the place and trying to punch each other while shouting unintelligible obscenities at each other. There went the bartender, young, healthy, tall, and well-muscled, from behind the bar. One hand on the collar of each offender and they were lying on the sidewalk outside. From experience Rudy knew they were being banned from the bar. He started to smile at the familiarity of the scene, then stopped. That really wasn't so funny, was it? He wondered if they had families back at home that they yelled at and hit, and little flashbacks of his own family violence darted through his mind, quick and relentless and sharp-beaked as hummingbirds. He really didn't want to think about that right now, but once those thoughts started coming, they wouldn't stop.

Would Anna really leave him? Did Hank know something he didn't? He thought back to the first time he had beaten her, and the empty two weeks without her. He had wanted to kill himself, he was so lonely. Rudy had hated to look in a mirror during that period of time. The sight of himself had made him nauseous.

He wanted a beer.

He *didn't* want a beer.

Okay, he'd have *one* beer and go home.

In the end he left the bar and went straight home without that beer.

He walked in the darkness. His driver's license was in the hands of the Minnesota State Patrol at the moment, for drunken driving. The clear, clean night air should have cleared up his head, but it seemed to make it fuzzier. A headache started, and his jaw ached where it had been fractured. *Too much coffee,* he thought. *A beer would take care of that. No, no beer. Just for tonight. Let's see if I can make it just to tomorrow night. Funny, the only time I get a headache is when I'm* not *drinking.*

Rudy kept his promise to himself that night. When he opened the front door, there was the aroma of baking. Anna had made an apple pie, which was set in the middle of the kitchen table to cool. She and the kids were sitting in the living room, laughing at some movie, all together—without him. He couldn't remember the last time they laughed in enjoyment in front of him.

When he closed the door, Anna came to the kitchen and flicked on the light. The brightness caused his headache to blossom. "What happened? It's only 8:30."

Rudy rubbed his hands over his face and eyes, more to hide them from shame than to alleviate any pain, and said, "I have a headache. Do we have any aspirin?"

Concern and a little fright flashed over Anna's face. "Sure. I'll get it. Why don't you go upstairs and lie down? I'll bring it to you."

Not waiting for a reply, she hurried to the living room. Rudy heard low murmuring in there. She was probably warning them to *watch out, Dad's got a headache.* He sighed, took off his jacket and started to throw it on the kitchen table, then corrected himself and hung it up on the peg by the door. As he passed into the living room, John and Larry were busy turning off the television set and picking up empty soda cans from the floor. Only Frankie came to him and looked up at him. "Hi, boys," Rudy said.

John and Larry stood transfixed like a pair of deer in the headlights, not knowing what to do. Finally John said guardedly, "Hi, Dad. We were just going upstairs."

Rudy regarded his older sons and saw watchful fear in their eyes. He sighed, and then said, "You were watching a movie when I came in. Sounded pretty good. Go on and watch it. I've got a headache or I'd sit down and watch it with you. I think I'll just take a shower and go to bed, though." He started up the stairs. "Good night."

John and Larry looked at each other, then back at their father. "Good night, Dad," John said.

"Night," Larry said.

"Night-night, Daddy," Frankie said. "I love you." And he

looked up at his father with wide, clear, blue eyes full of adoration. Rudy hugged his youngest son to his legs, tears welling up in his eyes.

"Love you, too. I'll see you all at breakfast," he called, turning toward the stairs to hide the emotion in his face. Halfway up the stairs, he heard Frankie talking to his brothers..

"You know what? Daddy smells different."

---

Anna hurried to get the bottle of aspirin and a glass of water for her husband. *Something's going on,* she thought anxiously. *Please, God, let it be all right. Let it just be a headache, and let him just go to bed.* On her way out of the bathroom she met Rudy, and yelped in surprise. "Oh, Rudy, I thought you'd be in the bedroom," she breathed, watching his eyes carefully to see if they were narrowed. That usually meant she would be beaten.

Instead, Rudy's eyes remained steady for a moment, and then he looked over her shoulder into the brightly lit bathroom. "Thanks, Honey," he said, taking the aspirin and water from Anna. He gulped three down with all the water in the glass while she waited uncertainly. "I'm going to take a shower and shave. And then I think I'll just call it a night. You go ahead and watch that movie with the boys if you want."

Anna now felt a different type of fear well up in her. Was it a stroke coming on? A brain tumor? Maybe they should call an ambulance. She couldn't remember him calling her 'Honey' since their early days of fighting and making up. And usually when he came in from a night out, especially a *Friday* night out, his whole body language said, "Go ahead and knock this chip off my shoulder and see how fast I can pound you into hamburger." His shoulders would be twisted to the side, his chest pushed out, and his thumbs would be hooked into the belt loops of his pants. Now he just looked . . . tired. And shaving! At this hour of the night! What did it mean?

"Rudy, sit down on the toilet lid and I'll take your temperature," she offered, moving out of his way. He took her shoulders and willed her to look at him again. She did. Under his hands he could feel her thin shoulders trembling slightly and sighed again.

"Look, Anna, I'm not sick. I've just got a headache, and I think a shower and some sleep would help. I'll be all right," he tried to assure her.

Anna plunged ahead. "Rudy, what happened tonight? You're so different!" Suddenly she realized that the smell of beer wasn't on him—there was only the usual smoke and . . . was that the smell of *coffee* on his breath? Confused, she stopped and looked at him.

Rudy grimaced in recollection. "A *lot* happened tonight. I'll tell you about it in the morning, okay?" With his hands still on her bird-like shoulders he started to bend toward her to kiss her, and stopped at the startled look in her eyes. "Good night, Honey. Go on now, go watch your movie." And he moved past her into the bathroom.

Anna stared at the closed bathroom door. She didn't know whether he really wanted her to enjoy herself, or if this were only a test, to see where her loyalties lay. If it *was* a little test, the minute she got settled on the sofa he'd be down there dragging her off it, telling her that her place was in bed with him. When she heard the shower start and the shower curtain close, she went downstairs to sit with the boys and wait. Their enjoyment was spoiled, however. Rudy's moods dictated full attention in this family. Instead of watching the movie on television, they whispered to each other and looked at each other tensely.

When the bathroom door opened, all of them automatically looked toward the stairs, but they only heard Rudy move into the bedroom and close the door. Absolute silence ensued. They tried to relax, but it was impossible. Anna put little Frankie to bed, and John and Larry followed soon after. Alone in the living room, she still felt uneasy, not able to concentrate on the television but not wanting to go up to bed and risk starting something with Rudy. She pulled a tattered paperback out of her knitting bag, one that she had read many times over, and forced herself to read it until she couldn't keep her eyes open any longer. It was only then that she crept up the stairs in the dark and slipped into bed next to her husband.

Rudy wasn't asleep. He had downed more coffee tonight than he ever had, and his body wanted—no, *needed* a beer. He tried to concentrate on other things. He thought of Anna, how thin and scared she had looked. Had *he* done that to her? Unbidden, images of himself flowed past his mind's eye: drinking, fighting, yelling, beating her and the kids, sleeping it off, being pissed off at everything and everybody. How long had it been since she had tickled him to see him laugh? How long since she had looked at him with smoky green eyes full of wanting him? When was the last time that the boys threw themselves on him when he came home from the job, delighted that, "Daddy's home! Daddy's home!"

He had no job, no prospects if he didn't quit drinking, and the bills were mounting up. Late notices were stamped on all the utility bills, and he hadn't paid the taxes on their house in two years. One more missed tax payment and the city would seize the house for back taxes.

It all came down to his beverage of choice. Bottles swam before his eyes, frosty and soothing. Just waiting in the fridge.

God, he couldn't stand this! He slipped out of bed and found his slippers in the dark. His mouth felt dry, *very* dry, and his eyeballs were hot. His headache was gone, but he felt off-balance, like he really didn't know what to do with himself. Rudy supposed he really *didn't* know what to do with himself unless he had a bottle in his hand or was going to get that bottle.

He went downstairs. Two o'clock in the morning! He guessed he'd sit on the sofa and wait to fall asleep there or greet everybody else in the morning.

Rudy turned on the TV with the volume off, staring at the images on the screen. He thought of the Richters and that awful feeling he'd had when he saw old man Richter coming after him. That anxiety—that all-consuming, knee-weakening, turn-your-guts-to-water feeling. Richter never drank; he was simply always pissed off or ready to be pissed off, and could quote chapter and verse from his ever-present Bible to demonstrate why Rudy needed a pounding. Rudy was sure that when Richter came charging up to him and his sisters, they all wore the same expressions on their faces that he had seen on his own sons' faces tonight.

He rubbed his hands over his eyes and face again, and got up to get something to drink from the kitchen. He deliberately poured a full glass of cold water from the tap, not even daring to open the refrigerator door. On the way back to the sofa, his eyes fell on the rows of family pictures Anna had arranged on the living room wall. Happier times. Of course, people always took pictures of the happier times, not the bad ones. Anna's high school graduation picture. His sons' school pictures. Anna with her family at a picnic. His parents, Jeremy and Sandra Baumann: an old black and white photo of a happy, married couple in front of an old-fashioned log farm house. Where had that been? Iowa, wasn't it?

He took a long drink of water.

Yes, Iowa. Near a place called Apple Springs. According to the stories, his own father had gone crazy and killed his mother and three older brothers. Then some bear ate him. Christ, *that* was a crazy lie! No wonder he drank. But hey, if he remembered correctly, that farm was still Baumann property. Something about one of his ancestors leaving a trust fund set up so that Baumanns could always live there. Well, his sisters were all married and living right here in Duluth ("Know 'em when you see 'em but don't have much to do with 'em," he'd been fond of saying about them lately). As far as he knew, that left *him*. It might be he could just move them all into that farmhouse in Iowa and try to find carpentry work in Apple Springs. He was all washed up in Duluth.

Maybe it was time to try some new turf. Maybe Hank would write him a letter of recommendation if he promised not to drink.

Rudy finished off the water and placed the empty glass in the kitchen sink. His reflection stared back at him from the kitchen window. His eyes still felt gritty and he was getting tired, but he felt generally better now. Looked better, too. On the spur of the moment he tried a deep-knee bend right there in the kitchen. There was a loud, double *crack!* of his knees and it took all of his strength to stand up again. Maybe a little physical labor around the farm would help him get back into shape, as well.

Suddenly Rudy knew that if he went to bed now, he could sleep. Things might just turn out all right, after all. He just needed a little time, and Castle Rudy would be right as rain.

---

The next morning Anna woke to the smells of coffee brewing and bacon frying. Her eyes flew wide open at once; something was terribly wrong. She turned and glanced at Rudy's side of the bed. Gone! *Oh my God! Is Rudy . . .* cooking? she wondered as she shot out of bed and into her robe. Picking up the alarm clock and staring at it, she saw it was only 7:00 a.m., far too early for Rudy to be up on a Saturday morning—or any morning, for that matter, when he wasn't working. She was bewildered. What in heaven's name was going on?

Out on the landing, she passed John and Larry, who were on the alert in their pajamas and waiting for what would happen next. Neither had dared venture into the kitchen. Larry whispered, "It's Dad, and Frankie's down there with him."

Anna whispered back, "Everything okay?"

Both boys shrugged and nodded, then followed her as far as the doorway to the kitchen. Anna combed her hair with her fingers on the way, wondering how bad she looked. She sneaked a peek around the corner at the stove. There was Rudy, *dressed and shaved and showered*, and actually *smiling* as he listened to Frankie's chatter. He glanced up and spied her; she was caught. Willing her galloping heart to slow down, she came fully into the kitchen with a trial smile. "Good morning, Rudy! You're up early today. What's going on?"

She stopped at Frankie's chair and gave him a hug and a kiss, then tried to help make breakfast, but Rudy said, "This is *my* project today. Sit down and have some coffee." He looked back at the entrance to the living room and raised his voice cheerfully. "Larry! John! Come on out here. You're not fooling me. I can hear you breathing."

There was a moment of silence in which the boys just looked at each other, and then they slid into the kitchen. John and Larry stood there, looking uncertainly between their mother and their father, who was in the act of pouring coffee for their mother. "Sit down, boys, breakfast is about to be served. We have scrambled eggs and bacon. There's no toast. I guess I forgot about fixing the toaster. But there's orange juice."

John just couldn't hold it in any longer. He burst out, "Dad, what's *wrong* with you? You're acting so, so . . ."

Rudy replaced the coffeepot and faced his family. "So *nice*? So *normal*?"

Desperately John tried to read his father's mood, but it was impossible. It *felt* like a trick, like so many Bait and Switch games his father had played with them all over the years. John was mightily tired of it. Tired, and deep-down, boiling *angry*. All right, he'd bite. He looked his father straight in the eye and said, "Yes."

He squared his shoulders. He had been the man of the house for a long time now, even though he was only sixteen years old. If Dad wanted to come after him, he was ready. He'd had enough, and so had his brothers and Mom. But Dad's first punch had better kill him, or he'd go after his own father and put him out of their lives, forever.

Rudy looked at his son's eyes and the flush starting up his neck, and the message was loud and clear.

He cleared his throat, and looked around at all of them. Anna, John, Larry, even little Frankie were watching him carefully.

"Sit down, son," Rudy said. "Let's eat a normal breakfast, and while we eat I'll explain."

John had been prepared for battle and adrenaline was already pumping through him. It took an enormous effort to back off from the emotions that had been welling in him, but at last he sat down and picked up the pitcher of orange juice. It shook in his hand, but he managed to get it all in his glass.

Rudy poured himself some coffee, and while everyone else was eating, he began talking. He had their full attention.

"Look, last night I went out with the intention of having myself a party, but it didn't happen. Instead, I ran into . . . a friend, and we ate and drank coffee. He told me some things about myself that I didn't like hearing, some pretty ugly things. I spent the rest of the night thinking about them, and I want to apologize to you all." Rudy's voice became thick with unshed tears of remorse. He cleared his throat and went on.

"I'm an alcoholic. I admitted it to myself last night for the first time, and now I'm admitting it to you. Last night I stopped drinking, and it's been almost fifteen hours since I had a beer. I'll never have another. I hear that alcoholism is a disease, that you can't help it, kind of like an allergy to alcohol. Well, I just can't have it any more."

John and Larry glanced at each other quickly. The look said, *What's going on?*

Anna looked down at her coffee. She had heard many speeches of this same type over the years. They meant little.

Rudy continued, "I also have an attitude problem. I've done and said a lot of really rotten things to you all over the years. I think that maybe I was just treating you all the way *I* was raised; I don't know. I *do* know I'm all washed up in this town as far as a job in building construction is concerned. I can't bring in a decent income. But I'm asking you all to help me through this."

John was the first to speak, and his tone was angry. "How, Dad? How are we supposed to help *you?* And why should we? You haven't helped any of us much."

Anna gasped, and John felt Larry stiffen beside him.

But Rudy was ready. "If you don't want to help me, I can't blame you. *Any* of you. But I have a plan." This was met with dead silence. "Can I at least tell you about it?"

Anna glanced around the table at the boys, who were saying nothing. She said, "Of course, Rudy, tell us."

He cleared his throat again, and looked gratefully at his wife. "Okay, here goes. My—*our* family has a farm in Iowa. I want us to move there. There's no mortgage and no taxes to pay, the land is fertile, and I hear there are plants and factories in the area."

John and Larry started talking at the same time.

"*Move?* Away from our friends and school?"

"I don't want to move! The only thing wrong with Duluth is *in this house!*"

Rudy threw up his hands in a defensive motion. "Just hear me out, okay?"

Both of the older boys stared down at their half-eaten breakfasts, which were growing colder and greasier-looking by the second.

"If we move there, I'll have a chance for a clean, fresh start. Nobody knows this family down there, or what I've done in the past. I can be a whole new man. I want us to be a real family, and learn to work and play together. I want us to have a chance at normal life."

John asked, "Why can't we just stay here and do all that? You can stop drinking wherever you are. It doesn't have to be on some farm in Iowa. And for your information, Dad, without you around, things *are* normal."

Tensely Anna broke in. "John, that's enough! Don't talk to your father that way."

"He has every right to talk to me that way, Anna, and worse. And for *your* information, John, it *does* have to be on the Iowa farm. Because that's all I have left, besides this broken down house that keeps getting worse, and welfare checks. Because I still love you all, and I hope and pray that somewhere deep down inside you, you each have some of the love you used to have for me," Rudy said.

Anna thought of the letter that Rudy had written to convince her to stay all those years ago, and a small, ironic smile trembled on her lips. Same arguments, different day.

"I'll tell you what. My next check comes in two weeks. Give me that time to prove myself. If I slide back into drinking or nasty remarks, if I hit any of you or even anybody else, deal's off. I'll go alone to Iowa. John, Larry, you can both still graduate with your classes. Frankie, you can stay here with Mom and she can cash my welfare checks." He looked at each of them in turn.

"Even then, even if I prove myself, you don't have to go with me. I realize I caused all my own problems and I'm the one who should have to pay the price. So just *think* about it for a couple of weeks, okay? We'll all sit down two Saturdays from now, and each of us will have a say."

Anna looked at him thoughtfully. This was the most convincing he had ever been in their years together. This was her chance to get out, if that was what she wanted. She lowered her eyes and moved to pour more coffee for herself. *We'll see,* she thought.

John and Larry looked at each other once again. "All right, we'll think about it," John said.

Rudy sighed a breath of relief. "That's all I ask," he said, blinking back sudden tears. "That's all I have a right to."

As the boys pushed themselves from the table and started to clear the dirty dishes, Rudy said, "Why don't you boys just go spend time with your friends? I'll do your chores today. It'll give us all a break. Anna, I'll help you with the wash, and then we'll take the rest of what money I have on me and get groceries. And I'll have a try at the toaster. Okay?"

Four surprised faces stared at him a moment, and then there was a general dash toward the stairs. Only Frankie hung back.

"What is it, Frankie?" Rudy asked.

Frankie looked back at him. With his clear blue eyes and blonde hair, Frankie looked so much like Rudy had as a boy that Rudy had to fight to keep his face from twisting into a grimace of grief. "*I* love you, Daddy. *I'll* go with you."

That was it. Rudy broke down and sobbed, kneeling and clutching his youngest son to him. Frankie patted him on the shoulder. "Don't worry, Daddy, it'll be okay." And the tears flowed even faster.

---

John and Larry fled out the front door still tying their shoes and slipping into jackets in the chill autumn morning. Neither had a destination in mind, but the chance to get out and about on a Saturday was too precious to waste.

"What do you think, Johnnie? Do you think he'll change?" Larry asked.

"Not for a minute," John laughed. "He won't make it. Life's too tough for him without the beer."

Larry weighed his older brother's words for a time as they walked down the sidewalk in the general direction of downtown Duluth. "He sounded pretty sure of what he was doing. I think he really *is* going to move to Iowa, with us or without us."

"Yeah, but you know what they say. One picture is worth a million words. I remember him telling Mom about a thousand times that he was going to stop drinking and hitting her. Kneeling on the floor in front of her in the living room or the kitchen, tears pouring down his cheeks—yeah, he's a good actor, all right," John snorted. "But he never could keep it up, and finally he quit apologizing. I say, 'Show me. Don't tell me, show me.' Then I'll believe it. But only then."

"What are we going to do if he *does* change?" Larry asked.

It was John's turn to think for a minute. His eyes were the slate blue of Lake Superior on a cold, cloudy day, and he looked off into the distance. "I don't know. Just between you and me, I don't have a lot of friends. In fact, I really don't have any at all. And I'm not doing so well in school, so it looks like I won't graduate with my class anyway. I've been thinking about dropping out."

"Holy crow!" Larry cried. "Dad would have a cow! Does Mom know?"

"No, and don't tell her," John warned. "She's got enough to worry about. Okay?"

Larry nodded, his eyes wide.

"I was thinking about waiting until my birthday in November. I'd move out and then join the Marines," John continued. "It's a good deal. They give you clothes, and food, and teach you how to do a job. And I figure that if I can take Dad for all these years, I should be tough enough for *them*."

"Wow!" Larry breathed. "But Johnnie, don't you have to have a high school diploma for that?"

"I don't know," John admitted. "I *said* I was just thinking about it."

They walked along, now passing through a neighborhood with steel bars on all the windows of the shops, most of which were not yet opened for Saturday business.

Larry tried out the words. "My brother, the Marine." He puffed out his thin chest and lifted his chin. "*John Baumann, United States Marine Corps.* Boy, that sounds good. Maybe I'll do it, too."

"No, you won't," John returned quickly, shooting a sharp glance at his fourteen-year-old brother. "You wouldn't like it, Larry. Besides, chances are they'd send me to Vietnam and I wouldn't be coming home."

Larry hadn't paid much attention to the way the Vietnam war was eating up the population of young men in the United States, but John's words sent a chill up his spine. "Then why would you go, Johnnie? Just to die?"

John smiled a small, sardonic smile. "Maybe. But first I'd get to fight, and I'm *good* at that."

Thinking about all the times that John had come home late at night and slipped into their bedroom dirty, with ripped clothes and bruised and bleeding knuckles, Larry had to agree. His big brother sure seemed to enjoy fighting. "I don't know why you like to fight so much," he mumbled.

John had heard him and stopped to face him. "It's because I get so mad."

"What makes you so mad that you have to hit somebody?"

John flipped a cigarette out of his pack and lit it. This was a habit that neither of their parents knew about, either. It made him feel tough, and whatever made him feel tough made him feel good. "Ask Dad," he said through the haze of smoke. "He taught me. I've been madder than hell at him for years, because of the way he treats us. I'd rather beat *him* up, but I never have."

"I thought you were going to do it this morning," Larry admitted. "That was a close one."

"Yeah, it was close," John admitted. "And I think he knew it. And I think it scared him. He sure backed off in a hurry."

"Johnnie, I don't have any friends, either. People make fun of me because I come to school in old clothes and never have any money to do anything, even eat lunch at the cafeteria. I'm doing okay in school, but I don't think anybody'd miss me if I left," Larry said. "I guess if you're going to join the Marines, and if Mom and Frankie move to Iowa with Dad, I'd go with them. At least I'd have a place to stay, and I'd be around people I know," Larry said.

"Well, I guess that's the right thing for you to do, then," John said with that faraway look in his eyes again. "You're a good guy, Larry. I hope things work out okay for you. But don't count on Dad changing."

They spent the entire day looking through stores and walking around downtown Duluth, two ragged boys without a dime between them, feeling totally alienated from the well-dressed and well-fed shopping crowd. Occasionally they'd see a homeless person begging for money, and once they even saw a homeless veteran dragging a filthy blanket behind him as a policeman rousted him from the shelter of a doorway. Despite the brightness of the day and the autumn colors that had begun to show, Larry's heart was heavy with the weight of his brother's words. Was *he* going to end up homeless and alone, too?

---

Frankie spent the day in utter bliss. He had accompanied both of his parents to the grocery store. His father had been in a good mood, and they bought more food that day than he had seen in the kitchen in his entire life. His mother had even smiled and laughed a little, and when they returned home, they both started supper while he watched cartoons. He could hear them talking, and once Anna even sang along with the radio. Five-year-old Frankie had not a care in the world. He adored his father. If he thought about the beatings he and his brothers and mother took from time to time, he was terrified, but he wasn't thinking about that now. Right now, all was right with the world.

In the kitchen, Anna had finally dredged up the courage to ask the questions that had been on her mind all day. "Rudy?"

"Yeah, Hon," Rudy answered, not looking up from peeling carrots.

"Don't you want a beer?"

Rudy stopped peeling carrots and looked up sharply, but Anna's face only showed puzzlement and concern. She wasn't baiting him. He relaxed and sighed.

"Yeah, I want a beer. I've wanted a beer all last night and all day today, too," he answered. "But I'm *not having one*." And he continued peeling carrots—this time, with a vengeance.

"Why did you really stop drinking?" she asked, her courage strengthening. "Why are you making all these changes? Why *now*?"

Rudy leaned on the counter. "You remember Hank Masters?"

"Yes, of course. He came to our wedding ceremony, and I've spoken to him on the phone a few times. He used to be your boss. Why?"

"Hank and I were never really buddies. Hell," Rudy laughed softly, "my only *real* buddies have been Budweiser and Busch for years. Those and my two fists." He looked down at his feet for a moment, then back up at his wife. "But Hank was one hell of a good boss. He knew what he was doing and told you when you were doing a good job as well as when you screwed up. He was always very fair, and I admired him. In all the years I worked under him, he and I never had a cross word."

"Was he the friend you were with last night?" Anna wondered aloud.

"Yeah, he was. And, among some other stuff I didn't want to hear, he told me I was doing all the right things to end up losing my family. I spent my childhood without a real family, and you and Johnny, Larry, and Frankie—you're all really important to me." Rudy swallowed, easy tears threatening at the thought. "I don't want to lose you and the boys. The loneliness would tear me apart."

Anna thought sarcastically, *Oh, I see. He just doesn't want to be lonely.* That was more like the Rudy she knew, thinking about his own needs. *Just another version of 'what Rudy Baumann wants, Rudy Baumann gets.'* She nodded in response to him, hiding her thoughts.

"And then I started thinking about how I've been treating you all, and how it must be horrible to just have me around—yelling at you all, putting you down, slapping and hitting you, drinking all the time and leaving you to clean up my mess. My foster father did all those things to me, only he didn't drink. He just waved the Bible at me while he was doing it. I built up a lot of hate in me, and I think that since I couldn't take it out on him, I took it out on you. I'm so sorry, Anna." His vision swam with tears now, and he swiped them away quickly.

"I had . . ." his voice was hoarse and low; he cleared his throat and began again, and Anna had to strain to hear him above the radio. "I had to be so damned *tough* just to survive, physically and mentally, that I never realized that I could stop once I left his house. You never did those things to me, and the only thing the boys ever did to me was be born."

Anna stared at him, holding her breath. This was new territory that Rudy had just entered.

Rudy continued. "When I met you, I thought you were the most beautiful, precious thing on earth to me. You still are, along with the boys. But last night I thought of how I took you in my hands like a beautiful, sweet bird and just crushed the life out of you. And do you know why I did it?" He didn't give her a chance to venture an answer, but went on. "It was because I was *jealous*. Jealous of the boys and all the time you spent with them. I needed you so much that I pushed you away."

Anna said in amazement, "You were jealous of the boys?"

"Seems stupid, doesn't it? After all, they were *my* boys, too. Anna, I'm not saying that it was right; it was just what I did. So when the boys came along I pushed them away and demanded more of you, and wondered what happened to all the love that was supposed to be in our family." He stopped, covered his eyes with one hand, and sobbed. Anna went to him and put her arms around him.

"Don't cry, Rudy," she begged. "You tried. At different times, you tried. And until lately, you always brought a paycheck home to provide for us. You never left us."

"I swear, Anna, I *swear*—this is it. I swear that I want my family and I'll do everything I can do to keep us together. Just give me one more chance. *Please*."

Anna thought of all their years together, their children, the passion that they had once shared. It occurred to her that despite everything, it might very well be that Rudy was doing the very best he could, and he was struggling to make some good come of their lives. It was hard to remember the love she had once had for him, that was true. But she did care about him, and, when all was said and done, she and the boys and Rudy only had each other. A rush of empathy washed over her.

Anna said, "Of *course* I'll give you that chance. You told me about being with that family who took you in, and how terrible it was. If you can live through that, you can live through anything."

Rudy wiped his eyes and looked at Anna. "Anna do you . . . do you still love me?"

Anna looked back at her husband. Did she? What was the truth?

"I think I might still love you, Rudy," she said. "I hope so."

He gathered her in his arms and held on for dear life.

---

John and Larry piled into the house just as Rudy, Anna, and Frankie were sitting down to eat supper. The smells from the kitchen were mouth-watering, and they were two mightily hungry boys from skipping lunch and all their exercise and fresh air. Anna called out, "We're just sitting down to supper, boys! Wash your hands and come on!"

They didn't have to be told twice. *Food, glorious food,* thought John as he helped himself to roast pork, carrots, mashed potatoes and gravy, and a biscuit. It wasn't until he was halfway through his meal that he noticed the eased atmosphere between his parents. For God's sake, they were even *smiling* at each other! He looked at his mother's shining eyes. *She isn't falling for this, is she?* He waited until neither of his parents was looking and poked Larry to get his attention. When Larry looked up, John aimed his fork in the general direction of his parents, and raised his eyebrows. Larry simply looked, shrugged, and went back to his potatoes. John dug in again. *Well,* he thought, *I might as well eat while the eating's good.*

It took him a moment to realize that his father was talking to him.

"John? Are you there?" Rudy repeated, a smile on his face. John's heart throbbed and he looked up.

"I was asking what you and Larry did today," Rudy explained.

John looked at Larry, who looked back. "Nothing," he muttered. He grabbed another biscuit and made a business of looking down at it as he buttered it.

"We walked around downtown, Dad," said Larry, giving his older brother's head a dirty look. "What did you do?"

"Your mother and Frankie and I did some chores and went shopping, and then Mom and I made supper. We had fun," Rudy said, still looking at his oldest son's head. "When the dishes are done I'd like us to do something together. You've got your choice: take a walk, or look at my pictures from Iowa."

It turned out that John *was* listening. "Dad, we just walked about fifteen miles! My legs are going to fall off!"

Rudy said, "Then it's decided! We'll look at pictures of Iowa!" and he and Anna chuckled together.

"Pretty slick, Dad," said Larry.

"I don't care," said John.

Rudy looked at John, who was avoiding his eyes. *Boy, does he hate me. Yeah, I know the feeling. John's going to be tough, all right. God, help me through this.*

When they had all eaten their fill, Anna announced she was going to wash the dishes and asked for volunteer helpers. Before anyone could respond, Rudy said, "John, I want you to help me with the trash. We'll let Larry and Frankie help with the dishes tonight, and you and I can catch them tomorrow morning."

John shrugged, and went to get his jacket. They worked silently as they filled large trash bags in the kitchen, then stuffed those in the trash cans and hauled the heavy cans to the curb. John turned to go inside, but Rudy stopped him. "Don't go in yet. I was going to have a smoke, and I don't want to smoke inside anymore, either. Here, have one." And he offered a filtered cigarette to his son.

"What makes you think I smoke?" John asked, trying to sound casual, but losing an interior battle. *Here it comes. He knows I smoke, and he's going to hit me. It's happening, right now. Get ready,* he warned himself.

"It's amazing what you notice when you aren't drinking. I could smell it on you when you sat down at the table tonight," Rudy said gently. "Here. It's okay, have one," and he offered the cigarettes again.

And John did take one, a little defiantly.

They smoked in silence for a minute, looking out at the street. Rudy said, "Thank you."

"For what?"

"For helping me with the trash; for spending this time with me. I know you're pretty mad at me, and it must be hard for you, so I'm thanking you."

John looked at his father for a moment. "You're welcome," he said shortly, not denying his anger.

"When we go back in there, I'm going to have you help me carry a chest down from the attic. There's a lot about me that you don't know, and it started in Iowa. Things from when I was a kid are in that trunk. If you see them and hear my story, it might help explain a lot," Rudy told him.

"Okay," John shrugged. He would be cooperative, to a point. He was also mildly curious about this chest his father wanted to bring down. He had never seen a chest in the attic; of course, he had never explored it. The only times he had ventured up there were to take down boxes of Christmas ornaments and put them away again.

When they finally tossed the cigarette butts aside and turned to re-enter the house, Rudy's heart was a bit lighter. At least John was listening, for now.

---

The chest was, in fact, pretty small, and it was no wonder that John hadn't noticed it before then. Boxes of canceled checks, a large, ornate bird cage, and dusty, folded blankets hid it from view. Rudy directed John in rearranging the clutter, and together they lifted it from the attic's corner. Cobwebs and dust festooned a very heavy, homemade chest made from oak. It had been sanded and was decorated crudely with carvings of tulips and leaves on the lid's center. The hinges were made from thick, aged leather, and an old-fashioned skeleton key was still in the lock. "This chest was handmade by Heinrich Baumann, an ancestor of mine and the first Baumann in America. It was passed on down through the family to me," Rudy explained. "Let's get it into the light and clean it up a bit before we take it downstairs."

Under the single bare lightbulb hanging from the rafters of the attic, Rudy dusted the chest with cleaning rags. When he was finished, the product was impressive only with its weight. "What do you have in here, gold bricks?" puffed John.

Rudy laughed out loud. "I sure wish that were true. Actually, there *is* some gold in there, but it's the wood that makes it so heavy. Let's try to make it downstairs without one of us falling and breaking a leg."

Minutes later they set the chest on the coffee table in front of the sofa and Rudy gathered the family around it.

"I'm going to tell you a story, and then we're going to open the chest and look inside," Rudy announced.

"Gee, Dad, how long is your story going to take?" asked Frankie doubtfully.

"I'll make it short. How's that?" Rudy smiled at his youngest son and ruffled his hair.

He told them then: the legend of the Heinrich Baumann family and the farm in Iowa—the story that had been passed down from generation to generation. In its repeated telling, details had been lost or changed. Now it was an Indian curse (a lie, Rudy declared) upon the land that brave Heinrich had tried to break. His own father, Jeremy, a veritable saint, tried to rejuvenate the farm but was killed along with his mother and older brothers by a rampaging bear. The strange pull that the land seemed to have on certain male members of the Baumann family, the very fertile soil that was so good for planting crops but so very poisonous to the Baumann men, and questions of madness or alcoholism in the Baumann line were not mentioned by Rudy. He also didn't mention the fact that the very weather on the Baumann farm was at times entirely different from that of the surrounding countryside, or that the Indians had named the land, "Heartless." His family listened, enraptured by the tales of extreme hardship and astounding bravery. Rudy painted a verbal picture of a veritable Garden of Eden, complete with hanging bunches of sweet, wild grapes. By the time he had finished, none of them could wait to open the chest and see what was inside.

John asked, "But Dad, if it was so great there in Iowa, what are you doing *here*?"

Rudy stood stock still, staring at the chest for a moment. He had the feeling that some important information had been overlooked, but for the life of him, he couldn't think of what it was. In his own mind, he was being thorough and truthful in the telling of the Iowa story. "I was adopted after my parents died, and the family moved here to Minnesota," he finally finished.

Anna broke in at this point. "I know you had a rough time with that family, Rudy. What was their name . . . Richter? Yes, that's the name."

Rudy bent his head. Yes, *that* story was fresh in his mind. He told his sons about Stanley Richter: his pettiness, cruelty, and abuses. He admitted wanting to kill the old man and that he held a deep, visceral hatred for him to this day. John listened, and felt a chill race up his spine. *Does Dad know he's exactly like Richter?* he wondered. When he looked up at his father, waiting for him to continue, his father was looking directly at him, a sorrowful expression in his eyes, and the chill was replaced by a flush of heat that radiated out from his chest.

And he realized that Rudy Baumann knew it and was ashamed of it. John looked back at the chest quickly and let the silence linger.

"Now, Dad?" asked Frankie, and the tension in the room was broken by general laughter.

Rudy nodded, and said, "Now!"

Frankie already had his hand on the key, and rattled it in the lock. With some assistance from Anna, the lock clicked, and Anna opened the heavy lid.

Inside was a sea of letters, newspaper articles, and old pictures. Rudy sat aside and let the boys sift through the pictures, answering their questions. There was one of Running Bear; another of the famed Dr. Leipmann and his wife. There was a stoic wedding photograph of Heinrich and Katrina Baumann. At the time, the style was for the man to sit while the woman stood behind her husband, her hand on his shoulder, and neither smiled. There were more modern pictures of Rudy's family, in black and white, but less formal and friendlier, from the very first days at the Iowa farm. And here was a picture of Stanley Richter himself. He stood alone in the photograph, scowling at the camera. He had insisted on having his picture taken with the Bible and providing each of the surviving Baumann children with a copy of the picture so that they would never forget him.

Anna was more interested in the written material. The more intriguing newspaper articles were about the original tragedy, and the reporter was fond of using words like, "mysterious" and "ill-fated" and "doom", without pinpointing exactly what these words were supposed to be describing. One headline article shouted, "*Heartless!*" and explicitly recalled the horrors that the Indian women had endured, and the curse of Bear Who Sees. It also mentioned the ill-fated White Feather, whose "ghost" appeared periodically to protect innocent children and women.

There were postcards of old Apple Springs and the Mississippi River, old, showy greeting cards, and a very old letter to

Stephan Baumann from his lawyers, stating that his money would be held in trust and invested so that the taxes on the Baumann farm would be paid in perpetuity as per his instructions.

At the very bottom of the chest was a dark red velvet lining, and as Frankie ran his hands over the soft material, he asked, "What's under here?"

Rudy said, "Pull it up and see."

Frankie did, and gasped. Fixed to the bottom of the chest by yellowing cellophane tape were fifty, twenty-dollar gold pieces arranged in rows. Anna stared, open-mouthed. There had to be a thousand dollars in money in this chest at face value alone, and the dates . . . why, the dates were all in the early 1800's or even earlier! There was a fortune in the attic all along, and she never knew it. With this money, they could have afforded so much more than they had.

"Rudy, you never told me about this," she started angrily, and then stopped as she saw the puzzlement on her husband's face.

"Anna, I don't know if it was the drinking or what, but I swear to you that I didn't even remember this chest until last night. Even then, I thought there were only *two* gold pieces. I didn't even remember old man Richter's picture being in there! I have no idea why I'd keep that. I could have *sworn* there were only family photographs and pictures of the farm with fields of corn and wheat. I don't see *any* pictures of the farm in here at all. In fact, I distinctly remember a picture of a pumpkin patch with huge pumpkins in it, and me sitting on top of one—but it's not there. And I *know* that I was the last one to look in there," Rudy said helplessly. He turned toward the kitchen and snatched his jacket from the peg by the door. "I'm going out for a cigarette."

As Anna sat there open-mouthed, John jumped up and said, "I'll go with him, Mom," and disappeared after his father.

Anna's mind whirled. *How could you forget this? How do you forget all this money when we were starving at times, letting the kids go without new clothes for school, without extra money for your damned beer? How does forty dollars grow into a thousand dollars in a locked chest?*

She stopped Frankie from pulling the tape away from the coins, then shut the lid and joined Larry on the floor to look at the pictures. No wheat fields or pumpkins or corn. Maybe it *was* the alcohol, and maybe by this time it was hopeless. Maybe Rudy was heading for the bar right now.

---

He wasn't. John found him pacing back and forth on the sidewalk in front of the house, smoking furiously and muttering to himself.

"Dad?" he called.

No answer. John approached him.

"Dad?" he repeated, and reached out and touched his father's arm. Rudy visibly jumped, and even in the poor light from the street lamps, John could see the hurt and confusion on his face. "Dad, are you all right?"

"No, I'm not all right! I've lost my mind!" Rudy cried, his voice strangled. "I've freaking lost my mind and I don't know if I can get it back!" He threw his spent cigarette to the sidewalk and ground it out with his shoe. He looked down the street, where the nearest bar's neon lit the night and promised forgetfulness. "I need a beer."

John shook his head. "That's a bad idea, Dad."

"I need a beer. You don't understand how I feel, John. You just can't quit something like that cold turkey. I was crazy to think I could." He dug in his pocket for his package of smokes, but it was empty. "And I'm out of cigarettes."

"Want one of mine?" asked John, offering a crumpled pack from his own pocket.

Rudy hesitated, and then took one. His hands were shaking too badly to light it, so John took it from him and lit it for him.

"Here, Dad," he said calmly, handing it back to his father.

"Thanks, son," said Rudy. "But I'm still going to have that beer."

John said, "Okay. Go have your beer. But if you do, you can forget me going with you to Iowa!"

Rudy stared at his son. "Were you thinking of going with me? I thought I had lost you."

"I was pretty mad at you before tonight. Maybe I'm still a *little* mad at you. But yeah, I was starting to think that Iowa didn't sound half bad," John said.

Rudy looked back down the street at the neighborhood bar and swallowed. His tongue felt fuzzy and a headache was threatening to split his head in two. He knew, he just *knew*, that just one beer would make him feel fine again.

"Don't go, Dad," John said softly. "Not tonight. Just put it off for one more night. I know you can do it."

When Rudy didn't answer, John desperately searched for some magic words to make his father stay home, and found them.

"I love you, Dad," he said.

Rudy threw away his cigarette and reached for John, and John put his arms around his father. "I love you, too, Johnny. I love you all so much," sobbed Rudy.

"I can tell now, Dad," John said in a hoarse voice, and together they turned to rejoin their family inside.

PART FOUR

# The Wrath of Heartless

# CHAPTER
## Twenty-One

It was touch-and-go for the next week or so for Rudy, who underwent a gallant struggle. Every morning he rose before everyone else, showered and shaved, and made breakfast. He was pleasant, funny, helpful—an all-around Boy Scout, in fact, much of the time. He and Anna went for long walks during the day, talking about their feelings, sharing, and planning. Visiting a coin dealer, they found that the treasure trove that Rudy had forgotten was worth tens of thousands of dollars. For now, Rudy would keep it where it had been all these years. If they moved to Iowa, they could use the money to start a new life. Rudy put a "For Sale" sign in the front yard, and a couple of prospective buyers had already been by to see the house. They even went out to a movie once, together as a family. Rudy had stopped entertaining the thought that there was a possibility that he would go to Iowa alone.

Anna was totally convinced after the first few days that Rudy would keep his word this time. His whole attitude had entirely changed. He never pressed for sex, which was a relief to her for now, but was attentive, caring, and gentle. It didn't take long for Larry and Frankie to relax around their father and do all the things that kids do: giggle, wrestle, tease, chase each other, argue, complain, whine . . . the Baumann house had changed overnight, it seemed.

Only John knew some of the details of his father's constant struggle with needing and wanting alcohol. He was the one who kept watch at night after everybody else went to bed. He knew that Rudy slept very little during this time, and would eventually rise and find his way to the kitchen. Rudy craved sweets and caffeine, and most nights John would come upon his father wolfing down chocolate or cookies with chocolate milk.

They would talk about the day, and Rudy would admit that certain things had bothered him mightily. He would describe how he kept a smile plastered on his face, gritted his teeth, and thought of beer. Not just beer generally; it seemed he could count each and every beer he'd ever had in his life and re-live the cold freshness, the bite and sting, and the easy feeling it gave him as he took the first couple of swallows. That was what beer meant to him: relief.

Rudy told his son how, without the alcohol, he seemed to notice *everything*, and that colors and sounds and smells and tastes and textures all made *noise* to him. It was impossible for him to watch TV, for instance, while Anna was doing the wash. The sounds of the washer and dryer, the smells of the soap and bleach, even the extra heat the appliances generated would break his concentration. He had just never noticed those things before, or at least not to that degree. When things got to be too much for him, he'd take a walk. He thought he might have walked the equivalent of a hike from New York City to Chicago by this time.

He now had his driver's licence back, and was officially off his parole officer's caseload, but Rudy found himself visiting just to talk. The officer had been delighted by Rudy's abstinence, and had suggested Alcoholics Anonymous. But Rudy wanted to do it alone. He found it unbelievable that *anyone* had as tough a time as he did without alcohol, and was deeply ashamed of what he had done to himself and his family. He couldn't bring himself to admit any of it to strangers.

John listened and listened, and eventually opened up to his father about his lack of friends, the fist fights, poor grades in school, and his general feeling of alienation. Most importantly, the two talked about the deep anger they had in common, and promised to help each other keep it in check. John asked his father to show him how to play poker, and they passed the wee hours of the mornings in this way until both of them were dog-tired and ready for sleep. During those long, long nights father and son built a friendship that had never before seemed possible.

That second week was much easier. Rudy found that coffee laced with plenty of cream and sugar had a calming effect, and he drank it throughout the day. He started sleeping through the night, and one night Anna woke to the familiar sounds of thundering snores, the heat of her husband's body next to hers, and a very hairy armpit placed firmly against her nose as she slept on her back and Rudy slept on his stomach with his arm draped over her. She lifted his arm in the darkness and tried to stifle a laugh. *Ah, the joys of married life,* she thought, and turned her head into her pillow to quash the sounds of her giggles. The more she tried to hide her laughter, the more the bed shook, and Rudy woke, oblivious to the reason for the bed shaking. He sleepily asked if there was an earthquake, and Anna burst out with peals of laughter.

That brought him wide awake, and instead of answering his questions about what was so funny, she snuggled against her husband. That night was the first time in at least four years that Anna and Rudy truly made love without Rudy forcing it, and it was sweet for both of them.

Their lovemaking rejuvenated them both, and the days flew by. That Saturday morning Rudy gathered his family in the kitchen as he had two weeks before, and asked the question: Who was going to Iowa with him?

It was unanimous. They all were going to Iowa. Again, there were tears, but they all wept. And these were tears of joy.

---

So it was that Christmas of that year found them happily living in the Baumann homestead in Iowa. To each family member, it was like a dream come true. Rudy had easily sold the Duluth home and cashed in all but two of the twenty gold pieces from his ancestor's wooden chest with a coin dealer. In all, the family now possessed a sizeable fortune.

Of course, Rudy had his little secrets.

First, he had never told Anna about her father's letter, or the telephone calls he had made when Johnnie was born, to Harold Christianson and to her friend Karen. As far as she was concerned, both of them had abandoned her, and that was fine with Rudy.

Second, he had told Anna that he had called his sisters and offered them equal shares of the money found in Heinrich's old chest, and that they had declined to have anything to do with the treasure. That was a lie. At the time, Rudy had figured that they hadn't wanted anything to do with him when he was penniless, and now that he had money, it was none of their business. He felt it was *his* money, left for *him* to find.

Last, he had paid a little visit to his old friends Bert and Cal before he had left Duluth. Late one night (or rather, very early one morning) while they slept unaware in their respective beds, he had methodically smashed the windshields and slashed the tires of their cars. He did this with feelings of great enjoyment and fulfillment at the time.

By the time he had reached Iowa, all of this was patently and conveniently forgotten by Rudy.

He had immediately opened checking and savings accounts in the bank in Apple Springs, and gave Anna a full quarter of the money to keep for herself, "In case you ever need it." Anna was stunned. In fact, she had never dreamed of having money of her own since she had married Rudy, and didn't know what to do with it. Instead of banking it, she hid it carefully away in a crock on the top kitchen shelf. She'd have plenty of time to decide what to do with it. There was no hurry. The wooden chest was placed under the original bed in the master bedroom, exactly where

Heinrich had placed it. The original mattresses were in wonderful shape for antiques, but Rudy had them replaced with new ones.

As a matter of fact, Rudy let loose a flood of money, paying teams of men for adding two bedrooms and two bathrooms, fixing the house up with electricity and telephone service, installing a septic tank and indoor plumbing, having the road from the house to the highway across the river graded and graveled, and affixing an antenna to the roof for their television. He took the whole family on a shopping spree to Des Moines for Christmas, giving each of the boys their own money to spend for presents and spending lavishly for clothes and comforts for the house. A second, used car was bought for Anna's transportation and for John to use upon occasion.

Rudy was bothered less and less by the need to drink. If he grew irritated at times, he retreated to the barn, which he was transforming into a carpenter's dream of a workshop. Before the family had left Duluth, he had visited his old supervisor Hank Masters, presenting himself clean and sober. Hank was delighted at the changes in his old acquaintance and former employee, and when Rudy walked out of Hank's house that day, he had a sterling letter of introduction to prospective employers. That letter had landed him a full-time job at a factory making pre-fabricated homes outside of Apple Springs. It was year-round, respectable work that brought health and dental benefits for the whole family with it. He would start work the week after the New Year holiday.

The boys had all been accepted into the Apple Springs school system, and were looking forward to starting after the New Year as well. John sought a brand-new start with his teachers and peers. Larry seemed to fit in easily wherever he went, and thought that things would work out all right in school. Frankie never mentioned school, or friends, or what he thought of them, but seemed content. For now, Anna was happily grooming their nest.

While the adult townspeople of Apple Springs seemed to welcome the family with open arms (and certainly were glad of the income they were enjoying from Rudy's various projects), they were astounded that Rudy should move his family to the farm. Given the land's history, particularly the *Baumann* history, it was a disaster waiting to happen. Gossip buzzed from one end of the town to the other, and the older citizens, now in their seventies and older, shook their heads. *They had to be warned.*

Despite the apparently happy family atmosphere that surrounded the Baumanns when they were seen on the street, dire predictions were made. It became such an issue that the subject was brought up at a town meeting: *someone* had to have a talk with Rudy Baumann, and it needed to be *soon*. There was unanimous agreement among those in attendance, and it was decided that Sam Fuller, the present sheriff, should do it. After all, he was an authority figure and was most likely to be believed. And, in the end, it would fall to him to organize the cleanup of the mess when the disaster *did* occur.

# CHAPTER
# Twenty-Two

Fuller planned that conversation with much trepidation and a lot of thought. Talking it over with his wife, Sandy, he wondered how he could tell a man who had just moved his family all that distance and who had just spent all that money making the farm his home—how could Sam tell him that he had just stepped into a potential nightmare? Didn't Rudy Baumann know *anything* of the history of the farm? How would he react? And it was Christmas time, for God's sake! But he had agreed to tell him and felt bound to this duty. He fully believed that it was something that must be done.

Sandy suggested that he let the Baumanns have their Christmas in peace, and plan his visit for two days after the holiday, in the early afternoon. The whole town knew that Rudy wouldn't start work until after the New Year. It was best to catch him at home during daylight hours, she thought, and to approach him alone, without a deputy.

Sam agreed. He'd keep it friendly and straightforward, and then if Rudy Baumann decided to stay, it was his right and his business as an adult. If he didn't want to stay, Sam could get some help organized to move the family. After all, they weren't working the farm. There was no need for them to live in such an isolated location.

So, two days after Christmas, on a crisp, sunny day with not a cloud in sight, Sam Fuller set out to do his duty. His stomach churned. At the age of forty eight, Fuller was in excellent physical condition and had over twenty five years of experience in dealing with people of all kinds, but the job that lay before him felt as formidable as anything he had ever faced.

He crossed the bridge over the river holding his breath. He had never been out this way before; there had never been an reason to do so. Transients *never* squatted here. Juveniles *never* broke out the windows or partied out here. The local grapevine told him so. Well, he didn't exactly believe that, but he'd never been called to send a car out here. Before he had left Apple Springs he had talked to some of the men who had done renovations on the property. None of them had sensed anything odd about the place. Well, he'd see. Fuller had substantial faith in his ability to use his cop's intuition, and he didn't doubt it now.

He drove at a slow speed up to the farm house, not wanting to alarm the family. He could see smoke coming from the chimney, and a snowman had been built on the front lawn. Even though no one from Apple Springs had been out to enjoy the sight, someone had strung multicolored lights in the form of a star on the front of the barn and along the eaves of the house. So far, everything looked just as apple-pie normal as he could want.

While Fuller parked the cruiser in the front yard between the house and the barn, the face of a small boy suddenly appeared in the driver's side window. Fuller was in the act of removing the keys from the ignition when he saw the face out of the corner of his eye and he started, dropping the keys to the floor. He took a couple of deep, calming breaths when he saw it was only a little boy, and rolled down his window.

"Hello there, son," he said, smiling. The smile felt fake and stiff, but it was the best he could do. "Is your dad home?"

"Is he in trouble?" Frankie asked.

"No, no, nothing like that. I just wanted to talk to him," answered Fuller reassuringly.

"Are Johnnie or Larry in trouble?"

"Nobody's in trouble, son. What's your name?"

"Frankie."

Fuller smiled a more genuine smile this time. This kid reminded him of his nephew—he had to have the dirt on his older brothers at all times.

"My name's Sam Fuller. Frankie, go get your dad for me, would you?" he asked.

"Yes, Sir!" Frankie said, and galloped to the barn. Fuller got out of the cruiser and closed the car door, looking around and squinting in the glare of the sunshine on the snow. A minute later, Rudy Baumann stepped out of the barn, zipping his jacket with a concerned expression on his face. Little Frankie Baumann made a mad dash to the house. If Fuller were a betting man, he would bet that Frankie was making a full report to the rest of the family right now.

"What can I do for you, Officer?" Rudy asked, extending his hand for a shake.

"You're Rudy Baumann, right?" asked Fuller.

"Yes," Rudy answered, still wondering why the sheriff was on his farm.

"I'm Sam Fuller. I guess you know I'm the sheriff for the county," Fuller said.

"Nice to meet you, Sam," Rudy returned. "How about coming into the house for a cup of coffee?"

"Thanks, but I really wanted to talk to you alone for just a minute. Is there a place we can go to get out of this glare?" asked Fuller, indicating the brightness of the day. He had sunglasses in the patrol car, but didn't want to use them. He wanted Rudy to see his eyes while he talked.

"Sure," Rudy said, and led the way to the barn.

They entered by a newly installed side door. Inside, the barn was lighted and heated, and Fuller saw that Rudy had made great progress in building his workshop. "Wow!" he exclaimed. "You must be quite the handyman. I'd *love* to have a workshop like this." He wandered around the benches, shelves, saw tables, and tools in awe.

Despite his concern, Rudy smiled proudly. "I guess I'm handy with carpentry—it's my trade—but I'm useless around a car or plumbing. Anyway, I did all this because it's my dream, and the space was just here waiting for me."

Sam Fuller turned to Rudy and asked, "Is it okay if we sit here and talk for a minute?" He pointed to a couple of wooden chairs near a desk full of papers and blueprints.

"Of course," said Rudy, and they both sat. Rudy waited expectantly. He had had various dealings with cops over the years, but none of them had gone like this. Mostly cops were picking him up off the sidewalk or breaking up a fight, fingerprinting him, or questioning him. Something pricked at his memory—something about Duluth—but he couldn't quite put his finger on it. What *was* it? Should he be worried?

Fuller took off his hat and placed it on top of the papers on the desk, then leaned forward with his forearms on his knees and studied his shoes for a moment. When he looked up, Rudy was sitting in a similar position. Good. He had all of Baumann's attention.

"Part of me is embarrassed at being here, and part of me says I have no choice in the matter," Fuller began. "I have to talk to you about the history of this farm, and let you know how dangerous it is to live out here."

Rudy hadn't been aware that he had been holding his breath, but it exploded outward in laughter. "You mean all those stories about the Indian curse and the bears?"

Fuller nodded, frankly puzzled at Baumann's attitude. "You know all about that already?"

"Sure I do," Rudy answered. "Stories have been passed down through the family for generations. You don't believe in them, do you?" He looked at the officer with incredulity.

Sam Fuller looked Rudy straight in the eye and said seriously, "Yes, I do."

"You're an intelligent man; I can tell that, Sam. And you've had a lot of experience as a cop, right?" asked Rudy.

Fuller nodded, never letting his eyes leave Rudy's face. "Over twenty five years."

"I can't believe that you're taking all that seriously!" Rudy said, and looked over toward the nearest workbench.

*You blinked first,* Fuller thought. *There's something there that tells me that maybe you do believe at least part of it.* He let the silence ride.

Rudy rose from his chair, and started hanging hand tools on a pegboard. "Well, I can see why you're embarrassed, Sam. But why would I move myself and my whole family down here and spend all that money on renovations to the place if I thought for a minute that we could get hurt?"

"I really don't know, Rudy," Fuller answered. "Frankly, I thought that maybe you had never been told. You were just a baby, really, when it happened the last time. Hell, I was just a kid myself. But the old folks remember it like it was yesterday, and they all swear the same thing: this place gets a hold of the Baumann men and poisons their minds. The men go wild and kill their families, and it only stops when they are attacked and killed by some big animal. People think it's one hell of a big bear."

"You're telling me there's a bear out there that has been around for over a hundred years?" asked Rudy, turning to look at Fuller once again. "That doesn't make sense."

"No, it doesn't. Now, here's the thing. This is the part I'm embarrassed about, because normally I'm not a superstitious man, Rudy. There's supposed to be something . . . supernatural going on out here. Something that wants this piece of land to be left alone. I don't know, I guess you'd call it something like the Bermuda Triangle."

Rudy just shook his head, smiling.

"If you talk to any of the folks who were around when your parents and brothers were killed, *any* of them, Rudy, *they all give exactly the same story.* This is the part that gets me as a cop. Say there's a holdup of a convenience store, or even an auto accident in broad daylight. Plenty of witnesses around, everybody saw the whole thing. When I go to interview them, each witness will have at least a slightly different story. They usually remember broad details, but not everybody is a good witness, and their memories of what happened will vary. The truth is in there, somewhere. It's my job to piece it together."

Rudy chuckled. "Sounds to me like all these old folks have told the story to each other so many times they've memorized it. Then they pass it down to entertain the kids."

Fuller sat back in his chair and sighed. "I was afraid you wouldn't take this seriously. Rudy, it's the worst mistake you could make. I'm only asking that you consider that there might be more to this world than we can explain."

Rudy only shrugged.

"Just one more thing, then. I have a challenge for you. I want you to just think about all this, and if you notice any strange incidents, any changes in yourself at *all*, call me." Here Fuller pulled out his wallet and took out his business card. "Any time of the day or night, call me, and we'll meet. If you come to believe that any of this is a possibility, you buy me a beer. If you don't, I'll buy *you* a beer. Okay?" He extended the card to Rudy, who took it and looked it.

"No beer." Rudy said it so quietly that Fuller could hardly hear him.

"What?"

Rudy drew a deep breath and exhaled it. "No beer. I quit drinking."

Fuller thought in awe, *Here it is. Here's the weakness. This is how it will begin.* He said, "Coffee, then. Okay?"

Rudy looked up at Fuller, then glanced to the side. "Sure. Just as soon as I notice anything."

Fuller rose, smoothed his hair, and replaced his hat on his head. "Good. I'll check back with you on that."

He led the way back to the cruiser and waved at the Baumann

boys, now lined up on the front porch of the farm house. He and Rudy shook hands one more time before he left, and he said goodbye.

Rolling just as slowly on the gravel drive away from the Baumann farm, Fuller thought, *He won't do it. He's already made up his mind.* He looked in the rear view mirror and saw Rudy Baumann slide his business card into his pants pocket and then wave again, as if his hand had been empty all along.

As soon as the sheriff's car bumped over the wooden bridge, Anna joined her husband in the dooryard. "What was *that* all about?" she asked her husband.

Rudy looked at his wife and smiled reassuringly. "Just wanted to introduce himself and say hello," he lied easily. "Sort of a community spirit thing."

Anna looked back at the disappearing cruiser. "Well, *that's* something you'd never see happen in Duluth." And they walked back to the farm house, arms around each other to help ward off the cold.

---

Fuller was right. Rudy had no intention of ever contacting *anyone* about his thoughts on anything to do with his life. He had enough on his plate. *Isn't that something,* he mused. *This is the first time in my life when everything is going my way, and someone wants to spoil it.* He took the sheriff's card out of his pocket and looked at it again, and shook his head. Oh, well. The farm was just fine; it felt *wonderful.* He could see changes in each of them here, but they were *good* changes. There was hope, and space, and freedom. Uh-uh, no way. He wasn't going to spoil all that. Still, instead of throwing the card in the trash, he placed it in his wallet. He didn't stop to think why he kept it.

And, as time wore on, it seemed that the community's misgivings were ill-placed. From all appearances, Rudy had no intention of farming the land. He worked a regular, company job like many of them these days. Although not much was seen of Anna, she seemed happy and content as she went about her business shopping and doing errands in town. The children were all enrolled in school, and Larry and Frankie seemed to be doing fine academically. John, the eldest child, seemed a little standoffish at first, but his English teacher soon discovered that he read very poorly. With a little free help after school, John was soon able to understand more of his course work, and no longer was failing. His self-esteem rocketed, and he was able to find friends among his peers. The Baumanns looked like they were going to make it, at the farm and in Apple Springs.

Whenever Sam Fuller saw Rudy on the street or in stores, he noted that Rudy was polite and friendly but avoided all mention of his visit to the farm. He also noted that whenever Rudy passed any of the three bars that the town sported, he hurried past with his head down, never looking in. In the end, Fuller and the town gave in. The Baumanns seemed fine, and there was no need to beat a dead horse.

Winter loosed its icy grip, and a lovely spring gave way to the humid heat of the Iowa summer. John passed with his class into his senior year, and got a job helping out at the truck stop, stocking shelves and cleaning up. Larry got a job delivering newspapers.

Strangely enough, and so subtly and gradually that no one in the family was alarmed, Frankie showed the first signs of change. Normally sweet-tempered and emotionally close to both of his parents, he now spent most of his time at home alone in his room, in the barn with his father, or in the woods by the river. When she thought about him, Anna noticed that he seemed to be pulling away from her and his brothers, but she wasn't overly concerned about this. Frankie adored his father and mimicked his every action and even his style of dressing. She thought that was normal. And if he preferred solitude to spending time with his brothers, that might be considered normal as well. After all, there was a large gap in his and the older boys' ages. It should be no surprise that their interests should vary.

Rudy himself seemed content with his job, and when he and Anna were asked to help the Apple Springs Community Coalition for Humanity in renovating a house for a widow and her children, they pitched in enthusiastically. Rudy's carpentry skills were top-notch, and he found himself as foreman of renovations, directing others instead of taking all the orders. Anna loved interior design, and had a talent for choosing window treatments, carpeting, paint, and wallpaper that blended together in a pleasing fashion at rock-bottom price. Frankie went with them, and was never found far from his father's side.

Sandy Fuller, the sheriff's wife, took the opportunity to get to know Anna better. They were about the same age, and Sandy was interested in the woman who, along with her husband, dared to ignore history. She invited Anna and Frankie to her house to visit after they had finished one day, promising to drive her and Frankie back to the farm afterward.

Anna liked Sandy, and wanted to accept the offer badly, but out of long habit, she immediately went and asked her husband's permission. From across the room, Sandy could see Rudy turn to look at her, then back at his wife. There was more discussion between them in low voices. Something was wrong. This was taking far too much time. If it were Sandy, she would have simply informed her husband of her plans, and that would have been the end of it, whether he liked it or not. She frowned, and started forward.

Just at that moment, Anna broke away from Rudy and hurried toward Sandy with a tight smile on her lips. "All set!" she said lightly. Behind her, however, Sandy could see Rudy just standing there, staring at his wife's back. There was no readable expression on his face.

"Is everything all right?" asked Sandy.

"Oh, sure," Anna answered. "Frankie!" she called, and Frankie dropped the hammer and the nails he was pounding into pieces of scrap wood to rush to her side. Sandy also found this odd. When her own children were Frankie's age and were in the middle of an interesting project, they seemed to grow gourds for ears. It usually took a lot of effort to get their attention and convince them to do something else. Unless, of course, it was shopping for toys.

Anna explained to Frankie that his father was going to finish up and go back to the farm alone, and that he was going to come with her to this nice lady's house to visit for a while. A strange, calculating look crossed his face, as if he were about to refuse, but Frankie obediently agreed.

On the way to the Fuller house, Sandy commented on how willing Frankie was to come along with them. Anna laughed, and told her that Frankie had always been the easiest of the boys to raise. He was *always* agreeable. Sandy stopped at a stop sign and kept her thoughts on the subject to herself. Frankie was a little *too* agreeable, clean, and quiet from her own experience, and there was something about him that seemed *cold*. She wondered if there were more to the story.

Sandy pulled to a stop in her driveway, and turned to Frankie. "You have your choice, Frankie," she said. "You can play outside on the swing set in the back yard; you can watch cartoons on TV; or you can sit and have milk and cookies with us old ladies while we talk and talk and talk." She winked conspiratorially at Anna, who looked a little puzzled.

Frankie stared at her, then asked, "What should I do, Mom?"

Anna turned around in her seat and said, "Why, whatever you want to do, Frankie. It's your choice."

He regarded Sandy seriously for a moment, then asked, "Is it okay if I play on the swing set and have cookies, too?"

Sandy said, just as seriously, "Yes, you can, Frankie. No problem."

Inside, she showed Anna and Frankie around her house, which was decorated in the style of "well-lived-in": it was comfortable and homey, but a little messy. She led them to the kitchen, gave Frankie a stockpile of cookies in a plastic bag along with a can of soda pop, and showed him the back door and the swing set. After Frankie went out the door, she turned to Anna.

"How about you, Anna? You can have orange soda, lemonade, coffee, or a beer."

Was it her imagination, or did Anna flinch at the word, "beer"?

Anna said, "Lemonade's fine," and watched Sandy pour them both glasses of lemonade. At Sandy's suggestion, they took their drinks and a plate of cookies out into the cool shade of the back porch to talk and watch Frankie on the swing set.

Although she was dying to pump Anna about her home life with Rudy, Sandy steered the conversation into general terms: events around Apple Springs, cooking, the weather. Anna commented that she liked the winter better in Iowa than in the northern reaches of Minnesota. It had been cold here, and there had been snow, but it never reached the bitter wind chills of Duluth.

Sandy said, "I think it's going to be a little too hot for you this summer. Did you get an air conditioner?"

"Rudy had one put in the living room last week. I don't know if we'll need it, though. So far it just seems pleasant," Anna commented.

Sandy did a double-take as she looked at Anna. Last week there had been three nights in a row where the July temperatures hadn't fallen below eighty degrees at night. Sam had turned on the air conditioning, or none of them would have been able to sleep those nights.

"What about those storms this last spring? How did you do out at the farm?" she asked casually.

"Oh, you mean those tornadoes? I couldn't believe it when I saw on TV how it destroyed those houses outside of town. At our place, it just rained," Anna said.

"Well, Anna, you sure are lucky," Sandy said, looking steadily at her friend. "Here in town the power lines were down, and it blew shingles off our roof. When they broadcast the tornado warning, we went down into the cellar and put mattresses over ourselves until the town siren sounded the all-clear. We were relieved to be alive."

"Oh, we don't have a cellar," Anna informed her, and took a sip of lemonade. "We just sat in the living room and watched TV until it was all over."

"Anna, I can't believe it! Do you know how dangerous that is?" exclaimed Sandy. "When they call a tornado warning, it means that one has been sighted *in our area*! You have to get to a safe place immediately! Don't you even have a root cellar on that farm?"

"No, nothing like that. Sandy, we were watching the skies. We didn't see anything out of the ordinary," soothed Anna. "We were really all right."

"Well, I'm very glad you were all right, but you ought to consider having Rudy build a root cellar. If not that, at least get away from all the windows and doors, and cover yourselves. Tornadoes can kill. It's happened *right here*, in Apple Springs, several times," Sandy urged.

"I'll talk to Rudy about it. But, Sandy—that farm house was built over a hundred years ago. The original roof is still on most of it, and the barn is the original barn. Why, it's still got the original paint on the barn, and you can hardly tell it wasn't painted just last year. I don't think a tornado has ever come near the place! Maybe . . . maybe it's the effect of the river, or something, but nothing there ever seems to age or break. I think we're terribly lucky," Anna asserted. "I really think things are *going to be all right*."

"You've been very lucky," murmured Sandy, and took a long sip of her own lemonade. She thought, *It's like she doesn't even live in the same world that I do. But one thing is for sure: she wants me to believe everything will be all right. I wonder what Sam would say about that?*

She changed the subject, and told Anna about her part-time job as a clerk in a local doctor's office. "I went to college, majoring in

English," she told Anna, "but then I met Sam, and we fell in love and got married. Maybe one day I'll go back and finish my degree. I know that when my youngest daughter started in the first grade and was gone all day, I was bored stiff around here with nothing but house work to do. That job has been a life-saver."

"I had a job once," Anna said wistfully, thinking only of the two weeks she had spent working in Duluth while married to Rudy.

"What did you do?" asked Sandy.

"I was a bookkeeper for a department store in Duluth. I really liked the work, and we needed the money," Anna explained.

"How long did you work there?" Sandy asked, thinking she was finally on safe ground with this subject of conversation.

"Not very long," Anna clipped out. "This was great lemonade, Sandy, thanks so much. But I think Frankie and I had better be getting home now. Can you take us?"

"Oh, Anna, are you sure? You've only been here a little over an hour."

"I wanted to put a roast in the oven for supper. If we leave now I can just make it," Anna responded. "Frankie! It's time to go now!" she called.

And Frankie came running, complete with the empty soda can and plastic bag. "Thank you, Mrs. Fuller. It was very good."

Sandy drove them out to the farm, and wasn't surprised to see that Rudy was sitting on the front porch waiting for them when she dropped Anna and Frankie off. It also didn't surprise her that Anna didn't invite her in, or offer a return visit.

---

That night a very impatient Sandy waited for her husband to come home, eat his supper, talk about his day, read the newspaper, and watch the news. She knew this was his "winding down" time, and she was glad to give it to him. She was also very glad that both of their daughters were spending the evening with friends, because she desperately wanted Sam's views on her conversation with Anna Baumann that afternoon. When the news program was finally over, she switched off the TV, folded the newspaper and sat beside her husband on the sofa.

"All right, what is it?" asked Sam, amused at his wife's obvious ploy to get his full attention. Sandy was brimming with news of her own, he could tell.

She told him about Anna's visit, from when she first invited her home to when she dropped the Baumanns off, and waited for her husband's response.

Sam drew a deep breath and sighed it out. "I knew there was something going on the day I visited Rudy Baumann out at the farm. I couldn't pinpoint all of it, but he did ring a couple of bells for me. He told me he had quit drinking. Now, that could account for how "good" Frankie is around adults and how Anna acts like a scared little mouse, especially if he was a violent drunk."

"You really think so? Do you think he beat her? Do you think he's drinking again?" Sandy peppered him with questions.

"Yeah, I guess I think he must have been quite the drunk, and he was probably abusive. You see that pattern of tiptoeing around in families that have been through hell with a drunk who is abusive. I don't think he's drinking now, though. You should see him when he walks by a bar or past the beer and wine in the grocery store—you can just tell it's taking everything he's got not to jump right in again. He might be having a hard time staying away from the stuff," Sam told her.

Sandy sat straight up, her hands on her hips, and opened her mouth to let out a torrent of her feelings on that particular subject, but Sam stopped her.

"I have no evidence at all that what I'm *guessing* is true, Sandy, and I don't think he's drinking now. I can't do anything about something I don't know about."

Sandy folded her arms across her chest stubbornly. "But you can keep an eye on him," she suggested.

"I can keep an eye on him, yes," nodded Sam.

"And I can work on giving Anna a little backbone," Sandy mused.

"Sandy, be her friend. Let her talk to you. Don't pump her or she'll shut up. And, *whatever you do*, do not get between them or between him and his kids. Domestic violence is no laughing matter."

"Okay," Sandy said lightly.

"I mean it, Sandy," Sam emphasized, taking her hand. "And if she or the kids need help, there are organizations that can help them, right here in town. Don't get things stirred up and don't get in the middle. Promise me."

Sandy took her hand back, smiled a reassuring smile at her husband, and turned the TV back on. "Don't worry, Sweetie. I won't interfere. I promise." She went into the kitchen and turned on the faucet to pour dish water for the supper dishes and thought, *And I had my fingers crossed when I made that promise.*

---

Sandy's campaign to socialize Anna Baumann was spectacular in its scope. She called to chat. She hailed her like an old, best friend at the supermarket or in the street. She invited her to lunch. She introduced her to several other women, of all ages. Throughout all this, Anna was circumspect in her choices of what she would or would not do. Sandy had a terrible feeling that it had nothing to do with what Anna wanted, and *everything* to do with what Rudy wanted. Whenever the subject of family dynamics came up, there was a burning *blank* on Anna's part.

Her curiosity was in flames, and Sandy tossed out the bait of an argument with her husband when the two women met in the parking lot of the local supermarket.

"He told me that if I ever used his policeman's flashlight to prop the window open again, I'd find it where the sun would never shine," Sandy finished with a giggle.

Anna gaped at her.

"So, the very next day, I decided to get him back," Sandy said, noting Anna's expression but choosing to ignore it. "I took his flashlight and propped the window open in the kitchen. When he came down to breakfast, he saw it right away."

Anna, her eyes huge, whispered, "What happened?"

Sandy laughed so hard she could barely get her words out. "I dropped my pajama bottoms and mooned him, right in broad daylight and in front of the kitchen window!"

Anna gasped. "What did he do?"

"He laughed and pretended he was going to do me over the kitchen table," Sandy said, breathless from laughing. "I was only saved by my younger daughter yelling from upstairs that she couldn't find her sweater!" She started to giggle again. "Sam's such a lot of fun, especially when I tease him."

Anna put her head down and looked in her purse for her car keys.

"So, Anna. Don't tell me you never tease Rudy! What happens when you tease him?" pumped Sandy.

"I don't usually tease Rudy. I did, when we were first married; then again, there was a time when we first moved here that I'd have fun with him, but that changed."

"Well, for heaven's sake, why? You can be married and still have fun, can't you?" Sandy prompted.

"Rudy doesn't really have much of a sense of humor any more," Anna replied, and looked at her watch. "Oh, my goodness! I have to get home. Glad to see you again, Sandy," she said over her shoulder, heading for her car.

Sandy looked after Anna's retreating back. As ominous as it sounded, there was nothing she could do about Anna's life to make it happy. It frustrated her endlessly. She put her cart in the parking lot corral, trying to think of a scheme to get Anna to open up to her, but nothing came. Anna was like a brick wall.

# CHAPTER
## Twenty-Three

Anna drove back to the farm with a lot on her mind. Yes, she used to tease Rudy, and yes, he used to be a lot of fun. She was mindful of the constant struggle he had to stay away from alcohol, and was thankful for his efforts. But she could not understand how, without alcohol and with the new job and different surroundings and Rudy's great start here in Iowa, things could be so much *worse*, so *fast*.

When they had first moved to the farm, Rudy had been so very generous: with money, with his time, with his affections . . . and with freedom, for herself and for the boys. When had all that changed? More importantly, why had it changed? She had no idea. She only knew that now, things were back to the same old routine they'd had in Duluth. Rudy got up, waited for his breakfast (which had better be on time), gulped it down in silence, and gave his orders for the day. Each one of them had jobs they had to accomplish each day, and if those jobs were not completed when he came home, Rudy could be very handy with his fists, his feet, or his belt. Then Rudy would eat his supper, quizzing them each closely on what they had done and who they had talked to during the day. After supper, he would disappear into the barn. And, by this time, they each knew better than to disturb Rudy when he was in the barn. Except for Frankie, that was. Frankie wandered in and out of the barn at will.

She had a feeling that they were about to lose John. Each day, her oldest son retreated into himself more and more, until not even she could tell what he was thinking. She thought he would probably run away, and if he did, she'd never see him again. That thought gripped her heart and twisted it painfully. And Larry—easy-going, rational Larry—was retreating from her as well. He looked at her with accusing eyes, as if this were all her fault. And he looked at John with something like panic. It was no use questioning the boys. That only drew blank stares or one-word responses. In Duluth, their roles had been clearly defined. She and Johnnie and Larry and Frankie were very close, sharing everything and enjoying each other. When Rudy came in, they helped each other in keeping Rudy's antics to as painless a threshold as possible. That closeness was gone now. Now, they each went their separate ways, like perfect strangers.

And Frankie. Of her whole family, there was something about Frankie that was the most disturbing. He adored Rudy, banked on every word he said—and then disappeared. He would have nothing to do with her at all unless his father told him to go with her to the store or to visit Sandy, and then he seemed like a shell of a child—all little boy on the outside, but watchful and guarded on the inside.

She sobbed aloud, and the sound scared her until she realized that she was making it. What had happened? She had lost everybody who was important to her, it seemed: her mother, her father, Karen, Rudy, the boys—and *she didn't have the foggiest notion as to why it had happened.* Maybe she should see a counselor. Maybe someone like that could explain it to her. She did have money of her own, so that there was no need for Rudy to know. Yes, maybe. It was early August now. Maybe in the fall, when Rudy was working and Frankie was back in school, she would get some help. Because she had a feeling that if Frankie knew about it, Rudy would know about it, and Rudy would kill her for talking about their family to a stranger. She sensed that Frankie knew *that,* as well. She shivered. *What a terrible thought for a mother to have about her own son, she chided herself.* Didn't they call that paranoia? Yes, she surely needed help. *First, help for me,* she thought, *and then, when I'm stronger and understand more, I'll get help for Frankie.*

Before she made the turn onto their property, she pulled over to the side of the road to check her face and make sure that no one could tell that she had been crying. She saw the tell-tale puffiness under her reddened eyes; that would never do. Anna dug into her purse, and from the bottom she pulled out a vial of eye drops. She applied a couple of drops to each eye, tilted her head back and closed her eyes to wait out the burning sensation, and then dabbed at her eyes with a tissue. It was like magic. Now just a little makeup, and she'd look all right, unless someone got right up into her face. That was unlikely, she knew. She drove on home.

Once there, she pulled up in front of the house and opened the trunk, preparing to take in the groceries. It was Saturday morning, and she knew she'd be hauling them in herself. As expected, Rudy stepped out of the barn to check on her. She waved and smiled an automatic smile, and he raised his arm in return before going back into the barn. John and Larry were both at work, and Frankie was probably in the woods again. She didn't know what he found so fascinating there, but he spent most of his time among the trees and along the river.

Anna unloaded the groceries, drove the car to the shade next to the house, and put a casserole in the oven for lunch. Then, instead of starting the laundry as she usually would on Saturdays, she went into the living room and sat on the sofa—a new one—in the silence of the house. She felt funny, as if she had so very much to do but couldn't think of a thing that needed to be done. After all, who cared if the laundry got done tomorrow instead of today? The house was spotless. There was nothing, nothing that had to be done. So, what did one do when all the necessary work was done? Again, she came up with a blank. *Rudy would tell me what to do,* she thought. *Oh yes, he'd have all sorts of ideas for me.* And that thought depressed her even more.

The telephone rang, and she rose to answer it. It was Sandy, sounding excited and out of breath.

"Anna, I just finished talking to Liz and Linda," she said. "We came up with an idea, and we all thought of you!"

"What is it?" Anna asked, a little alarmed. Rudy wasn't here to tell her what she could do or what she couldn't do.

"Well, tomorrow we're going to Des Moines. They're having a *gigantic* arts fair there, with fabulously expensive stuff *and* starving artist specials. We'll go to the fair, have a nice supper out—maybe Japanese, if you like that—spend the night at a hotel, and then go shopping. It'll be like a girl's holiday! How about it? Want to come?"

Anna paused. "What does Sam say about it?" she hedged.

Sandy laughed. "Sam doesn't know about it yet. I'll tell him tonight. If he can't take care of the kids, I'll have my neighbor watch them. He'll probably tell me that he starved to death when I get home from Des Moines, but I know how to deal with that. So how about it?"

Anna glanced at the kitchen clock. Rudy wouldn't be in from the barn for another forty five minutes, and she didn't dare make a decision without him. Or did she? Two whole days away from this farm and a family who had become foreign to her. Art and a supper out. Time with women. Shopping. *Are you out of your mind?* she thought. *Rudy would kill you.*

"Sandy, can I call you back?" she asked.

"Sure, Anna, but doesn't it sound great?" Sandy persisted.

"It sounds like heaven. But let me call you back this afternoon, and I'll tell you for sure then whether you can count on me or not, all right?" Anna pleaded.

"Okay. Call me back," Sandy ended, and hung up.

When Anna hung up the phone, she turned immediately to her bedroom. There she changed into jeans and walking shoes, and walked right on past the kitchen and out the front door, even though she should probably have checked on the casserole. Outside, Anna turned toward the woods and the river. *Frankie will see me,* she thought. *Well, let him see me. It's supposed to be my woods, too, isn't it?*

She walked straight through the fields and took the path to the river. There she followed the bank downstream a little way, until she found a spot where she could sit and watch the rushing water from under a tree. It was so soothing. Why hadn't she ever done this before? Her mind turned to the art fair. There would be paintings, and sculpture. Tapestries, weaving, pottery. Hand-made jewelry. She had been to a giant art fair in Chicago once, many years ago, and it had been captivating. She wanted so very badly to go with Sandy and Liz and Linda. She wanted to pretend that her husband and her sons didn't exist, that she was twenty one years old again and in charge of her own life. She wanted things to be clear to her again.

Anna sat and daydreamed, the rush and gurgle of the river in the background. She remembered the old Anna, the one who was alive and sure of herself, and strong. She had liked that Anna—she had liked her very much. *If I'm really alone in this world,* she considered, *then I only have myself. Shouldn't I spend my days being the person I like?* There was a tiny, inaudible *snap!* In the back of her mind, and the old Anna was fully remembered.

Anna had no idea how long she had sat on the bank of the river, but she woke from her reverie when she became aware that someone was standing across the river, looking at her. Why, it was an Indian woman, young and beautiful, and somehow radiant in her old-fashioned native dress. Anna was overcome by a sense of pure peace, and she smiled at the woman. The woman smiled back, then crossed her wrists in front of her chest and bent her head. *What a wonderful sight, Anna thought.* Wasn't there an Indian woman named in the newspaper clippings? Yes! I remember. Her name was White Feather.

Suddenly a shadow fell over her, and she started as she saw Frankie from the corner of her eye, just standing there at her side looking down at her. "Frankie!" she cried, her heart jumping painfully in her chest. "You scared me. Where did you come from?"

Frankie pointed across the river. "Over there."

Anna followed his finger with her gaze; the Indian woman was gone. Had she imagined her?

"Oh? Is there a bridge to get over there?" Anna asked, getting up from the ground and brushing herself off.

"You have to walk across on a log," Frankie told her. "Mom, it's time for lunch."

"Well, come on then. You can walk your old mother home," Anna said, trying to make this a light moment.

Frankie came with her, but would not walk at her side. Instead, he walked behind her, even through the fields where there were no trees. Anna pretended not to notice. She would have loved to have asked him if he had seen the woman, but something told her that could be dangerous for her. They walked back to the house in silence.

She entered the front door, and immediately knew that she was in trouble. Rudy stood at the open oven door, taking out a very burnt casserole. He had opened the windows, and smoke was pouring from the casserole dish.

"You burned the casserole," he said accusingly.

Anna stepped into the kitchen, picked up a couple of potholders, and took the burnt mess from Rudy. "Sure looks burnt to me, too," she said, smiling to herself.

"Well, I'm not going to eat that!" Rudy shouted.

"Me, either," Anna said, and dumped the casserole, dish and all, into the trash. It lay there sizzling.

Rudy's eyes bulged.

"I'm hungry, Anna. What am I going to have for lunch?" demanded Rudy.

"Well, I just went grocery shopping this morning, so there should be plenty to eat. Why don't you open the refrigerator and see what there is?"

Rudy gaped at her. Frankie disappeared into his bedroom and slammed the door. Anna heard it with a tiny thrill of terror, which she squashed immediately.

"Are you telling me that I'm supposed to get *my own lunch?*" he asked incredulously. "Is that really what you're saying? Because, by God . . ."

"And are you telling me that you're so helpless that you'd stand around like a chicken and starve if I didn't put your food in front of your nose?" Anna asked. In the back of her mind, a small voice moaned, *Oh no, no, no;* but in the front of her mind, Anna wanted to go to the art fair, and she was determined to go, even if she had to pick a fight to do it. It might cost her a black eye, or a kick to the kidney, but surely it couldn't be as bad as when Rudy had been drinking. After Rudy beat her, he always made up by trying to please her, and this time she knew what she wanted. She forced a laugh. "Come on, Rudy. I was gone on a walk too long and made a mistake. Big deal. It's not the end of the world. Let's see what we can have to eat." And she made a move toward the refrigerator.

Rudy reached from behind her and slammed the door shut. Anna turned, bracing herself, and looked straight into his furious face.

"What's gotten into you? It's that Sandy Fuller, isn't it? She's put ideas in your head," Rudy accused.

"I'm more interested in what's gotten into *you,*" Anna said, trying not to flinch. *No fear. Show no fear,* she chanted to herself. *You've started, now finish it.* "What happened to the Rudy who promised that he would change? The Rudy who *did* change, for a while? Because I want him back, Rudy, wherever you've put him. I liked that man. I *loved* that man. That was the man I believed in enough to follow to Iowa. What happened?"

Rudy reeled back as if she had slapped him. He opened his mouth once, twice, then whirled and slammed out the front door. Anna watched him re-enter the barn from the living room window. Her heart was pounding, and she was out of breath, as if she had been running hard. Suddenly the hairs on the back of her neck rose up, and she turned quickly to find Frankie right behind her.

"Isn't Dad going to eat?" Frankie asked.

"Guess not," Anna said with false brightness. "Come on, I'll fix you a sandwich." She made a gesture to take her son's shoulder, but he shrugged it off.

"I'm not hungry now," he said.

"All right. I'll make a sandwich for myself, and a sandwich for you. You'll find yours in the refrigerator if you get hungry later," Anna told him, and turned back to the kitchen. She was taking bread out of its bag when she again heard the front door slam. She looked out the kitchen window and saw Frankie heading back to the woods.

Only then did she lean against the edge of the cupboard and allow the tremors to pass through her. Her teeth chattered, despite the hot wind blowing in from the open kitchen window. She got an afghan from the sofa, wrapped it around her, and laid on the cushions.

*You'll pay for that, Annie,* she said to herself. *But what's the worst that could happen? He could kill you, I guess. On the other hand, you can only die once. And is this living? No, I don't think so. I think it's like a walking death right now. As long as you live on this farm, there's not a friendly face you can turn to.*

Eventually she got up from the sofa, made the promised sandwich for Frankie (even though she doubted he'd touch it), and put a roast in the oven on a low heat setting for supper. Then she picked up the phone and called Sandy.

"Sandy? It's me, Anna. I'm going to go with you tomorrow," Anna informed her friend.

"Oh, Anna, I'm so *glad!* Here's the plan: you drive to my house and park the car here. Liz is going to drive us all in her big Cadillac. Can you be here early, like 7:00 a.m. in the morning?"

"Sure," Anna said.

"Oh, I can't wait to tell the others! We're going to have so much fun!"

"I can't wait either," Anna said. "Well, you can plan that I'll be there at your house, 7 a.m. sharp, tomorrow. Take care." And she hung up. She felt like taking another walk along the river.

---

In the barn, Rudy was in a frenzy of activity. He had been making storage bins for the root cellar he had dug out behind the barn (at Anna's suggestion), and he followed through with his plans automatically. The change that had come over his wife had left him off balance. There seemed to be trouble in Castle Rudy. *You bitch!* he screamed at Anna in his mind. *Who do you think you are, talking to me that way? I ought to wring your neck!*

In the forest, Frankie was at the river's edge, throwing rocks straight down into the water as hard as he could.

Rudy stopped long enough to wipe the sweat from his head. *God, it's hot in here! I've got to get something to drink.* He walked over to the tiny refrigerator he kept in his workshop for snacks and drinks and opened its door. *Now how in the hell did* that *get in there?* He was looking at a six-pack of beer. Nothing else was in the refrigerator. He took the six-pack out. It was ice-cold; it had been in there a long time. He pulled one of the bottles from the cardboard carton and rolled it over his forehead and the back of his neck: *Aaaahhhh. Nothing like a cold one.* Without another thought he took the church key from the top of the refrigerator and lifted the top off. He chugged the beer, then looked at the empty bottle in his hand. *Say, didn't I give up drinking?* he asked himself, and then answered, *Guess not.* He tossed the bottle into the corner, where it landed on the hard-packed earth there.

Now, what was he thinking about? It seemed to him that something was upsetting him, but he couldn't remember what it was. While he thought about *that,* he opened a second beer and returned to work. Well, it would come to him in time.

Rudy had himself a work marathon going. Plywood and 2" x 4" lengths of wood were turning into storage bins in his skillful hands. The sweat poured down, and he finished the last of the beer. In the middle of sanding the ends of one of the bins, it came back to him. *Anna! She got her fresh mouth back, didn't she? Well, I'll see about that.* Rudy Baumann was the professor in his house, and that bitch was going to get a lesson that she'd never forget, that was for sure. No little split-tail was going to tell *him* to get his own lunch, not while he was paying her way—not to mention the bills for her three little rugrats.

*Rudy!*

Rudy whirled and almost fell to the floor. The barn stood empty. Funny, for a split second there he thought he had heard old man Richter calling him. He turned around to his workbench again. Now what the Christ was *this?* It looked like a box of some kind. When did he start on *that?* He ran his hand over the end of the box, and felt a rough spot. Well, whatever it was, it needed to be sanded. He started the electric sander and applied it to the wood.

*Rudy! You're still a screwup, you know.*

Rudy gasped as he started guiltily. He switched off the sander and turned around slowly. There was Richter, coming in from the fields with a pitchfork in his hand just has he had hundreds of times in years long past. He didn't even look at Rudy. Instead, he turned his back and started pitching hay into the horse stalls.

"I didn't do nothin', Sir! I swear!" Rudy backed up against a pile of boards. "Ask 'Lissa! Ask Sarah! I been workin' hard all day!"

*Sarah and Melissa have been out of your life for years, Rudy, get a grip on yourself. I'm talkin' about your wife.*

"You mean Anna?"

*Now who in the hell else would I be talkin' about? Jesus wept, boy, are you gonna be slow your whole life?*

"What'd I do, Mr. Richter?" Rudy asked, confused. Now that he thought about it, he didn't think that Richter had ever met Anna. In fact, the reason he hadn't met her was that Richter was *dead,* just like

Mom and Dad. Only, Mom and Dad had died a long time before Richter did, or at least that's what he *thought* he remembered . . .

*Don't give yourself a stroke standin' there tryin' to think too hard, Rudy. I always had to do your thinkin' for you, didn't I?*

"I can think for myself, Sir," Rudy said, but it came out defensively, a little like a whine. Rudy didn't like that sound, but he was helpless to control it.

*Don't think, just listen, Rudy. That Missus of yours really thinks she's somethin' special, doesn't she? Pretty and trim and proper and prim, that's her. Missus Goodie Two-Shoes. And she's got quite the mouth on her, doesn't she? And an attitude!*

"Yeah, you're right," Rudy admitted.

*Of course I'm right! And here you are, lettin' her live here outta the goodness of your heart, when you're tryin' to work the work of a man and provide for her and her three pups.*

"That's for *God damn* sure," Rudy said. The whine was gone from his voice. Now here was someone who understood the situation.

*DON'T BLASPHEME!*

"Sorry, Sir."

*You know what the problem is, don't you, Rudy? She's on her high horse, and you need to take her down a peg. You need to teach her what her place is, because, Rudy, she just doesn't know. And it's your place to teach her, you bein' the husband and all, like the Good Book says.*

"God Damn right!" Rudy agreed, and opened the little refrigerator. By God, there was another six-pack in there, all fresh and ready to go! He took one from the carton and opened it, drinking deeply.

*You take the Lord's name in vain one more time and I'm going to shove this pitchfork right up your ass, Rudy-Patooty!*

"Sorry," Rudy mumbled. Then the matter at hand came back to him. "She was okay for a while, but all of a sudden today she's not *normal* any more, Sir. She burned my lunch! And then she threw it in the garbage! And *then* . . ."

*Yeah, yeah, yeah, she told you to get your own food, right? Well, then, it's up to you to change all that, isn't it, Rudy? Show her what kind of a man you are!*

"How am I gonna do that, Sir?" Rudy asked, wiping his sweaty hands on the front of his pants.

Richter chuckled, wiped the sweat off his brow with a dirty red bandana hankie, and stuck it back in the front of his biballs. *You'll think of somethin', Rudy. Yep, you'll think of somethin'. But you'd better hurry, Rudy. Because she's plannin' on leavin' you. Tomorrow, Rudy, early in the mornin'.*

Rudy's chin dropped. "She *wouldn't* leave me! She wouldn't *dare!* She loves me! She *needs* me!"

*Haw, haw, haw!* Richter chuckled richly. *You've been lax, boy. Lazy! You'd do best to put her on the top of your list. And you'd better add Johnnie and Larry, while you're at it.*

"Johnnie? Larry? Are they going with her?"

*Nope, they got their own plans.*

"Frankie—what about Frankie?"

*Now, don't you worry about Frankie none. He's mine. Just like you're* mine.

Frankie stopped throwing rocks into the river and went upstream, looking for his log to cross over.

And Richter walked out of the barn, carefully setting the pitchfork up against the closed barn door as he went.

When the old man was gone, Rudy turned back to his work. Yes, these bins were going to be just the ticket for the root cellar. This one was almost ready, and he could put it out there with the other two. Suddenly he felt light-headed, almost like he'd been drinking. He wiped his forehead with his hand and it came away soaking wet. Droplets of sweat flew onto the workbench. He decided to go into the house early and call it a day. It was just too damned hot out here to work any more. Next time he was in town, he'd look up the price of an air conditioner.

# CHAPTER
## Twenty-Four

John waved at his co-workers as they dropped him off at the bridge at the foot of their property. *Man,* it was hot today. The traffic at the truck stop had been unending, with loads of tourists and truck drivers. His muscles ached, and he gleamed with sweat, but he was in a great mood. Today his boss had shown him how to work the registers. John felt certain that he was about to get a promotion and a raise. *If only life at home could be this good,* he thought.

Outside the house, he saw Larry's bicycle propped against the side of the porch. He was proud of his younger brother. Larry had made friends here easily, and worked to deliver papers seven days a week. He was up before dawn on most days, on his bike and gone. John wished he could be a little more easygoing, like Larry, but he didn't think it would happen in *his* lifetime. Sure, there was a while there, just before they moved to Iowa and when they had first moved in, when Dad had been so easy to live with. They had all made a good start out at the farm. But soon Dad had started slipping into his old ways, all except for the drinking. In fact, in some ways he was even nastier now.

And then there was Mom. It was funny, but in Minnesota, John had felt sorry for her. He had seen her take more beatings and verbal abuse than he thought a woman could take and still be alive. Then, when Dad had stopped drinking and made all those promises, she had turned into a different person. John had loved being around her then. She had seemed a lot younger and happier, full of laughter and teasing. She talked back to Dad, and gave her opinions freely. He could even remember her singing as she went about her house work. But now she was back to the scared little mouse she had been during most of his life. He was disgusted with her and with himself for putting up with Dad, and he hated Dad most of all for that—for taking Mom and beating her back to the way she had been. Now it was all he could do to look at either of them, or even face his own eyes in the bathroom mirror.

Frankie . . . Frankie gave him the creeps. He was like a little robot; when Dad told him to do something, he did it, perfectly, the *first* time. Otherwise, he didn't listen to Mom or him or Larry—he just . . . went away. Now, he sat in his room with the door closed, hung around Dad in the barn, or went to the woods. Once, Mom had let John use her car to pick Frankie up after school, and he had watched the other kindergartners burst out of the school doors, yelling and playing with each other. Frankie had come marching out and straight to the car. He totally ignored the other children. And he was always, *always* clean. His room was never a mess. And Frankie totally adored Dad. He followed him around like a puppy. John shook his head as he got changed into his work clothes for his afternoon chores. Yeah, Frankie definitely was very weird, and neither Mom nor Dad seemed to notice it.

He passed Larry's room on the way outside, and saw him sitting on his bed with his baseball card collection spread out around him. "Hey, Larry! Did you do your chores yet? If you didn't, and Dad sees you sitting around like that, he's going to tan your hide."

Larry looked up from the cards. "Don't you ever get tired of this, Johnnie? Chores every single day of the week—and it's *summertime.* We only have a few weeks left before school starts again."

John sat beside Larry on the bed. "Of course I get tired of it. I'm tired of *all* of this. But you and I know it's not going to be forever, right? I'm just waiting for graduation."

Larry nodded, his face unhappy. "What am I going to do *then*, Johnnie? Without you, there's just Dad and Mom and Frankie here."

John put his hand on Larry's shoulder and squeezed it. "I told you, Larry, you *can't* come with me, and I can't stay here. Just try to wait it out, like I did. You know, with your grades, I wouldn't be surprised if you got a college scholarship. You could probably do anything you want to do for a career."

That brought a grudging smile to Larry's lips, and dimples shown in his cheeks. "Well, I wouldn't *mind* being a marine biologist."

"Oh God, here we go again! If you mention fish or plankton or the secret language of the dolphins to me one more time, I'm gonna puke! And it's gonna be . . . on your pillow!" John bent over Larry's pillow and made fake gagging sounds. Larry grabbed the pillow and beat his brother over the head with it. Baseball cards flew to the floor as they wrestled and jostled each other.

Suddenly the front door of the house opened and closed. It was a small, almost stealthy sound, but they both were attuned to the slightest strange sound from years of living around Dad. They stopped, still as statues, each holding his breath for the next sound. Dad and Frankie usually slammed the front door. Mom came in with a bustle. Who was down there?

John got up and motioned for Larry to stay put. He carefully looked around the corner toward the kitchen. And there was Rudy, looking straight at him. He was wearing old jeans and a strappy T-shirt, and at that particular moment he looked *really old,* like maybe a hundred and one. "Hi, Dad," John said, partly in greeting and partly to warn Larry. Very quietly, Larry got off the bed to straighten it and pick up his baseball cards.

Rudy looked at him as if he didn't recognize him.

"Dad? You okay?" John asked tensely.

Rudy blinked, and it was as if the blink turned him on. He said, "I don't feel good. I'm going to take a bath." He then went to his room, took his wallet, keys, and change from his pockets, and laid them on his dresser. John followed him uncertainly.

"Do you want me to call a doctor?" he asked.

"No, I'll be all right. I just got overheated in the barn. You know, I don't think you boys should be doing your chores outside in all this heat." He picked up his wallet and keys from the dresser and tossed them to John. "Why don't you and Larry take my car and run into town for some ice cream? Bring some home for all of us."

And Rudy went into the bathroom and closed the door. John heard him turn on the water in the bath tub.

He went back to Larry's room. *"Did you hear that?"* he whispered.

*"Yeah,"* Larry whispered back. *"What's going on with him?"*

*"Sshh. Let's just go."*

As the boys walked past the bathroom, they could hear their father talking to himself. They glanced at each other quickly but kept on going.

Once outside, John looked around for his mother's car, and saw it parked in the shade. "Larry, where's Mom?" he asked, a knot of fear forming in his throat.

"I saw her going into the woods when I got back from my route. She's probably taking a walk."

"I think we'd better tell her that Dad is in the house early and acting funny," John decided.

"Yeah, I think you're right," Larry agreed.

The boys found Anna easily enough, and told her what had happened. "He said for us *not* to do our chores, and gave us his wallet and keys to go get ice cream," Larry emphasized. "He's acting really strange, Mom."

To their surprise, Anna simply sighed and smiled at them. "He and I had some words earlier. He's probably just in shock."

"You had a *fight?*" John asked incredulously. His mother seemed at ease, and there didn't appear to be a mark on her.

"No, we didn't have a fight. I just said, 'we had words.' In a *normal* family, that's where one person disagrees with another person without somebody getting a black eye," Anna said evenly. She looked at her sons. "I'm sick of this, boys. Sick of his moods and orders and worrying constantly about whether each of us is doing the right thing. Your Dad made some promises before we moved here, and I think that he's going to start keeping some of them." Anna looked at the boys thoughtfully. "Listen, I'd better let you know now: I'm going to leave for a little vacation early in the morning. Your father doesn't know yet, but I'm going. I'll need someone to make sure Frankie is okay while I'm gone."

"Are you *leaving* Dad, Mom?" Larry asked, his eyes wide.

"No . . . at least not right now. No, tomorrow I'm going to go with some of my friends to Des Moines to an art show and to do some shopping. I'll just be away overnight, and back on Monday. Do you two think you can handle things around here for me while I'm gone? I don't know whether I can count on your father."

John looked at Larry, who nodded. "Yeah, between the two of us we can work something out. But, Mom—is he going to let you go?"

Anna looked at her oldest son steadily. "Oh, yes, John, he's going to let me go. One way or another, he's going to let me go."

"Are you going to be all right if we leave you for a little bit? I mean, I think we should be around when you break the news to Dad, just in case he doesn't take it very well," John said.

"I'll stay out here until I hear your Dad's car coming back, and I'll wait until supper to tell him. Does that suit you?" Anna asked, still smiling.

"Yeah," John answered.

"That's a good idea," Larry said.

The boys started back toward the path to the house, but John stopped and turned around. Anna was still looking at them, still smiling. A sunbeam had slipped through the trees and dappled her golden hair. She looked *beautiful,* and *happy.*

John shivered in the heat.

"I love you, Mom," he said, and meant it.

"I was hoping you did," she answered. "I always loved you both so very, very much."

He looked at her for another moment, capturing the picture in his mind's eye, and then followed Larry out of the woods.

---

John drove, and Larry opened his father's wallet, looking for money for the ice cream. John figured they could make it to the store and back in about thirty minutes, if he pushed it. Gravel ground out from under the tires, and dust billowed in through the open windows.

"Hey! Take it easy!" Larry cried, poking John in the arm. "You're choking me to death!"

"I think we should hurry," John told his brother. "I've got a feeling that things are coming to a head, and I want to be there for Mom when they do."

"Well, slow down so I can breathe. Anyway, Mom said she'd wait to go back into the house until she heard us come back, and she promised not to say anything about her trip until suppertime. We've got about three *hours,* Johnnie," Larry said.

Reluctantly, John slowed to a more normal speed. Still, he didn't intend to dally. His gut told him that things were about to blow.

Beside him, Larry held his father's wallet open. "How much for ice cream, do you think?" he asked John.

"Couple of bucks, maybe."

"Hey, Johnnie, there's *tons* of money in here! Jeez, there's nothing under a twenty!" Larry exclaimed. "There must be a couple of hundred dollars in here."

"So? It's Dad's. Just take a twenty out and leave the rest. We'll put the change in there before we give it back."

"Okay," Larry said, and pulled out a twenty from the middle of the stack. A business card fluttered to the car's floor, and he bent to pick it up. "Wow, Johnnie. Do you remember when that policeman came and talked to Dad?"

"Yeah. Why?"

"Here's his card." Larry handed the card over to John, who read the name off while he was steering the car.

"'Sheriff Samuel Fuller,'" John read. "I wonder why that cop gave Dad his business card? I always wondered what they were talking about in the barn that day," John said, and then glanced in the rear-view mirror. "Oh, shit!"

Larry followed his brother's gaze to the mirror and then turned around in his seat. "It's a cop with his lights on, right on our tail!"

"I know, Larry," John said. "Shit. I've got to pull over. I don't think I was speeding."

His heart pounding in his throat, John pulled to the side of the road and stopped the engine. He had never been pulled over by the police for anything before. So far in Iowa, he had led a pretty quiet life. He had been hoping to keep it that way.

He watched the cop get out of the cruiser; the lights were still twirling.

It was Sam Fuller.

The Sheriff bent to look inside the car through John's open window. "Hey, it's John and Larry Baumann! Hi, guys!"

"H-hi, Mr. Fuller," said John.

"Hi," said Larry. Although he was a little nervous, he was mightily interested in what was going to happen to John.

"I just pulled you over because you were driving your father's car and you looked a little young to be your father, that's all," Fuller smiled. "I didn't mean to scare you."

John blew out his pent-up breath. "Whew! I thought I was speeding or something."

Sam Fuller automatically let his eyes roam over the inside of the car as he bent to talk to the boys, and spotted Rudy's wallet with a wad of money in it. John also had his business card in his hand—the one he had given to Rudy Baumann a few days after Christmas.

"What are you boys doing with all that money?" he asked casually.

"Oh, it's not ours. It's our Dad's," Larry said helpfully.

John shot Larry a look that said, *"SHUT UP!"* and then turned to Fuller. "He tossed us his wallet and his keys and told us to get some ice cream," he said, and then winced inwardly. *Boy, you in a heap o' trouble,* he thought. Who in his right mind would give his sons his whole wallet to go get ice cream? Well, Dad wasn't in his right mind, but Fuller didn't need to know that.

"Everything all right at home, boys?" Fuller asked.

"Sure. Why?" John asked.

"Just wondering. I see you've got my card in your hand, John."

John jerked, almost dropping the card. "This was in his wallet," he said, showing it to Fuller. "We were just interested because of . . . well, because of the day you came to talk to Dad."

Fuller straightened to his full height and looked up and down the road. It was empty. He looked back toward the Baumann farm; not a cloud in sight. Well, if the stories were true, it meant that things were indeed fine on the Baumann farm right now.

The boys were afforded a good look at Fuller's tight, muscular abdomen, obviously protected by a bullet-proof vest. John swallowed nervously and glanced at Larry.

Fuller popped his head down to window-height once more. "You boys come on out of there. I want to talk to you."

John's legs were like jelly as he got out of the car. Larry was starting to feel a little more nervous. They stood by the car, hearts sinking, as Fuller walked back to his cruiser, got in, and spoke on his mike. To their surprise, however, he then turned off the lights and the engine, got out of the cruiser, and walked over to where they were standing. "Let's sit over there in the shade," he said, indicating some trees about twenty feet from the side of the road. "I just called in to let them know I was taking a break."

John didn't know if he could walk to the trees, but he did. He and Larry sat on the ground while Fuller dusted off a large rock to balance himself on. He set his portable radio on the ground near him.

"You boys are young, but not *too* young," Fuller began. "John, you're a senior in high school, right?"

"Yes, Sir."

"Just call me Sam, okay? And Larry. How old are you?"

"Fourteen. Almost fifteen," Larry said.

"Old enough, then," Fuller nodded to himself. "Did your father tell you boys why I came out to the farm after Christmas?"

"He told us you were welcoming us to the community," Larry said.

Fuller smiled. "Well, yeah, that too, but mostly I went out to warn him about that piece of land. I didn't think it was safe for him to have his family out there, and I told him why. He didn't believe me. I gave him my card in case he ever wanted to talk about it."

John looked at him, wondering where this was going.

"It's not really my job to tell you this, but I think it's my duty as a human being," Fuller said. "Believe it or not, that land your family is living on is like a Venus fly trap. You know what that is?"

Both boys nodded.

"It draws people in, it attracts them. And then when it's too late, it eats them."

"That's crazy," John said.

"Whoa!" exclaimed Larry.

"It does sound crazy, I'll admit. I don't know exactly what 'story' your father told you, but I'm going to tell you the whole thing as the old folks in town have told me."

Fuller then proceeded to give the entire known history of the Baumann land to the boys. They listened, fascinated. When he'd finished, Larry said, "Wow! It's just like a movie!"

Fuller smiled. "Yeah, it's pretty fantastic, all right. But this isn't a movie, Larry. This is real. It's like a piece of the Twilight

Zone right here in Iowa. We've taken soil samples, water samples—we even tested the air and the vegetation for poisons, but we can't find any scientific explanation for what happens there. We've searched those woods for Indians and bears, and I swear *there are none.* As far as I'm concerned, there are just things in nature that we can't explain, not with the tools we have, anyway. And until we can, we're going to have to learn to just stay away from them."

John shook his head. "This is just too much. Indians and bears and murders. I'm sorry, Sir—I mean, Sam. I appreciate you talking to us, but this is all ancient history." He glanced at Larry and plunged ahead. "Back in Minnesota, Dad had a drinking problem and he used to beat us, but he's stopped. No beer. And the farm is fine. We *live* there, remember? It's *normal.* We haven't seen anything or heard or even *felt* anything wrong on the farm.

"Neither did your ancestors. It came out in the men of the families, and that was the first warning that any of them had," Fuller interrupted. "Did you ever stop to think that your father's meanness might be part of all of this?"

John shook his head emphatically. Larry forced his face to look absolutely blank. Sam put up a hand, forestalling John from talking, while he thought. *What are the magic words? How can I make them see?*

"Okay. Let me ask you this: do you believe that weird things happen in the Bermuda Triangle?" Fuller asked, directing the question at John.

John thought a moment, then said, "Yeah, I guess so. You see stuff about that on TV all the time."

"And they've never been able to fully explain it, right?"

"Right," John agreed slowly. "But what does that have to do with our farm?"

"What if they never put that stuff about the Triangle on TV? What if there were no actors telling you about it, or books about it—only stories that folks told? Would you believe it then?"

"I guess I'd have to see it, first," John said.

Fuller slapped his knee in frustration. "All right then. I'm not going to try to convince you of anything. I'm just going to repeat what happens and let you boys go on and get your ice cream." He counted the steps out on his fingers. "First, a man has close contact with the soil of the land by digging in it or lying on it. Second, whatever his weaknesses are, those are magnified, and he gets obsessed with them. Third, he goes crazy and spills human blood, in anger, on the land. Fourth, the weather goes crazy and every cloud in creation starts heading to your farm—we'll be able to see it from town. There'll be a hell of a storm over there, and nothing in town. Last, when the guy's killed everyone he can, he heads to the woods by the river. *Something* in there kills him and drags him across the river, off Baumann property."

He looked both boys in the eye. "That's it. Five steps to tragedy. And it's happened too many times to ignore." He stood up to lead the way back to Rudy's car, and when the boys had settled themselves in the car again, he went on talking.

"I'm a cop, so I've been trained to follow the facts. But every cop who's been in the field for a while will tell you that there's more to life than the eye can see, and we learn to pay attention to those feelings we get from time to time when things don't fit together quite right. And boys, I am telling you that I have one *hell* of a feeling about your Dad."

John and Larry looked at each other. Larry looked troubled, and worried.

"The only thing you can do when real trouble starts, and don't worry, you'll know *exactly* what I mean when it does, is get your family off the land." Fuller's radio, silent until now, squawked in his hand, and he turned to answer it. When he turned back, he said, "I've got to get going now; I'm needed. But if either of you boys ever wants to talk about this some more, just call me. Any time." And Sam Fuller hurried back to his cruiser, started the engine, and tore off toward the far side of town with lights revolving and the siren wailing.

John sat there behind the wheel of his father's car for a moment, staring straight ahead.

"Johnnie? What do you think?" asked Larry, looking for guidance from his older brother.

"Well, a lot of weird things have happened today. But I think the weirdest thing so far has been a cop stopping us to tell us a fairy tale," John said. "I think Dad drank so long that it's affected his mind, and I think that maybe Mom is going to leave him. And, as far as I'm concerned, that's a good move. Should've happened a long time ago." He started the car's engine and pulled back onto the blacktop. "Maybe that cop's got a screw loose."

Larry kept his thoughts to himself and looked out at the passing scenery. Maybe John was right, maybe Sheriff Fuller was the crazy one. But *he* wasn't the one who was talking to himself in the bathtub right now. An involuntary shiver ran through his body.

"Let's hurry up and get that ice cream, Johnnie," he said, and John agreed.

---

Frankie was confused. Just a few minutes ago, he had been angry, throwing rocks into the river as hard as he could. Now, he felt as if he were floating aimlessly on his back in a big swimming pool. Since they had moved to Iowa, things like this had happened occasionally. Lately, however, they happened more and more often. Gradually, the weightless feeling left him, and he could feel that he was lying flat on his back on the ground in the woods. *Mom's here, in the woods again,* he noted, and turned away from where he knew she was. He walked upstream a little way to the log that had lain across the river for many, many years, and crept across it. There was another one downstream from here (he had explored these woods thoroughly), but he didn't like using that one. It felt bad to him. So he used this one, even though its bark had been worn slippery smooth over the years, and he had even slipped from it and fallen into the river once.

On the far side of the river he halted, looking in all directions. He picked up as many stones as he could find that were about the size of a chicken's egg, and filled his pockets with them. He carried the last few in his hands. And then he went hunting.

There was an Indian woman in here, dressed just like they looked on TV westerns and in his comic books. She never spoke. She only looked at him sorrowfully. Frankie *hated* her. He didn't know why, nor had he ever stopped to think about it; he just knew it. And this woman would kill Dad, if she could; he could feel that, too. Frankie spent his free time slinking through the woods on this side of the river, stalking the Indian woman. She would appear suddenly in the trees, and then Frankie threw rocks as fast and as hard as he could at her, but he could never hit her. The rocks bounced harmlessly off the trees or landed in the woods behind her.

One time, and one time only, he had thrown a rock at her and heard a squeak of surprise and pain. He had felt elated, and ran to where the woman had been standing. It turned out to be a chipmunk, just a dumb chipmunk, lying there with its sides heaving and its eyes turned toward Frankie with the whites showing. Frankie was immensely disappointed that it wasn't the woman lying there. He stepped on the chipmunk's head and squashed it flat with his shoe. There was a satisfying *crunch* as he finished the chipmunk off, and then wiped his shoe on the grass and resumed hunting.

There were many days when he didn't see the woman at all, but he felt lucky today. He thought that maybe today, or tomorrow, or sometime soon, something *big* was coming, and he thought that it would be him finding and killing the woman. He slipped through the trees, easing himself around the larger ones and darting to cover to watch and wait. A giggle slipped out. Dad would be so surprised, and so *proud* of him when he found out that he had killed an Injun all by himself!

---

Sam Fuller raced to the scene of an auto accident, on the highway outside the western city limits of Apple Springs. Sounded like two teenagers playing "Chicken" with their cars on the highway on the other side of town. *Damn,* he hoped they weren't hurt too bad. He hated scraping up the remains of people off the road and he hated giving relatives and loved ones the worst of all bad news. In a small town like this, all too often it involved people he had known.

Fuller steered the cruiser carefully through the halted downtown traffic, and then picked up speed again. Something was tickling him at the back of his mind, something about his wife, Sandy . . . he glanced up at the photo of her that he had placed on the cruiser's visor. It would come to him, but he didn't have time to think about it right now. Right now, he had to pay attention to his job. He rounded a curve in the road and felt dread wash over him. It was a head-on collision in the middle of the two-lane blacktop highway. Two cars were mashed together and two groups of medics from the ambulance and the fire department were working desperately. Traffic was piled up around the scene of the accident, and people had gotten out of their cars to get a better look. He could never understand why people just *had* to see the blood and guts and gore, but they did. He picked up his microphone and called into the station. "Two-two-one to thirty-eight."

There was a burst of static, and the station replied, "This is thirty-eight, go ahead."

"TX Sandy and tell her I'm at the scene, and that I'll be late tonight."

The station came back, "Clear."

He stopped the cruiser and got out with his portable radio. *Sandy,* that nagging little voice persisted at the back of his mind. *Well, at least she'll know not to expect me for supper,* he thought, and he went forward to do his grim business. And to do that, he had to push Sandy from his mind.

---

John noted the slowing of traffic ahead of him, and decided to get the ice cream from the truck stop instead of going all the way through town to the supermarket. He swung into the lot and pulled to a stop. Well, it could only be a choice of chocolate, strawberry, or vanilla here—God knew he had stocked enough of it—but at least they wouldn't get stuck in traffic.

Larry came in with him. John waved hello to the clerk behind the cash register and went straight to the freezer section. While he was mulling over his choices, he caught snatches of conversation. From what he could gather, there had been a big car accident on the highway on the other side of town. When it was his turn to pay for his purchase, he offered the twenty that Larry had pulled out of his father's wallet, and asked the clerk about it. "Hi, Greg. Hey, did you hear what happened?"

Greg took the money and rang up the purchase, dropping the change into John's hand and reaching for a paper bag for the ice cream. "Yeah," he said in a low tone. The manager didn't appreciate his employees gossiping on the job. "I heard that Tom and Butch were in one *hell* of a smash-up on the highway." Greg glanced around to see if anyone was listening, but no one seemed to be paying attention at the time. "They say that they'll both probably *die,* man."

John was just about to ask another question when Greg looked beyond him and said, "Yes, Ma'am, will that be all today?"

He took the paper bag of ice cream and handed it to Larry, and they walked out of the store. Once outside, Larry said, "Aren't Tom and Butch in your class, Johnnie?"

John's throat felt too tight for his voice to come out; he nodded silently. Tom had been in several classes with him this last semester, and he knew Butch by sight. He also knew that they both had dated the same girl, and were constantly at each others' throats about her. Andrea didn't care. She was dating someone else now.

He got behind the wheel of his father's car again. When he

didn't move to start the car, Larry said, "Johnnie, we've gotta get home with this ice cream before it melts, right?"

John looked in the rear-view mirror and caught his own gaze in its reflection. He looked scared. For Larry, he wiped the expression off his face and started the car. "Yeah, right."

His mind was still on Tom and Butch, though, and he accidentally drove into a big pothole with the right rear wheel as he reversed in order to position the car to get back on the road. The back end of the car fell with a thud, and the whole car rocked. John slammed on the brakes, and was thrust forward into the steering wheel. Larry slid off the seat onto the car's floorboard. At the same time, John heard the clatter and tinkle of glass colliding and breaking in the trunk.

He swore and turned off the car's engine. "You all right, Larry?" he asked, helping Larry pull himself back onto the car seat.

"Yeah, but what was that *sound?*"

John sighed. It had been quite the day, starting off so well with the manager showing him how to operate the cash register, and then getting worse and worse. Now it sounded as if he had broken something his father had put in the trunk of the car. All he wanted right now was to be at home in his bedroom with the door closed and the pillow over his head to block out all the noise of this awful day.

He started the car again, eased the wheel out of the hole in the pavement, and drove over to the side of the station, where the pavement wasn't pocked with holes. He parked and grabbed the keys. "I've got to look in the trunk, Larry. Something broke back there."

Where John went, Larry followed. John twisted the key in the trunk's lock, and swung it up and open.

There lay a sea of both empty and full beer bottles. The reek of fresh beer from smashed bottles made his eyes water. Disappointment stabbed at him. But John had *known,* hadn't he? Somehow, he had felt it for a while now, and he wasn't really surprised.

"Holy *shit,*" Larry breathed.

"Guess Dad's drinking again, after all," John said.

"What are we going to do, Johnnie?"

John slammed the trunk lid down hard, bringing the sounds of more broken glass. "We're going to go home and give Dad his ice cream, *that's* what we're going to do. And we tell Mom, but only Mom. Don't tell Dad and *don't tell Frankie.*"

They got back into the front seat of the car. "Yeah, I know," Larry agreed. "That little creepoid tells Dad *everything.*"

John drove home as fast as he dared.

---

In the delightful dappled shade by the rushing river, Anna was enjoying her solitude and her plans for the trip to Des Moines on the morrow. She hugged her knees and smiled. *Things will be all right,* she thought, *because* I'm *going to be all right. I can't change Rudy, but I can change me, and I've already started.* Her heart skipped a beat as she thought how she had coolly handled Rudy's anger over the burnt casserole. Part of her could scarcely believe that she had the temerity to stand up to him and that she further would shock him at supper. Part of her applauded herself, and reminded her of the way she used to be. It felt *right,* and healthy.

Seventeen years of marriage to Rudy Baumann had made her unsure of herself, scared, unhappy and cynical. However, those years of marriage had also given her three sons. If she *did* end up leaving Rudy at some point in the future, she thought she could count on John and Larry to be part of her life. But Frankie was another matter entirely.

The thought of Frankie clouded her day. *Each of my sons is an individual. I should love them each equally for who they are,* she scolded herself. *But why can't I love Frankie? Why does he make me feel like he's capable of . . . well, of evil?*

A chill wind rushed through the trees and reached her. *Now I know I need help,* she thought. *Any mother who thinks her own son would hurt her or others needs to have her head examined. In the fall*

*... in the fall I'll get some help.* She thought of the money that Rudy had given her, safely hidden in the crock on the top shelf of the kitchen cabinet. She had never even counted it to see how much was there, but Rudy had told her it was a quarter of the money he had received from the sale of the coins. *Did he lie?* Anna shook her head as if to clear it. Now where had *that* thought come from? Rudy may have his bad qualities, but being a liar wasn't one of them. Was it? Nope, she decided, Rudy Baumann was, if nothing else, predictable, or she wouldn't have survived with him all these years.

Well, tonight at supper she would tell Rudy about her trip to Des Moines. She would face whatever he did, and then he would stomp off to the barn for whatever he did there alone. While he was gone, she'd pack an overnight bag and stow it in the trunk of the car. Before he was awake in the morning, she'd be out the door and gone with the money from the crock jar. And by the time she got back, he would have had time to get over his tantrum and get on with life, she thought. *And if I do it once, I can do it again. There'll be something to look forward to once in a while besides Rudy and this house, and thinking of the boys slipping away from me. And if I do it twice, maybe I can take the boys away from this dreadful home.*

The sound of an automobile's engine broke her reverie. She got up, stretched luxuriously, and swept grass and old leaves from her jeans. Anna thought that this had been much better than a nap or watching television for a rest. She should have done it long ago.

There was a rustle in the trees behind her, and she turned with a smile. Instinctively, she knew it wasn't Frankie or Rudy. It turned out to be John and Larry, beckoning to her to come with them, and she joined them on the path.

"Mom, I have to talk to you," John said rather breathlessly. And then he stopped, because Frankie had appeared right behind his mother in the time it took for her to walk the few steps to the path.

"What is it, Honey?" she asked, aware of Frankie's presence by John's warning glance and the prickle of goosebumps on the backs of her arms.

John thought quickly. "There was a car wreck on the other side of town. I heard that two guys I know from my class were in it."

They walked toward the house in an odd group, with Anna and her two older sons in front, and Frankie lagging behind a few feet. Anna was filled with concern. "Are they going to be all right?" she asked.

"The way I heard it, it doesn't look good for either one of them," John told her. "Someone said they needed the ambulance from the hospital *and* the guys from the fire department to handle it. Traffic was backed up all the way through town."

"Are *you* all right, John? Did you know these boys well?"

They had reached the house, and John opened the door. Larry scooted inside with the ice cream and put it in the freezer while Frankie lagged behind, standing near the dining table and running his fingers over its surface. To look at him, he had nothing on his mind at all. John stood by Anna as she checked the roast and pulled out potatoes to peel. "I knew them both, but not very well. I guess I'm okay, but it's still a shock."

"It's a terrible thing when someone so young dies or is hurt so badly," Anna said, hugging John. "But sometimes things are meant to be, I think." She handed a paring knife to John. "Care to help your Mom peel potatoes?"

He took the knife and a potato. Behind them, Larry walked to his father's bedroom and replaced the wallet, complete with the change and receipt for the ice cream, and Rudy's keys on his father's dresser. He then went to the living room and lay on the floor with his chin propped in his hands, watching television. Frankie had started tracing widening circles on the surface of the dining table with his finger, humming a single note under his breath. Grabbing a second potato and starting to peel it, John said to his youngest brother, "Frankie! Why don't you get washed up for supper?"

Frankie stopped humming and stared at John. "Dad's in the bathroom," he said, in a matter-of-fact voice. He started his humming and tracing again.

"Dad's *still* in the bathroom?" John exclaimed, looking quickly at Anna, who looked alarmed. They both dropped what was in their hands and went to the bathroom door. John knocked on the door loudly. "Dad!"

From inside the bathroom came no answer; but if they listened carefully, they could hear the identical hum that had come from Frankie. Larry appeared nervously behind John.

John pounded the door furiously. *"DAD! Are you all right?"* he shouted, shaking the bathroom door in its frame.

This time, the humming stopped, and they could hear the stirring of bath water as Rudy rose from the bathtub. "I'm fine," he said, in a calm, reasonable voice. "I'll be out in a minute."

John and Anna looked at each other. He had sounded pretty normal. *Well,* thought Anna, *then that's the way I'll play it.* Aloud she called, "Supper will be ready in about a half hour or so." She walked back to the kitchen to continue to make supper. As John turned to follow her, Frankie walked past him to his bedroom and slammed the door behind him. Larry resumed his position in front of the TV.

"What did you want to talk to me about?" Anna asked John, in a very low tone. "I can feel that there is something that you didn't tell me yet."

John picked up the paring knife and starting peeling potatoes quickly while he whispered, *"While we were gone, we found out that Dad . . ."*

There was the scrape of a dining chair behind them, and Anna turned to see that Frankie had returned with a comic book. *"Later,"* John mouthed to Anna, and she nodded.

A half hour later, they were all sitting at the dining table with a veritable feast in front of them. Anna had learned, from long practice, how to put a meal together in a hurry. Instead of the supper conversation that one might expect at such an ordinary family gathering, however, there was dead silence as each individual tried to be as quiet as possible while chewing and swallowing. That is, all except for Frankie. Abruptly, in the middle of reaching for a slice of bread, he said, "Mom's going to go to Des Moines tomorrow, Dad."

Anna's eyes flew wide, and she gasped involuntarily as Rudy looked up from his plate and stared at her. John and Larry kept their heads down, working systematically at finishing this meal without adding to any trouble that might be coming.

"Frankie! You spoiled my surprise!" she laughed shakily. "*I was going to tell your father myself.*" *How did he know?* she asked herself wildly. *How in God's name did he know?*

Rudy put his fork down, folded his hands in front of him with his elbows on the table, and stared at her. This was not a good sign. "So, tell me, Anna, why do you think you are going to Des Moines?" he asked in a voice that was deadly calm.

She took a deep breath. "Oh, some of the girls and I are going to an art fair there. We'll spend the night at a hotel, go shopping and come back on Monday night," she said airily, as if this were something normal for Anna Baumann to be saying to her husband Rudy. "Kind of like a girl's holiday," she added weakly when Rudy didn't immediately reply.

"Well, now. Do you feel like you need a vacation, Anna?" Rudy asked in that same voice, picking up his fork and looking at the tines.

"Sure. Why not? John and Larry can handle things here while you're at work," she answered, and then bit her tongue. She had meant to keep their collusion a secret, asking them for help in front of Rudy, but it was too late now.

John tried to act his way out of the spot. "Well, yeah, I guess I can help out. What about you, Larry?"

"Sure, I'll help. Just tell us what to fix for meals," Larry said innocently.

Anna flashed them both a brilliant, grateful smile.

Rudy pushed his chair away from the table and sighed. *Oh God, here it comes,* thought Anna, and braced herself.

"I know you've got ice cream for dessert, but I'm full. I guess I'll just go on out to the barn right now," Rudy said, and walked right out the kitchen door. Frankie followed, slamming the door in his customary manner. To Anna, Rudy's reaction was suspicious. No angry outburst? No broken furniture, or broken bones? Somehow, she thought that Rudy's reaction would be much worse than usual when it finally came. Well, she would be ready for it.

Anna and Larry and John looked at each other in confusion. They hurried to finish their meals and do the dishes, and then the boys went to John's room for a game of chess while Anna raced to her bedroom to pack with her heart hammering against her ribs. Somehow, she felt like a criminal, trying to sneak away with a big bag of money. She chose a few different outfits, including what she would wear the next morning, and her night things. She would carry her makeup in her purse.

That reminded her: it was time to get some money from the crock in the kitchen. She pulled a chair over to the counter and climbed on it to reach the crock. The rime of dust on the lid told her it hadn't been touched in quite a while. That was good. Quickly, while still standing on the chair, she counted out four hundred dollars in fifties and hundred dollar bills. She started to put the crock back on the shelf, and then stopped thoughtfully. On impulse she fished her hand into the crock and took the entire wad out. It was huge! How much money did she *have* here? She couldn't stand here and count it. Anna felt vulnerable in this position, and she wouldn't like to have Rudy (or Frankie) walk in on her like this. She replaced the crock, climbed down, and pushed the chair back to the table. Two more things to do, and she'd be ready for her trip.

Anna always left her purse on the kitchen counter next to the toaster, in the little nook between the refrigerator and the kitchen wall. She fished out her car keys from the side pocket, then carefully straightened the stack and stowed the money away deep into a zippered compartment inside her purse, wrapped in facial tissues. A casual glance would only show a slightly messy purse with a wad of white tissues for her nose. She replaced items on top of it, zipped her purse closed, and set the purse back into its original position. That done, she fetched her overnight bag from the bedroom. She wanted to get it into the trunk of the car without Rudy knowing about it. Things just felt more secure that way.

She slipped out the kitchen door and around to the side of the house, where her car was parked. Anna placed the suitcase in the trunk, eased the trunk lid shut, and was back in the house in a matter of seconds. She replaced her car keys in the side pocket of her purse. Now, all she had to do was wait for the morning.

---

It was as hot as a blast furnace in the barn, and when Rudy opened the door, it rushed at his face. He opened the front doors of the barn just a crack to let some of the cooler evening air in, moving a pitchfork to rest against the door on the house side of the barn in order to do it, and then sat down at his desk. He wasn't exactly sure what it was, but he had to figure something out, quick. His desk is where he did his figuring. He searched through the papers on his desk and emptied the contents of his drawers on top of his desk, but nothing occurred to him. He then turned to regard the rest of his work shop. What *was* it that he had to work so hard on?

A fly with the breadth of a nickel buzzed his head, and he swatted at it. He got up and strolled around, but still nothing clicked. Finally, he started work on his storage bins again, thinking that it would come to him in time, but a half hour into it he was sweating like a pig. He opened the little refrigerator and looked in. Empty! Well, he could do something about *that*. He turned to the side door of the barn and picked up the pitchfork in his right hand while he turned the knob in his left hand. Anna was standing there, right outside the door.

She froze on the spot, a vanilla ice cream cone in each hand, staring at her husband holding the pitchfork. Rudy smiled at her playfully. "Whatcha got there, Anna?"

"I . . . I was bringing you an ice cream cone, Rudy. Here, take it before it melts," she said as she shoved one toward his right hand.

"Well, isn't that nice of you," he said, closing the barn door and locking it behind him. He took the ice cream cone in his left hand and gave it an enormous lick. "M-m-m, is that good!"

"Rudy," Anna said shakily, "what are you doing with that pitchfork?"

He looked down at the wicked tines at his side. "You mean, this?"

"Yes. Where did you get it?"

He smiled reminiscently at the tines, bringing them up to the level of his face. "It was in the barn." He flashed a huge smile at Anna. "Hey, your ice cream is dripping all over your hand! Better eat it quick!"

Anna backed up, looking at the ice cream flowing down her hand. "I'll go clean up," she said, and fled into the house. She quietly closed the kitchen door and backed away from it, until her hips hit the dining table from behind.

Rudy followed her, but not immediately. He crunched his ice cream cone in three enormous bites, smacking his lips and wiping his hand on his pants, and then looked around thoughtfully. There! There behind the lilac bushes up against the side of the house! It was just the *perfect* place for a pitchfork. He plunged it behind the bushes and stood back to admire his handiwork. There. That was the first thing he had to do. Now for a beer.

He entered the house without looking around and headed

straight for the refrigerator. No beer there, uh-uh, not in Anna Baumann's refrigerator! He laughed to himself *(what do you expect from Mrs. Goodie Two-Shoes?)*, rummaged a bit in the refrigerator, then closed it and went to fetch his wallet and keys. Maybe tonight he needed a little company with his beer. In fact, he thought he might be able to think and remember with a few brews in his gullet. Yep, that was the ticket. Rudy whistled as he slammed the kitchen door on the way out.

If he had bothered to look in the shadows of the living room, or turn on a light, he would have seen Anna crouching in the corner watchfully, but he didn't even think about looking around. Tonight, Rudy was one busy man.

---

Anna heard Rudy's car engine roar to life, and ran to peek hopefully through the kitchen curtains. He was leaving! She breathed a great sigh and lifted her shaking hands to her face, trying to calm herself. When she saw that his tail lights were almost at the bridge, she left her place at the window and turned on the lights in the living room.

*I have to find that pitchfork,* she decided, *find it and get rid of it. At least when he drank before, he never came at me with one of those.* She opened the kitchen door and stepped out on the porch, searching for it. Not there. She went to the barn, but the side door was locked. In frustration she rounded the side of the barn and looked at the front doors. She was in luck, because Rudy had left the front doors propped open slightly. She squeezed herself through the opening.

It was quite a workshop, she decided, but there definitely was not a pitchfork anywhere in here. She examined some of the hand tools and hefted each in turn. These could *all* be potential weapons. There were chisels, and hammers of different types; saw blades and a nail gun; *everything* seemed sharp, or heavy, or so . . . *handy.* Anna noted the litter of empty beer bottles in the corners of the barn warily. *He didn't just start drinking today,* she thought. *Nope, it's gotten to be his hobby again.* She moved over to Rudy's desk, and picked up two pictures from the top of the pile there. They were the pictures of Heinrich and Katrina Baumann and the hated Stanley Richter. Anna dropped them immediately. They felt older than old, ancient maybe, and somehow *slimy.* She looked around some more. If Rudy were going to come at her with a pitchfork, she needed something she could handle easily. She found a can of paint thinner and a box of wooden matches, and looked at them grimly. If it were a matter of stopping Rudy in his tracks, then squirting thinner on him and lighting a match might make him think twice. And if it didn't stop him? Could she actually light her husband on fire? She shivered, but turned off the lights, and left the way she came still carrying the thinner and matches.

In the house, she secreted her weapons in the bedroom, down below her side of the bed. Anna then sat on the sofa in the living room with the television on and the volume turned down low, to wait for whatever came.

---

When Sam Fuller pulled his personal Ford Bronco into his double-wide driveway, he was very thankful to see Sandy's blue Chevrolet already parked there. It had been a *terrible* day, and he wanted nothing more than to just be around her and talk about normal things for a little bit. Sandy opened the front door as he climbed the steps, and embraced him. She led him inside silently, then closed and locked the front door.

He put his flashlight and radio on the kitchen counter and sat at the table, allowing Sandy to bustle around him. She was chatting non-stop to him about the kids, but he wasn't really listening. Instead, he was immersing himself in her warmth and the pleasure she gave him in just being *alive* and *there* for him. She poured him a cup of coffee and halted at the look in his eyes. "Was it that bad?" she asked quietly.

"It was the worst," Sam answered, and pulled her to him.

She held his head to her breast and kissed the top of his head. "*Sshh*. Just relax and eat for now. You can tell me later, if you want to," she soothed. He lifted his head, and said, "I love you, Sandy."

"And I love you, too, Sam," she said, looking at her husband with sorrow. It was her experience that he took it badly when somebody died "on his watch," even though he couldn't possibly have prevented it. When Terry, the dispatcher, had called her to tell her that there had been a possibly fatal collision and that Sam would be home late, she had turned on the police-band radio, learned the names of the two boys involved, and the fact that neither of them had left the scene alive. Tom Albertson and Clarence (Butch) Black had had run-ins with each other before, each getting more vicious, over the affections of a girl. Sam could have been sitting right in the spot where the boys finally died, and they would have just driven peacefully past and found another spot to continue their war. And Sam was left to clean up the mess they made. She clucked in sympathy and anger at life's occasional brutal unfairness, and turned back to the kitchen counter for Sam's sandwich.

While he was eating, she poured him a bath and laid out his robe for him. She had sent the girls to the neighbors' house already to spend the night, and no television news program would be turned on in this house tonight. No news of the Vietnam War, or crooked politicians, or protest marches or rioting. Not tonight. She chose some soothing background music on the radio, and left the lights in the living room on low.

After his food and bath, Sam sat up in bed with a book while Sandy nestled against him with her own book. After a few minutes, he said, "This is nice. Thanks for understanding, Sweetheart."

"Nothin' to it," she quipped. He slipped his arm around her and told her about his day. The boring paperwork. Another complaint from Mr. Beecham (who *always* thought he detected the smell of burning marijuana coming from the house next door; it had turned out to be burnt toast this time, and Fuller doubted that Beecham had ever smelled real marijuana in his life). News from around town. Pulling over the Baumann kids and talking to them (which evinced quite a bit of interest from Sandy). His call to the scene of the two-car collision. Handling traffic while he waited for the deputies to arrive. Finding out that both boys had died. Calling the coroner. Getting details from witnesses who hadn't actually *seen* the collision, but had heard them arguing earlier. Finding skid marks where the cars had each started and aimed straight at each other. Measuring distances and collecting evidence. Arranging for tow trucks and the cleanup of the scene. Taking upon himself the duty of telling Mrs. Black, a divorced woman, that her boy Butch would never cause her any more trouble. Writing it all up with the other officers who had been on the scene. On the way home, he had gone back to the scene. All that was left to tell the tale were the skid marks, smears of blood on the pavement, and a shower of broken glass by that time. The cleanup crew was still working on it.

"I thought of you today," he said.

"Oh, gee, thanks," Sandy answered pertly. "Of course, once a year ain't bad, I guess."

"No, I mean when I was talking to the Baumann boys. It just occurred to me that you had the Baumanns pegged. Rudy *did* have quite the drinking problem in Minnesota, and he did beat Anna. But the boys said he's not drinking any more."

Sandy slapped her book closed. "I *knew* it. I *knew* something like that was going on. Anna never opened up and told me, but you can sense when a person is holding something back. That *son of a bitch.*"

Sam put his hand on hers. "Yeah, but for all we know it's in the past. I did a little side-investigating of my own. He was arrested several times for bar fights and driving under the influence back in Duluth; he even spent jail time there for it. He had his driver's license lifted for a while. But since he's been here, there's not been a peep out of him. I had a friendly conversation with his boss at the factory. So far he's had perfect attendance, and a perfect work record. So try to hold off on any judgments right now, all right?"

"Why in the world would she stay with him when he treated her like that?" asked Sandy plaintively. "She can't *want* to live like that."

"There are all sorts of reasons that people stay in those kinds of relationships. Sometimes, they just don't know that anything better exists. Sometimes they've been threatened with murder if they ever leave, and they believe it. Some stay for the kids, or because they have no other place to go. With Anna, I'd bet he cowed her into believing that the world began and ended with Rudy Baumann, and nobody else mattered. And, Sweetheart, there are a lot more families and relationships out there like that than you'd ever dream possible. People just don't talk about it."

"Why would he do it to her?" Sandy asked. "Anna is sweet, and caring, and lovely."

"From what I've read and been taught, the abuser has been abused himself or herself, or needs to have absolute control over the other person because of feeling helpless in other ways," Sam told her. "It's a huge subject, Sandy, and it's not cut and dried. In my job, I see the darker side of human nature much too often, and many times it comes out with the people who are closest to us."

"Sam?"

"Yeah?"

"I had almost made up my mind to cancel this, but Liz and Linda and Anna and I were planning on going to Des Moines for a couple of days. We were going to leave in the morning. It would have been a wonderful time for Anna to get out and have some normal life," Sandy said wistfully. "Would you mind? The girls are already next door, and the Nelsons said they wouldn't mind watching them until I get back."

"I think it's a *great* idea, for you as well as for Anna. Go ahead and go. And the girls don't have to stay next door. I have tomorrow off and I can take Monday, too, and they can have a taste of being with Dad for a change. We'll eat take-out, watch movies . . . and it isn't often that they get to beg me in person for spending money. I'll spoil 'em rotten. It'll be good for me, especially after the day I had today."

"Oh, Sam, thank you, Honey, thank you!" Sandy cried, throwing her arms around his neck. "Just don't mess up the house *too* much, okay?"

Sam opened his book again. "Let's see. I wonder if the tattoo parlor is open tomorrow?"

"Sam! You tease!" laughed Sandy.

"What's so interesting in Des Moines? I know, shopping."

"Yes, shopping, and there's a big art fair. Mostly it's just the idea of getting out with the girls and being away for a little bit."

Sam reached over and kissed the top of Sandy's head. "Have a good time, and I know I don't have to say this, but take care of yourself."

Sandy looked up into Sam's eyes. "I am so lucky to have you," she murmured, and let him know she meant it with a kiss.

Within a minute, their books had dropped to the floor, while Sam and Sandy Fuller made the best of their time together.

# CHAPTER
# Twenty-Five

Since Sam Fuller was off work for the night, and not cruising the streets of Apple Springs, he missed Rudy's big old Ford sitting in front of The Rusty Bucket. Of the three bars in town, the Bucket was the least savory, but it had what Rudy craved: dimness, a rowdy Saturday night crowd, and plenty of beer on tap. He pulled open the door giving on the sidewalk and inhaled deeply of the fumes of alcohol and cigarette smoke, like they were the finest perfumes dabbed on the most intimate places of a beautiful woman. *This* is what he needed. *This* is what he had been waiting for.

The place was noisy and packed with people, so he stood at the bar and lit a cigarette while he waited for the bartender to notice him. In such a small town, it wasn't long before two of the men he worked with at the factory spied him, and invited him to join them. A few minutes later, a pitcher of beer appeared on the table with fresh glasses. Rudy's acquaintances had just turned into his best friends when they stood him a round.

"So how do you like Iowa, Rudy?" asked Herb Stenley. "Is it much different from Duluth?"

"I love it," Rudy answered earnestly. "The farm's great, and the work's not bad."

"I've never lived anywhere else," said Cliff Barham. "No need to. Apple Springs has everything I want."

Rudy drained his glass and poured another beer from the pitcher. "Either of you have wives?"

"Used to," muttered Cliff. "She divorced me two years ago and took the kids with her. Said she didn't like my style."

"Sorry, man," said Rudy.

"Well, I don't exactly miss her, if you get my drift. I like to get out and party at night, and she wanted me home with those two little brats of hers. And she was really big on church. I'd rather sleep in on Sundays," Cliff said.

"What about you, Herb? You married?" Rudy asked. For some reason, this topic was very much on his mind tonight.

"Nope. Never really found just the right girl. I must have fooled around with every possible chick in this town. Some of them are okay, but *marriage?*" He gave an exaggerated shudder.

Rudy waved the now-empty pitcher at the waitress, who caught his gesture and nodded. "You are *lucky*. Both of you."

"Why do you say that, Rudy? I've seen your wife. If you don't want her, I've got dibs," laughed Cliff.

*"Watch your mouth,"* Rudy growled.

Cliff and Herb thought he was kidding and laughed, but their laughter dried up when they saw the look in Rudy's eyes and the set of his shoulders. "Hey, Buddy, we were just having some fun. Lighten up!" Cliff clapped Rudy on the back. "No harm meant."

A full pitcher of beer arrived. Mollified, Rudy said, "Okay, okay. It's just a bad time for me."

"Why is that, Rudy?" asked Herb.

"Because my wife thinks she's going to leave me in the morning," Rudy ground out, drinking half of the beer in his glass in one gulp. He set his glass down on the table with a little too much gusto, and beer sloshed over onto his hand. He licked it off absently.

"Jeez, Rudy, that's terrible," said Herb. "What do you mean, she *thinks* she's leaving you?"

Rudy leaned back in his chair and dug into his pants pocket. He dangled a set of car keys in front of the men. "She ain't leaving if she can't drive her car," he said with a smirk. The other two men smiled uncertainly.

"I hate to say this, Rudy, but if she wants to leave you, she'll find a way. That's one thing I learned from my divorce: when a woman's mind is made up, she's *gone*. Unless you give her a good reason to stay," Cliff offered seriously. "You'd better put some sweet moves on her."

"Oh, I've got some sweet moves planned for her, all right. You betcha. Anna's mine, and she's not going *anywhere.*" Rudy stood up. "Gotta make some room. Get us another pitcher, okay?" He slapped a twenty onto the table and walked toward the back of the bar.

Herb and Cliff were silent for a moment after Rudy left the table, and then Herb said, "I've got a bad feeling about this."

Cliff eyed him doubtfully. "Oh, come on. They probably just had a little tiff, and the man's in a drinking mood. I remember times like that from when I was married to Betsy. We'll just stay out of it, okay?"

Herb sipped his beer, then nodded. "Okay. But Cliff—have you ever seen anybody drink so much beer so fast and still walk and talk so straight?"

Cliff considered this. "We might have to drive him home."

Herb laughed. "Hell, *he'll* probably have to drive *us* home." And he poured himself another beer.

---

In John's room, the chess board had been put aside, and he and Larry were talking. "I wanted to punch that little bastard at the supper table," John said quietly, indicating the wall between his and Frankie's room. "Telling Dad about Mom going to Des Moines before she had a chance to say something. And how did he know? I don't think Mom would tell him."

"He's creepy, Johnnie. He knows *everything* that's going on, even if he's been in the woods all day," Larry said.

"Well, maybe I'll teach him a little lesson while Mom's gone. It's time he paid for his mouth. He treats Mom just like Dad does, and Dad thinks it's funny."

Larry looked at his older brother, alarmed. "Dad would *kill* you."

John rose from the bed. "Yeah, well maybe I'd like a piece of *him*, too."

He opened the door to his room and walked down the hallway toward the kitchen, leaving Larry to follow him. The living room light was still on, and he peeked around the corner. "Mom! What are you still doing up?"

Anna had been lying on the sofa staring at the television, not really comprehending the show that was playing, and she started guiltily at the sound of John's voice. "Oh! John, you scared me. I'm waiting for your Dad to get home, I guess. I'm a little nervous." She sat up and smoothed her hair. "What time is it?"

"It's after midnight, Mom. Look, you need your rest or it'll spoil your whole day tomorrow. I'm not tired. If you want me to, I'll sit up and watch TV, and if I hear Dad coming I'll wake you up."

"I can stay up with him," Larry volunteered.

"Don't you two have to work in the morning?" Anna asked. "Larry, I know you have to deliver the papers."

"Piece of cake, Mom," he grinned.

"Go on and get some sleep. Remember, the bars are open until two o'clock, and when Dad was drinking he never left until they asked him to leave," John reminded her. "You've got plenty of time."

"I don't even know if I *can* sleep," Anna said ruefully. "I've been sitting here thinking about it, and you know, I can't *picture* myself in Des Moines at the art fair. I have a feeling it's not going to happen."

John sat next to his mother. "Mom, I can't ever remember your taking a trip alone, without Dad. You should at least try to get out and have some fun."

Larry sat on the other side of her. "And bring us something back," he said with his charming smile.

Anna put her arms around her two older sons and hugged

them to her. "Okay, okay, I give up. I'll try." She got up from the sofa and headed toward the bedrooms, turning to smile at the scene of John and Larry arguing over which channel to watch.

She went into her bedroom, flicked on the light, and closed the door. She didn't immediately lie down. She lowered the shades and turned on a small bedside lamp, and then turned off the overhead light, throwing the room into dimness. It was good enough for what she wanted. She knelt next to her side of the bed and pulled out the can of paint thinner and the matches. Good, they were still there. She jiggled the can, trying to judge just how much was in there. She thought that it was at least two-thirds full. She checked the match box, and found that it was almost full. Anna carefully replaced the items and got into bed, fully dressed with even her shoes on. If Rudy came home in an angry, drunken rage, she wanted to be mobile as fast as possible. She turned off the bedside light.

John and Larry talked softly into the night, but neither thought of the Sheriff's words. And later, as they dozed in front of the television, neither saw Frankie sneak into the house and to his bedroom.

---

At 1:45 a.m., the bartender called, "Last call!" and flicked the lights of the Bucket, leaving them on. Music from the jukebox halted. The few remaining patrons blinked blearily in the sudden light. Rudy had been declared officially drunk by Cal and Herb about an hour before that. At this particular point in time, he wouldn't be able to drive, but he could still walk. To their amazement, he turned and waved at the waitress.

"Hey, Sweet Thing, two more pitchers over here!" he yelled. His voice echoed in the nearly empty bar. Sweet Thing glanced at the bartender, who shook his head and came out from behind the bar.

"Hey, Buddy," he said easily to Rudy.

"Hey there, Whoever-You-Are!" Rudy blasted back at him.

"I'm Jim, the bartender. I've gotta tell you, I'm cutting you off. You've had too much to drink already."

"You can't cut me off! It's still Last Call!" Rudy argued.

"Not for you. You're through, and I'm asking you nicely this one time to leave. Can you guys help him?" the bartender asked Cliff and Herb.

They nodded and rose. "Come on, Rudy, let's go," said Cliff. "We'll leave the rest for another night." He put his hand on Rudy's arm.

Rudy swiped at his hand angrily and shouted, "I'm not going anywhere! Leave me alone!"

The bartender looked over Rudy's head at Herb and Cliff. "I'm going to call the cops for some help here," he said. "Maybe you two had better clear out before I do it."

"Rudy, come on," Herb urged. "You don't want to go to jail."

At the word, "jail," Rudy staggered to his feet. He wobbled a bit in place, then tucked his shirt into his pants, trying to assume an air of injured dignity. "Okay, I'll go."

"Just a minute," the bartender said. "You can't drive. If you won't let one of these gentlemen drive you home, I have to take your car keys."

Herb offered, "I'll drive you, Rudy, or you can stay on my sofa for the night. I just live in an apartment around the corner."

Rudy stared at him, then nodded and led the way to the door of the bar, staggering slightly at one point. Cliff put out a hand to steady him, and this time, Rudy didn't shake him off.

When they were outside, the warm, humid August air robbed him of his breath, and Rudy was suddenly very, very tired. He wobbled with each step. "I don't think we're going to get him into a car," Cliff told Herb.

Herb agreed, and they led Rudy to Herb's apartment. The second Rudy sat on the sofa, he passed out. With little difficulty Herb and Cliff laid him out horizontally, and Herb stepped back outside with Cliff.

"Never again," he told his friend. "That is one serious boozer."

"You've got my vote on that," Cliff snorted. "I had a good time until he showed up. I feel sorry for his wife. I hope she does leave him."

"Come on by about noon if you're up," Herb said. "If he's still here, we'll get him home somehow. I don't really care to have him in my place. He's got weird vibes." And he wiped his hands on his pants, as if he had touched something he didn't care for.

It turned out that neither of them had to worry about Rudy the next morning. Rudy Baumann, it turned out, had his own inner alarm clock.

# CHAPTER
## Twenty-Six

Something was bothering Anna. She was drowsing in a twilight between the deep, unrestful sleep of the last few hours and full wakefulness, when the concept of *time* came to her. She was at once fully awake, with the feeling that something was deeply wrong. She put out a hand in the darkness toward Rudy's side of the bed, and when she felt only the smooth, untouched bedspread there, she sat up and turned on the bedside lamp. The clock said 5:32, which meant that she had actually slept for several hours, and the house was silent.

She went to the bedroom window and pushed the shade aside. It was not yet dawn, but she could see that the spot where Rudy usually parked his car was empty. With a sigh of relief, she went out to the living room to find John and Larry.

Anna smiled at the sight. Both of her sons were draped over opposite ends of the sofa, snoring loudly, while static blared from the television set. She turned down the volume, but left the TV on for a bit of light, and gently shook John awake, then Larry. They both woke slowly, and sat up groggily. Obviously they had a long night on their watch. Putting a finger to her lips, she gestured at the clock on the fireplace mantel, and whispered, "He's not back yet."

Larry yawned and stretched. "I wasn't really sleeping."

"I know," Anna grinned, "you were just resting your eyes. You two did a good job, and I did get some sleep. Now it's time for me to get ready and go."

The boys nodded, and Anna hurried to the bathroom. She took a quick shower and put on makeup, then dressed hurriedly in pink shorts, a white sleeveless top, and white sneakers. She was excited. It looked as if she would actually make it out of the house before Rudy got back. Her thoughts turned to the promised pleasures of the day ahead, and she relaxed her tense posture as she took her purse from its spot in the kitchen to slip her makeup into it. *I did it!* she congratulated herself. *I'm almost gone!*

In the living room, neither John nor Larry had moved from their spots on the sofa. She pranced up to them, twirling and smiling. "How do I look?"

"You look great, Mom," Larry said, smiling himself. "What time is it?"

"It's not even 6:30 yet," she answered. "I'll leave now. You two can do whatever you like now. It's going to be all right, after all."

"I don't have to work until 11:00 this morning," John said. "I'm going to bed. What about you, Larry?"

"I have to get ready for my paper route, but when I'm done I'll come home and sleep. What about Frankie?"

What about Frankie, indeed. As if on cue, Frankie shuffled into the living room. He was already dressed in jeans, a T-shirt, tennis shoes, and his favorite, red cowboy hat. He didn't look sleepy, not at all. In fact, he looked as if he had been up for hours.

"Where's Daddy?"

Anna took a deep breath. "Daddy isn't home right now, Frankie. It's time for me to leave on my little trip. I'm glad to see you up already! Now I can say goodbye."

John and Larry just looked at each other. "We'll walk you out, Mom," John told her.

"That would be wonderful. I'll get my purse and keys, and I'll be going." Anna walked to the dining table, where she had left her purse, and put her hand in the side pocket where she usually kept her car keys. They weren't there. *They must have gotten bur-*

*ied while I was rearranging my purse yesterday,* she thought, and dug deeper into the compartment. There was no familiar jingle, and she couldn't find them.

She bit her lip, and opened the main compartment of her purse to check there. No keys. The money was still in there, however. What *did* she do with her car keys?

She turned to her sons. "Anybody see my car keys?" she asked, looking at each in turn. John and Larry both shook their heads, but Frankie only smiled. "Frankie, did you see my car keys?" she asked pointedly.

"Nope."

"Then why are you smiling?"

"Daddy's coming," he said, and produced a plastic horse from his pocket. He made it gallop over the surface of the dining table.

A flash of red-hot irritation shot through Anna. She put her hand over Frankie's hand and the horse and knelt on the floor by the table. "Frankie, listen to me. I am going to Des Moines today. I'll be back on Monday night. But I can't go unless I have the car keys. Do you know where they are?" she asked sharply.

"Yep."

"I thought you said you didn't take them!" John exclaimed, raising his voice. "You lied!"

"I didn't take the keys, Johnnie. Daddy has 'em," Frankie said, looking up at his brother with an angelic smile.

Anna got up from the floor, feeling like she might faint.

"How do you *know* that Daddy has the keys? Did you see him take them?" Anna asked Frankie in a softer, calmer tone.

"I don't *have* to see him. I just know," Frankie shrugged. He went into the kitchen. "Mom, can I have a biscuit?"

Larry put out his hand to stop Anna. *"I'll* get it for him," he said with disgust. He went into the kitchen and opened the bag of biscuits, watching as Frankie reached in and took one out. "Here, have *two,* you little shit," he muttered under his breath, and stuffed another into Frankie's hands. Crumbs dotted the kitchen floor, but Frankie only grinned broadly. He walked to the kitchen door. "I want to go outside," he said in a demanding voice.

John stepped to the door, unlocked it, and opened it for Frankie. Frankie started outside, but his brother put his foot and leg in front of him. "I think I'll just see if you don't have those keys on you," he said, and patted Frankie's pockets. They were empty. John stood up, looked at Frankie, and said, "Okay, go on. But I think I'll look in your room for them."

Frankie looked up at John and said, "It really doesn't matter any more." He left the house, and John slammed the door behind him.

"Mom, I'm sorry, but there is definitely something very wrong with Frankie," John said as he passed his mother on the way to Frankie's room.

She stopped him. "Don't bother."

"What do you *mean*, don't bother? The chances are, Frankie stole your keys, and I'm going to find them!"

"John, Frankie knows things that he shouldn't know. I don't know how he does it, but he does. If he says that your Dad has my keys, that's probably right. And you're right, there *is* something terribly wrong with him. I think it's your Dad's influence on him, and I don't think it can be fixed until I can get him away from Rudy."

"You're not just going to give up on your trip, are you?" John asked her angrily.

"Not at all. I'm going to call Sandy and ask if she'll come and pick me up," Anna said. "Don't worry so hard, John. Nothing's that much out of control here."

John sat at the table and fumed while she called her friend. Sandy picked it up on the first ring.

"Anna, is that you?" Sandy asked. "Are you coming? Liz and Linda are already here."

"Sandy, I've had a little problem. I've lost my car keys, and I don't have another set. Is there any chance that you could come out here and pick me up?"

"Of course! There should be no traffic on the road at all," Sandy agreed. "I'll be there as soon as I can make it."

Anna put the phone down and sighed. "My clothes for the trip are locked in the trunk. I'll get a few things to change into, and then I'll wait outside," she told John. "Larry, you'd better get going on your paper route."

"I'm going to stay until you leave, Mom," Larry said stubbornly, crossing his arms over his chest to emphasize his point.

"And I'll wait with you outside," John said. When Anna opened her mouth to disagree, he held up his hand. "No arguments. You left *us* in charge today, remember?"

Anna closed her mouth again and smiled gratefully at her sons. Then she hurried off to find suitable substitutes for clothing in Des Moines, and stuff them into a paper bag. *I guess I'm not alone here after all,* she thought with a thrill of delight. *I still have John and Larry.*

---

Rudy was lying, soundly asleep on his back, on the sofa in Herb Stenley's living room. He was having one *helluva* dream, and it was taking all his attention.

*He was in the barn, working on a chest of drawers for Frankie's room, and concentrating hard on getting the corners just right. Dad was watching him in awe. "I'm proud of you, son," his old man said. "I was worried you wouldn't amount to anything, but you've got yourself a real way with wood. It's like money in the bank!"*

*Rudy's heart thumped to attention. He whirled toward the desk. "Daddy? Is that you?"*

*"You bet your ass it is," Dad grinned. Most of his teeth were missing, and the few that were left were black stubs stuck in doughy, red gums. "I been watchin' you."*

*"Watchin' me? Where've you been all these years?"*

*"I've been right here, waitin' for you, Rudy." Dad's breath smelled like rotten chicken, and his skin was splotched grey and yellow.*

*Rudy was puzzled.* "But everybody said you run off and got killed, Daddy. One mornin' you were out here in the barn. I remember, 'cause I was with you. You were . . . you . . ."

*Dad chuckled wetly.* "I was havin' myself a little talk with you, wasn't I, Rudy? You were on the floor, pounding nails into some scraps of wood, and I was explainin' how to do things the right way, because, Rudy, you weren't too bright. You always took several explanations before you got things right." *He guffawed and slapped his knee.* "You never did too good at rememberin', so I had to repeat things with my fists and my feet. Damn, boy! At first it gave me some whores of headaches to explain things to you, but after a while, why, it cheered me right up!"

In his dream, Rudy remembered. He swallowed and tossed his head on the arm of Herb's sofa. Sweat broke out on his face and neck, and a low moan escaped his lips. He could feel a long-forgotten hot ball of pain deep in his gut where his father had once kicked him. He turned onto his side and wrapped his arms around his belly.

"You scared me bad, Daddy, and I ran out of the barn. You were chasin' me with the pitchfork, and Mama was screamin' after you to stop. 'Lissa and Sarah came and got me, and we hid in the corn. We could hear Mama screamin' and screamin', and you were yellin' that you were gonna kill us all. Sarah said that Mama would come and save us, but Mama didn't come. You were lookin' for us in the corn with the pitchfork, stabbin' at the corn and yellin', and you almost got us, but we ran to the woods and . . ."

"HAW, HAW, HAW!" *Dad laughed.* "You kids sure could run! Yep, you outfoxed me then and I lost track of you, boy, but I found you now!" *Suddenly the old pitchfork appeared in Dad's hands.* "Better run, Rudy! Go get your sisters to hide you again!" *And he threw his face into Rudy's and ROARED, moldy spittle and bits of rotted teeth spraying over Rudy's face.*

On the sofa, Rudy's knees rocketed as if he were pumping a bicycle in a race for his life, and his thrashing arms knocked newspapers from Herb's coffee table onto the floor. He struggled up, up, up and out of his dream, *forcing* himself awake, and opened his eyes to an unfamiliar room with his heart pounding.

He sat up, looking around and wondering where he was. Rudy looked at his watch. With the luminous hands, he could see it was just a little after 6:30 in the morning. He sat there a moment, and then he had a sudden clear image of Frankie in his head: Frankie was grinning and wearing his little red cowboy hat. *Now* he knew what he had been trying to remember the evening before. *Now* he knew what he had to do.

He groped his way out of the apartment in the bright, cloudless light of a new morning, recognizing the main street of Apple Springs off to his left. He staggered a bit, but purpose drove him, and he made it to the corner and to his car. He felt in his pocket for his keys, and pulled out Anna's car keys as well. A cheerful smile split his face, but his good humor was replaced almost immediately by an all-too-familiar, head-smashing throb. *Oh, goodie. A hangover on top of everything else. Oh, well, a man does what a man has to do,* he thought. It was time to set his family straight.

---

Sandy replaced the phone on the hook softly, not wanting to wake her husband, and went to the front door. Out on the steps, she motioned to Liz and Linda, who were leaning on their cars with mugs of coffee, talking. She explained quickly that she was going to pick Anna up, and asked them to wait there.

"I shouldn't be too long. She's all ready, and there's no traffic at this hour. Go ahead and get more coffee if you like, and use the bathroom. Just don't wake Sam up—he needs his rest," Sandy finished.

Liz and Linda nodded their understanding, but as Sandy backed her car out of the driveway, Liz asked Linda, "Where does Sandy have to go to pick Anna up?"

Neither of them realized it, but Sandy was going to have to go to hell and back to get her friend.

---

Rudy tossed his half-smoked cigarette out the window of his old car as he rounded the turn onto his farm's driveway. He took it a tad too fast and wide. Road dust blew in the driver's side window, threatening to choke him and blind him at the same time. From the trunk there came a series of thumps, clatters, and the smashing of glass. *Oh, for Christ's sake,* he thought. He floored the accelerator to outdistance the dust, and sure enough, way down at the end of the driveway he could see Anna in her cute little shorts and white top, her purse slung over her shoulder. She was standing on the porch with her hands on her hips and *oh my God, is that ATTITUDE?* He laughed at the thought. *Oh, yes, let it be attitude, and let her open her perfect little mouth. Just once. Oh, please.*

The sight of her pissed him off, even though he had been expecting it. He pulled up in front of the house in a cloud of dust, but before he could stop the engine, Anna was off the porch and stalking down the steps. John followed right behind her. He looked like he was trying to call her off. *This is going to be a dandy,* Rudy thought, looking forward to laying some satisfying hurt on his family. He opened the car door and bounded out of it, ready for action. He came face to face with his wife next to the lilac bushes at the bottom of the porch steps, right where he wanted to be.

"Get out of my way, Anna. I'm not in the mood," he growled and made as if to pass her.

Anna grabbed his arm. "Give me my car keys," she demanded. Her green eyes sparked fire.

Rudy stopped and looked at her hand on his arm. "You want to take your hand off me?" he spat, jerking his arm away. "You're not going anywhere, Anna. Not today, not any day." His eyes darted to the left. All he had to do was reach out his hand, and the pitchfork would be there. Oh, what a surprise she had coming to her!

Anna tried to step in front of him again, and his reaction was immediate: he back-handed her across the face, and she fell back and to her left on the porch steps. A small trickle of blood ran from her nose. She shook her head to clear it, and one single, tiny drop flew off her face and sailed through the air to land on the ground in the dooryard.

John shouted, "Stop it!" and placed himself between Anna and Rudy. Larry appeared on the porch behind Anna, his face white and set grimly, and he helped his mother to her feet.

Rudy stood there, grinning at his family. He gestured widely. "What are you all going to do? *Beat* the keys out of me?"

"*I'm* not interested in the keys," John ground out as he faced his father. "I'm interested in you getting the hell out of here and out of our lives. You've made our lives miserable for years, Dad, and this is enough. Now get OUT!" and he shoved Rudy backward as hard as he could.

The move surprised his father. He had been expecting a roundhouse swing of John's fist, which he could have ducked. Instead, he pinwheeled his arms and stumbled backward, landing in the dirt. He lay there flat on the ground, gaping at his son.

"You little son of a bitch," Rudy growled low in his throat. "Have *I* got a surprise for *you*."

---

Sandy made the turn onto the farm road easily. She squinted ahead. The bright sunlight made it difficult to make out details, but it looked like the whole family was outside the farm house. *That son of a bitch is NOT going to stop her,* she thought, her jaw set, and she pushed the accelerator closer to the floor. She flipped open the glove compartment as she steered the car with her left hand, searching for some type of weapon. Sam was a cop. *Surely* he'd have a gun or *something* in here that she could use. Her hand closed around a small cannister. Pepper spray! Sam had gotten it for her years ago for self-protection, but she hadn't liked to carry it and had tossed it in the glove compartment instead. She put it in her lap and searched some more, but came up with nothing more useful. Well, it would have to do, unless she wanted to slap Rudy across the face with a map. She hoped she'd be able to figure out how to use the spray easily, because she never had read the instructions.

In the back of her mind was Sam's voice telling her not to get in between Anna and Rudy, but she ignored that voice. It was easy to say that when . . . and then she was close enough to see: Rudy had reached out and slapped Anna across the face with the back of his hand! As she watched, one of the older boys pushed Rudy to the ground.

Nobody had even looked at her coming toward them yet. About thirty yards from the house she veered into the empty corn field to the left, bumping and slamming the car across the old corn rows. Sandy shut off the engine and got out, holding her tiny cannister in her hand.

---

Sam Fuller woke with the distinct feeling that Sandy was in real trouble.

He looked at the clock: 7:30 a.m. She should already be on the road. *Let's see. If they left at 7:00 like they planned, they should be around Fennville by now,* he thought. As he sat up in bed, he had a sudden, terrible feeling that Sandy wasn't in Fennville. He got up out of bed and looked out the window overlooking the street. Liz and Linda were standing by their cars, sipping coffee and glancing at their watches. He opened the window and called down.

"Hey! Liz! Linda!"

"Hi, Sam!" they called, and waved, smiling.

"I thought you'd be gone by now. Where's Sandy?"

Liz shielded her eyes and looked up at him. "Anna called; she lost her car keys. Sandy went to pick her up."

Sam slammed the window shut and threw on his clothes, service belt, and holstered service revolver. He took the stairs at a gallop, stopping only long enough to grab his radio. Throwing open the front door, he raced to his Bronco and turned to the two shocked women standing in the street. "When did she leave?" he asked, opening the vehicle's door.

Liz and Linda were gaping at him, their mouths making perfect little "o" shapes.

"WHEN DID SHE LEAVE?" he shouted, and Linda was galvanized into speech.

"About f-fifteen or twenty minutes ago, Sam. What's the matter?" she called after him as he screeched backward out of the driveway, touched his brakes, and shoved the automatic transmission into Drive. There was no answer from Sam, only a shower of tiny gravel and dust from his spinning tires. At the end of the street, before he turned, they saw him reach his hand out of the car window and affix a flashing red light to the top of the Bronco.

Liz looked at Linda. "What should we do? Stay here?"

"I don't know," Linda replied, her hands held to her chest protectively, "but I don't think he wanted Sandy to go to Anna's house."

---

Sam was speeding past the truck stop on the far side of town when he saw the first clouds zooming from out of nowhere to gather over the Baumann farm. "Fuck!" he swore, and blared his horn as he passed a slow-moving sedan holding two very surprised elderly women, probably on their way to church. He checked the sky again. *Holy Christ,* he thought in awe and dread, *this is it! This is what it looks like!*

Nasty, green-grey clouds were streaking across the sky, coming from all directions to convene above the Baumann farm. The pile of thunderheads was enormous. He couldn't see the top of them, and he was still miles away. Flecks of lightning shown through the nearest clouds. He slid his police revolver out of the holster and put it on the car seat beside him. Glancing at his left arm, he noted that the sun was showing full strength on his car—for now. He turned his radio on. "This is two-two-one to thirty-eight."

"This is thirty-eight, go ahead."

"I am proceeding to a domestic dispute at the Baumann farm off old 7114 East. Request backup."

He made the turn onto the Baumann property and bumped across the bridge. He was now beneath the sick, slimy skies that spelled disaster.

Only static came from his radio, punctuated here and there with what might have been the dispatcher's voice. He swore again, then said into the radio, "Repeat, proceeding to the Baumann farm, request backup!" Only static answered him. He tossed the radio onto the car seat and concentrated on what was ahead of him.

He slowed as he passed Sandy's car. She had left it a few yards off the driveway after driving directly into the corn field. The driver's side door was open, and Sandy was gone. *Sandy!* he screamed in his mind.

---

John stared at his father, lying spread-eagled on the ground with a silly expression of utmost surprise on his face. Rudy was red-eyed and unshaven. His shirt hung out of his pants on one side, and at some point, he must have urinated in his pants. A wet stain marked his crotch and the inside of his legs. Feelings of revulsion and shame washed over him: *this* was his father. "You're nothing but a stinking, worthless, mean old drunk. Now get out!"

The wind picked up and the sky darkened. Old leaves and dust skittered up restlessly into mini-cyclones. Rudy seemed to deflate, and he turned on his side. John stepped forward threateningly. Rudy raised his hands in supplication. "Okay, okay! Maybe you're right. Maybe I ought to just get out of here and leave you all alone." John relaxed, and allowed his father to regain his feet. Behind him, Anna huddled with her arm around Larry. Rudy looked at his wife.

"Anna."

She looked away.

"Anna, I'm so sorry."

"Just go, Dad," John said forcefully, "and leave Mom's keys!"

"All right," Rudy agreed, a woeful expression on his face. His shoulders slumped, and he appeared beaten. "I can't fight you all." His hand fluttered down to his pocket, and he pulled out the keys to Anna's car. "Here, John, you take 'em."

"Toss them."

And Rudy tossed them. They sailed to John's side. He put out his hand but missed them, and they landed on the ground.

In the space of time it took for John to look away and follow the flight of the keys, Rudy disappeared around the corner of the house. Anna saw it, and cried, "John!" in warning.

John swung his head back around, but his father was gone. Vaguely, he heard his mother beg him to stop and come inside the house, but a rush of adrenaline sent his blood pressure skyrocketing, and all that was left was the sound of his own heart thundering in his ears. He rushed around the corner and came face to face with Rudy. His father's expression was a Halloween mask of mixed fury and good cheer, and he held a pitchfork in his hand. He roared, an inhuman roar, and in that moment he looked like Satan himself.

John backed up, and ran into Anna and Larry, who had followed directly behind him. Anna screamed and pulled at her son, but John shook her off wordlessly. This was the ultimate confrontation between father and son. He put his hands out to the side and hunched his shoulders, looking for a weakness and a chance to attack.

Behind him, Anna and Larry were shouting at Rudy to *stop*

*it, stop it!,* but John paid no attention. Rudy made a few experimental jabs with the pitchfork, giggling as John dodged and weaved. Then his face grew deadly serious. It was time. He lunged with the pitchfork, and grazed John's ribs with one of the tines. A sizzle of fire flashed across John's side, but it barely registered. At lightning speed he reached out and grabbed the shaft of the pitchfork, and father and son were locked in a desperate struggle to gain control of it.

Larry rushed forward, his head lowered, and butted his father in the side. Rudy staggered but held on to the pitchfork, viciously kicking Larry away. Larry gave a muted *oof!* as he hit the side of the house hard and bounced off. He slid to the ground. White-hot pain shot from his shoulder, and he fought to stay conscious. Rudy didn't even turn to look, because his and John's eyes were locked in a fearsome gaze. Neither of them would give up.

---

Sandy was tiny but athletic in build. Making a bee-line for the side of the barn furthest away from the house, she heard further male shouts but ignored them. She had enough to concern her in attempting to leap the old corn-rows without falling and injuring herself. A wind had picked up, and the sky darkened, but she barely noticed these facts. When she reached her goal, she sank down to her knees and looked at the four-inch metal cannister. "Twist cap off, discard, point and spray," the instructions read. Well, that seemed easy enough. The cannister had lain in the glove compartment of her car for years, alternately freezing and baking with the passing seasons. Sandy wondered briefly if it still worked. Wistfully she wished for a good, old-fashioned wooden baseball bat. Rudy was twice her size, but she was *very* good at softball, and she thought he wouldn't be able to do much damage with two broken knee caps.

Peering around the corner toward the house, Sandy had to squint against a whirlwind of dust kicked up by the rising wind.

She heard a roar. *Oh my God,* she thought, *it sounds like the lions in the cat house at the zoo! But where had everybody gone? There!* She saw Anna and one of her sons back up from between the house and barn, and they were both screaming. She crept forward across the front of the barn, twisting the cap off her cannister as she went.

---

Ahead, Fuller could see the house and barn with two vehicles, one parked directly in front of the house, and one to the side under some trees. Between the house and the barn were a group of people. More importantly, he could see Sandy peeking around the side of the barn. His hair stood on end and he floored the accelerator. To his horror, Sandy sprinted across the front of the barn, approaching the group. He had intended to cut her off and stop her, but he was going to miss her; he was just a little too late. He cursed, slammed the steering wheel with his hand and drove around the side of the house, flashing past the car parked under the trees. He stopped the Bronco and leapt out with his revolver, heading for the space between the house and the barn and, most importantly, Rudy Baumann's back.

He peered around the corner. There was Baumann, all right, struggling with John for control of a wicked-looking pitchfork. He knew he could take Rudy with his gun; it was almost point-blank range. Still, Anna and Larry and John were beyond Rudy, and the way the man was bobbing and weaving around, Sam might hit one of the others.

His cop's powers of observation had noted a shovel leaning against the back of the house. He ducked back, holstered his gun, grabbed the shovel, and then headed back around the side of the house.

---

Frankie was playing his favorite game in the woods, Hunt the Indian Lady. He noted the darkening day and the wind picking up, but he thought it would be all right. Dad was home, and Dad was in charge there. In his mind's eye, he could see Dad with a pitchfork in his hand, and he giggled. Yep, Dad would fix everything. Still, when the normally peaceful river seemed to come alive with waves and froth, it occurred to him that *this* side of the river might not be too safe. He ran to the log lying over the river and started across.

But the wildness of the river had spattered the log with water, and it was slippery. Frankie was forced to wrap his arms and knees around the log and creep slowly forward. Below him, he saw whirlpools form, and the river suddenly looked a lot deeper than it had ever looked before. Just as suddenly, the picture of his father that had he had become accustomed to seeing in his mind's eye was *gone,* like a blank screen at a movie theater. At that same moment, his mind heard his father scream at him, *Frankie! Frankie, help me!* For the first time in his life, Frankie Baumann experienced the emotion of mortal fear. He struggled the rest of the way on the log with his heart in his throat.

On the Baumann side of the river, Frankie ran through the familiar trees and full out down the corn rows. He could see the house in front of him, and called with his mind. *Daddy! Daddy, where are you?* This time there was no answer, which frightened him even more.

Then he reached the edge of the porch, and he could hear his father and his mother and brothers yelling at each other. He crept across the front of the house, and spied someone else—Mrs. Fuller—crouched at the edge of the barn, watching. She wasn't even looking at him, and he moved slowly to position himself behind his mother and John. His hand crept to his pocket and the store of rocks he kept there. Daddy needed help.

In fact, Sandy was looking in mixed relief and fear at her husband, Sam, who was stealthily approaching Rudy from the rear with his gun in his service belt and a shovel in his hands. Anna had seen him too, and her hands flew up to her throat. The wind blew more fiercely, sending fresh leaves now, and twigs, and dirt from the dooryard to pelt her unprotected legs. She turned her body slightly toward the house to shelter her face, and her hair whipped in front of her eyes. Anna pulled it away, and gasped, because in front of her now was Frankie, Frankie with a rock in his hand the size of a hen's egg and a huge grin, and he was looking at John.

"BANG, BANG! YOU'RE DEAD!" Frankie yelled at the top of his lungs, and bulleted the rock at John's head. All his practice had paid off, because the rock connected squarely with the back of John's head. He let go of the pitchfork and toppled to the ground, conscious but stunned.

Rudy roared in exultation, and hefted the pitchfork for a killing blow. And Sam Fuller hit *him* across the back of his head with the shovel.

The blow stunned Rudy. He wobbled, but didn't go down. He dropped the pitchfork, and turned to face Fuller. "What are you *doing?*" he asked plaintively.

"I'm saving your fucking life," Sam said, and punched Rudy in the jaw. This time, Baumann went down, and stayed down.

Frankie disappeared back the way he had come, as fast as his legs could carry him.

Sandy ran to Anna and put her arms around her friend, and together they helped Larry up from the ground. "I think his shoulder's just dislocated," Sandy commented. Anna didn't answer; she just stood there in shock. Sandy took her by the shoulders and shook the stunned look off Anna's face, and clarity snapped back into her friend's eyes. "We've *got* to get him to a hospital," Sandy said loudly and carefully, and Anna nodded her understanding.

Anna found the keys to her car and her purse in the front of the house, and drove her car around to the front yard. By that time Sandy had helped John to his feet, and Sam had handcuffed Rudy's hands behind his back. Sam checked Rudy's pulse. It was slow, but steady and strong. Rudy was still alive.

Lightning struck the ground in the corn field. A deafening thunderclap accompanied it. It was as dark as dusk.

Sam drove the Bronco up to Rudy's motionless body. He opened the door to the back, and with John's help, heaved the man in. Once that was done, he yelled (and he *had* to yell over the roar of the wind), "Okay, everybody, here's what's going to happen. Sandy, you get back to your car and drive as fast as you can to the highway. *Stay there.* John and I'll take Rudy here. Anna, you take Larry in your car. Stop at the highway and stay with Sandy."

Anna yelled back, "Where's Frankie?"

They all looked around, but Frankie was gone.

Another bolt of lightning hit the ground, closer to their group.

"FRANKIE! FRANKIE!" his mother screamed.

"Anna, we have *no time!*" Sam cried.

Anna turned to struggle up the steps of the porch, but the wind pushed her back. From the sky came three simultaneous bolts of forked lightning, and the earth shook with the report of the thunder. Sandy grabbed her and forced her into her car. "Frankie's in God's hands now," she told Anna, kissing her friend roughly on the cheek and standing back. "NOW GO!" As she stood back and watched Anna steer down the driveway toward the highway, she thought, *And may God have mercy on his soul.* Then she followed, dashing down the driveway to her own car.

Sam got behind the wheel of the Bronco, and turned to John, who was sporting a huge egg on the back of his head. "I want you to watch your Dad. Let me know right away if he makes a move. Right now we have to get off this land."

John turned in his seat and looked dispassionately at his father. "Okay, Sam."

They raced toward the highway. Ahead of them, Sam could see that a forty-foot tree had been ripped out of the ground and lay against the bridge. Water sloshed up and over the bridge itself.

"Hold on," he ordered John, and gunned the engine. They made it to the other side just as the bridge finally gave way with a loud cracking and splintering. John looked out the back window of the Bronco, and saw that the bridge was *gone*.

---

The group gathered on the side of the highway, where two sheriff's department cruisers and three deputies awaited them. As Rudy was taken into custody, Sam found that his radio now worked again. He finished reporting in and then the entire group stopped and watched the Baumann farm in awe. The storm clouds were one with the earth, and from the very heart of it, they heard a flat *whumpf!* and a ball of fire appeared where the house had been. Anna thought guiltily of the paint thinner she had left under the bed, but soon realized that it didn't matter. At the place called Heartless, where the weather was never too severe and where nothing ever rotted or aged, a twister appeared. The barn, Rudy's old Ford, fully grown maples and elms and oaks and locust trees—all were pulled from the earth toward the center of that enormous cyclone and then up, up, until they disappeared. The very soil of the farm went as well, spiraling around the perimeter in front of their faces and disappearing into the center of the maelstrom. Balls of lightning zipped along the earth, singeing what was left. The thunder could be heard throughout the county.

It lasted for a full fifteen minutes. In that time, the sun shown on them all, and not a breeze escaped toward this side of the river to relieve the heat of full August in Iowa.

When the twister lifted its fury from the ground and disappeared back into the clouds, the water from the river welled over its banks and flooded the pit that was once the Baumann farm. The clouds dispersed quickly, like a movie running backwards in time, and soon the sun shone as brilliantly across the water as it did on the side of the highway.

In the quiet that was left, they could hear Anna sobbing, "Frankie! Frankie!" John and Larry looked at each other, and then away. Both were thinking the same thing: *It's better this way.*

The entourage made its way back to Apple Springs proper, and to its promise of peace, at last. The curse and the story of Heartless appeared to be over.

# CHAPTER
## Twenty-Seven

Rudy awoke in the hospital, chained to his bed and with a guard in attendance. When he found he was restrained, he grew so violent that he was medicated. In short order he was transferred to the psychiatric unit. He eventually ended up in a state hospital for the emotionally disturbed. Psychiatric observers reported that he suffered full-blown auditory and visual hallucinations of his father, step-father, and his youngest son, who each urged him to kill, and he tried to act out their orders. He was judged to be mentally incompetent to stand trial for attempted murder, and, according to the testifying psychiatrist, it appeared to be hopeless for the foreseeable future. No amount or type of medication could completely calm him, and he was obsessed with the thought of finding and killing Anna.

Anna used the money in her purse to rent an apartment for herself and her two remaining sons. With Sam Fuller's influence, she was soon gainfully employed in a local bank as a loan officer, and life went on. On impulse one day, she called her old landlady, Mrs. Sherwood. With relief, she found that not only was the older woman alive, she was still living in her house. She poured out her story of life with Rudy, omitting the finer details of the very end of their relationship, and learned that her father was still alive (and married to Sylvia Sherwood!). Anna talked to him, and it was as if the years melted away. She promised to visit soon, bringing both of her remaining sons with her.

She also learned her old friend Karen's married name and contacted her. Stiffly at first, then gradually with more warmth and sympathy, Karen listened to Anna's story. "God, Anna, if I'd only known! I'm so sorry I listened to Rudy!"

"Well, we all did," Anna admitted. "That was part of Rudy's personality. He made you believe that down was up and that yesterday was today. But he's gone now, out of my life for good."

"You're divorced?"

"It's pending, but I shouldn't have any trouble finalizing it. There was plenty of evidence as to why I shouldn't be Rudy's wife any more."

"Because I know someone you should meet. He's your age, tall, dark, and very handsome, and *employed* . . ."

"Karen!" Anna stopped her friend, and laughed. They would reunite in Minnesota when Anna visited her father.

As for Anna's future, it was somewhat unclear, but it felt exciting instead of dangerous. She didn't know if she would stay in Iowa, or go back to Minnesota, or maybe try another place. She knew that she could count on keeping in contact with John and Larry. She was *herself* again, and for that, she was happy—that was the best part. The only clouds in her mind were connected to her memories of her youngest son, Frankie. Although her head told her that nothing could have prevented his death, her mother's heart ached for the loss of her smallest child and wondered what she could have done better with him. A memorial service was held for him, and an empty child's coffin was buried in the Apple Springs cemetery with Frankie's name on the headstone. She would carry that emptiness in her heart forever.

John finished high school, and joined the Marines. He spent part of his tour of duty in Vietnam, managing to live to see the end of the American fighting in that conflict. Under the guidance of Sam Fuller, John started college courses in law enforcement when he was once again a civilian.

Larry went to college, avoiding the last of the United States' draft, and studied to become a marine biologist. He planned to earn his doctorate in environmental studies, and was very interested in environmental issues concerning the effects of human lifestyle on the marine ecosystem.

No sign of Frankie Baumann, other than his battered red cowboy hat, was ever found.

Now, the Baumann property itself was another story. On that August day, it was as if the poisoned earth, water, and wind, furious at being cheated of a banquet of blood, had turned on itself. The forks of the river spread until they were present only as muddy trickles, joining to make a small creek at their juncture. In the middle was a marsh of stagnant, malignant water and quicksand. It stank of decay and death, and why shouldn't it? In the end, it showed its true nature.

Now, there's a story that folks tell of a wooden box holding a treasure of twenty-dollar gold pieces that are rare and *growing* in number and getting more precious by the day, sitting somewhere in the middle of that marsh, with the wood rotting around it to spill its golden temptation beneath the stinking slime and murk of the marshland. No one has ever looked for it, however.

Would you?

THE END

# ABOUT THE AUTHOR

Author Farral Bradtke was born and raised in the United States' Midwest and has traveled extensively throughout the United States and Canada. She has a special interest in both the human psyche and in paranormal events and how the two sometimes interact. Ms. Bradtke has worked in medical and educational fields for thirty-six years and enjoys writing about all of the possibilities of the human soul: good, evil, and all there is in between.

She presently lives and writes in western North Carolina.